the winter knight

JES BATTIS

ECW

Published by ECW Press
665 Gerrard Street East
Toronto, Ontario, Canada M4M 1Y2
416-694-3348 / info@ecwpress.com

Editors for the Press: Jen Knoch and Jen R. Albert
Copyeditor: Crissy Calhoun
Cover Artwork: David Curtis

LIBRARY AND ARCHIVES CANADA CATALOGUING
IN PUBLICATION

Title: The winter knight / Jes Battis.

Names: Battis, Jes, 1979- author.

Identifiers: Canadiana (print)
20220477566 | Canadiana (ebook)
20220477574

ISBN 978-1-77041-720-5 (softcover)
ISBN 978-1-77852-105-8 (ePub)
ISBN 978-1-77852-106-5 (PDF)
ISBN 978-1-77852-107-2 (Kindle)

Classification: LCC PS8603.A8785 W56
2023 | DDC C813/.6—dc23

This book is funded in part by the Government of Canada. *Ce livre est financé en partie par le gouvernement du Canada.* We acknowledge the support of the Canada Council for the Arts. *Nous remercions le Conseil des arts du Canada de son soutien.* We acknowledge the funding support of the Ontario Arts Council (OAC), an agency of the Government of Ontario. We also acknowledge the support of the Government of Ontario through the Ontario Book Publishing Tax Credit, and through Ontario Creates.

Canada

PRINTED AND BOUND IN CANADA

PRINTING: MARQUIS   5 4 3 2 1

MIX
Paper from
responsible sources
FSC
www.fsc.org   FSC® C103567

To my mom, who gave me the Middle Ages.

To my students, for showing me endless possibilities.

*And to the Book Man—Chilliwack's oldest independent
bookstore—for offering me a whole world of stories to discover.*

HILDIE

§he felt it hovering like a moth above the great fireplace.

Hildie squinted at the musicians as they tuned their instruments. The cellist was arguing with the pianist about canons, which had something to do with infinity, but Hildie was distracted and couldn't follow the conversation. The musicians were safe. Their deaths were curled tightly within them—dark threads better left undisturbed.

Someone else would die tonight.

Hildie could see death coming but couldn't stop it, which made the investigation all the more bittersweet.

She heard her mother's voice. *I need a status update.*

Hildie exhaled. Her mother was First Valkyrie, the boss. She already watched Hildie with an attention bordering on paranoia. She was even more fixated tonight: a death was about to bloom in Morgan Arcand's centuries-old mansion. The haunted house was on university grounds, which meant a lot of bystanders who had no idea that they'd just walked by a reincarnated knight on the way to the sashimi. It would be hard to keep things out of the public eye. But Morgan had her tricks.

Hildie tapped her earpiece. "Update: the snacks are amazing at the dean's fall semester party, and this dress I got from Winners looks like a trash bag."

Knights were myths stuck on repeat—a battle song that just kept streaming. Stories that kept being told in different times and bodies. Valkyries had a wild family tree, stretching back to the time when this whole place was covered in boreal forest. People loved reading stories about King Arthur and Morgan le Fay, but the reality was a lot more complicated. Arthur was in prison, Morgan was a university dean, and Hildie spent most of her time untangling blood feuds and breaking up fights on the beach. When a knight died under suspicious circumstances, it was her job to separate the facts from the stories. And everyone had a long story.

Myths loved places hemmed in by water, like Vancouver. They shimmered in the depths. This place used to be called Terminal City, because it felt like the edge of the world.

Hildie could hear Grace's disapproval over the Bluetooth connection. *I told you to buy something strapless from Holt Renfrew.*

"Have you seen their plus-size section? It's just a sign with a sad face emoji. Besides it's a crazy runesmith's party, not the Junos."

Don't call her crazy. She hates that.

Beautiful people were handing their beautiful coats to staff at the door—probably grad students who'd been roped into this for extra money. Hildie found a space behind a pillar with an old woman's face carved into it. She seemed to be sticking her tongue out. Maybe it was one of Morgan's guises, or just some bit of medieval weirdness.

She pulled up the dean's file on her tablet. Some of it was redacted—instead of black lines, those sections were just blurs on the screen. Everyone had secrets, and Grace restricted access to the more sensitive information. Sometimes, Hildie thought her mother simply didn't trust her. Maybe she was right to withhold. Here was what she knew:

Morgan Arcand (no middle name). Aliases: Morrígan, Morgana, Sheela na Gig, the Very Black Witch, Queen of the Outer Islands. DOB: sixth century? Age of current myth: [blank]. (Guess she didn't want anyone to know.) Family: Igraine of Tintagel (paternity disputed); Arthur (half-sibling). Appearance: sometimes thin, tall, and pale; other times short and thick; occasionally a stone. Runesmith. Always dangerous. Current occupation: dean of arts.

Her known associates were essentially everyone. A squire couldn't take a piss in this city without Morgan Arcand knowing about it. She'd thrown herself into academia for the last few decades, and that made things quiet. Rumor had it that she was gunning for the job of university provost, currently held by Mo Penley. Short for Mordred, but you didn't want that name attached to your school's strategic plan. They were two old conservatives butting heads for control of knowledge, control of how their stories might be framed.

Hildie spotted them talking to each other, near the entrance to the kitchen. She ignored the smell of puff pastry and moved closer to hear their conversation, but the party noise swallowed whatever they were saying. Morgan wore a green Balenciaga gown with a chain of intricate gold knots around her throat. Hildie remembered that her nan—the previous First Valkyrie—had once described Morgan as a *difficult knot*. She felt a flash of grief, but pushed it down. Penley was leaning in close, whispering in Morgan's ear. He was tall and pencil-thin, with graying blond hair. His tiepin was a small dagger that gleamed under the lamplight, and he wore a suit effortlessly, as if he'd been born in a double-breasted jacket. His eyes were cold—like an empty hearth.

Morgan gave him a long look and walked away. Penley went upstairs, pausing briefly at the banister, as if he'd stopped to study something. Hildie made a note to investigate the second floor. This was the oldest house in Vancouver, and it kept its secrets close.

Her mother compressed a lifetime of subtle disappointment into the audio feed, which was uncomfortably clear. *Keep your eyes open. Don't get distracted.*

Hildie switched off the earpiece. It wouldn't stop her mother for long, but it was satisfying nonetheless.

She checked her notes on Mo Penley. University provost—a fancy title that meant an academic vice president. (The actual president was always on a plane somewhere.) Alias Mordred; questionable family connection to Arthur. (This family tree was like a wild baobab with giant roots stretching everywhere.) Conservative. Liked to deny tenure. There was a note about a harassment case, but she didn't have time to read it now. Most of the good stuff in Grace's notes was password-protected. It interfered with Hildie's job, and more than that, it pissed her off.

What she needed was her nan's notebook; it had years' worth of cryptic data written in her delicate hand. It was tucked away in Hildie's closet—she'd stolen it after the funeral, but couldn't yet bear to look at it.

She gazed up at the soaring roof, where ancient timbers were locked in an embrace. It reminded her of being a kid, when she used to crane her neck to stare up at the clouds in search of snow. Hildie glanced around to make sure nobody was watching. Then she laid her hand against one of the beams. It was warm to the touch. She could feel the echo of life in the wood grain. The house itself was a ghost, inclining toward her. Colonizers had brought it on ships from Europe to preserve their own aesthetic. Now it was frozen in time, remembering winters, politics, interminable wars, and all those words that rose like smoke to settle in the rafters.

Hildie watched the cater waiters bustling around in their crisp uniforms. They were essentially invisible. A person in a uniform could get close without arousing suspicion, the same way you might allow a ladybug to alight on your finger. This was the problem with being a valkyrie. She could smell death but couldn't exactly pinpoint it. Anyone in this house could be the killer or the victim. She didn't have much time. The Wyrd Sisters would be studying the thread, too, about to cut. It wasn't personal for them. Valkyries were the ones who cleaned up the mess and dealt with the survivors.

Not that Hildie minded the sisters. One of them was her best friend.

Nice try—turning off the earpiece. Did you forget about what I can do?

She sighed. "Let's not."

Don't trust Morgan.

"That's your advice? Be scared of the big bad wolf? Why don't you actually help me in person instead of judging me from a distance?"

I'm dealing with the perimeter. And she's more of a crow than a wolf. The line was silent for a moment. Then Grace added, *I can call for backup if you—*

"I can handle a party just fine, Mother."

You've got a short memory then.

Hildie didn't want to talk about Morgan's last party: she'd been drinking vodka out of a thermos when she should have been watching the crowd.

You broke that knight's nose—

"Yes, I was there; I don't need a recap."

Just watch for traps. And don't eat anything.

Hildie shoved two salmon puffs into her mouth and switched off the earpiece again.

In an ideal world, Grace would have had several strong daughters to follow in her footsteps. But in the end, there was only Hildie, and she didn't want to be First Valkyrie. The family tradition would die with Grace. It drove her mother nuts. Why couldn't Hildie just grab a spear and fall in line with the rest of her kin?

Sometimes she wondered what her own thread looked like. Could she twist it in another direction? Or was it woven this way for good?

Vera Grisi and her nephew are here.

"Maybe I'll throw this earpiece into the ocean."

Her mother didn't rise to the bait. *Keep an eye on her.*

Hildie saw a middle-aged woman in a gray coat, gently guiding a kid through the crowd. Not a kid exactly—probably eighteen or so. He squinted at the lights and looked uncomfortable. A man leaned close to Vera, whispering something. He had curly black hair and merry eyes, but there was a tiredness there as well. She'd have to look him up. Vera said something inaudible in reply, and her expression remained closed. Her eyes were the same color as her coat. She was beautiful and somehow distant, like an aging film star who'd grown wise enough to deflect personal questions during interviews.

Hildie slipped upstairs, noting a clever rune on the balustrade. It made her sweat, but she brushed past it. The floorboards groaned. She stepped into the library, which was a baroque paradise with intricate honeycomb shelves. Some of the books were behind glass. Hildie opened a nearby volume, but it was written in Old Welsh—not her strongest language. She heard a soft click—perhaps one of the cabinets quietly closing. She was just about to duck out of the room when Mo Penley emerged from behind the shelves. She listened to the space around him, but there was so much interference. He was holding a thick volume with an engraved leather cover. Hildie saw something like a medieval illumination on the page. A grotesque with several heads and tails. Then he closed it.

"Sorry—" Hildie moved to edge out of the room.

"Not at all." His smile was a bit conspiratorial—as if they'd both caught each other. "I should get back down there."

"Hiding from donors?"

His mouth curled. "You must feel out of place here."

She wasn't sure what that meant. "Well, it's not my first choice for a Saturday night. But I'm out of gin, so—" She gave an exaggerated shrug.

"Of course." His expression hardened. "Like mother, like daughter."

Hildie felt as though she'd been slapped. Before she could reply, he gave her a curt nod, then replaced the bound manuscript and left. She heard his footsteps on the stairs. Counted to fifteen, until she knew he must have rejoined the crowd. Then she walked back down the hallway.

There was an office near the end of the landing. She passed by, then stopped when she heard voices coming from within.

"—shouldn't have come," Morgan was saying. "This was a mistake."

"—our mistake—"

Something inaudible. Then Morgan's voice, clear and cold: "It can't be stopped."

Hildie heard footsteps approaching the office door. She ducked into the spare room, just as Morgan's mystery guest emerged. She couldn't see him through the crack in the door—just a shadow moving down the stairs. She smelled his sweat and, beneath that, something like decaying leaves. Was it him? Corpse or killer?

Hildie looked around the guest room. Everything clean and crisp, with Berber carpet. But the duvet was slightly uneven, as if it had been made up in a hurry. Someone had slept there—maybe last night. The knight who'd just hurried downstairs? Hildie could smell the history on him, even if she didn't know who he might be.

She saw a framed photo lying facedown on the desk. Morgan Arcand in jeans—*jeans?*—and an apple-red blouse. Her look gave nothing away. Beside her, Vera Grisi was making a face, as if to say *Take the photo already*. A man had his arm around her, and Hildie realized it was the cute, tired-looking knight she'd seen earlier with the merry eyes. He looked pleasantly stoned in the photo and wore a Manu Chao T-shirt and ripped jeans. Aging punk with a soft exterior.

It was the strangest thing to find in this beautiful old house. Why hadn't it been on display? Had someone rescued it from a drawer? The frame was old wood, not a cheap imitation. And who had taken the picture? Hildie couldn't imagine a world in which Morgan and Vera shared the same space so comfortably. Their rivalry was legendary, though Vera had been off the radar for a while.

Even queens had to make a living sometimes.

Hildie made her way downstairs. Her mother's voice chimed in. *I need an update.*

She deliberately stood next to the crackling fireplace. "Sorry, you're breaking up."

Is that popcorn?

She stuck the earpiece down the front of her dress.

The sun went down, and lanterns winked to life outside. The cool air was inviting. As she grabbed her jacket, she noticed Vera Grisi's nephew coming downstairs. Why had he been upstairs? They made eye contact for a second. He looked away quickly, and she noticed that he was carrying his shoes like someone doing a walk of shame. She reminded herself to check his file, but he seemed harmless, like an awkward puppy.

7

The musicians were shifting from one piece to another. She swayed slightly, flushed from the heat of the fire.

Hildie heard footsteps. She turned and saw a youngish guy in a green blazer, standing next to the nephew. The dean's assistant—she forgot his name. He had a bushy hipster beard. The expression on the nephew's face was rapture.

What were those two doing together?

Bach's Goldberg Variations, her mother's voice said from her dress.

"Since when do you like classical?"

What you don't know about me could fill Stanley Park.

The music transformed. It sounded like thunder.

Until she realized that it *was* thunder. A storm was shaking the windows. Caterers flew in all directions, trying to shut out the weather, as guests streamed in from the patio. The glass turned black, and the rain began.

Hildie looked back at the stairs. The nephew and the dean's assistant were gone.

She looked for Morgan but couldn't see her either.

She let her mind go unfocused for a second. Shadows played around her. Dark threads that linked people, or pulled them apart. Lives echoing, some long and loud, others quiet and too short. One about to snap.

Something moved past the window. She felt it. Beneath the storm, she heard something that might have been breathing.

It was very close. The death, the taut thread, the thing in the margins.

Hildie thought of what she'd seen in the manuscript image. The grotesque with too many heads and tails.

She tried to take in the entire room, but there were too many guests. Vera and the tired knight were near the piano. Was the nephew still upstairs? Someone darted through the sliding glass door, and she caught a whiff of dead leaves again.

It was coming.

But where? She let her senses move outward, like roots beneath a forest floor. Trees spoke to each other that way, hearing news from far away. She listened deeply, but the music and the storm and the rattling glass and murmured gossip were all too loud.

The piano soared.

Then she heard the scream.

She was already running. The sound echoed in her ears, along with her mother's voice, bellowing orders. Hildie took the stairs two at a time.

It wasn't a human scream.

She burst into the spare room. The dean's assistant—*Bertram*, she finally remembered his name—and the nephew stood on the opposite side of the room, by the desk. The nephew's face was pale.

The body was arranged on the sheets, arms crossed, haloed in blood. Hildie drew closer.

She knelt down. Warmth still clung to him. She ignored the smell and leaned in further, until her face hovered near the space where his head used to be. Mo Penley's cold blue eyes couldn't stare at her in death. But his gray suit and aristocratic long fingers were unmistakable. The cut along the neck was clean. Spine and marbled fat, bright as stained glass.

Beneath that, teeth marks. A ragged wet chunk taken out of the torso.

Hildie leaned in closer. Beneath the rough wound—a tattoo. No. Someone had carved it into him. Neat lines, still welling with blood.

A rune that she'd never seen before. Something from the old alphabet. It made her stomach hitch. Twisted something inside of her.

Morgan appeared in the doorway. Her expression, as always, inscrutable.

"Nobody leaves," Hildie said.

2

WAYNE

ayne sucked in his breath as he entered the strange old house with all its secrets.

The living room had a vaulted ceiling, made of ancient timbers that reminded him of a forest canopy. They stretched high above him, locked in wild cruxes that made him dizzy for a moment. The trees held up everything, and he imagined the roof as a sky made of curling moss and weathered stone. The ceiling of some odd green chapel that had grown all around them. Storm clouds gathered in the bank of windows that surrounded him. There were bronze busts placed evenly on side tables, wreathed in candlelight. Faces that he didn't recognize. They seemed to turn toward him, with expressions of mild interest.

Things that Wayne knew:

1. He loved lists.
2. This house belonged to Morgan Arcand, who was terrifying.
3. Morgan Arcand had once tried to kill Aunt Vera with an exploding apple. (Weird flex but sort of biblical?)

4. His shoes were torture chambers and he *needed* to throw them in the fireplace.

Uncle Gale was limping toward the puff pastries. He wasn't really Wayne's uncle—just his favorite of several people he called uncle, and sometimes *nuncle*. Gale lived with Aunt Vera in a tiny apartment that always smelled like books. They were both academics, though Gale was more of a translator, and Aunt Vera taught as an adjunct at the university. Now that Wayne had started his first semester, they both wanted to have serious chats with him about research methods and where he saw himself post-graduation. He'd just started! He could barely imagine surviving the next few months, let alone walking across a stage to collect a degree.

He pulled out his phone to text Kai. She'd asked for pictures of Morgan's haunted house, and texting her would calm him down. But he forgot where he was for a moment. Someone in a green blazer bumped into him, and he pressed himself against the wall.

Force field. Force field.

Wayne imagined a sphere forming around him, like his therapist had taught him. He could expand or contract it at will. Nobody could get in without his permission. Too bad people didn't seem to follow the rules.

Aunt Vera appeared at the edge of the sphere. He let it shrink—Vera was family, and he didn't mind if she stood close. She'd just handed her dove-gray coat to someone. He hadn't noticed the blue dress she was wearing underneath, because the coat was so compelling. When he was younger, he used to rub the silver lining.

He reached into his pocket, closing his hand around a stim toy his dad had given him years ago—a ball of interlocking chains that made a soothing *snick* sound when he played with it. The ring mail was cool against his sweaty palm, and he felt his blood pressure going down. *Snick. Snick.* It probably looked like he was doing something indecent with his hand stuck in his pocket, but he didn't want to take it out and risk dropping it or—worse—having to explain it.

Aunt Vera was wearing his favorite earrings: the gray opals. In this ancient house, with the firelight throwing her long shadow against the stones, he could imagine her as a queen. A queen who got laid off whenever the university decided that there wasn't enough teaching to go around, even though she'd been there forever.

She looked at him kindly. Aunt Vera was always harried and kind, though Wayne knew she had a temper she kept on a leash. "Ready to mingle, love?"

"I have never—in my entire life—been ready to mingle."

"That's the spirit." She lowered her voice somewhat. "Be careful. I brought you here because it's time to connect with this part of your life. Plus, you might make some allies who can help you during your first semester."

"I've got Kai." He felt a pang of guilt, as if Kai could hear him considering other friends to interview. She wasn't jealous, but she did have a way of making the world quiet down so it was only the two of them. He couldn't imagine a third party. That's why meeting her boyfriends and girlfriends was always a bit of a disaster. He and Kai would exchange significant looks over coffee while the other person just looked politely confused.

"Kai would kill for you," Aunt Vera said, "but you also need friends who don't set things on fire."

"That was barely her fault."

A woman in an emerald dress walked by them. For a split-second, her eyes raked across Aunt Vera. He knew how looks could punch through you, and this one felt like a gauntlet to the face. But Vera just raised an eyebrow. She was the kind of person who'd do your taxes, skin a deer, and correct your term paper, all without breaking a sweat. She got things done and had no time for people who played games or couldn't say what they meant. A raised eyebrow could very well mean war.

His eyes widened. "Was that—?"

"Stay away from her. Go wander, but not too far. And if you get overwhelmed—"

"Not my first rodeo," Wayne said.

Vera looked like she was about to say something else. Then she smiled and walked toward Gale, who was already getting distracted by the paintings.

Reflexively, Wayne checked his phone.

Kai had messaged him. *How's the capitalist orgy?*
If I don't come back, tell my story.
She replied with a gif of Cookie Monster narrating *Monsterpiece Theatre.*
Kai was his person. She distracted him when he was on the edge of
a panic attack. She translated for him when he forgot how to use words.
She deftly kept people from touching him, and she'd threatened more
than one bully with immolation. The perks of knowing a runesmith.
But he was in university now. He needed to strike out on his own.

His mother would have had something pithy to say about this. She'd
laugh and call him Wort—her pet name for him. *Just point and look confident, Wort—it adds an air of mystery.* She never would have wanted him
mingling with knights and runesmiths. She'd tried to create a normal
life for him, within the parameters of their wild family. But she'd been
gone for five years now and wasn't coming back. It was moot.

"Moot," he whispered, liking its sound.

A man stood in the hallway, in a suit that matched the gray clouds
outside. He must have heard Wayne talking to himself, because he had
an odd expression. It looked like he might touch Wayne's arm in a
friendly way, and that absolutely couldn't happen. They both stared at
each other for a weird moment. Then the man's expression changed,
became colder—studying Wayne like he'd been studying the paintings
a moment ago.

Wayne had to squeeze around him, nearly knocking one of the
frames off the wall. It took a moment to steady himself after that.
He went into the living room and approached the soaring fireplace.
The hearth crackled, and the heat was a surprise for a moment, like
the world intruding on this curated space. There were faces carved into
the stone. Bearded men with wild eyes. He could feel the heat of the
flames and hear the pop of green wood burning. This hearth had
warmed people for centuries. It knew exactly what people needed—
what would keep them alive.

He held his hand out, feeling a bit silly. But he could feel something.
Deep in the fire, he saw a version of himself, looking out. A memory, or
a premonition.

13

"Sorry about earlier."

Wayne jumped. A guy stood next to him, carrying two glasses of red wine that gleamed in the lamplight. He wasn't one of the catering staff. The color of his blazer reminded Wayne of moss. He almost wanted to touch it but resisted the urge. The guy's expression was playful. At least Wayne thought it might be. Guys were tricky, and he didn't want to get trapped in some sarcastic conversation about sports.

"I mean bumping into you. The dean had me on a wild errand involving little cakes and—" He shook his head. "Never mind. I'm Bert." He held out the wine glass. "This is really very good, and you should try some immediately."

"I'm Wayne." He took a sip. It tasted like fire and flowers and precious things. "Wait," he said. "Bert, as in—"

Bert raised a hand. "You're going to want to say something about *Sesame Street*, but I'll just stop you there."

"That's your right."

They clinked glasses. Bert was grinning at him. Not a wide grin, but sort of a quirk, like he'd decided that Wayne might be interesting but wasn't sure yet. He'd seen that smile on a number of people. *You're weird, but I could definitely like you.* It didn't always go in a positive direction, but that was how he'd met Kai, after all. Kai, who was brilliant even at eight years old, who had looked at him as if recognizing an old accomplice.

Wayne realized that he should say something, but saying the right thing wasn't a particular talent of his. Right now, he was thinking about Bert's brown eyes, which he could sort of look at if he squinted slightly. Which probably made him look like he was about to sneeze.

"I hate parties," he said at last. "But I love fireplaces."

Brilliant, Wort.

"Interesting stance. I love parties, as long as I can choose the music."

"You'd have to fight me." Wayne was slightly surprised when those words came out of his mouth, even though they were true.

"Oh yeah? You like to DJ?"

"My friend says that I have control issues, but I think of it more as a public service."

Bert gestured to the musicians. "What are your thoughts on Schubert?"

Wayne listened to the mournful key, which would speed up in a moment. "He wrote this for ghosts—shortly after ending up in a sanitarium. I can relate."

He wasn't sure why he'd said that last part. He sucked at flirting. That was why.

Bert shrugged. "No reason to fear ghosts."

"No?"

Bert looked thoughtful for a moment. Then he said, "Let me show you something. We have to sneak though."

"I can sneak," he replied, not quite sure if it was accurate. He was pretty clumsy, and the dress shoes weren't helping. He had the habit of bouncing off doorframes, like a bat with broken echolocation.

Bert led him to a staircase that he'd noticed before. Wayne put one foot on the bottom stair and immediately felt a sense of dread.

"Um."

"Trust me." Bert grabbed his hand.

The contact was so unexpected that he nearly yanked his hand away. But Bert was already dragging him up the stairs, the way you'd drag a kid somewhere.

"Where are we going?"

Bert let go of his hand once they were at the top of the stairs. He put a finger to his lips. Wayne saw a slice of light from what looked like an office. Someone was inside, shuffling through papers. Bert motioned for him to walk on tiptoes. They both did it, but after a moment, Wayne started chuckling in spite of himself. Bert was laughing, too, but trying to suppress it, and it came out more as a snort. They hugged the wall and kept going, past what looked like a guest bedroom, which smelled of lavender. It was dark, and Wayne almost reached for Bert's hand again but thought better of it. Bert was probably straight and this would all end with a moment of supreme awkwardness that he'd be telling Kai about later. *I put my hand on his knee and he told me that a centuries-old mansion was an inappropriate place for romance.*

Wayne knew it was going to be a library before the door opened—he could feel it. When he stepped inside, his heart exploded. The built-in shelves rose nearly to the ceiling and were full of hardcovers. Clouds swirled above the skylight; Wayne pictured a castle of books under a veiled moon, secure against the storm. There were old volumes under glass (which he'd pictured), but also oblong atlases and encyclopedias and manuscripts stacked in honeycomb alcoves. There was a tapestry of a unicorn on the wall, dark and frayed, so that it looked more like an original than a reproduction.

There was a manuscript on the desk, nestled in a velvet container to protect the delicate folio. Someone had left a wine glass nearby, carelessly. Wayne grabbed it without thinking and moved it away from the ancient book. The leather binding was the same color as the wine, rich and dark, casting blush shadows against the desk. Wayne could see little imperfections in the vellum—tiny hairs—and realized that the page had once been a living animal.

Bert used a funny tassel to turn the pages. They had a familiar scent. He stopped on a page with an illuminated image. It was a beast with too many heads and tails and eyes. Its mouth was full of fire. Wayne stared at the impossibly deep reds and golds. The colors hadn't faded. The cramped script around them skittered before his eyes. One of the capital letters seemed to extend like vines, shivering.

The room changed.

Everything was underwater. Bert was no longer next to him. As he watched, frozen, the unicorn stepped out of the tapestry. She wasn't kind or pristine. Her coat was dark and matted, like a wet ram, and she gazed at him with bloodshot eyes. Her horn glistened. Wayne couldn't move.

Bert had a hand on his back. "You okay?"

The unicorn shimmered and was back in the tapestry. But its shadow was still moving across the floorboards.

Wayne tried to catch his breath. "I don't know. I don't know."

He knew he should say something reassuring to Bert. Maybe send him outside for a glass of water, as if that would help. Anything to make him leave, so he wouldn't see the meltdown that was coming. Wayne closed his eyes. Someone had affixed two giant bolts to either side of his head and was slowly turning them. He felt the words logjamming in his mouth. It was impossible to figure out where each sound was coming from. His mother used to calm him down. She'd tap out messages on his back or hold him firmly. *Tell me*, she'd say, *about every bird you saw today. Every book you touched, every raindrop, every animal that seemed friendly.* But she was gone now. She'd left and blown a crater in their family. He felt like an uncorked wine bottle, spilling everything.

Bert said something inaudible.

The storm rushed over him. He felt his knees starting to buckle. *Don't fall. Don't—*

Then he was moving, but not on his own. They were in a different room. The guest room, he realized, though his vision still swam.

Bert sat him on the edge of the bed.

Then he heard a soft drumming on the nightstand.

"Match the beat with me."

"What?"

The drumming continued, gentle but persistent. "It's pentameter. Five beats, unstressed, then stressed. Like this. Match it."

Da-DUM-da-DUM-da-DUM-da-DUM-da-DUM.

There was music coming from downstairs, but all he could hear now was the five-beat rhythm. Slowly, clumsily, he tapped along with it.

"Good. That's it. Once more."

They both drummed in unison. By the time he got to the fifth beat, he could breathe again, though the nausea was still prickling in his stomach.

Bert tapped a half line gently on Wayne's knee. "That's called a bob and wheel," he said. "See? Your anxiety turned out to be a teachable moment."

"Thanks."

"Poetry saves lives." He smiled slightly. "You're good?"

"Not precisely. Better though."

He thought he recognized the music that was drifting up the stairs. He wanted to listen more closely, but this whole situation felt unresolved. Bert didn't seem to be humoring him, exactly. His expression was open and patient.

"Why did you want to show me that book?"

"I don't know. I just thought—it felt like you'd want to see it. I'm not even sure why I thought that."

Dim light cast the shadow of branches around Bert's head. Wayne kept sneaking side-eyed looks. He was stocky and bearded and had a quirky smile. He'd risked getting fired, just so that a stranger could see something magical.

Or maybe he knows who I am. The famously awkward nephew of royalty. Maybe Bert just wanted to know about his legendary Uncle Arthur, who was in jail.

Bert stood up. "I should put that book back—we don't want anyone else having a panic attack. Give me a minute." He smiled. "No more than three shakes of a rabbit's tail. Six at most." Then he left the room.

Wayne stood there for a second, uncertainly. His feet were killing him. He took off his shoes and padded downstairs to follow the music. His toes could breathe again.

There must have been nearly a hundred people crammed into the great room. Everyone was gathered around a single pianist now. She swayed gently, fingers dancing with each crossover. Wayne knew he'd recognized the music. He felt it on a cellular level. The Goldberg Variations.

He loved both Glenn Gould versions—the 1955 LP with all its youthful ferocity, and the wiser 1981 version with different pauses and links. You could tell that he'd learned things in the interim, and the immensity of that knowledge was burned into the vinyl. The pianist had reached the fifteenth variation, which was his favorite. Gould called it the "most severe and beautiful that I know."

It played with you, startling with its lush, blue tones—like a friend who was smiling and then began to cry, unexpectedly. The folklore was that Bach wrote the Variations to soothe a count's insomnia, but if anything, they were designed to pull you in, confuse you, worry you, hold you.

Gould had probably been queer and on the spectrum. Wayne loved the picture of him on the '55 LP, eyes closed in ecstasy, hands crossing over on the keys. The crossover technique meant that his hands were gradually moving away from each other, a series of sad departures.

Wayne turned slightly and saw that Bert was standing behind him. Looking at him, but saying nothing. Was his expression full of possibility? Or just politely blank?

He swayed in spite of himself. Let his hands move back and forth, the way you'd thrust your fingers through water and marvel at the resistance. Let himself melt into the endless changes that the music promised—the spectrum of love and desire and singularity, holding out the idea that we were all variations, dancing toward and away from ourselves.

He was startled to feel Bert's hand in his.

Not pulling him up the stairs this time. Not yanking him out of a bad situation. Just delicately holding on, so that they became a swaying circuit. Wayne's smile was electrified. Not the social smile he put on, or the awkward smile that people demanded for pictures. It burst out of him, crooked and joyful.

That was when they heard the scream.

Someone flashed by him. Wayne's heart flipped. It looked like—but when he squinted, they were gone. Just a ghost. And there was no time to think about it.

They ran upstairs and stumbled into the guest room—where Bert had calmed him down moments before—and the world turned to a confusing negative.

It took him a moment to connect the images. The body on the bed. The blood spreading like a snow angel, soaking the sheets. The blank space where the head had been. It was the man who'd glared at him and refused to move. He recognized the blood-spattered suit.

And rising from the bloody ruin, a rune. Had he seen it before? He tried to remember.

Something put a paw on his heart, and he shuddered.

3

HILDIE

Hildie remembered Nan trying to explain it to her when she was a girl. *Knights are reborn,* she'd said, *like flowers in spring. Only not as consistently. Sometimes you get a whole generation intact—other times they need to find one another, stitching their family back together. It's our job to watch over them, as they live, again and again.*

And what about us? She'd stared at Nan. *Are we like that?*

The flash of mischief in her eye. *Niblet, we're a whole other catastrophe.*

Hildie returned her mind to the scene. Mo Penley was a celebrity in death, as he'd been in life. Youngest provost in the history of the university.

Now that job would likely go to his rival, Morgan Arcand. Interim for now, but she had ambition. *A fact that absolutely won't haunt us,* Hildie thought, without much humor.

Her mother arrived shortly after they discovered the body. She came alone. This was a sign of respect, but also a message: *I don't need backup, and we should keep this in the family.*

It was her job, more or less, to keep the knights safe, keep them from killing each other, remind them of past lives and myth cycles. She could intervene sometimes, but not always. Some things—often the hard things—just had to happen. Some of the knights were flaming racists who saw themselves as the pride of some imaginary Saxon race. Medieval proud boys. No such thing as chivalry—just survival.

She hadn't asked for this. Like them, she'd been born into duty.

Hildie didn't wear armor, sing dirges in Geatish, or dance with giants. Not usually. But she did carry a weapon, and her ancestors had a lot of advice to give. Mostly about dating, which was a whole other story.

Her mother was talking to Dean Arcand. Grace wasn't impressed by power. She'd look down her nose at a star destroyer.

Hildie had to interview most of the guests. She began with a string of older knights. No horses in the game. They were just really into classical music, and Morgan had probably invited them to keep up appearances.

Eventually she got to Bertram, the dean's assistant. He looked tired, but not particularly shaken by the event. Hildie glanced at his file. It was riddled with holes. Not gaps—actual holes in a scanned PDF of some old vellum manuscript. It looked as though bookworms had been nibbling away at his life.

Aliases: Bertilak, Bercilak, Ysbaddaden, Tarquin, the Host. Place of birth: Chester? Castle Hautdesert? Family: parents ?; Gog and McGog (distant relations). Appearance: barrel-chested, beard, smiles a lot, likes to brag. Untrustworthy. Occupation: dean's assistant (grad student).

Hildie almost added *bear cub* to the description but knew it would confuse Grace. If only she had access to her mother's file—but it was hidden. All the more reason to take a peek at Nan's old notebook.

She looked up at Bert. He was staring out the window. His green blazer was ill-fitting, and she wondered if it still had the tags on.

"How long have you worked for Dean Arcand?"

"Forever." He ventured a smile, then tamped it down, as if realizing that he was being inappropriate. "Two years, officially."

"What does your job entail?"

"Mostly arranging her GroupWise calendar. And finding her these weird Cornish pasties that she loves."

"Do you spend a lot of time upstairs—near your employer's guest bedroom?"

He shifted in his chair. "You were there too."

"I was doing my job. What were you doing?"

After a beat, he replied, "I just needed a moment to myself."

"What about your buddy?"

"Who?"

"Vera Grisi's nephew. You were both awfully close to a dead body."

Bertram shrugged. "He seemed anxious. I was just being nice. When we heard screaming—we were the closest to the stairs." His expression didn't change, but his eyebrow twitched.

"I'd stay away from the nephew," she said, in a casual tone. "Until this all gets sorted out to everyone's satisfaction."

Bertram inclined his head. "Whatever you think is best."

If a shadow could thumb its nose at someone . . .

Little shit.

"Give me your phone for a second. I'll put my number in. Just in case you remember something."

He handed her the phone a bit warily, set to the new contacts screen. Hildie used one finger to type in her number, smiling apologetically. "I hate these touch screens. Must be the elder millennial in me."

She used her other hand—ink-stained from signing forms—to trace a faint rune on the underside of the phone. One of Nan's tricks. In case she needed to track him.

She handed back the phone. "Don't leave town."

He tilted his head, as if considering this. Then he walked away.

She wanted a cigarette but didn't want to justify it to Grace. Her mother wasn't buying her theory that nicotine could replace all of her other vices.

Hildie ducked outside. It was still raining, but there was a stillness that made her relax somewhat. The freezing rain made little divots in the pond. She opened her umbrella and studied Mo Penley's file again.

What was he looking for in the library?

She found Vera's friend by the pond—the older knight who'd been with them. Gale. Aliases: Galehaut, Amiloun, Amadís de Gaula. Soft-spoken, middle-aged stoner. Some kind of translator who'd been close with Vera and her ex back in the day. Gale seemed harmless. Just here for moral support.

Hildie went back inside. There was espresso brewing in the kitchen, so she drained a tiny cup and inhaled a handful of crackers. She wanted to sleep. She wanted to fly somewhere that had no Wi-Fi. Or back in time. She'd liked being eight years old. Listening to her nan sing from the kitchen while she made tea. Now the house belonged to Grace, and some of the warmth had vanished. She had a new space-age kettle, though Hildie had rescued Nan's, which now sat in her own kitchen, rimmed with light rust and memory.

Vera Grisi walked over to her. She'd been speaking with Grace a moment before, which was never a good thing. "We're leaving," she said. "Forward me any questions." She said it imperiously, like a professor explaining assignment guidelines.

Her gray eyes had a quiet power. She wouldn't be pushed. Hildie went unfocused for a moment and let Vera's expression hold her. For a moment, she saw a rocky wasteland, the wild emptiness of the Wirral, trees cleaved by lightning in a Welsh landscape. A woman in a tower, watching a horse tear across a green swarth. A sly smile. The name Gwenore on a knight's lips.

Hildie blinked.

"Where's your nephew? If you send him my way, I'll make it quick."

"There's no need to speak with him."

"One of exactly two people who were in the room with the body?" She saw Vera flinch slightly at the word. "As I said, I'll keep it quick. He's been through enough."

Vera relaxed slightly at this. "He's just a boy. I've always—" She sighed. "He's barely part of this world. His mother, Anna—she always protected him. But then she left, and—I shouldn't have brought him."

"But he is family, no?"

23

She spotted Wayne making his way across the room.

"Just don't alarm him," Vera said quietly. "He's got anxiety."

Wayne was hovering on the edge of their group, as if unsure how to proceed. He smiled politely, but she could tell that he wasn't feeling it. Just trying to look compliant. His gaze hovered slightly above her nose.

Hildie pulled up his file quickly. Young knight, untried, nephew to Arthur. Aliases: Gwalchmai, Gauvain, Walewein. Apparently he fought a dragon once—a *baby* dragon, if she was reading it right—though she couldn't believe it. A note said *good at conversation*, which nearly made her laugh. This kid wanted to run. He wasn't like the Gawain who existed in older records. The one who always seemed to have the answer to everything.

"Hildie has a few questions for you," his aunt said. "Just try to answer as best you can. We'll go afterward."

Wayne sat down across from her. "You're a—" He raised an eyebrow. "Yes, I'm that," she said.

"Can I see your credentials?"

She almost laughed. But it was a fair request. Hildie reached into her pocket and withdrew the badge. It was more of a brooch, engraved silver and studded with garnets. Her name was written in runic script on the reverse side. Knights used to respect valkyries. Carrying the mark really meant something. Now they barely noticed her kind, even when she was saving their lives. They'd forgotten the songs of the spear women, the old maxims, the charms to preserve a blade's edge. Nobody respected the canon.

"You and"—she glanced at the file—"Bertram reached the guest bedroom at the same time, correct? What did you see?"

He looked down, as if considering his response. Then he said, "The provost was on the bed." He glanced at Vera. "His body. It looked—I mean, he couldn't have been there for very long. We walked by the bedroom earlier, and it was empty."

"You and Bertram."

He nodded.

"Had you met him before tonight?"

His expression flickered slightly. Was it embarrassment? "No. He introduced himself when I was standing by the fireplace. Brought me a glass of wine."

Vera's eyes narrowed. "I told you not to drink anything here."

"Sorry, Auntie."

"Are we done here?" Vera put a hand lightly on her nephew's shoulder. Hildie shifted her tone. "What were you and Bertram doing upstairs?"

Wayne actually blushed.

"I wanted to see the library," he admitted. "I convinced him to take me up there."

A lie. No way he'd convinced Bert to do anything. Why was he lying?

"And what did you look at?"

"Just—this book on herbs and animals. A medieval book."

Only part of the story was a lie, and she'd need more time to sort that out. She'd have to look up his mother's file. Why had she left exactly? And what was she protecting him from?

"You can go," she said. "But don't go far."

More than anything, she wanted to have a bath and wait for that moment when the water temperature was the same as her body's. She'd turn off all the lights and pretend that it was one of those isolation tanks, where posh people floated around in the dark and stopped thinking about their hundred-year mortgages.

Her greatest hope was to find an unattended tray of vol-au-vents and shotgun them all. What she found, instead, was her mother. Grace was leaning against the marble counter. There were two goblets of wine next to her. Grace pushed one toward her. "Relax. You're done." Her hair was streaked with silver. She was short, but when she spoke, her voice carried. Her mother had always seemed to take up an impossible amount of space, like a mountain squeezed into a small landscape.

Hildie held the glass with both hands. The wine tasted like summer. "My brain will start the second shift as soon as I get home."

"Get some sleep. You'll be busy tomorrow."

She hated when her mother used that matter-of-fact tone to say what she'd be doing. Like Hildie's life floated before her in a crystal ball. Though she was right, as usual. As soon as the news hit the larger community, there would be calls and drop-ins and threatening notes and crackpot theories and endless distractions. She'd never realized, until it was too late, that being a valkyrie was more outreach than battle. She hadn't drawn her weapon in months. Her hands were itching for a fight, and for the purity that always came after. The exhausted, blood-in-your-ears rush, followed by a feeling of peace.

"How were the interviews?"

Hildie resisted the urge to drain her glass. "A few leads. A lot of dead ends. Plenty of bullshit evasions that I'll have to deal with later." She felt a bitter knot in her throat—decided not to say anything, then changed her mind. "You know, it would be a lot easier if half the data in these files wasn't redacted. How are any of us supposed to do our jobs this way?"

Grace's expression was impassive. "Maybe just your copy is redacted."

"Amazing."

"Hildegard—"

"Please don't call me—"

"I trust you," she said, slowly and deliberately. "But some things are sensitive. Even I don't know everything. These people protect their own." Grace seemed to be looking at something invisible. She took a long sip. "Morgan is shook. I can tell. She's being far less sanctimonious than usual, and earlier I saw her washing a dish. One of the caterers had to take it away from her."

Hildie felt their thoughts synching up, as they did sometimes when they were working a case together. A familial telepathy. "You don't like her for this, then?"

"If she did plan it"—Grace finished her glass—"the plan went awry."

She tried to look untroubled as she watched her mother pour another glass. She'd had problems with addiction in the past. Most women in their line of work had to deal with that sooner rather than later.

Grace looked steadily at her as she set down the bottle. "You're worried?"

"No." Hildie realized that she might be asking about anything. The case, the morning, the wine. She chose the most logical topic. "I think we've made a good start."

"*You've* made a start. I spent hours calming donors and making sure that no alliances were forming."

Hildie looked at her funny. "I thought you liked that. The high-powered stuff."

"I miss fieldwork." She set the glass aside. "Vera's definitely hiding something. And I don't trust Morgan's assistant. You should go after them both."

"I will." She tried to keep the note of irritation out of her voice.

Grace tapped the rim of the glass. "You know the drill. These people love to fight. We deal with the aftermath."

"Like a mythic cleaning service," Hildie muttered.

Grace almost smiled. "Someone has to do it. Night, kid."

She flinched but managed to smile. "Don't stay up too late reading trashy historical fiction." She knew this was the vice Grace was most embarrassed about. For a moment, she imagined something more bleak. Her mother drinking straight vodka from a coffee mug, the way she used to some nights when Hildie was still a girl. Nan's dark stare. Grace red-eyed and trembling as she feverishly wrote down case notes. Hildie used to wonder if she'd become her mother, if all children did as well. She thought of the vodka in her freezer. The condensation on the glass, chilling her fingertips.

They weren't the same. But, like parallel runes, they touched in places.

Hildie finished the wine, grabbed her coat, and stepped outside. It had stopped raining, but everything was storm-touched. Fat blades of grass bowed, heavy and wet. She took off her shoes and walked barefoot down the driveway.

Morgan Arcand was standing there, watching the last guests make their way home. For a second, she didn't seem to see Hildie; she had that distracted look you get when you're trying to find your glasses. Then she said, "You're satisfied?" Her voice had a musical quality, but there was something darker beneath it.

"Excuse me?"

Morgan looked up. "With the interviews."

"We've got some leads." She sounded less confident this time. The dean was making her nervous, like a fire that was about to spread.

Morgan assessed her for a moment. Hildie felt naked. Then the older woman split in two. One Morgan stayed exactly where she was—holding her purse, smiling. Another Morgan whispered in her ear, *Don't wake the beast.*

Then the dean was gone.

Across the street, a fox emerged from a blackberry bush, looking oddly surprised.

4

WAYNE

Kai sat with him on the porch, drinking Growers Cider because it
was all that remained in the fridge. A fizzy, guaranteed hangover.
Wayne picked at the peeling deck chair. Kai played a game on her phone.
The stars burned coldly above Grandview Park. Mo Penley was dissolving quietly somewhere. A family of raccoons made their way across the
parking lot below. *A gaze*, he thought. *That's what a group of raccoons is
called.*

He'd never seen a corpse before—let alone a headless one. The sheared
bone white against the yellow fat, like a strange mural. The ragged edge
of the bite, as if something had tasted him, then spit him out.

"I can't believe you didn't take a picture," Kai said.

"Of his *neck*?"

"No. The teeth marks." She was using her quiet, thinking voice. "My
mom says there are lots of monsters that feed on knights, but they haven't
been around for ages. And none of them are particularly interested in
heads. If you dream about it, you can give me an artist's rendering."

He didn't bother to say that he only dreamed about a few things. The suspension bridge where he'd screamed his mother's name. Her sword in the snow. Sometimes a green-tinted memory of a castle that he could never escape from.

And a beast with eyes like rooms on fire. But he didn't like to think about that.

"Gwalchmai." Kai nudged him.

"Don't use my knight's name," he murmured. "Something could hear." Besides, that was an old version of him. Welsh and warm-blooded. He had a dim memory of shaving Uncle Arthur's beard. The water in the basin, the red of his cheeks. How he'd trusted the blade in his nephew's hand, though some other part of him had been watching, waiting for the slip, the bloom of blood.

"You can't be afraid all the time."

Easy for you to say, he nearly replied. But, of course, it wasn't. She had lots of things to be afraid of. White dudes in trucks, for starters.

She was texting someone. She'd been furtively texting for the past week, but he hadn't asked her about it yet. Kai could be a fortress. She seemed to notice him noticing for the first time. A shy smile played across her face.

"It's just a boy."

"Oh?"

"His name is so embarrassing I can't even tell you."

"More embarrassing than Gwalchmai?"

Her phone buzzed. She read the message, and her eyes lit up, though she didn't laugh. People often took her smile for a smirk, but Wayne knew what it meant. One of the only smiles he actually trusted.

"It's probably nothing," she said. "He's sweet—that's usually a bad sign." Then her smile dissolved as she got another text. He could almost feel her annoyance as she typed something rapidly, so it must have been directed at her mother. For a second, he saw a string of Pinyin characters flashing across the screen, but then she shifted position, and he couldn't get a clear angle on her phone. He shouldn't be eavesdropping anyhow. Kai always had secrets.

"Mama drama?"

Kai closed her eyes briefly. "We play a fun game where, every thirty seconds, she asks if I'm studying runes, and then I say, 'No, Mom, I write epic poetry now.' And then I learn a new horrifying phrase in Cantonese."

Wayne thought of asking a tricky question about Kai's dating life—then decided not to. Instead he asked, "Is there a rune for seduction?"

Kai laughed, and it sounded like bells. "There's a rune for joy. Wyn." She traced a symbol in the air; it looked like a sharp *P*. Just an outline. There was no intention behind it. "Closest thing. It's actually suuuuper dangerous. Fucking magic."

They worried about each other. That had always been part of their friendship. That, and other things. It was always changing. They surprised each other. Plus, they'd both lost a parent. Sometimes Kai's mother wanted her to be a particular kind of runesmith. But Kai needed to do things her own way. Wayne's mother had always just wanted him to be safe. But now she was gone, and his father wasn't talking about it anymore. Wayne needed to know things.

Kai had to work on her computer science project—something to do with arrays. She left and immediately sent him a picture of a handsome dog leaning on a couch. They kept sending it to each other, and it always made them laugh. That dog knew something.

After she'd gone, Wayne made sure that his father was snoring. He checked on all the leaks—brown patches spreading across the balcony. If their landlord decided to renovate and then flip the place, they'd end up homeless. But that was like worrying about rain or traffic. Just the daily ruination of this city. He went back to his room and fished for the box in the back of the closet. The one his dad didn't know about. Put on the Variations, at low volume. Lifted the lid and breathed in. Some of the papers still smelled faintly of smoke.

Before his mother left, she made sure to destroy anything she couldn't take with her. She was thorough that way. But then she'd sent him the key to a post-office box. His dad hadn't seen the key—one of her old allies must have slipped it under the door. Over the years, he'd collected what she sent him in secret: old photos, lists, scraps, and cryptic notes.

He didn't know why she sent the letters. There were no return addresses, no clues for contacting her, no way to reconnect. Maybe it was guilt. Maybe she was preparing him for something. He always felt a mixture of warmth and bitterness when reading her words. The last letter had arrived months ago—nothing since. He felt the absence like the ghost of a meltdown in his brain. White noise building, and with it, the fear that this was it—the end of their correspondence. The final stroke in her departure.

Wayne found what he was looking for almost immediately. A Polaroid photo of Uncle Lance, mugging for the camera. He was raising a glass of wine, as if toasting the photographer. His eyes sparkled, with a hint of danger. Always hard to tell with him. Wayne studied his jaw and dark eyes. There was no mistake.

Uncle Lance had been at the dean's party. Wayne had seen a flicker of him.

But why? He'd been gone for years. His departure was one of many, as their family scattered to the winds. His mother's exit was the last and most final.

He found one of her old papers—something about eye tracking and the visual cortex. That had been one of her research areas. Ironic, since his own ability to make eye contact was so sketchy. He'd grown adept at regarding people's noses and shoulders. He could look into Kai's eyes, because he knew her so well, but it was intimate. Not something for strangers, and even with those closest, it could be too much.

The paper was silken. The first letter—the only one where she tried to explain herself.

It's hard to find the words. Like drawing something from a dark well. I was in exile—that's how it felt. It doesn't mean I don't love you both, unbearably. My life was a cave with walls pressing in. I hope you know that this decision doesn't negate our wonder, our song together. A part of me will always be with you both. And as you get older, I'll try to explain. I was becoming so hard-hearted, and I had to make a choice. I chose myself, and I hope that someday you'll forgive me, leofest.

Wayne reread the letter slowly. Leofest, he knew, meant dearest. It was Anglish—a language she'd rarely spoken in front of him. She'd always wanted to shield him from that world. The world of knights and valkyries and runes that could heal or destroy. *I was in exile.*

Was that how their life together had felt?

She lied about trying to explain. Nothing she said after that came close to an explanation. But he still hoarded the letters. They were all he had.

Dearest Wort,

You must be fourteen now. I can't believe it's been a year since I've seen you. This is the hardest thing I've ever done. I miss your floppy hair, your dancing eyes. I miss the glow of the light under your bedroom door, when I know you're reading. I'm so glad you have Kai in your life. She has a great deal of power, but don't forget that she can be fragile. Take care of each other. When she pushes you to be more social, don't be afraid. But there's also a place for your thoughtful distance—the two of you are halves of a perfect rune.

You were born to be exactly who you are. Things will be very confusing now. I'm sure the dreams have begun. I know you'll be brave enough to be kind.

A knight is more than a sword.

min leof,

Anna

His father used to talk about her—about their old life, among family. But it was harder now. He didn't like to remember. He worked two jobs to afford the rent on this place—their crumbling East Van tower.

Wayne put the box back in the closet. The needle skipped on the record. He replaced the album in its sleeve and crawled into bed.

She was right. The dreams had started around that time. Nightmares where a beast hunted him, and his sword was too heavy to lift.

⟶⟨⟩⟵

He FaceTimed with Kai while making eggs. She was walking from her mom's place near the SkyTrain station. People shivered in their wool coats, and he could hear yelling outside the McDonald's on Broadway. The B-Line bus was a constant rumble in the background. Once he put the phone too close to the stove, and Kai yelled, "What's that noise? Is your apartment on fire?" The eggs popped and snapped.

Kai showed up as he was plating their breakfast. He heard her boots on the stairwell, then the sound of her key in the door. She walked into the kitchen and deposited a paper bag on the table. "Almost got into a fight over these cannolis, so you'd better enjoy them."

"What happened?"

Kai sat down. "Trust-funders in line at Fratelli Bakery. Staring at me like I was on the menu."

"I'm sorry that boys are monsters."

"Me too." She drowned her eggs in Tapatío hot sauce. "Did you go straight to bed last night, after I left?"

He raised an eyebrow. This was Kai's way of asking about his emotional state, which she rarely did. She wasn't the hug and sympathy type. More like the Slurpees and video games until dawn type.

"I sort of feel like an origami creature that got folded one too many times."

She bumped her foot against his. "Sorry, Bear."

She'd started calling him Bear in high school, after he'd put on weight. *Embrace it*, she'd said. *You're a mega bear babe, and everyone wants your honey pot.*

He felt more like a hungover Winnie the Pooh. He even had the right outfit: a striped shirt and boxers. Though Winnie didn't wear bottoms at all. Just let it all hang out, flashing the Hundred Acre Wood like the perv that he was.

34

He made Kai a third egg, in spite of her protests. She always wanted a third egg, because there was never enough yolk to saturate the rye bread. By the time he was done washing the dishes, Kai had already picked out an outfit for him. She'd avoided his collection of graphic tees and chosen a black shirt that he swore was too small.

Kai stared at her phone while he got changed. "There's so much drama on my queer Discord channel," she said. "Between that and the trans femme group chat, I feel like I'm trapped in an emotional car chase." Finally, she looked up. "Put it on. *All the way* on, Gwalchmai."

The tag on the shirt made his skin crawl, and the belt was a torture device, but he had to admit that Kai was right. He did look pretty okay.

"I like that skirt," he said.

"Thanks. I stole it from H&M."

"*Kai.* You can't keep doing that."

"After the security guard leered at me for a half hour, I felt that I deserved it." She dug through her bag while he finished getting dressed. "I don't want to code anything. I want to stay home and watch *Euphoria.*"

He tried to make his hair look like anything other than a wet terrier. "You could probably do that and still ace the course."

"Nah. Some of it is actually tricky. I'd like to get a job someday, and they tend to frown on applicants who slept through Java Programming and Applications."

"I still don't understand what Java is."

"A super boring thing with a delicious name." Kai scowled. "It's like—I can do this stuff without breaking a sweat. I'm decent at it. But sitting in a lab surrounded by nerds and future MRA boys is giving me rage face."

Kai usually kept her eye on the normal world. She rarely talked about traditions. They'd gone to a mainstream school, where Kai tried and failed to fit in. Sometimes, in exasperation, she'd sketch runes with him in an empty field.

Kai picked up her *My Neighbor Totoro* bag. "Honestly. We could ditch. Compassionate reasons."

"I can't really miss this class."

"Ah. It's *that* one, is it?"

He nodded. "Plus, I've got an appointment at the Student Success Office."

"Oh God. Steal one of their motivational posters for me."

"If I don't go, it could mess with my financial aid. Plus, if I really want to—" He shrugged. "Anyway. I should go. I said I would. Maybe if I tell them I saw a dead body, they'll give me an advance on my student loan."

"Is the valkyrie stalking you?"

"I haven't seen her."

"And the other fellow—what was his name? Ernie?"

He felt the warmth rise to his cheeks. "You know his name."

"*Bert.*" She chuckled. "Hard to imagine an epic romance with someone named after an oatmeal-obsessed puppet with OCD. But to each his own."

"Uh-huh."

She snatched the comb out of his hand. "Have you formed a trauma bond? With Ernie?"

"I know what you're doing. I'm not going to feel optimistic about some moment at a nightmarish death party. I mean, there's a real Valkyrian investigation happening. That's the priority. Not—"

"Cruising in the provost's library?"

"Exactly. It was nothing."

"I thought he held your hand."

Wayne's stomach fluttered. "He was just being human."

"You know the last time a guy held my hand in public?" Her expression turned bleak for a moment. Then she smiled. "Did you get his details? Let's message him on Scruff."

Wayne grabbed his keys and Compass card for the bus. "I doubt we'll talk again."

Kai said nothing. But she had her resolve face on, which was not good. He'd have to keep an eye on his phone all day.

Commercial Drive hummed as they made their way to the SkyTrain station. Pigeons dive-bombed them in search of stray fries. They scrounged up enough change to buy coffee from Continental, which was already full of students on laptops. Kai ducked into Pulpfiction and bought a copy of Casey Plett's *Little Fish*. Wayne found a Tiffany Aching novel, because he was a champion enabler of book-buying. Part of their friendship had always been justifying each other.

They'd both always lived here. Kai said that Commercial Drive was the only place where she felt like herself.

They piled onto the bus, squeezing their way to the back. They found two seats, and Kai used her bag like a spear to defend them. Students were packed so tightly that no one needed to hold on to anything. Their bodies melted into each other. A woman read skillfully, her boots planted against the rumbling floor. A hundred phone conversations gathered like smog above their heads. Word clouds that he couldn't quite shut out.

After a while, he became aware of someone staring at them. A group of guys were chuckling in a sinister way that he'd learned to recognize from a young age. The sound of boys hunting in a pack. One of them pointed at Kai. He heard the guy snicker.

Kai's expression remained neutral. She stared out the window.

The guys kept staring.

Wayne felt a stab of anger. He made a move to stand up, but Kai put a hand on his knee. "Don't," she said. The resignation in her voice made his heart ache. He seethed, but said nothing. Instead, he pulled out his earbuds and split them with Kai. Phoebe Bridgers sang a techno dirge as they drove up the mountain. The engine was whining now. They were nearly at the top.

His mother had once told him that a dragon lived in the heart of the mountain, breathing steam and sizzling in the rain.

The university came into view. It looked like a castle—the kind you'd see on a cliffside, guarding against some force that had long ago crumbled to dust. Apparently, when the university opened, it had been full of Marxists and deconstructionists who wanted to dismantle the whole system of teaching. It didn't feel particularly radical to him now. Or maybe the radicals had retreated to hidden caves to live with the dragon.

They walked up the stairs that led to the quad, hemmed in by concrete and Escher-like steps that led off in all directions. There was a line outside the library, which had installed a new automated checkout system that never worked.

Wayne muttered something beneath his breath.

"What was that?" Kai dug around in her bag.

"I should have hit those assholes," Wayne said.

"Perfect. You'd get to be the cis white boy hero, without any of the consequences."

He looked away. "Sorry."

"It's fine, Bear. I mean, it's not. It's daily and fucked and it's why I hate leaving the house." She forced herself to grin. "But check *this* out. I get a free muffin because I've gone through this punch card like a hurricane."

As they walked by the garbage bins, Wayne thought he saw a fox tail sticking out of the recycling. He frowned and drew closer, but it vanished inside. He was going to lift the lid, but feared that Kai might think he was losing it. Foxes didn't stalk people. Besides, maybe he was actually the one stalking the fox. Whatever that meant.

"I'm off to conquer Java," Kai said. "In an anticolonial way. Good luck."

"You too."

He watched her stride across campus. She could take a lot. She was much stronger than him. But sometimes he wished they could just lock themselves in a library.

The lecture hall was halfway across campus, and he was carrying a fifty-pound knapsack and dodging through more crowds. He would *not* be late. He would become the smiling student in the posters—the one without any issues.

It was nearly full when he got there. He paused to take in the space. It had vaulted ceilings, and in the dim light, he could make out at least one hundred students. The light of their smartphones reminded him of votive candles in the dark.

Dr. Grisi stood at the podium, shuffling through papers. He had to think of her as a professor, not his aunt. But she didn't even have a laptop. Dear God, was that a pencil behind her ear?

He sank into a seat near the back, feeling slightly mortified. He was actually related to this person. The last thing he wanted was a close relative marking one of his half-baked essays.

The lights dimmed further, as dark as if they were in a movie theatre. The students next to him were playing an online game that seemed to involve hot dads. One row down, someone was quietly FaceTiming.

Dr. Grisi projected an image on the giant screen. It looked Victorian or something. A woman in a garden, with long braided hair. She had a crown, but it was understated. Like there was no need for opulence. She *was* the crown. She held a flower, and her eyes knew something precious. Wayne felt like she could see right through him. There was a castle in the distance, but she was at the center of the illustration.

"Does anyone know who this is?"

Wayne closed his eyes. *She can't be serious.*

There was murmuring in the crowd.

"Anyone? Wild guesses?"

She was silent for about five seconds. He watched a hundred phones light up as students searched for *old woman* and *medieval times*.

"Her name," the professor said, "is Guinevere. The queen of Camelot. Howard Pyle depicts her in 1903 with an air of natural mystery. We tend to see her as this background figure, but she was a powerful politician in her own right. Now she's most famous for being involved in a kinky sex triangle."

There was some nervous laughter in the audience. He saw one guy stick out his tongue suggestively and high-five a buddy.

"Part of what we'll be talking about in this class," she continued, "is how figures like this are remade over time, distorted, adapted by the people who read about them. You may think you know the story behind King Arthur and Queen Guinevere, but the *real* story is a lot messier than that. It can't be contained. And it's still being rewritten in all kinds of adaptations."

He ducked out halfway through to make his appointment at the Office for Student Success, Financial Aid, Diversity, and Academic Recovery. The office was located in a glassed-in atrium, where sunlight poured in, making the tableau of desperate students waiting look like a Renaissance painting. A student using a wheelchair was politely arguing with one of the clerks, who seemed surprised that the cafeteria turnstiles might be a problem.

Wayne made it to the front and submitted his paperwork. The clerk looked it over, then made a funny noise, sort of like a printer that was out of paper. "You'll need a clinician's letter," he said, "if you want this accommodation."

His heart sank. "Look. That whole thing is sort of in progress. Isn't this enough? I have a doctor's note and I've filled out all the forms—"

"You'll need a note from a *psychiatrist*." He said the word so loudly that a few students looked over, mildly interested. "We require proof of—"

Wayne snatched away the forms. "Right. I'll be back."

He could feel his cheeks burning as he ran back to the lecture hall, hoping to catch the second half of class. If one more person asked him for proof of anything, he'd lose it. Though that's what his documentation was supposed to prove in the first place. That he was *losing it*.

Kai texted him. *Bear! How's the big scary lecture hall? Does Vera grow horns when she teaches?*

His aunt teaching medieval studies—like she wasn't a medieval study herself.

He thought about Uncle Lance, who could always make them laugh. Why had he been at that party? Had Vera seen him?

Wayne just wanted to survive his first semester. But the body kept shimmering in his memory, like a shadow at the edge of his vision. How close he'd been to something dead. How it hadn't really been the first time, and wouldn't be the last.

5

HILDIE

Hildie thought about past lives as she walked through campus, which seemed to be made of endless staircases. Her nan went to university—one of the first women to graduate in her program. Grace had thrown herself into the family business. Hildie's time in college was a blur of survey classes and sleepless nights. Trying to juggle psychology and philosophy and literature and forensic science meant burning through highlighters at an alarming rate. She'd dropped out in her second year. She hadn't fit in with the other students, and she didn't fit in now. When you can see death everywhere, it's hard to relax at parties.

Now she was here to follow up. She didn't have leads, exactly. She wasn't even sure if Dean Arcand—*Provost* Arcand now—would meet with her, though Bertram had politely made the appointment. It would give her the chance to see both of them in their natural habitat. And Vera Grisi as well. Queens and runesmiths haunting a castle on a mountaintop.

Once, Nan had been investigating the death of a local runesmith, who seemed to have spontaneously combusted in their apartment.

A perfect Sherlock Holmes sealed-room case. She'd written in her notebook, *folc trust their eðel.*

That's what all her notes were like—a mixture of English and older Anglish. The word *eðel* meant home turf. People trust home. Through years of investigation, her grandmother had learned that what people told you depended on where you talked to them. Lies for every space, but occasionally a truth snuck its way in. Hildie hoped that speaking to Arcand and Bertram at work might reveal new details.

The thing with knights was that they needed jobs. You couldn't live off a myth. Some never actually figured out that they were knights, while others came from a long cycle of stories, hearing about their birthright as young as possible. Penley had come from a cycle of dicks. People who tended to choose positions where they could abuse their power. They left a paper trail.

Hildie walked into the former Faculty of Arts building, which had been renamed Human Arts—whatever that meant. There were panels missing like gap teeth in the drop-down ceiling. It looked as though nothing had been renovated in years. Dr. Vera Grisi shared an office with various other adjunct instructors. The door's sign simply read *Sessional Office.* Hildie thought it was an odd word. Like people who were teaching from one season to the next, rather than scholars who'd devoted their lives to teaching, without making anything close to a living wage. She found Vera at a nondescript desk, marking essays.

Vera looked up. "Oh. When I wished for a break from marking, you weren't what I had in mind." She had a wry smile, but the mild combativeness was still there. She may just be an adjunct professor, but she still had powerful connections. And royal blood.

"Answer a few questions and I'll be out of your hair." Hildie glanced at a ficus, which was struggling to survive in the windowless office. "Which words come to mind when I say Mo Penley's name?"

"Several." Vera put down her pencil. She looked tired, but strong. Her eyes were alive and energetic. "Some people take this job to teach. Some like research. And some just want power. That was Penley."

42

"He was destined for administration?"

Vera laughed. "Perfect way of putting it—given who we are. Obviously he was stealth, for the most part. Morgan knew who he was, where he came from. She was threatened by him. Not at first. But he rose quickly through the ranks. He could be a wild card."

"Or a wild myth."

Vera almost smiled. "Indeed."

"Morgan isn't afraid of much."

"She's old and stubborn. Mo was young and arrogant. I know he was pushing for some kind of break with tradition."

That was news to Hildie. She'd thought of him as conservative—someone who wanted the status quo.

"He wanted *less* tradition?"

Vera did that thing where you try to take a long pull of coffee, only to realize that the cup is empty. She stared at it for a second, then put it back down. "Do you know what my last teaching evaluation said?"

It was an odd question. "Do I want to?"

Vera smirked. "It said, 'Lady was very knowledgeable.'" She laughed darkly. "*Lady.* Like I was a substitute teacher. If they only knew the schools I've attended—the things I had to learn, painfully, permanently. The price of that knowledge. But as soon as I appear, they see a mean old lady. At least no one threatens to burn me anymore. The number of times I got tied to a stake—" She shook her head. "Those days were never dull."

Hildie saw a different side of her in that moment. Vera was a former queen, and she had the reputation for being imperious. She got shit done and didn't really care what people thought of her. But this Vera was also dealing with her own future. Nobody bowed to her anymore. She worked at a university that saw her as expendable. But she hadn't stopped caring about anything.

Hildie thought about how people must see her. A valkyrie who'd inherited a job, rather than earning it. Close to power without any of her own, except for the spear that was her birthright. Some version of Vera, some past shadow, must have known her nan, and her nan's nan, going all the way back to a cliffside in Cornwall. Exchanging uneasy glances. Did Vera see her as an actual person, or just a faint echo of greatness? Hildie was so tired of proving herself to ghosts. She wanted to be simple and ignored—the kind of person who worked on a laptop in a coffee shop with concrete floors. Someone quietly creating whatever she wanted to.

Or maybe she just wanted to want that. To be the kind of person who'd be happy like that. She seemed nice and self-contained, that Hildie.

"Why did you bring your nephew to that party?"

Vera's expression flickered—as if she was deciding on something.

Hildie said, "One second."

Hildie went down the hall to the lounge that said *Faculty Only*. She'd noticed it on her way in. There was a fancy coffee maker there— candy-red, like a sports car. Hildie grabbed a pair of mugs and made two cappuccinos. Several professors looked at her in surprise. She gave them a winning smile as the frother made a mad sound.

Hildie returned to Vera's office, handing her a coffee.

Vera took the mug carefully at first, like it was a poisoned apple.

Then she took a sip, and smiled. "That was daring of you."

"I grew up in a tricky part of town. I'm used to people telling me to keep out."

Vera held the mug with both hands. It was a soft gesture. "Anna—his mother—she wanted a normal life for Wayne. Whatever that meant. But then she left him adrift. Gale and I half raised him. His dad's always been around, but he works so much." She stared at the crema, like a foamy, fairy-tale castle floating atop the mug. "I wanted him to know where he came from. And maybe I was looking for protection."

"From Morgan?"

Vera chuckled. "Her favors tend to have fangs. But Mo Penley—" She glanced outside, to make sure the hallway was empty. "He had a lot of power. He could make Wayne's life at school a bit easier." She shook her head. "I shouldn't have done it. I took him to a fancy party, and he ended the night standing next to a headless body. The medieval irony isn't lost on me."

Hildie tried to keep her tone neutral. "You and Gale used to be friends with Morgan—back in the day."

Vera's eyes shone. "So *that's* what the coffee was about. Trying to get under my fortifications to dig out the real dirt."

"I saw a photo of you in her guest room."

For the first time, Vera looked surprised. "She kept that?"

"Seems like you were close at one time."

"The four of us were a little myth on our own."

"Four of you?"

Something in Vera's expression slammed shut. "I have to get back to marking. Please don't pester my nephew too much. He's had a shock."

Hildie showed herself out. That was all she'd get.

Provost Arcand kept her waiting for twenty minutes. Bert was actually doing his job as her assistant. They'd recently moved to her new office, which was palatial, with a marble floor. His eyes were glued to multiple screens, and he answered one call after the other while updating her calendar. She'd expected him to be resentful of the position, but he was actually good at his job.

Finally, there was a lull. Hildie approached his desk.

"Sorry about the wait," Bert said, flashing her a grin. "Can I offer you bottled water, or a university-branded granola bar?"

She shook her head. "What should I know about your boss?"

He glanced at the double doors that led to her office. It wasn't fear on his face, precisely. More like reticence. He minimized several windows on the screen, and his fingers tapped the desk absently. The phone rang. Surprisingly, he ignored it.

"She has a vision," he said slowly, as if he was sounding out the idea behind each word. "She'll do what she has to, in order to make that happen. She can be difficult. But people respect her. I think she would have—"

The double doors seemed to open on their own. Bert cut short whatever he'd been about to say.

Hildie stepped into Morgan's office. There were furs on the floor, tapestries on the walls. Artifacts under glass. She saw what looked like an ancient belt buckle, with gold animals swirling around each other. A garnet brooch shimmered next to it—similar to her badge, though perhaps older, more elaborate. A broadsword hung on the wall. She wondered if security had anything to say about that.

Morgan didn't rise from her desk. Runes crawled along the edges—they might just pass for foliate carvings, if you didn't look too hard.

"I owe your mother a favor," Morgan said. "You get five minutes. After that, I have to attend a dean's council meeting." Her voice was smooth and neutral, like water moving across stones. Where Vera had a hidden warmth to her, Morgan seemed like an administrator to the core. Professional but impatient, always coolly assessing whatever came before her.

Not all myths were alike. The knights—they tended to repeat across generations. Sometimes they were reborn into loving families, and other times, they were dangerous anomalies within an otherwise unremarkable family tree—a sudden genetic tweak that came out of nowhere. They had to find each other. Recognize each other like animals in a forest. But myths like Morgan—they were different. She seemed always to be herself, or all of her selves. She lived and died and awoke more or less the same, only with a longer shadow. Hildie would have known more, if those parts of her file hadn't been blacked out.

What had Grace said about that? *They all have secrets.*

Morgan gestured to a teapot on her desk—the most human thing in the room. Hildie poured herself a cup in the name of hospitality.

"So. Who wanted Penley dead?" Hildie sipped. "Besides you, of course."

Morgan didn't raise an eyebrow at the accusation. "I didn't want any of this, Grace's daughter."

That stung. "But you did want to be provost."

"I have ideas for revising the school's strategic plan. Mo had different ideas. That does not mean I wanted his headless body in my guest room."

"What about the rune on the body?"

Morgan's hands were still on the desk, but another part of her seemed to be moving, gathering into itself. "An unusual choice," she said. "One doesn't see that particular rune very often. At least not in that context."

"What does it mean?"

She narrowed her eyes. "I don't teach anymore, Detective. You'll need to investigate that on your own."

Hildie tried not to let that rankle her. "And the rune on your banister? What was that one protecting?"

Morgan's expression didn't change, but Hildie could see that she'd gained a bit of ground. She'd asked the right question—the irritating one.

"I have a manuscript library upstairs. It's worth a great deal—and some of the titles are more dangerous than others. It's no crime to protect what belongs to me."

Hildie kept her voice neutral. "Fine. I'll do my job. I'll consider everyone. But give me a general direction here. Who could have done it?"

Morgan glanced, almost unconsciously, at the sword. Light from the vast windows made it gleam like a molten filament.

"Someone is working from the margins," she said. "Someone who cares little for the careful hierarchies that we've built."

"What about the beast?"

Morgan blinked. "I don't follow."

"Back at the house, you whispered in my ear, 'Don't wake the beast.'"

She smiled in a polished way. "You must have misheard. It was a long night."

"Something took a chunk out of Mo's body."

"Someone also took a fifth of him as a souvenir." Morgan lifted up a folder. "Perhaps you could start looking for rogue knights with a cranial fetish. I have a budget meeting, so we need to wrap this up."

"Thought it was a dean's council meeting."

Morgan looked through her. For a moment, Hildie saw something standing beside the woman at the desk. Something with feathers and eyes and hooked beaks. It opened its mouths and shrieked. The sound froze her blood.

Then time skipped forward. Morgan was standing by the open door.

"If I think of anything pertinent," she said, "my assistant will be in touch."

Hildie tried to keep the thorn out of her voice. "It's in your best interest to be honest with us. To help us in this investigation as much as you can."

"Or what?" Morgan's inflection didn't change, but her shadows swirled. "You'll put me in front of a tribunal? A council of spear women? We both know those days are gone. You're mostly bureaucrats now. Filing paperwork for the fates."

She gestured to Morgan's desk. "You've got a lot of paperwork yourself."

"Well. Myths used to cut. Now we administrate."

"But there's still power." Hildie held her gaze. "In all the old stories."

Morgan simply smiled.

She'd get nothing else.

It took a half hour to find her car in the underground parking lot. Everything looked the same. Not for the first time, she wished for a palfrey.

Stuck in bridge traffic, Hildie looked through Nan's notes, to see if she'd ever recorded anything about Morgan Arcand. She found a brief interview from decades ago, but most of it had been aggressively redacted in black marker. Unlike her to be so cagey. In the margin, she'd written *wings and possibilities*.

Hildie stared at it for a long time but couldn't decipher it.

Their office was in the old Sun Tower on Pender Street, with its greening cupola that marked an older skyline. When it was built at the turn of the century, the sculpted women that encircled the roof made quite a scandal. Imagine if people had realized that they weren't just seminude decorations. They were stone guardians that you didn't want to cross.

Hildie pressed the button for the eighth floor. The old, creaky elevator rose. She had an affection for it. It was like a floral couch that had once been beautiful; you couldn't quite throw it away.

The doors opened, and she was met with a familiar hallway. The thing about the Sun Tower was that it had seventeen floors, but the elevator couldn't get to the dome. That left nine floors left to climb the old-fashioned way. Every. Single. Day.

The first flight was always easy. She'd actually feel a sense of accomplishment when she hit the first landing. The second flight felt a bit excessive. By the time she reached the third, her calves were barbed wire. Not for the first time, she wondered what the fine was for puking in a heritage space.

The dome was much larger on the inside. Stray cobwebs rippled from the steel girders, and there was a smell that she could only describe as river rock. The ring of oculi, looking out on the city, reminded her of porthole windows. You could see little circular flashes of the skyline. A ladder rose into the center of the dome, leading to the uppermost point of the cupola. Her mother's office.

Valkyries worked at scattered desks. All of the furniture was salvaged, since they got so little funding from the community. They were a fading myth now. Most people didn't even know they existed. Women sat around old dining room tables, converted nightstands, ruined IKEA furniture that had been cast off. Most were entering data on rescued Pentium and Compaq desktops that took a century to boot up. Some were reading through case files, studying maps of the city, or squinting as they tried to decipher their own handwritten notes.

There were a few waves as she entered the workspace. A few stony looks. Mostly silence. Everyone knew her mother was the one with the rooftop office.

Hildie didn't want the office. She wanted a real life. Most days.

Grace wanted her to marry someone loyal and have little valkyries to keep the legacy going. Neither of those things was going to happen.

Hildie sighed and climbed up the ladder. It was like a reverse firehouse scene, designed for maximum humiliation. Some of her colleagues could do it with dignity, but Hildie felt like a benched athlete who'd suddenly been thrown on the ice as she wobbled her way up to her mother's unfathomable level.

Grace sat at a table made from a blasted tree. It was a Douglas fir, at least a thousand years old, and lightning had traced scar tissue along its surface. She worked on a touch pad, clicking with efficiency.

"You've dealt with the sisters, I trust."

She bit down on what she'd been about to say. "Not yet."

"Hildie." Her mother pronounced her name like it was an off-brand product on sale. "The clock is ticking."

She tried to clear her mind. It didn't work. Her mind was a hoarder. "Why am I listed as secondary on my own case?"

Grace looked up at her. "You've decided to take this personally."

"How can I not?"

Grace didn't quite set down her tablet, but she did move it slightly to the side. "You know this is high profile. The community is a hornet's nest right now. If I list you as the lead, considering all the variables—"

"Then you'd have to admit that I can do my job?" Hildie kept her expression neutral. This was an endless fight they'd been replaying since she was a teenager. She felt herself settling into well-worn footprints and familiar phrases. Why did five minutes alone with her mother always hurl her back in time? She was thirteen again, Grace pounding on the door. *I will not be spoken to like I'm some kind of monster. Hildegard, let me in!* Under the covers, drawing out her spear from the darkness where it lived. Feeling its cold perfection in her hand. Letting it appear, then disappear, as her blood shivered.

Grace was unmoved. "You'll prove the latter by solving the case. And you'll have plenty of help. Whatever you need."

"Except for records without holes in them."

Grace gave her an odd look. Maybe it was protective? But that sometimes looked like annoyance on her.

"It's dangerous to know everything," she said. "There are places even I can't go. But I'll keep you in the loop as much as I can."

"While taking all the credit."

Something flashed across her eyes. "Is that what you want? Fame? Because you chose the wrong line of work."

I didn't choose it!

Hildie let out her breath slowly through her nose. "What I want is your trust."

"And you have it. Think of me as a silent partner."

A silent partner controlling my every move.

Grace had returned to staring at the tablet. "Better get a move on."

"What about the provost? She wasn't exactly forthcoming in her interview. Do you think she's messing with us?"

Grace smiled thinly. "Darling. She's living for it. That's what she does. You've got to catch her in the knot, and pull it tight."

Hildie climbed back down the ladder, which was impossible to do in a dignified fashion. She didn't wave at anyone on her way out. She walked down the endless stairs in silence.

She didn't even know where to start. The menacing provost. The weird personal assistant. The queen marking essays. And the clueless nephew.

Hildie cut across Cordova and walked down to Water Street. Gastown was in full swing. The windows of the Black Frog tavern were already steamed up, and the bouncer was scanning the line for beautiful faces. A group of film students was shooting a project that involved light-up masks and dancing. They leaped around like monsters in a wild rumpus, while a drum track echoed in the background.

She imagined this neighborhood how it once was, at the close of the nineteenth century. Traders and sailors and mill workers partying it up in cheap saloons. People meeting up for clandestine sex in flea-bitten rooms, tangled in sour sheets. The cry of the mill in the distance, like an axe being ground to fatal perfection.

The sisters worked out of Hotel Wyrd, near the site of the original Hastings Mill. Railtown was one of the oldest neighborhoods, and the hotel had been there since before the nineteenth century. From the outside, it resembled a block of crumbling apartments in a neighborhood whose borders were indistinct.

The hotel side-eyed anyone who came too near. Imagine if a Victorian building had a drunken fling with a dignified bed-and-breakfast. Add some crumbling marble and a chandelier that might have escaped the wreck of the *Titanic*. People stayed here when they wanted to vanish. People who weren't entirely people. The sisters enabled a variety of gray market activities, but they kept things safe and clean, for the most part.

Hildie felt something like spiderwebs brush her face as she walked into the lobby. Best not to think about what they really were.

True to its name, the lobby was weird. A kelpie basked in her indoor koi pond. It was hard to interview a carnivorous aquatic horse, and Hildie didn't mind leaving that particular case as pending.

Shar was working the counter. It helped that she liked people. Hildie wondered how that would feel. She imagined a warm, oozy feeling of contentment, like marshmallow fluff. Strange to feel that way, especially with the knowledge that they had. Her real name meant shear in Anglish, because she cut souls like thread. Her sharp edge created the future. She'd modified the spelling for customer service.

As a valkyrie, Hildie's gift—more of an inconvenience—was smelling death. She didn't know whose exactly—just that she was close to it. As gifts went, it was a bit shite. Often, the details of the death were obscure, but if she tugged on that invisible thread, she always saw something. The sisters had a lot more thread to work with.

Shar waved at her as she approached the desk. Her head was shaved on one side, and a long purple braid hung down the other. It moved slightly; there was an entire ecosystem in there. She was wearing a tapestry repurposed as a skirt.

"How's business?" Hildie asked, knowing the answer.

Shar put her head on the desk. "Burst pipe on the third floor. Phoenix ashes in the bathroom. Any idea how difficult those are to clean? Plus, a *certain horse* keeps eating all of our fish as a midnight snack. We only let her stay because kelpies have the best gossip."

The kelpie snorted water and seaweed onto the carpet.

Shar closed her eyes for a second. Then her smile returned. She was a cheerful person who only wanted to murder people occasionally. "I take it you're here about Mo."

Hildie nodded. "Grace is breathing down my neck, so I'd like to get this over with quickly. He's in the undercroft?"

"They're prepping him now."

She put out a sign that read, in Anglish, *The sisters will be with you shortly.* Then she said, "Come on. Let's head to the basement. You can't keep a body waiting."

They squeezed into the ancient elevator. Shar turned a key in the panel, and the art-deco coffin made its way to the subbasement. The undercroft was cold and had a dirt floor. Normally that wouldn't be a problem, except that it was raining. Weather in the undercroft tended to be idiosyncratic. Shar and Hildie shared an umbrella as they made their way carefully across the chamber.

"If I'd known it was raining," Hildie said, "I wouldn't have worn these shoes."

"Tell me about it. A few hours ago it was snowing, and I ruined a pair of ballet flats." In between the raindrops, Hildie could make out glittering particles of dust. They settled like a mist around the vaulted ceiling. She smelled earth and, beneath it, the sweet tang of decay. Penley's body was laid out on a stone bier. A canopy shielded him from the rain. He was naked, and she glanced quickly at him, then away. He had a light dusting of blond hair on his chest, now shattered by the wound.

The eldest sister, Clywen, gently washed the headless body. She sang beneath her breath while winding a black cloth around him. Her name meant the ball of thread that connected people to the past. Braeda, the middle sister, washed his pale hands. She was the braided present, eternally now, so she kept glancing at the newsfeed on her phone (to Clywen's annoyance). When Braeda was done, she reached into a vacant fireplace and withdrew a fistful of ashes. She brushed them across what was left of Penley.

That left Shar, the baby: the future.

Together, the sisters saw everything, forgave everything, and rarely freaked out.

"You're late," Braeda said.

"Are they?" Clywen always looked like she was remembering something. Her gray hair was a bit wild. "I thought they were early."

"*Late*," Braeda repeated. "We've got too much to do. I have to check on a soccer game, a dissertation defense, and an open-heart surgery in the next"—she glanced at her phone—"*two minutes.*"

Braeda had the energy level of an overcommitted mom who was trying to secure world peace while arguing with the PTA. If they hadn't been so close to a dead body, she'd be double-fisting two cold brews.

Clywen simply nodded in agreement. When you spent most of your time in the past, no amount of calendar alerts would keep you tethered.

"Hi, Hildie." Braeda didn't look up from washing his foot. "How's your mother? Is she sleeping well? I have a tonic if she isn't." Braeda always spoke like she was on multiple conference calls.

Hildie pointed to the ragged wound below his breastbone. "Any teeth marks that we could possibly identify?"

"Reminds me of a dragon wound I saw once," Clywen said wistfully. "Those were the days. Baby dragons everywhere."

"No match in our files." Braeda gestured to a cabinet overflowing with papers, papyrus rolls, clay tablets, bark inscribed with runes, stained glass, and a few vellum leaves that looked a little *too* much like skin. "Lots of monsters to check on though. Could be a gryphon—they're bitey—or a pissed off wyvern, or—" Her phone chimed. "Just give me—"

"*Braeda.*" Clywen gave her a surprisingly coherent look. "We need you."

Braeda stared longingly at her phone but nodded. "Right. Right." She had a soft, heart-shaped face, and her expressions went a mile a minute. You always knew where you stood with Braeda because she wouldn't stop telling you. She also appeared to have tied back her hair with an old fan belt, or maybe an elastic waistband?

The sisters were like coroners, only much older and more dangerous if you crossed their jurisdiction. They didn't always provide clear answers. But they were the closest thing the valkyries had to a microscope. People in the community had the habit of being reborn, and the valkyries were the only ones who kept decent records on who they'd been before, what they'd done, and how they were likely to manifest again. Myths had no absolute beginning or ending, so some of the records were closer to poetry than data, but that was all they had. Like stories and cities, they changed with the times. The sisters were the oldest myths of all. They were like volcanoes. You respected them above all else, and got out of their way.

Hildie stared at the white of Mo Penley's spine. The ghost of his head, as if someone had chipped off a piece of stained glass. "Where do you think it ended up?"

"There are all sorts of things you can do with a head," Clywen said, almost absently, "if you like rituals. Or games."

Hildie shivered, then decided not to ask a follow-up question.

They formed a circle around the body. The undercroft stilled, as if someone had placed a hand over the world. Even the raindrops froze. Hildie felt the power in her bones. She could just make out a black thread tied to the body's toe. It fluttered. Clywen tugged on it, gently. It unraveled, like floating black silk. In the void, she could see his memories. Neural strands that trembled, already fraying and coming apart. A sturdy boy reaching for a flower. A woman with silver hair and laughter that was tinkling bells. A sword, surprisingly heavy in his hand. All the years rushing by like water, years upon years, then centuries, until he was drowning. Every shadow of him, all those boys and some girls and some who were beautifully in-between, reaching for the flower and the sword. Fear and desire braided.

To her surprise, Vera Grisi's face flashed across the skein of memories. There was blood and dirt on her face. She stood in a high tower, holding a sword, as Mo banged a heavy fist against the door. Two armies crashed into each other. Vera said something to Mo, and his face flushed red with anger, maybe shame.

Then she saw the outline of something else, but there were no details. Just a blank slash.

Shar took the last of the thread in her hands. The end of his future. It was strangely backlit, all the colors distorted by a garish filter. He was in a snug room, alone. Hildie recognized it as Morgan's spare bedroom. The only sound was rain and music from downstairs. She looked through

Mo's eyes at the photo on the desk. Morgan Arcand in her red blouse. Vera Grisi looking happy and exasperated at the same time. Gale Amadís with his arm around the queen, as if he was her one true knight. It was the last thing Mo ever saw.

What was he looking for in that picture?

Something screamed in the distance. Not a human scream.

Then it was over.

Shar opened her hands. The thread was fire now, throwing off sparks that rose to the ceiling and joined the dust motes. Then it was ash. Shar let it fall to the ground.

"He's not exactly dead." Hildie cleared her throat. "Right?"

"No one's exactly dead," Shar replied. "But his particular thread is cut. There will be other Mordreds. But this one is ash and rain."

Shar pointed to his neck. "Clean cut. Sharp axe, I'd say."

"Very sharp." Clywen traced a finger down Mo's chest. "What else?"

His body parted at her touch. Like an X-ray, her fingertip shone into him. Hildie saw the dark contents, red and wet. Not just his scars, but the scars of every Mo before him. Knife bites and sword strokes and crushed ribs and ruptures. An appendix scar. A seam along his ankle, from a fall. The scar tissue of countless lifetimes. Some of the wounds were reckless. Some came from love, or hate. Some were cosmic accidents. The natural shocks of being almost human.

Clywen paused at the base of his breastbone. She was still for a moment. The folds of her dress reminded Hildie of a waterfall in negative colors. Then she nodded. She beckoned to her sisters. They placed their hands on his chest and closed their eyes.

Their voices were eerie. The sound of a glacier cracking, of a fox walking gently on snow. Barely a whisper, and also vast. A susurrus of leaves and background radiation. They sang a familiar charm.

> Out little spear, wherever you may be.
> Out, out, little spear.
> Out of breast, out of bone, heed our song.

Hildie felt it in her marrow, in her mitochondria. Her grandmother and great-grandmother, joining in. Blowing through her like breath shaping molten glass from the inside.

In a sudden daydream, she moved through the underbrush. In the clearing up ahead, she saw three giant women dancing in a circle around a tree. They had spears, and they were singing in a language that she could only partially understand. The tree was massive, and its branches extended in all directions, blotting out the sun. Even from a distance, she could see the great leaves rustling, the breath pushing up from the roots. The women kept dancing, and their spears met at odd angles, forming shapes that also seemed familiar.

The giant women spoke, *You are the charm. You are the dawn-watcher. You are the crow's gift and the riddled earth.*

Hildie frowned. "Is this a Tolkien thing?"

Wake up.

They flung their spears.

Hildie threw up her naked hands.

But the giants were gone. It was just the sisters in the room with her and Mo, or what had formerly been Mo.

Shar looked at her with concern. But this was ritual space, and she had to remain neutral. People were already suspicious of their friendship. You didn't casually share a pint with an immortal spirit-weaver. Everything caused ripples.

"You saw something," Clywen said. Her tone was bemused. The way you'd speak to a child who was figuring out gravity.

"Just an old nightmare," Hildie said.

"Your ancestors speak to you that way. Always listen to them, and don't be afraid."

Even when they try to skewer you?

Clywen held something up. Hildie couldn't quite see it. Shar took it from her, squinted at it, then nodded.

Hildie craned to get a better look. "What is it?"

Shar held out a pale white sliver. "Ylf shot."

Hildie didn't like where this was going. "Ylves don't hunt us. Not anymore."

"Something's gone skewy," Braeda said. "As if we have time for this. What with everything happening at the hotel. Now it's your job to find out what. We don't investigate—just report."

Hildie frowned. "To *whom?*"

Shar whispered in her ear, "You don't want to know." The brief contact made her shiver, but whether it was the words, or Shar's breath, she couldn't tell.

"Start with the old," Clywen said. Her voice sounded kind but also as if she was hiding something, the way a parent told you the needle wouldn't hurt. "Work your way forward."

Hildie knew better than to ask what the hell that meant.

"Come on," Shar said, leading her away from the body and the rain. "I could murder some nachos."

6

WAYNE

Kai seemed to have it all figured out. But then she'd give him this look that mingled pain and wonder, and he'd remember that this was happening to her too. This weird stage in their lives that would one day be fuzzy memories and the smell of burning coffee. He'd watched countless movies about college, but it wasn't like the movies. He never stood in the quad and felt that life was wonderful and knowledge was pouring into him. Knowledge was giving him panic attacks.

The crowds between classes were painful. His force field kept malfunctioning. He could feel every hair on his head, every cell dividing.

They walked to the reflecting pond. It was really just a big rectangle full of brackish-green water, but the campus refresh program had promised that it would soon be a hypoallergenic eco-study space. Wayne preferred the pond in its current state. A chair was growing lichen at the bottom. The closest thing they had to a coral reef. Students were reading and watching videos on their phones. A couple made out brashly, then stopped. Maybe they'd realized that nobody was watching.

Kai had staked out a space by the Egg. It was a sculpture from the '80s. From different angles, it resembled a dragon's egg or a giant avocado. She and Wayne burrowed in between its two halves, the stone cool against their backs. Kai pulled out her tiny pink vaporizer, and they got high inside the space egg. Wayne coughed. He always sucked in too much of the cool vapor, which tasted faintly of bacon, for some reason.

They split a bag of free mini doughnuts, which they'd snagged from some event about student marketing. Kai hugged the egg, pressing her cheek against its mysterious surface. Wayne ate some grass by accident with his doughnut. They shared her earbuds and listened to Charli XCX sing about boys making her head spin.

Kai leaned against him. Wayne didn't like when most people touched him, but Kai was an exception because they'd shared beds since they were eight. Sometimes she also didn't want to be touched. But often they'd drift together like this, two anxious magnets, pulled back into a familiar field.

They watched cloud formations. His stomach rumbled, from all the eggs and coffee and doughnuts. Kai farted and made a face, like she'd surprised herself. That made him laugh.

Then he remembered the body.

Fear coiled within him. Sometimes his emotions were planet-sized and they terrified him. What terrified him even more, though, was feeling nothing. Sometimes when your world was collapsing, it looked like nothing. You felt nothing because it was beyond words. Once, he'd caught his dad playing an old song that Anna used to like—"Freight Train" by Elizabeth Cotten. It was about moving on, beyond death even, to a place where nobody could find you.

"You hardly ever talk about her," Lot said. It wasn't meant as an accusation. Maybe he was even a little bit drunk. His gentle, broken dad.

Wayne had said nothing. There was too much to say. The silence was thick inside of him, like something he might cough up.

"Where did you go?"

He turned back to Kai. "I was thinking about Mo Penley."

She nodded slowly. Waiting for him to continue.

"It sort of—" He squinted at the sky. "It sucked everything out of the room. I know that knights"—he lowered his voice on the word—"I know we're supposed to focus on the battlefield. But I've never seen anything like . . . *that* before."

"Do you think Morgan did it?"

"I don't know. She's kind of terrifying."

"I get we're all supposed to be scared of her." Kai rolled a blade of grass between her fingers. "But once, when I had to leave comp sci early—due to the fact that I was about to shit myself from too much iced coffee—I saw her standing outside in this empty common area." Kai smiled slightly at the memory. "She was drinking tea from an actual mug. Just sipping slowly and staring at the trees. Like she was having a conversation with them. Obviously, she was perfectly put together, every strand of hair in place. But she kept dunking that tea bag, wanting to squeeze out every drop, and it reminded me of my mom when I was little. After she moved from Hong Kong in the '90s, she was always reusing things, worried that we'd run out, that something would happen, and we'd have to move again. Morgan had that same look for a second. Standing so still—but thinking about running."

"She still freaks me out," Wayne said.

"A lot of things do," she said, not unkindly. "But also. There's this girl in my class."

"Uh-huh."

"All I know is that she listens to Sophie, which, like, um, here's my heart on a platter? . . . And she wears these fantastic tights with, like, literary scenes on them. And one pair that's just *The Garden of Earthly Delights* by Bosch. I want to run away with her."

"Have you two spoken?"

"I praised some of her code." Kai put a hand over her eyes. "I was like, 'Dope call.' It's a piece of—never mind. It was ridiculous. And she was like, 'Thanks, Kai.' The really significant thing is that she knew my name."

"You're at the top of your class. I'm sure everyone knows your name."

"That's not why." She stared at the clouds. Then her phone buzzed. She read the text, and her face lit up. She quickly wrote something back, then frowned, revised it, and hit send.

"Garden Girl?"

"Nope. Funny Name Guy."

"It's a whole menagerie."

"Well, Garden Girl's intentions are unclear. The dude is—*something* maybe?"

"Straight?"

"Bi guy. Sometimes that helps." Her face clouded. "Not always. Queer cis guys can also be shithawks. But he hasn't said anything racist yet, so—" She gave a weak thumbs-up. "Unlike the dude who asked where I was *really born*. Um. Coquitlam? There's no exotic answer here."

"When are you going to meet?"

"Soon, I think. He invited me to dinner. Like, a real, public dinner." She looked thoughtful. "He's kind of pure. Like, we don't really talk about sex. He might even be ace. Which would be fine honestly. Fierce snuggling could be exactly what I need." She put her phone away and smiled. "What about your dude? Bert. He fancies you."

"He doesn't."

"You said he held your hand."

"That was because of the music. There was—a mood. I don't know."

"It's just funny. How a terrible thing and a lovely thing could happen within minutes of each other. At a party you didn't even want to attend."

Wayne processed this. He was silent for a while. Then he said, "I don't know how to feel. I never know. It's like other people are following a recipe, and I'm just destroying the whole kitchen with no plan."

Kai squeezed his knee. "You're a beautiful disaster."

Wayne thought about the chaos of the party. He tried to replay those moments, before he'd seen the body. His breath caught as he remembered—seconds before—what he'd seen flash past him. There'd barely been time to register the person. But he had. It was a face he'd not seen for years, but you never forgot the people you grew up with.

"I think—"

But Kai was frowning. "Is that a fox?"

The fox was about twenty feet away from them. Tail like a pointing manicule tucked between back paws. Golden eyes narrow, but also somehow inviting. Like someone who can't figure out if they're going to enter an unfamiliar restaurant, or go home and eat familiar . . . whatever foxes eat. Voles? Wild hamsters? Wayne realized he knew nothing about foxes, except that they got a bad rap for their cunning. This one was kind of cute.

The fox moved closer. Sort of sidling. Time went out of joint. The fox was near and far, near and far, like that *Sesame Street* skit with Grover. The fox seemed to dance between frames, close enough to touch but impossible to pin down.

He remembered something. Another version of him, in another place. Yelling at a fox. *You clawed through my armor, you little shithead!* Holes like windowpanes in the ring mail. The fox laughing, as only foxes could.

Then the animal was running across the green.

Kai was grinning. "We have to follow it! This could be our fairy tale!"

Did they deserve a fairy tale?

She was already running. He had no choice but to follow.

After a few seconds, he could feel the blood returning to his legs in painful pins and needles. He ran through the pain, aware that it wasn't the smart thing to do. He should call someone. He should make an appointment. He should check with Aunt Vera about his essay. Why had he agreed to take her class? The last thing he wanted to do was write a research paper on his life as a baby knight, or failed myth, or whatever he was. Aunt Vera was playing at something, skirting the edge of disaster with her lectures on chivalry. Or maybe she was just using her knowledge to survive. He needed to talk to her. To finally ask the right questions, which he'd never been able to ask his parents.

Instead, he ran.

The fox led them across the green. They wove among students who were reading, sleeping, talking on phones, covertly sipping from travel mugs filled with vodka. Kai's boots pounded grass and gravel. They'd given up on subterfuge. Now it was only about the chase and what it could mean.

As his legs pumped, he remembered learning to ride a bike. His dad lost patience early on—Wayne was too scared of falling—but his uncle Lance had stepped in. He built makeshift armor out of towels, shammies, and pillows. He even borrowed a pair of ski goggles for a visor. Wayne peddled like mad. He had still been scared of falling, but then the wind had caught him. Lance's hand was pressed to his back. *I've got you. I've got you.*

For a second, he was a comet.

Then he fell, almost immediately, into a ditch.

He remembered Lance bending over to disentangle him from the bike. *You flew.*

Wayne's whole life cracking open into light. *I flew.*

He'd seen Uncle Lance at the party. He was sure of it.

And now he was chasing a fox.

Kai flying ahead of him. If you froze that moment, it would throb with happiness and pain, like a bloody knee.

He'd gone back to the box of letters. A few mentioned Uncle Lance.

He loved you, and I know that he misses you. He had to leave. It was the sanest possible choice for him—staying would have put us all in danger. Sometimes people leave because they have to. I'm not fumbling for your forgiveness. We left for different reasons. But Lance always comes back. It's part of his story, and you'll see him again. You'll understand so much more. I promise.

Were they all just stories being retold? Leaving and coming back, like characters who dipped in and out of the margins?

He ran after Kai running after the fox.

Lance had come back.

Maybe everyone would. Even her.

They could face each other in silence. Blood boiling. Parts of them swam through each other, remembering when they'd been one body, one heartbeat. She'd always know him.

But what if the words didn't come? Or he said everything and the world exploded?

7

HILDIE

She dipped her nacho in bloody sour cream. It was salsa, but Hildie kept thinking about the body. Judging by his case file, Mo Penley had been a difficult person with a colorful history. But in many ways, he'd also been the public face of his community. A knight who spoke for the old families, the most exclusive bloodlines.

Shar waved to her. "Your chip is on the verge of collapse."

Hildie blinked and realized that there was sour cream on the back of her hand. They were in Mary's, in the middle of the lunch rush. Their booth was a shade of teal that made her eyes water. There were pink highlights everywhere, like a gender reveal party. Everything used to have a layer of grit to it before they'd renovated. She missed the Formica tables, the grease-coated tiles. Like most of Davie Street over the past decade, the diner had found a way to make itself marketable and inoffensive.

She ate the chip. "Sorry. I'm in the thick of it now."

"You mean Penley."

She nodded. "My head feels like a trash folder."

The server came by, and Shar ordered two margaritas before Hildie could protest. Shar had the alcohol tolerance of an immortal. She could probably drain a keg doing a headstand and still do complex algebra.

"Tell me about the nephew," she said.

Hildie gave her a flat look. "Don't you already know the answer to everything?"

Shar flicked an ice cube at her. "I can see the future—sometimes. That doesn't mean I can give you an accurate metaphysical forecast."

"When's the last time you took a day off?"

Shar rubbed her forehead. "Point taken. Though I could ask you the same question. You've been maxing out on overtime lately."

Hildie laughed. "Imagine if we got paid for overtime."

The margaritas came. They clinked glasses, and everything was normal. Until Hildie thought about the body again. "Vera Grisi has kept her nephew out of the game. The mother left when he was in middle school, and we don't have much of anything on the dad. Some kind of hedge knight. The mother's line is what matters."

"I've heard mainstreaming is becoming more common," Shar said, draining a third of her glass.

Hildie shrugged. "There's a certain appeal to it. Some of us were handed a spear at nine years old. It might have been nice to have more flexible career choices."

"What would you do?" Shar's eyes sparkled. "If family wasn't an issue?"

"There's no point in thinking about it."

"I beg to differ. Thinking about it keeps me sane on days when I have to clean up after a malicious lobby horse."

Hildie chewed thoughtfully.

She knew what she was supposed to answer. Marriage and kids. That was the default. But it wasn't that simple. Some days she wanted a cute girl to read books with. Some days she wanted a boy who was up for adventures. Some days she wanted herself: a quiet apartment, a winter's night, a perfect glass of wine. Did those desires have to be contradictory?

Grace cared about legacies.

Except there was no guarantee that Hildie's kids would even be valkyries.

Those gifts often skipped generations. Or they showed up randomly, in families that were ordinary in every other way.

It might have skipped me. I could have just been . . . me.

Would her mother have accepted her? Would Grace even love her if she wasn't a valkyrie?

So much of it felt like accident and chaos. A storm that either uprooted your life or missed you entirely. You carried on and barely noticed it in your rearview. The past few years had been chilled, like a drink. She'd stopped thinking about what she wanted.

Hildie took a sip. "If family wasn't an issue—I don't know. Sometimes I imagine traveling. The freedom of being on a train. Like you could be anyone. Walking through cities alone. Waking up whenever you want. Maybe I've always been more of an observer, that way. But sometimes I'm happiest by myself."

"In this scenario, have you also won the lottery?"

Hildie smiled. "I'm independently wealthy. It's my fantasy, right?"

Shar raised an eyebrow. "Solitude can be sweet. But what about a partner?"

It was weird of Shar to ask. Maybe the margaritas were actually getting to her. "You know that rarely works."

"I don't just mean a physical partnership. Someone who gets you. A shoulder to doze on, while the train takes you to some fabulous destination."

"Maybe I'm my own partner." As she said it, she liked the idea. "Or maybe I'm dating the whole world in some way. The train and the books and the ocean."

"You're dating the *ocean* now?"

"You know what I mean."

Shar smiled. "Yes. Dating doesn't have to be speciesist. And I don't know why I pressed about the partner thing. My life isn't exactly typical."

From the stories she'd told, Shar had a very broad dating pool, which included ghosts, elemental forces, and, once, a pansexual quasar. *Exhausting,* she'd said. *Don't date anything that has a radioactive corona.*

"I get it," Hildie replied. "We're all works in progress."

She'd had more traditional partners. People who'd expected a reasonable amount of sexy times. It was a basic compromise, like going to a hockey game when you didn't really care, or taking an interest in your partner's poetry. The problem was that they didn't like thinking of it as a compromise and tended to be hurt when she just wasn't that into it. They resented the rules that she created to protect herself and feel okay within her own body. And they never believed her when she said she was in love, because love was supposed to include sex, right?

Love was also supposed to include talking and eating and sleeping and cuddling and watching shows and doing laundry and counting down the minutes until you got to see each other. But all of that seemed to pale when you removed sex from the equation, or put rules around it. She'd lost track of all the liberal queer girls who'd raged at her *lack of intimacy*, or the feminist boys who'd lost their shit when she wouldn't immediately go down on them, like that was as casual as a text.

She watched Shar watching her. They'd known each other for a long time. Whispered in the dark. Stared straight ahead while sitting in a car, in the middle of an empty parking lot, as their lives imploded. Carried each other through grief, and worse. For a moment, Hildie allowed herself to imagine Shar on that train. Sitting across from her, reading, or watching the patchwork of buildings as they flew by. Fitting like jigsaw pieces.

But what would that look like? She didn't even know what she wanted, let alone what Shar wanted. She wove the future. She saw everyone at their worst and best. Why would she follow Hildie around on some journey of self-discovery when she was busy making sure the universe didn't fall apart?

"What about you?" She clinked Shar's glass again. "If family wasn't an issue, and you could do anything—what would it be?"

Shar looked faraway for a moment. Maybe she really was staring into the future.

"Dog-walking," she said after a beat. "That's where it's at."

"Sounds great. Let's walk dogs on the edge of the world."

Shar smiled. "Terminal City, remember? We're already here."

Later, in the car, Hildie flipped through Nan's notes. She rarely talked about the city. She'd had the old country in her bones. Hildie did find one note, scrawled after she'd dealt with a case in Stanley Park. Two angry runesmiths had met in an honest-to-goodness duel, in the pre-dawn hours, which she'd described as *uht-ceare*. The time of dawn-cares. You weren't supposed to duel with runes, especially when you could burn down an old-growth forest. Her notes indicated that it had been about love, not magic, though they were so often the same.

She'd written, as a kind of afterthought, *The city is the modern court.*

Hildie puzzled over this, wondering if it referred to something legal. Then she realized that Nan meant Camelot. Whatever that was. She thought about courtly culture, with all of its politics and gazes and betrayals. The city, like the court, followed its own rules. The rules weren't necessarily the problem. They could be changed, even broken, in useful ways.

The problem was when there were no rules at all.

There was no Magna Carta for knights, valkyries, and runesmiths. Just oral traditions passed down over time, stories that were also rules for living well. Punishments for those who threatened the community's survival. The city was as confusing as any court. She remembered her conversation with Morgan—how she'd rolled her eyes at the thought of a valkyrie tribunal. But at least she remembered the time when they'd maintained order through iron and blood. The days when wars were endless, and someone had to manage all that slaughter. Now they watched and kept records and occasionally intervened, but they rarely drew spears. They'd become more of a long memory for knights, reminding them of the rules that kept them from descending into chaos. They were closer to the fates and acted as their officers in the world.

Now someone had ignored those rules. Refusing to acknowledge city or court. Digging up the bones of the past, all those forgotten kingdoms, and the wars that set them on fire.

Shar had told her about an ylf who was staying at the hotel. Hildie was supposed to interview one, about the ylf shot, but it's hard to pin down someone who barely occupies your reality. Shar assured her that the ylf would resurface eventually, but in the meantime, Hildie needed to knock on some doors.

Grace wanted her to follow up on Vera's interview, which had been sketchy to say the least. There was also Bert, who'd be easy to find. He kept regular hours in the provost's office, and—if she was right—he'd be pretty invested in keeping any weird side of his life private. She'd been surprised to hear Vera say that Penley might have had radical plans for the community. She'd scoured his online ratings on various sites, but all she could gather was that he was a bit of a prick who didn't give extensions. Something didn't add up.

Had he been working on something, beneath the cover of his job? Now that Morgan held the reins, she could push through all kinds of decisions. What would she do next?

Hildie wanted to fast-track things. And that meant making a Very Bad Decision.

Her grandmother had taught her that, and she had known what she was talking about. When she was First Valkyrie, she'd taken on recreant knights without flinching. She'd apologized with a wink, absently wiping blood off her twinset as if she couldn't figure out where it had come from. But that had been a different era.

Grace preferred order. But Hildie had never fit into her mother's tapestry of rules and traditions and family debts.

If she was going to do this, she'd do it her way.

Morgan Arcand's house was nestled at the top of the mountain, and she liked watching the city fall away. The bustle of Hastings Street turned into suburban sprawl, into areas heavy with development that looked like skeletal space stations looming over the neighborhood. *For Lease* signs tattooed the corridor. She was driving her mother's car and mindful of the fact that she could destroy the deductible with one wrong move. But if you're going to commit to a VBD, you have to go all-in. Otherwise you're just half-assing your own doom.

Tracy Chapman sang through her mother's expensive speakers. Her velvety gravel voice filled the car. "Talkin' Bout a Revolution" on the radio. She remembered wearing out the CD.

By thirty-five, you were supposed to have a plan. She had roughly two thousand dollars in her checking account, an impressive book collection, and a yearly lease on her apartment that she didn't trust would be renewed. It felt like more of an outline than a life. But in her line of work, it wasn't easy to put down roots. She kept odd hours, dealt with dark shit, and was banned at several dry cleaners because she'd brought in too many bloodstained dresses.

She'd never finished college. The option was there for a while, but her training took up a lot of time, and Grace wasn't a huge fan of the liberal arts. Back when Nan got her law degree in the '60s, the campus had been a magnet for riots, and her grandmother had seen her fair share. She'd bailed out her friends. Hildie imagined her showing up at the jail, wearing an aura of rage. *I'm sweet*, she used to say. *Not soft.*

Sometimes Hildie felt like both. Hard and soft. Sappho's *Sweetbitter*.

All she knew was that Grace's blue Camaro handled like a dream, and hopefully that was worth the trouble she'd just invited into her life.

The engine roared in delight as she drove up the steep incline. The university's chrome sign declared *A Place of Knowledge. A Place for Everyone.*

If it was a place for everyone, why was it on top of a bloody mountain?

As she neared the top, the sky seemed to devour her. The North Shore mountains gathered around her like a curious audience. From this perspective, Vancouver looked small and manageable below.

The house was on the edge of campus. It was ringed by residential developments—towers designed for people who'd fled the city. A mixture of blue mountains, scraps of sky, and ever-moving cranes, like the mountain itself was being rearranged by giants.

Historians speculated that it was the oldest residence in Canada, though that depended on your perspective. The Musqueam people had built settlements over ten thousand years ago. This was all unceded territory.

The campus gradually gave way to forest, as if it was being reclaimed. Hildie parked and walked down the shaded path that led to the house.

She clocked a few security guards, but they were mostly distracted by their phones.

The driveway was empty. Hildie knew Morgan wouldn't be there, because she'd scheduled a fake meeting with her for precisely this time. She'd disguised her voice and yelled a lot of buzz words at Bert, until he'd scheduled the meeting to get rid of her.

From this vantage point, the house resembled an abandoned villa. Curtains shaded the massive windows, and the reflecting pond was still. Like every old thing, the house attracted ghosts and a kind of subtle trilling energy that raised the hairs on the back of her neck.

Knights had a code. They didn't always follow it, and it was an ever-changing set of rules, but at least they acknowledged it. People like Morgan were different. They lived in the margins. Her grandmother would have been called a witch, and Morgan—with her multiple PhDs—was still dealing with sexism on the daily.

She'd been called worse than witch.

Hildie felt an awkward kinship with her. She wasn't exactly rooting for the provost. Morgan—all the Morgans—had been a thorn in their side for as long as anyone could remember. But her knowledge and her power had value.

She approached the old door. *Old* didn't quite cover it. The foliate engravings were at least seventeenth-century, and the wood might have been a thousand years old. It was dark and scarred and lined with memory.

Hildie studied the surface carefully. There was a rune engraved near the bottom. It was Morgan's signature rune—five vertical lines against one horizontal, which translated roughly as apple in the Ogham dialect, which you generally saw on trees, rather than stone or iron. One of her incarnations used to trade in explosive apples, which wreaked havoc at courtly dinners. Hildie wouldn't touch that rune for all the money in the world.

She crossed over to the frozen reflecting pond. Nobody had come through to search the grounds. Morgan would have gone over the place with a fine-toothed comb if she was concerned with physical evidence. Hildie followed the gravel path around the pond, where pansies and witch hazel were doing their best to thrive in the cold. There was no sense of death. She scanned the grass for more ylf shot, but all she found was a displaced snail, which she carefully moved away from the path.

The real story would be inside the house.

Valkyries followed the trail of death. At one time, they'd been able to *choose* who died. But that was a different world. Now, they just sniffed it out, then stayed around to pick up the pieces. Most of her job involved details. Fragments of memory, blood-spattered clothing, stories that shifted depending on who was telling them. If she broke into Morgan's house, there'd be hell to pay. The question was—how close could she get before she was actually trespassing? This was still on university endowment land—settler code for stolen—which meant that the outside of the house was fair game.

She remembered the sign on the way in. *A Place for Everyone.*

Just call me Everyone.

Hildie walked around the back of the villa. There was a carriage house, surrounded by withered vines. The door was unlocked. She poked her head in. The air was cool and smelled like moss, with something underneath that she couldn't quite place. She used the flashlight on her phone to scan the interior.

It was more of a shed, really, which didn't match the grandeur of the house. There were tools stacked in one corner and an antique drafting table with a single chair. Everything looked broken down. What was she building in here? Hildie toed the wastebasket in the corner. It was metal and scraped the ground. Heavy. More like a cauldron than a trash bin. She peered inside and saw a layer of fresh ashes, along with a few fragments of paper.

Hildie used a pair of tweezers to recover some of the paper. It was glossy. She held it up to her phone light. She saw a gray eye; a slash of red blouse; the corner of someone's mouth. Hildie used her phone to magnify the scrap of fabric. It was Morgan's outfit, now torn into pieces. She was looking at the photo from the guest room—the photo of Morgan, Vera, and Gale. Someone had tried to destroy it. Hildie pocketed the fragment and left the shed.

She heard something. A shuffle. Her senses weren't warning her of anything yet. But she'd definitely heard it.

She thought she saw a figure retreating along the path.

Hildie walked with purpose. You don't run toward a dangerous thing, but you don't creep toward it either.

Something vanished into a snarled hedge. Maybe it was just a shadow. Hildie listened. She could feel the frost in the air. She searched for a tell-tale thread. Something that couldn't be hidden. Tried to still the blood pounding in her ears.

There was something. Like a scrap of spiderweb, worrying her face. She couldn't see it, but she could feel it.

She stood still for a long time. Breathing. Waiting.

Then she heard the crunch of a shoe on gravel.

Hildie reached. She plucked her spear out of thin air. It gleamed like the event horizon of a black hole. It was cold to the touch.

Her blood boiled. She heard the giant women singing.

She leveled the spear.

The skeletal branches danced back and forth. Hildie parted them with the spear. Nothing. Had she actually heard it? Maybe her nerves were getting to her.

The spear chilled her hand. It never warmed up. It belonged to another place, older than everything, where all the myths settled. Along with other things that you wouldn't ever want to meet. Hildie knew the spear was part of her, but it still made her nervous—the same way a flash of your own temper might surprise you. What she was capable of.

Another crunch.

She turned, and something slammed into her shoulder. It threw her off balance. She reached out and came away with a handful of cold leaves.

Hildie saw the trees shake. Like something had pushed through them.

Had it been real?

She noticed a drop of blood on her hand. Hildie stared at it, uncomprehending for a moment. Then she remembered the bushes. It wasn't her blood. A thorn must have caught them. She rubbed her aching shoulder. Valkyries were strong, but whatever had struck her had felt like a truck. A hockey player or a linebacker, maybe. Hildie parted the flowers again, scanning the ground. Something winked back at her.

She wrapped a handkerchief around her hand. Delicately, she picked up the object. Light flashed against gold.

It was a brooch.

Hildie felt her breath catch as she examined it. There was an ancient pin, designed to fasten to a cloak. It was unquestionably gold, with writhing animal designs. She thought she could make out horses, birds, possibly dragons. Alien eyes regarded her coolly. There were runes on the underside, but time and motion had rubbed them into soft nothing. The thing belonged in a museum. But the tingling in her fingertips told her that it would never end up on public display. Some power had touched it. Something as old as her spear. She'd have to ask the sisters.

She wondered what the letters spelled. A name, or a motive?

Something orange flashed past her vision.

Hildie frowned.

Was that the same fox?

8

WAYNE

They're thirteen and dancing on the bed to "Bad Romance." It came out a while ago, but Kai loves it now more than ever. The video is super confusing—someone keeps pouring champagne into Lady Gaga's mouth and then she's in bed with a skeleton—but Kai loves it and they watch it on a loop. Even at thirteen, Wayne is sort of a vinyl snob and would prefer something classic. But Kai has instituted a ban on opera and big band, telling him that he needs a pop music education. She probably had a fight with her mom about the exact same thing, and now she's winning on different grounds. Wayne hates dancing because it makes him feel out of control. He's already clumsy. Any movement involving both hips *and* arms feels way too advanced. But he climbs on the bed and they dance while Kai screams, *Want your bad roooommmmance!*

Wayne's mother knocks on the door and tells them to keep it down. She's been wearing the same denim dress with pockets for days, and looks tired, but the hint of a smile plays on her mouth. Very soon she'll be gone. He feels that somewhere but doesn't know it for sure, not yet. Their apartment sags against the premonition. Even the bookshelves are waiting. His dad spends a lot of time in the burnt-orange chair, listening to Steely Dan on giant headphones. Occasionally he practices guitar, but his heart's not in it. Years later, he'll pawn the acoustic Epiphone, then retreat to his bedroom with a six-pack.

Once, his mother came into the living room while his dad was playing. It was one of his own compositions—a rarity—and his face was a mask of concentration as his fingers moved along the frets. She handed him a chocolate-chip cookie that she'd just baked. She never baked, which only made it more surreal. He couldn't take his hands off the guitar, so she popped the cookie into his mouth. He grinned around it as he played, crumbs scattering down his shirt. When he started to drool, she laughed brightly. It was summer, the house smelled safe, and his parents were actually married for a moment instead of just pretending.

Kai presses repeat and the song plays one more time. Lately she's been withdrawn and hard to reach, but dancing seems to put her at ease. Wayne's feet get tangled in the duvet and he bounces against the wall. It makes her laugh. They finish the dance on their knees, and Kai shouts the French lyrics into his pillow. Her face is flushed and glowing, and her newly shoulder-length hair fans out.

The song ends. Kai pulls out a compact and repositions herself by the light. She fixes her makeup, scowling. He notices that her bag is full of MAC Cosmetics, which are pretty expensive. He knows because he wanted to buy her some for her birthday, but the Sephora in Metrotown mall was so loud and smelled too weird and it gave him a panic attack. He had to stagger outside and suck in the fresh air.

"Did you go shopping?"

She carefully reapplies lip gloss. "In a manner of speaking."

"You swiped those."

"Not *all* of them. Mom bought the mascara." He can see her resisting the urge to roll her eyes. "She's being super cool."

He runs through a list of safe responses. Her dad died a year ago, and everything is still raw and complicated and full of dark subtext. "Was it on sale?"

She laughs. "You're being diplomatic. Good boy."

"I'm not a dog."

"It's a joke, Wayne."

He barks.

She's laughing. "Careful. You'll make me look like Pennywise."

Kai loves horror novels. She reads more than anyone he knows, even his mother, who's constantly reading.

She sees him eying her lip gloss. "Come here."

He hesitates. "Does it taste funny?"

"No." She's already applying it, before he can reconsider. The brush is cold. She swipes it across his mouth. "Now plump your lips."

"What?"

"Like you're about to kiss someone."

He makes a face. "You said it didn't taste like anything."

"Just toxins."

She spends the next ten minutes giving him a smoky eye. "We don't want to go full drag queen," she murmurs. "Just halfway there."

Her confidence is infectious. Whenever Kai puts her mind to a subject, she can learn it completely. He'd love that power, but his brain is a traitor. Some things he learns right away, and some things elude him completely.

When she's done, she hands him the compact.

"It's like the Eye of Sauron," he complains.

"Good. That's power."

"Your makeup doesn't look anything like this."

"I'm not a drag queen." Her voice has a thorn in it.

"I know."

She's silent for a while. Her sleeveless blouse reminds him of sun-dappled water. It's acrylic though. The fabric would make him scream.

"How did the meeting go?" She wants to change the subject.

He folds his arms. "Dr. Dick says I'm a borderline case."

It was his mother's idea. *Just some general tests*, she'd said. Like it was normal to fill out psychological inventories in an office that smelled like burnt coffee. His dad hated the idea. His hands were white-knuckled on the steering wheel as he drove Wayne to the office in Coquitlam.

"Borderline what, exactly?"

He didn't want to say autistic. Nobody else wanted to say it either. There were lots of euphemisms and the suggestion of ADHD, then something called PDD. An army of acronyms.

"The doctor called it a spectrum," he said quietly. "But I'm not sure where I am on it, or what it means. There was a weird test, with flying frogs and monopoly pieces, and I couldn't tell if I was saying the right thing or not. The room smelled. I just wanted out."

Kai traced a rune on the duvet. It flickered for a moment. It looked like a tree with two branches. "Feoh," she said. "That means abundance. Or lucky. Which is what you are."

"Lucky to have some weird diagnosis."

"No." She brushed the rune away. "Lucky to know yourself."

"Maybe."

"Did the doctor make you draw things again?"

"My anger."

"Ooh. What did it look like?"

He shrugged. "A beast. Nothing."

"Do you really want to be put in a different class?"

"I want to be homeschooled, but it would interfere with my parents' fighting schedule."

Kai brushed off that detail. "You can't hang out in the library forever, babe."

"Last week, I started hyperventilating because my clothes were too tight. I went to the library and Craig Widows followed me."

"He's cute. For you, I mean."

Kai was more open to his boy crushes than he was. The thought of kissing a boy terrified him, as did the thought of kissing anyone.

"I was worried. He was smiling. That can be a trap sometimes."

Kai nodded slowly. He didn't need to tell her that.

"He rubbed my back. It was scary at first but then okay. His hand on my back. He kept smiling. Then he whispered something that I couldn't hear. When I leaned in closer, he spat in my face."

Her eyes went dark. "I'll set him on fire."

"Kai—"

She leaned in, lowering her voice so his mom wouldn't hear. "I've been working with fire runes. I could do it."

Wayne crossed his arms so tightly that he could feel pins and needles. He shook his head. "No point."

"Boys are broken."

"I wouldn't have to worry about that if I was homeschooled."

"But look at all the valuable social skills you're learning!"

He stared at her for a moment. Then she cackled. Her laugh was one of the only things that made him laugh. For a minute, they both wheezed.

A few minutes later, they heard the apartment buzzer.

Uncle Lance's voice echoed in the hallway. Wayne was excited. Uncle Lance seemed so over his parents; he was always rolling his eyes affectionately at them. Wayne didn't understand every eye roll, but at least they weren't aimed at him. Uncle Lance made it feel like they were coconspirators in some drama. Like *Grey's Anatomy* with less blood.

He started to get off the bed. Then Kai frowned and shook her head. His mother was talking in a weird voice. Sort of hissing.

What have you gotten yourself into?

She kept repeating this. Lance's reply was hazy through the door.

His mother's voice rose. *Don't bring this into my house. Unlike you, I have a family to think about.*

I've got a family too, Lance shot back.

His mother's laugh was ugly. *You've got an experiment. Not a family.*

Wayne didn't know what that meant. It was true that Lance didn't have kids. He lived with Aunt Vera and Uncle Gale, who wasn't anyone's uncle. His parents were the kind of liberals who didn't bother mentioning what this arrangement could mean. Kai called it a power throuple. The truth was that nobody really knew what it was or how it worked, but it seemed to stress his mom out.

Lance said something inaudible.

They must have been close to the bedroom door, because he heard his mom whisper, *Don't say his name.*

Then Lance was stomping out.

81

Wayne threw open the door and ran after him. His uncle was half-way out the door when he turned around. His mother stood in the door-way of the kitchen. Her eyes flicked from Lance to Wayne, then back to Lance again. She seemed poised to say something, but she just stood there, frozen in anger.

"Take me with you," Wayne said.

He didn't know why he said it. But Lance's warm, cluttered apart-ment seemed infinitely more comfortable than this tense, silent house.

His mother walked into the kitchen.

Lance's hand hovered over his shoulder. "You're going to be fine."

Wayne's face twisted. "I'm *not*." His voice was soft.

Lance leaned in close. "You're a knight," he whispered. "Don't forget that."

❦

They'd lost the fox, so Kai settled on following Bert.

Not stalking exactly. She called it P.I. work. She was in the middle of a Kristen Lepionka book about a hard-boiled queer detective, so she had stakeouts and other bad decisions on the brain.

"Plus," she said, "I'd rather self-immolate than go to this class on algorithms."

Wayne agreed because her momentum justified it. He probably wouldn't have done it on his own. He'd just take the bus home, get lost in a fierce internal monologue, and spend the rest of the day staring at a blank screen. Kai was often the instigator because she knew that he didn't need much encouragement beyond a liberal nudge.

Now they were low-key tailing Bert as he made his way across campus. He seemed almost aimless. He'd start off in one direction, then stop, as if he'd forgotten where he was going. Was he stoned? Wayne didn't know enough about him to tell. He made mental spreadsheets for everyone, and so far, Bert's only said *smells nice, great beard,* and *good with panic attacks*. They hung back and kept to the darker spaces. It was Kai's idea for them to share a set of earbuds while they walked, so it looked like they were absorbed in music and therefore totally incapable of stalking someone. But the cord kept getting tangled and Wayne demanded why she didn't just buy wireless headphones, which resulted in an argument that nearly revealed them.

"Googling," Kai said, thumbs flying as they stumbled forward. "There's not much. Almost nothing, really. Just his email on the dean's office website. He's listed as an *advisor*, whatever that means."

"I think it's a glorified personal assistant." Wayne took out the earbud. "I'm going to either trip or strangle myself on this cord."

"Fine, fine." She put them away. "Okay, what did you glean at the party?"

"What did I *glean?*"

"I'm not trying to be flippant. Just—did he tell you anything about himself?"

"He hates *Sesame Street.*"

"We'll need more than that when we're eventually put on the stand for this."

Wayne thought back to that night. It ended with horror, but he also wanted to go back to relive those moments before everything went sideways.

"He showed me this book. He knew the dean would be mad, but he said I'd get it. I wasn't sure what he meant. But it felt like he was defying her, and that made him happy."

Kai nodded. "So he's got some authority issues. Same."

Bert stopped abruptly.

Kai pulled Wayne into a hedge.

"Subtle," Wayne said, with leaves in his mouth.

They waited a beat, then climbed out of the hedge.

Bert was on his way again.

They followed him into the Human Arts building. He took the stairs, which surprised Wayne, because Bert hadn't seemed that body-conscious. Kai stabbed the elevator button and they rode in tense silence. They got off on the top floor, where Morgan Arcand's office was. It used to be the periodicals section of the library, but the offices of various administrators had spread across it like vines. They walked through an open-plan office where everyone looked miserable. Then down a concrete corridor. The air was stale and cool, like they'd entered a secret cave.

The door was open slightly, and Wayne saw a flash of marble floor. Bert was talking to Morgan.

She looked pissed.

Bert kept nodding, the way you do when you're not really listening.

Then she said something that must have struck a nerve because his eyes narrowed. He got really still for a second. Wayne could almost see flames flickering around him.

Then he turned to leave, and they ran for the elevator.

"Do you think she's got him picking up her dry cleaning?"

"I'm not sure," Wayne said, as the elevator descended.

"Clearly he doesn't like her."

It was more than that though.

His defiant stance. The visible struggle for control. It was the kind of anger that flashed out of you when you were dealing with someone close. Not with a manager. More like a family member.

How were they connected?

They followed him to the Z lot, which was the lowest in the parking lot hierarchy—practically an open field. He got into a beat-up green Pony, which roared to life. Kai was pulling Wayne with one hand while she frantically swiped through apps on her phone. She found Car 4 U and stabbed in her details. A tiny car flashed its headlights. It was about the size of a tricycle.

"Come on!" She pulled him along. "This is a chase, bitches!"

"You're way too excited about this."

"It's no *Gran Turismo*, but it'll do."

"I told you not to—"

They were already squealing across the parking lot.

Kai swiped one-handed through her playlist as they made a hairpin turn. The voice of Hayley Kiyoko filled the car.

"Shit. Sorry. Wrong chase music."

"Give that to me before we crash!"

Wayne found it soothing to shift through her playlist. It was better than watching cars flash past them. He chose "Levitating" by Dua Lipa. The car whumped with bass.

"Excellent," Kai said.

Bert's green car shot forward. Kai wove in and out of lanes, oblivious to drivers honking and making rude gestures.

Soon they were deep in the university's residential space. The development was called Mountain View, though the rising condos would eventually obscure the view itself. As they turned up the road, things changed. The skeletal condos fell away. The road was shaded by trees.

"I know this," Wayne said softly.

"Really? I have no idea where we're going."

"It's Morgan Arcand's house."

Kai raised an eyebrow as the tiny car struggled with bumps in the road. "She must really need that dry cleaning."

Why would Bert be going to the provost's house? Was Kai right? Had she simply sent him on an errand? Or was it something else?

Kai hit the brake.

Wayne stared at the line of trees. Everything was still.

"I don't see him anymore." She shook her head. "How did I lose him?"

Kai got out of the car. She seemed to be sniffing the air. Then she walked over to a stunted tree nearby. Wayne followed. She was staring at a burn mark on the tree. Wayne squinted and realized that it wasn't a random mark. Someone had burned a rune into the wood. It looked like an *h* with a diagonal slash through the center. It didn't give him the willies, like that rune on the banister had. But neither was it comforting.

"Hægl," Kai said.

"Bless you."

"No. That's the rune." Kai peered at it. "And see this?" She pointed to another black smudge. "They've woven it with something else, but I can't make it out." Then her eyes widened. "*Oh.* I forgot—it can mean bad weather. If you weave it right, you can use it for concealment. Almost like a mist. Or a shadow."

He thought of the rune he'd seen on Mo Penley's body. It had almost been part of the shattered flesh; he couldn't distinguish the blood from the design. But there'd been something familiar about it. Something big. Almost giant. He couldn't quite remember. He needed to tell Kai, but it was still like smoke in his mind.

Wayne tried to pierce the line of trees. "They could still be here."

Kai nodded slowly. "We should go."

"What about Bert?"

He could be in danger.

He could be the danger.

"We're not prepared for this," Kai said. "I need to do more research."

There was a funny note in her voice. Wayne realized he hadn't heard her excited about research in a long time.

He took one last look at the black smudge on the tree.

Runes, like people, could be more dangerous in numbers. Weave them the wrong way, and anything could happen.

What would his mother think of this? He was deep in the life that she'd tried to protect him from. Wayne thought of his dad, burnt out from working double shifts, just trying to keep the balance that she'd insisted upon. Trying to keep a roof over their heads.

He followed Kai back to the car. They drove back in silence. But when he looked over at her, she was smiling, ever so slightly.

In the sweet exile of his bedroom, he read another of Anna's letters.

Dearest Wort,

You're only as good as the people who claim you, the people who will go to war for you. Kai is one of those friends, but you also need more than only the two of you. Seek out people who give you space and make you feel more like yourself. Avoid those who make you feel small or false. When you find a true friend, the reaction is almost chemical. Forgive the science metaphor—that's how I think.

Lovers will come and go (I know, I know—you have a mum who says "lovers," how gross!) Girlfriends or boyfriends will enter and leave the scene. But friends stay behind and help you clean up the mess. Someday, you may find a person who does all of those things. Or it may never cross your mind. Being alone is an act of love too. Loving yourself. But whatever happens, don't be afraid to connect. It's hard. It never gets easier. But you can do it.

leof,

Anna

She was right. It didn't get easier. She'd made it worse by leaving—made everything worse. For years, she'd been his interpreter, his litigator. Snapping at people who said *look me in the eye* or *shake my hand*. Delicately weaving him out of bad situations. Making excuses for his silences. He'd grown to depend on that gentle interference. And then she was gone, and the uncertainty came rushing in. She'd left him with half a manual for understanding life, and the rest was indecipherable. Like walking out on a half-built castle, as its foundations were still settling. What if there were dragons underneath? Real ones?

Still. Kai's smile filled him with sly confidence. She was his coconspirator.

And Bert. What the hell was he?

9

HILDIE

Hildie spent the first nine years of her life waiting. She didn't quite know what she was waiting for, but she could feel it coming and knew that it was inescapable. Like when you wake up with a tickle in your throat and otherwise feel fine, but you know what's about to happen. Her future as a valkyrie hovered like a shadow.

It was an ordinary life in some ways. They'd shared a house with her grandmother in Strathcona, a lively neighborhood on the edge of the Downtown East Side. Her grandmother would often take in people who had nowhere else to go. Hildie saw early on that there were forces in the world beyond your control, things that could rule you and destroy you, things that howled at the door. But she also saw kinship and love and people doing small things for each other when they could have simply turned away. Her mother's drug was alcohol; she ruthlessly judged anything else. But her grandmother accepted that drugs were part of the neighborhood, like cracked pavement and dandelions bursting out of empty lots.

Hildie didn't realize what her grandmother was. She was just Nan. She had smiley wrinkles around her eyes and a laugh like a sparrow. It would trill out of nowhere and echo through every room in the house.

One day she found Nan in the kitchen, holding something in her lap. She was polishing it with a rag, moving in endless circles across the wood. Every time her hand drew near, the wood sang.

"Nan, what's that?"

She smiled. "Oh hello, doll. It's a spear."

Hildie must have been very young. Five, maybe. "A spear? Like in the wolf poem?"

Nan used to read *Beowulf* to her, because it pissed off her mother.

"Exactly. Their word for it was *gar*. Tricky spear Danes. Our word is older."

"Our word?"

"In the language, yes. Though there are even older words." Nan delicately polished the spear, her hands working from memory. "Words buried under sarcophagi and lost to time. Words forgotten in darkness and never written down, though once they were song."

Her mother came into the kitchen. "What are you doing?"

Nan didn't look up. "What's it look like?"

"Are you using Pledge?"

"I like the lemon."

"Jesus."

"Don't bring him into this." Her eyes sparkled. "You know, yours could use some work, too, Daughter."

Hildie's eyes went wide. "Mum has a gar too?"

Her mother's look was cold. "We've talked about this."

"You've talked," Nan said, still polishing.

"I'll teach her in my own way. It's my choice."

"Not much time left." Nan touched a fingertip to the lozenge-shaped blade. When she drew the finger away, a bead of blood danced on it. "She'll find out soon enough."

Hildie reached for her grandmother's finger. Her mother pulled her away.

"It's just blood," Nan said, smiling. "Nothing to be afraid of."

But her mother was already bustling her out of the room.

She did get a spear eventually. It was a hard thing to hold. You didn't own it, really. It barely existed in the world, though when it appeared, it was more solid than anything. A singularity pressed to an elegant line, warping her fingertips. Her grandmother taught her that *warp* was a funny word that meant a lot of things, including a story. It wasn't a bad thing, being warped. It was a shared way of living.

Her mother had only explained the job once. Grace sat down on the edge of her bed, looking tired, as always. There was a wine glass in her hand, and Hildie watched the liquid sway back and forth like a kind of fire. She'd learned to be wary of her mother in these moments. Grace had never laid a hand on her, rarely even yelled, but there was a strangeness to her when she was drinking—a kind of wild openness. Like anything might come out.

"We used to be slaughter-companions," her mother said. "On the battlefield, we shadowed the warriors. The greatest among us would choose who lived and who fell. But over time, our power contracted. Like ink fading in a copier. Now we can feel death nearby. We can even retrace a life that's been cut short. But not much else. Mostly, we watch, and wait, and make sure the warriors obey the fates. Sometimes they try to escape what's been woven. You can change a story, Niblet, but you can never avoid it completely."

Hildie had absorbed this. "And we're also warriors?"

"Yes. Only with more paperwork." That seemed like a joke, but Grace's voice was too frayed to land it.

"But we can't change anything. Or bring anyone back."

Grace must have known she was thinking about Nan. She shook her head.

Hildie felt the spear. It was whispering to her. She shook her head as if to clear it.

"Then what's the fucking point?"

Grace didn't even seem shocked when she swore. They both just looked at each other for a while. The glass in Grace's hand. Hildie's hands empty.

90

How long did they stay like that?

Nan's notes had this to say about spears: *the exposed part of you—it feels pain, but, like you, it's unbreakable.* One of her clearer notes.

⚬⚬

Grace was calm, and that meant trouble.

Hildie expected her mother to start yelling right away. But she sat silently at the desk, oddly still, as Hildie settled into a chair. There were a few points in her favor. She hadn't totaled the car. She hadn't run afoul of the provost. Valkyries had been popping in and out of history forever. Nobody believed a report about a spear-wielding woman. Really, she was just carrying on a tradition of being unapologetic. Nan once pulled out her spear in a Bonanza Steakhouse because an ylf was stealing all the pickled beets from the buffet, or so she claimed.

Hildie put her hands delicately in her lap. She wanted to appear contrite, but not guilty. After all, her instincts had been correct. You always turned up something when you looked at a crime scene with fresh eyes. This time, she'd turned up a shadow with a very solid build. And a brooch that she could hopefully trace to someone. She'd given it to the sisters. Clywen had snatched it from her with great interest, but Hildie hadn't yet heard an update from her.

Grace scanned a file in front of her. Whatever she was reading made her eyebrow twitch, almost imperceptibly.

That wasn't good.

Finally, she looked up. "I'll give you ten seconds to tell me why you were skulking around Morgan Arcand's house like a raccoon," Grace said.

Hildie swallowed. "Only ten?"

"That's a poor use of a second."

She ignored the ice in her gut. "I didn't come back empty-handed. Someone else was skulking too. And now we've got some trace for the sisters to examine."

Grace said nothing for a beat.

Hildie ran a hand through her hair, which was greasy and sticking up in weird horns. She imagined how beautiful a shower would be, and how very, very far away she was from being able to wash away the entire day.

Grace leaned over the desk. "You revealed yourself to someone who could be the killer. And if you'd done a better job of concealing yourself, we might have more to go on. Now they'll just be more careful. Especially around you."

"They hid in a hedge," she murmured. It sounded ridiculous.

Grace had a hungry look.

There's something she knows that I don't.

"Guess who visited the house after you did?"

Hildie couldn't see the file. "Girl scouts?"

Grace slid the file over to her. A grainy security camera showed two people. One she recognized as Wayne. The other was a tall girl she hadn't seen before.

"The nephew." Grace pronounced the word like it was a curse. "And a runesmith. We don't know much about her yet, but she's another complication. What if they'd arrived while you were tussling with the rose bushes?"

She felt like this was a rhetorical question, and unsafe to answer.

"Hildie . . ." Grace sighed. "What's the first rule of this job?"

She shrank into the chair. "Trust no one."

"That's the first rule of *The X-Files*." Grace shook her head. "The first rule of this job—our family tradition—is that death is messy. It spreads into every corner of your life, and it involves people on the margins. If you'd been following the nephew, you would have seen this coming. Instead, you were haunting the dean's house, against my orders. Now the kid is involved, which means I'll soon have Vera Grisi looming over me."

Hildie was getting angry now—another family trait. "The kid can do what he wants. His aunt shouldn't be controlling him."

Grace's voice got very low. It was like a vicious purr. "He is a knight. You don't get to mess with a knight's future."

"The way you messed with mine?"

Grace looked as if she'd been struck. "What do you mean?"

"Nan was always trying to tell me things, and you'd talk over her.

You'd push me out of the room like it was a car accident and I shouldn't look. But she was trying to prepare me. I wanted to learn from her."

Grace passed a hand over her face, like she was impossibly tired. And maybe she was. Her job was unenviable. The overtime was infinity, and the pay was shit.

"Your grandmother had a lot of old ideas," she said, after a beat. "Not all of them were good for you. I was trying to give you something else. Something normal."

"You put a spear in my hand when I was nine! How's that normal?"

"Yes, I put the spear in your hand, but I also left a door open. I wanted you to take on the responsibility in your own way. You've had a lot more choices than I did."

Hildie almost laughed. "Right. You gave me so many options. Be perfect. Uphold the traditions. Don't shame your ancestors. Fates forbid I try to have a life."

"I never said you had to be perfect."

Hildie couldn't listen anymore. She'd reached the saturation point where everything Grace said felt like a thorn against her skin. "Now you've got the perfect excuse to freeze me out of my own investigation. I'm doing the work. Doing it my own way. But what's the point if you're just going to be the critical voice in my ear the whole time?"

Grace raised an eyebrow. "You want to quit? Slam your badge on my desk? This isn't Special Valkyrie Unit. It's your blood."

Hildie was silent. Then she laughed. "SVU."

"Stabler. *Such* a putz." Grace sighed. "You're not quitting, and I'm not firing you. I need you."

"Then what are you going to do?"

Grace reached into her desk, pulled out two glasses, and filled them with Scotch. Hildie didn't want to think about the fact that her mother was drinking at work.

"Are you promoting me?"

"God no." Grace slid the glass across the desk. "But I am going to ruin your life in a different way."

Hildie sipped at the Scotch. It tasted like a storm.

WAYNE

In the dream, they stood on the Capilano Suspension Bridge. Wind tossed it from side to side, like a strand of pearls between a giant's fingers. Back and forth, the rain and the wind, and his heart hammering. He clutched her hand. His aunt said something, but the wind carried her words away.

A shadow moved at the end of the bridge.

A raven shrieked at him. *Hwæt! Hwæt!*

He was shaking and crying and waiting for the shadow to come.

His mother's note, written in a clear hand. The empty space where her car had been. His father's closed face. The records she'd left behind. A mug half-full of cold tea on the living room table. The sweet smell of her cigarette smoke, drifting underneath the bathroom door. The sound of her deciding.

He'd jumped on a bus at fourteen without telling anyone. The bridge was where Anna used to take him when things were hard. He loved the sway of it, like a giant stim, back and forth. Realigning the plates of his life. The last time they'd come, she'd been quiet. She kept staring into the mossy darkness below. There was a crowd, but Wayne had felt like the bridge belonged to the two of them. She was giving him something, leaving him with something.

Aunt Vera found him, in the gloaming light, swaying. Hands white-knuckling the edges. The wires digging into his palms. She said nothing. Then the raven came.

The beast was there, and it knew him.

Dearest Wort,

There is a beast in all of our dreams. We live for the hunt—I'm sure you feel that by now. Sometimes you're hunting the beast, and some-times it's the other way around. You'll see it like a flicker, in the corner of your eye. You'll hear it in an empty house, in leaves falling, in the glow of your phone.

You don't have to be afraid of the beast. Respectful, but not afraid. Like all things older than us, it teaches us something about ourselves. We're all questing—even the beast. And it will always be with you; you can't live your life trying to avoid it. Perhaps I ran from it, and that was my mistake. Or my truth. Only time will tell.

There's always someone who goes after the beast and tries to tame it. Some knight who thinks they'll turn it into a trophy. But you can't. It's as old as shadows, as old as flickers on the cave wall, as old as graves. You can't bind that. Only live with it.

leofest,

Anna

⁂

They were deep in the old-growth forest of Stanley Park. They stood by the hollow red cedar, whose skeleton had sheltered people for seven hundred years. It remembered a precontact landscape that was radically

95

different from the Vancouver that he knew. Territory stewarded by the Squamish, Musqueam, and Tsleil-Waututh Nations.

The forest smelled like camping and moss and the sawdust of an East Van playground that he remembered, from years ago. Kai was there, but he also felt piercingly alone, beneath the canopy of leaves. They stretched above him like a church's vaulted ceiling. Fluorescent lights gave him a migraine, but forest light was a balm. It made him feel that something more than fear was possible.

He walked over to Kai, who was sitting on a stump. She'd brought lunch. She had Tupperware for all occasions, including two forks. She speared some bao and handed it to him. They ate in silence.

Wayne broke it because he was nervous and needed to put his energy somewhere. Normally he could have been silent with Kai for hours. "Any texts from Mr. Funny Name?"

The ghost of a smile played across her face. "Okay. Let me show you one. *Don't* be Judge Judy though."

"I swear."

She showed him a text exchange. She'd called the guy Hot Tinder in her phone, which answered the question of how they'd met.

Kai: listening to SOPHIE and really feeeeeeeeling shit

Hot Tinder: listening to Leonard Cohen on vinyl

Kai: babe no

Hot Tinder: bird on a wire

Kai: ofc the one song that mentions knights

Hot Tinder: we'd be cute birds

Kai: would 100% be the agro owl from Sword in the Stone

Hot Tinder: you'd be a lovely owl

Kai: what bird would you be . . . don't leave me hanging on a wiiiire

Hot Tinder: swan

Kai: we'd both be prickly

Hot Tinder: swans don't fear death

Kai: cuz of their freakish swan strength

Hot Tinder: they sing when it comes

Kai put the phone away. "He's weird, right?"

"We're all weird. He seems quick enough to keep up though."

"With my moods?"

"With your beautiful owl brain."

Kai stared into the woods for a moment, like she was searching for something. "For now, it's a bubble. Once we meet"—she made a popping motion—"he'll be just another dude that doesn't keep his promises."

"But you won't know until you meet."

"I'm tired of boys and their myths."

"Don't leave him hanging on the wire."

She laughed. "Plus he has a nice—"

"*Nope.*"

Kai stood, brushing off her skirt. "Okay. Rune defense lesson one," she said. "There are good runes and bad runes. Put them together, and you get gray. That's how most power works." She made a face. "White supremacists think they can bend runes to their cause. Calling themselves Sons of Odin. Please. Like Woden gives a shit about their fake-ass Anglo-Saxon nation. Runes are as old as fire. As old as the darkness in caves and burial cairns. They've got personalities. Like little gods. We share the world with them. And sometimes, if we know how to speak, they listen."

She took out a lighter and charred the end of a stick. Then she traced a rune in soot on the surface of the log. Two right angles, locked in an embrace.

"This is Dæg. It means fruitful," she said. "It's a welcome rune. If you see it on a door, it means a safe house. My mom says there aren't many left though."

Wayne felt slightly ill. "Should you be telling me this?"

"Do you want to be prepared? Or do you want to be dinner?" Her expression softened. "I know it's not the life you expected. But it's here. It's breathing down your neck. And you need to be able to protect yourself."

He nodded slowly. "Okay. Generous."

"Right. On its own. But weave it with Nyd—" Kai sketched an *x*, or maybe it was a slantwise cross. She joined the runes at the edges with a kind of dark flourish. Wayne felt the wind shift around them. He tasted ozone. Then the two shapes sputtered with green light. Wayne nearly jumped. The light reminded him of discount fireworks. He'd seen her weave runes before, just not this close.

"It's a homing beacon," Kai said. "Do it right, and you can use it to call for help, or to find someone you're connected with."

The fire didn't consume the wood. It popped a bit, then flickered out. She handed him the stick. "You try."

"But I'm not a smith like you."

"A sword isn't a knight's only weapon," Kai said. He wondered if her mother had told her something similar when she was a little girl. "A rune is a whisper. They're just really old words for talking to the world. Knights don't have access to the whole alphabet, but there are certain letters and combinations that your family hones over time. Like iron against a whetstone." She raised an eyebrow. "Plus, whetstone is a great drag name."

He tried to copy the first rune that Kai had drawn. It came out lopsided. Then he traced the next rune and linked them with a shaky line.

Nothing happened.

"Just wait," Kai said. "It's a basic protection rune. It should listen to you."

"Do runes have ears?"

She silenced him with a look. He hadn't seen her this focused in a while.

Wayne stared at the sloppy shapes. They weren't runes. They were an embarrassment.

Then he felt something. Like a hand tugging him.

There was a pop of green light.

Nothing more. Just a wee flash, like a fire you thought had gone out, until it suddenly hissed at you from the ashes.

Kai hooted. *"See?* You did it!"

"I barely did anything."

"But that's how all knowledge starts. And you've got it in you. Not like a smith, but like—someone who's been around the anvil. If that makes sense."

He thought of someone pounding runes on an anvil. Crafting words and whispers. A line flashed across his mind. Then another. It was part of what he'd seen on Mo Penley's body. The shape like a staff with a spike sticking out. Or a witch's nose. A fake witch, obviously. Real witches had unremarkable noses.

He drew the shape in the ashes. "I remember now," he said. "This is what I saw on"—he swallowed—"on the provost. Or part of it. The rune. It was . . . pointy? Almost like a tooth."

Kai sucked in her breath.

"What?"

"That's a thorn," she said. "It's . . . a tricky rune."

"Tricky how?"

"It can mean a lot of things. A claw. A giant's fist. A poke in the right—or wrong—direction. Something that gets stuck like a burr in your heart."

"Does it have to do with death? Giants are monsters, right? So it's bad?"

"Monsters are all about perspective." She tucked her hair behind her ears. "I need to think about it more. Like every rune, it can be good or bad. It's always something *big* though. Not to be used lightly. For now, all we know is that someone's weaving a lot of dangerous power for an unclear purpose." Then she smiled. "Look at you. Being a lil rune detective."

"That's the valkyrie's job," he murmured. "I don't feel like a detective. Or a knight. Or a wizard, for that matter."

Kai snorted. "Wizards are male fantasies. Horny old men with twisty beards. We're, like, interpreters. The word *rune* used to mean murmur, and you're tuned to that frequency. It's a difficult blessing. Like anything magic, it can kill you."

"You're the one with the magic."

Kai handed him her last piece of bao. "There's enough to go around."

⸎

He huffed up the stairs, across the quad, and was nearly late getting to the Student Success Office. His neuro Spidey sense tingled. Wayne looked around and saw a woman with headphones, trying to shrink herself into invisibility. Her backpack was covered in convention stickers, and she was reading a copy of *Squirrel Girl* while also trying to move with the line. He gave her a shy smile, which she returned.

The receptionist waved him into a honeycomb of small, concrete offices. Wayne hated the campus psychiatrist, who wore boxy blazers from Tan Jay and frequently interrupted him to cite the *DSM*. She meant well but had the habit of referring to him in the third person—"people in his situation"—which made him doubt that she actually meant *people*. He sat down on the lime-green chair, which was the only cheerful thing in the office. He needed these meetings to go well. He needed to know that there'd be some modicum of support, in case he had a meltdown in class or failed to understand a mumbly prof. In case he froze up during a presentation. He couldn't afford a failing grade, and it sucked that people couldn't see when he was trying his best. They wanted him to be like everyone else, communicate in short polite bursts, smile and nod, and make intimate eye contact while completely ignoring that one light in the lecture hall that would. not. stop. flickering. How were people not writing their essays on that light?

The psychiatrist who walked in wasn't wearing a Tan Jay blazer. He looked like a banker who'd just survived a long weekend—his tie was askew and he had a cowlick. He'd ironed half of his J.Crew shirt, but the other was a forest of wrinkles. Wayne stared at his shoulder, then willed his eyes to move up to the guy's nose. Noses were safe. Noses were his greatest allies. The psychiatrist looked vaguely familiar.

He extended his hand. "Hi, Wayne. I'm Dr. Hadley."

Shake his hand. It's not a claw. It's just a hand, and it'll be over in three-two-one.

He pumped the hand once for good measure, then withdrew. A ghost of the contact remained in his fingertips, like mild shocks. "Where's Dr. Tan J—? I mean Dr. Astolat?"

Dr. Hadley looked faintly amused. "She's on mental health leave, so I've taken over a lot of her files. I'll try to be as efficient as possible and pick up where she left off, so we can reach a positive accessibility outcome for you."

"What does that mean?"

Dr. Hadley looked up from his file. "Our goal is to ensure support. We want to be certain that you're getting the classroom assistance that you need for optimum—" He suddenly smiled, and there was something goofy about it. "Sorry. The jargon can be a drag. We're here to help, is what I mean."

Wayne zoned out for a moment, then realized that Dr. Hadley was still talking.

He willed himself to smile and say, "I feel confident about what you've said." Dr. Astolat had loved that. It always disarmed any tension.

The counselor's expression was quizzical. "You feel confident about free coffee?" He gestured to the machine on the desk. "Not the response I was expecting, but sure. Do you take cream or sugar?"

Wayne kept his expression neutral while dying internally of shame. "Black. No, cream. I don't know why I said black. It tears through me like a rocket."

This is going well. Why don't you tell him that your best friend is a runesmith? Or that you're hallucinating foxes? Can foxes also be runesmiths? How would their little paws make the—Focus, Wayne.

Dr. Hadley pressed the button, and they both said nothing while the machine threw up. Wayne didn't want to take the coffee, but he couldn't refuse free caffeine. Plus, he enjoyed the feeling of a warm mug in his hands—it reminded him of those aimless nights with his mom, edging closer to sleep as they kept each other company. They both shuffled a bit awkwardly in their seats. Dr. Hadley was cute in a rumpled way. There was something innocent about him, though his eyes looked like they'd seen things.

"So"—Dr. Hadley was studying his file—"you've never had a diagnosis."

It was a statement rather than a question. Wayne said, "I was sort of . . . between diagnoses as a kid."

Hadley digested this without comment. "It's possible for you to receive partial accommodation without an official diagnosis. The extra time on assignments we can do, as well as a private room for exams. But if you need more, we'll have to work with a clinician who's more experienced with—"

"People in my situation?" It came out before he could stop it.

Dr. Hadley managed to look somewhat contrite. "It's not my field. I'm more of a generalist with youth issues. If you want to label this as anxiety, then we can file some of the paperwork now, but it'll take time to process."

The concrete walls seemed to shimmer. Wayne could feel the anger rising through him and coming off in waves. He tapped the chair, but under his coat, so Dr. Hadley couldn't see.

"It's not just anxiety," he said slowly. His voice sounded tinny and distant. He struggled to bring it back, to ground himself.

"The diagnostic process is complicated, especially at your age. You've likely"—he paused, as if searching for the proper phrase—"picked up strategies for dealing with social difficulties or sensory issues."

"You mean I know how to mask."

His expression softened. "Sure. That's one way of looking at it."

"So, in order for this to work, I have to—what—perform, like, a text-book definition? Should I say 'cool, cool, cool' and uplift you with physics?"

"Nobody wants you to be a stereotype, Wayne."

"But that's exactly what you're saying. You know how many tests I've done? I've got high marks in weird, I assure you."

"That's not a word we'd—I'd—use."

Wayne focused on breathing. "Hiding is survival," he said. "Passing for normal. I'm pretty good at it by now, yeah. But I'm not asking for something special, something *extra*. I don't want to be accommo-dated. I just want an equal playing field. Though I regret using a sports metaphor."

He half smiled. "I hear what you're saying. I'll file some of the paper-work today, and we can modify things as they evolve."

Dr. Hadley seemed about to say something generic, but instead he made a face, like he'd tasted something sour. "College is awful. Everyone's a hero for surviving it. Can we meet next week?"

Wayne had never heard this phrased as a question before—as if it was his choice. "I could do an afternoon meeting."

"I'll pencil you in. Figuratively speaking. It was nice to meet you!"

The uptick at the end confused Wayne. He legitimately seemed to mean it, as if they'd just connected over craft beer rather than ableism.

Wayne left the office feeling confused, which was nothing new. He pulled out his phone to text Kai. Then he stopped in his tracks, like a frozen cartoon character.

Bert was in the waiting room, texting someone.

He looked up and grinned. "Well, hello."

He wore a shirt with a medieval manuscript screen-printed on it. Wayne peered closer at the illumination, then blushed when he real-ized it was a nun with a penis tree. Bert's hair was tilting to one side. It looked as though he hadn't slept. His knapsack was spilling over with books, including a behemoth with tissue-paper pages that cheerfully boasted *online content*. If the content was online, why did he have to pay $100 for a book like a bowling ball?

Bert stood up. "Exorcizing demons?"

Wayne blinked. "What?"

"I mean"—he shrugged—"never mind. These places always make me nervous as fuck. Like someone's scanning me with poor OCR."

"Yeah. I get that."

"Were you seeing Dr. McHotPants?"

He looked away, slightly embarrassed. But also secretly pleased that they might have the same type. "I just met him."

"He's a peach. Don't get him talking about archaeology though. He's super into amphorae and dirty chalices." Bert grabbed his knapsack. "Well, I'm off to spill my secrets. Nice running into you."

Wait!

He tried to think of something to say—something that would convince Bert to stick around for a few more seconds. All he could come up with was "There's free coffee!"

"Yup. One of the perks of psychoanalysis, I guess."

"Well . . ." *Ask him about literally anything!* "Foxes."

Bert raised an eyebrow. "Is that . . . a topic?"

"Foxes," Wayne repeated. *Dear Lord.* "I've been seeing them."

"You've been seeing foxes." He smiled slightly.

Were they just going to keep repeating each other like characters in a mumblecore movie? In a second, the counselor would reappear, and who knew if he'd ever see Bert again? This was fate. If that's what fate meant. Wayne wasn't sure about anything now, except that he was terrified of the future and also wanted to see Bert again.

"Around campus," Wayne said. "Maybe just one fox?"

"Are you sure it wasn't a raccoon in disguise?"

"He might have been going to a masquerade party."

"The raccoon ball scene is amazing, or so I hear."

What would Kai do?

She'd be assertive AF.

Do that.

"I saw you on campus—the other day." *Stalked you* was more accurate.

Bert cocked his head. "You're sure it was me?"

This wasn't going quite how he'd imagined. Was Bert making it a joke? Or was he actually being evasive? It was so hard to tell when you didn't know someone and hadn't built a database of their weirdness in your mind yet.

"I think it was you," he said uncertainly.

Bert was smiling now. "Were you possibly following me in an obvious way? Because I might have noticed when you stopped to tie your shoes for the seventh time."

His face fell. "Clocked us, did you?"

"Just a bit." He kept smiling. "You should have said hi."

Dr. Hadley appeared in the doorway. "Bert?"

Shit.

"Doctor." Bert flashed him a grin.

Dr. Hadley seemed unimpressed—like they'd dealt with each other many times before. "Come in."

Bert's smile turned fake. "I heard there was coffee!"

Wayne didn't know what to do next. Then Bert grabbed his phone, tapping in his number. "Here. In case you need to interview me about Vulpes later."

Then he disappeared into the office.

It took about five minutes for his heart to stop pounding.

Dearest Wort,

I never got the hang of marriage. I love your father, but sharing your life with someone is never easy, like a game whose rules are always being reinvented. Living with you was simple, though sometimes you reminded me of a past I wanted to forget. That wasn't your fault. You've always been self-sufficient, but relationships are full of talk and bewildering silence. Don't be afraid to ask questions. Don't be afraid to fail and try again and fail harder. That's really all any of us are doing.

When you meet someone in our community, there will be things that you simply understand. But that won't mean you'll know each other completely. Prepare for confusion and hurt feelings and broken things. Don't run from the cracks. They're necessary. They're making you stronger. If you look at a sword under a scanning electron microscope, you can see how many times it's been broken and reforged. The most interesting surfaces are imperfect.

If you fall for a girl, remember that she's been hurt before, that she has to move through a world that's violent, a world that wants her to fail. Be the person who lifts her up and makes her feel held, known, respected.

If you fall for a boy, I won't be much help—I fell for one and broke his heart. Just don't ever think there's only one way to be a boy. We're all riddles with no answer, just untold possibilities, depending on which words you focus on.

leof,

Anna

HILDIE

I t stung.

Not being saddled with the task of watching some knight pup who didn't know his ass from a hole in the ground. That was just so typical. No. What stung was the feeling of being managed by her mother.

She'd discovered that Wayne's new counselor at the university was Galahad—a knight with a long history of pacifism who'd eventually settled into therapy. In most incarnations, he died young, so she made a note to keep an eye on him; even oblique involvement with this case might shorten his myth cycle.

It was a crime that she hadn't inherited her mother's organizational skills, or her grandmother's talent for getting to the point. Instead, she was a fire of awkwardness and uncertainty and side-eye.

She ducked through the entrance of Hotel Wyrd. The invisible spiderwebs brushed her hair, and she resisted the urge to wipe them away. It felt a bit like the universe sniffing you, and she wasn't a fan.

The kelpie swam around the fountain in lazy circles. She nodded a greeting. The kelpie snorted a bit of seaweed. Seahorse wasn't her first language, so she had to assume that meant either *hello* or *I'm ignoring you*.

Shar was working the front desk. Her long forelock was aquamarine today, and she was frowning at a stack of papers.

"Heya."

Shar looked up. "Welcome to my nightmare." She gestured to the documents. "City rezoning application."

Rezoning was code in Vancouver for demolition.

Hildie frowned. "Wait. How can they rezone something they can't even see? I thought this building was veiled."

"The hotel is more or less hidden," Shar said, "but buildings in Gastown are old and twisty. It's technically connected to an old garment factory that *does* have a physical address. The lines between the lots are fuzzy. You'd have to know a lot about this particular place in order to strike that way."

"So you think it's an inside job."

Shar's eyes went dark. "Someone from the community is gunning for our destruction. If they reveal the hotel and bury us in paperwork, and visits from curious structural engineers and property management companies—they'll disrupt the sacred space." She lowered her voice, as if someone might be listening. "That puts my family in danger. And if we can't do our jobs, then the universe crashes. Like bad Wi-Fi, or the Canada Revenue website."

Hildie tried not to consider the enormity of that. "Who would be willing to risk that?"

Shar shrugged. "Not everyone accepts their fate. Some people take it personally. And we've made a lot of enemies." She rolled her eyes. "Knights. Such babies."

Still, Shar looked genuinely worried. This was the woman who'd once used dark matter to brew moonshine. If she was shaken, then the sisters might really be in trouble.

Hildie leaned on the counter. "On a scale of one to cosmic reno-viction, how bad?"

Shar frowned. "I mean, it's not great. We've faced this sort of thing before. There's always someone who thinks they can expose us. But this feels more focused. They've already requested a forum discussion, which means that someone high up in the community is on board."

She tried to get a glimpse of the papers. "Any idea who's behind it?"

"Something called Caerleon Corp. Could be a shell corporation. Could be a bloodthirsty developer. I know nothing at this point." Shar shook her head. "Anyways. Don't worry about it for now. You're here to question the ylf, right? Room sixteen." She slid an electronic key across the counter.

"What are the chances that they'll actually be there?"

Shar returned her attention to the documents. "I'm not a nanny cam. Fifty-fifty? I saw them not too long ago."

In Shar's world, that could mean a century ago. But Hildie wasn't going to press.

"Okay. Thanks for this."

"Oh, and Clywen's now obsessed with the brooch you dropped off. Says it's spooky."

"Spooky?"

"Big magic. Someone with power made it—and apparently it has a twin somewhere. That's all she knows at the moment. Something to do with how its molecules are vibrating." She returned her attention to the paperwork. "My molecules are exhausted."

"Thanks."

Hildie wondered about the brooch's twin. Was this a two-person job? Then she thought about the sisters and their home.

Her mother had brought her to Hotel Wyrd at nine years old, when she first got her spear. Grace thought she should meet the sisters, since they were kind of like regional supervisors. Clywen gave her some toffee that was so prehistoric it was fused into a ball. Braeda kept checking her Casio Databank and sorting through a blizzard of Post-its. There were no bodies in the undercroft, or maybe they'd just been hidden for her visit. Shar was watching an unusual weather system—a hailstorm that only existed in one corner of the croft. The pellets swirled, like they were in some kind of surreal fish tank. Shar saw her and smiled. It wasn't a shy smile, but there was something she held back. At the time, Hildie couldn't have said how old Shar was. She was both young and old, always on a slightly different track, with the expression of someone who'd seen the beating, quantum heart of things, and maybe wished that she hadn't. Her hair had an iridescent streak.

"Can I watch the storm with you?"

"Sure. But watch out for stray stones. They hurt like you wouldn't believe."

Hildie couldn't imagine Vancouver without Hotel Wyrd. It was one of the only places where you could seek asylum, regardless of whatever blood feud your family was engaged in. The sisters had always kept the peace without asking questions. And Shar was right: they couldn't destroy the site just by demolishing the building. The plan didn't quite make sense, unless its only purpose was to distract the sisters and render the guests vulnerable.

Who might profit? Morgan Arcand had a deserved reputation for trafficking in Badness. Who was she willing to destroy to get what she wanted?

Room sixteen was at the end of a hallway that seemed to gradually slope in several directions at once, until Hildie was thoroughly disoriented. The hotel had a penchant for swaying softly, like a loosely tied ship. Parts of it weren't, strictly speaking, *here*, so much as straddling a divide that she couldn't cross. Not yet, anyhow.

Hildie knocked on the door to be respectful. There was no answer, but ylves didn't always notice things like doors. She scanned the keycard, and the door opened with a click. She stepped in.

The room was an old-growth forest—what Vancouver might have looked like before settlers invaded. There were towering Douglas firs, their crowns hidden by mist. It was dawn-cold and smelled like rotting leaves.

Okay. Forest suite. Got it.

She could barely make out the bed, covered in roots and fungi. The TV was entirely obscured by a wall of ferns.

Hildie reached into her bag and withdrew the typical offering. She placed it on the bed—a bowl of Stovetop instant stuffing (better than bread crumbs) and a probiotic yogurt. She wasn't sure if ylves needed any help in the digestion department, but it combined both milk and fruit, so that was a bonus. All of nature's bounty.

She cleared her throat, and said in Anglish, "I respectfully ask for parlay." At least that's what she thought she said. Her Anglish wasn't fantastic. She might have asked for a parsnip by accident.

A red light was blinking on the phone, which was partially covered by a colony of mushrooms. Maybe they had a message from the front desk. She briefly imagined what an ylf would order for room service.

For a while there was just demi-silence: branches creaking and the sound of birds nesting in the ceiling. Then Hildie felt something brush against her leg. She resisted the urge to scream, remaining absolutely still.

She watched the probiotic yogurt disappear in small, invisible bites. The stuffing vanished, first slowly, then with gusto. Old World ylves tended to prefer milk and bread baked on holy days, but those who'd adjusted to the digital age weren't as picky. They appreciated what you could whip up with a microwave.

The duvet rustled. It was half-covered in moss, and she could only see parts of the pattern, striped in living green. There was nothing there. She waited. The light in the room shifted, and the nothing darkened, turned to smoke. Eyes like Christmas lights reflected in the mirror. The rest of the ylf was . . . somewhere else. A mix of dust and shadows and the smell of rotting leaves.

Nan's notes said it best: *Never run. And never, ever insult them, because their memories are as old as the first trees.* One of the few things she'd written out in complete sentences.

Hildie noticed, for the first time, something gleaming on the bed. It looked like a quartz filament at first, a sliver of something. But it was an arrow. The same type of arrow used to incapacitate Mo Penley.

Ylf shot was unpredictable. It could kill you, or drive you crazy, or make you sleep for a hundred years until you were a pile of bones.

The lights in the mirror flickered. Hildie felt something touch her hair, like a raven's feather. The smell of leaves filled her up.

She repeated her initial greeting. Then waited.

Finally, the ylf said, "Saga hwæt þu hætst."

Hildie frowned. It took her a moment to translate the phrase. It wasn't the usual greeting. Then she remembered that it was the modified first line of a riddle.

Say what you're called.

The ylf wasn't just asking her name. They were asking about her family, her ancestors, all her relations. Every mother and grandmother who'd made her what she was, infusing her with stardust and memory and the strength of warrior women.

She could feel them purring to life around her. Nan in the shadows, with a wry smile. Her great-grandmother, bent double like a tree struck by lightning yet still formidable. A shadowy outline that might have been her great-great-grandmother, watching with hooded eyes. And near the back of the room, a shimmer that she couldn't make out. Perhaps one of the giant spear maidens from her dream. An arch-grandmother from her family's deep history, slowly materializing to get a glimpse of what would happen next. They rustled in her mind. They whispered and sang and gently scolded. But Nan was silent, as usual.

She spoke haltingly in Anglish. It would not have been the ylf's first language. But it was the closest lingua franca they could manage, since her Breton was absolute shite. Tough to learn a language when all you had to go on were a few names of rivers and ancient shrines.

"I am the daughter of Grace. Granddaughter of Cyneðryð. Great-granddaughter of Aud the Shaper. I humbly greet you-two, as a herald of the Spear-Sworn."

Hildie stumbled a bit over the second-person form of the dual pronoun *uncer*, which meant we-two. Ylves used the dual pronoun, always at least two people. *Spear-Sworn* was the old-timey word for valkyries, which she thought was a nice flourish.

The ylf was silent for another moment.

Then the whole room made a strange, silky, bubbling noise. Laughter.

They switched to accented English. "You said *gaar* instead of *gar* for spear. That means you're sworn to garlic."

Her face went red. "Shit. I mean—sorry. My Anglish is rusty."

"The state of the humanities."

Hildie wasn't sure how to respond.

"Why are you here, daughter of Grace and granddaughter of Cyneðryð?"

She spied Nan sitting on the edge of the bed. She winked. Hildie felt a wordless sense of dread. Like she was trying to hold up a crumbling tower.

What was she doing with her life? Would her grandmother be proud of her? Stubbornly single and living in a studio apartment that cost her entire salary? Hating her job most of the time? Ignoring the advice of her mother, which—though brisk, like an ice bath—was usually sensible and good?

Nan's wink had done nothing to answer these questions.

She whispered and sang but rarely spoke in Hildie's mind, as she had in the first days after her death. When Hildie was out of her mind with grief, the old woman's voice had risen like a kingfisher and flown over the dark.

Now she was inaudible, except for the odd note carried on the wind.

Carefully, Hildie reached into her bag and drew out a small parcel, which she unwrapped and set on the bed. It was the shot that she'd taken from the sisters.

"This felled a knight," she said. "We're trying to discover where it came from."

"And by we—you mean Grace and her Garlic-Sworn?"

At least the ylf had a sense of humor.

"The Office of Valkyries, yes." Hildie stayed tense, though the ylf was teasing her.

She heard a sniffing sound. Felt hot breath near her fingers.

"Not a killing barb."

"So it was meant to incapacitate." Hildie considered this. "Something took his head off, and then took a bite out of him. But this was just the appetizer."

Hildie didn't want to lose an opportunity, but she also feared that saying more could be dangerous. Their truce with the ylves was on shaky ground. What if she said the wrong thing and insulted her only informant?

Hildie inhaled.

Go big or go home, right?

"Look," she said. "Mo Penley was, by all rights, an asshole. But whoever killed him is up to something much bigger—I think. Someone is also trying to shut down this hotel. The community hasn't been this unstable in a long time. I think something's moving, and it wants to pull down the old order. Penley won't be the last victim. So if you have any ideas about where this dart came from—anything would help. Respectfully."

The ylf seemed to consider this for a moment. It felt more like ten long moments. Hildie wanted to scream, but she kept quiet, kept her expression open. *Don't be afraid of silence.* It was Grace, actually, who'd told her that. *People learn in the gaps between words.*

"I knew Cyneðryð."

Her grandmother's name startled her. When the ylf pronounced it, the *th* sounds were rippling liquid growls.

"You did?"

Nan smiled slightly on the edge of the bed. Then she returned her gaze to the trees, which towered above them all.

"She rescued my kin from a—how would you call it—a *pesticide*. Brewed medicine and watched over them until they were well again. She was a decent valkyrie."

"She was," Hildie said, feeling her voice thicken.

"She's watching you now."

"I know."

"She says she's always watching you."

Hildie blinked. "You can hear her?"

The ylf sounded momentarily confused. "You can't? Ah, well, we hear differently. We shall discharge our oath to your grandmother." The ylf shot abruptly disappeared. "We shall find the owner. It may take [ ] time."

Hildie frowned. "I didn't quite get that word. *How* much time?"

"More or less." The voice was already fading. "We shall find you, daughter of Grace."

"Wait! I'm on a deadline! *How* much time?"

But the ylf was gone.

Her ancestors were fading as well. She could see the trees through them, as if she was looking through steamed shower glass.

Nan still smiled.

"Why don't you talk to me anymore?" Hildie's voice broke. "Say something. Please. Tell me to fuck off. Tell me I'm wrecking it all—the potential and the love and everything you gave me. Tell me *something*. I don't know how to do this."

Nan had always been a cushion between her and Grace. A kind of interpreter, weaving over awkward moments, dismissing old feuds. Grace hadn't been a bad mother; she could be fiercely protective. But there'd always been a distance between them, like miles of blacktop, and Nan was the one who connected them. Now they were just drifting.

She remembered Nan reading her *The Cat in the Hat*. Her wide eyes. A sense of dread over what Thing One and Thing Two might do. And afterward, Nan telling her, *Niblet, don't fret, the world belongs to you.*

But what did she want? What had she ever wanted, except for Nan to read that book to her one more time? To grin like the cat as they floated in her old bed, the ragged nest of her childhood, which was now a spare room with Grace's treadmill?

Vines had completely covered the bed now. She heard the crowns of trees crackling above her, readying for a storm.

Hildie looked around the forest room. There was nothing to search. Nothing left behind. Just a dream of wilderness that would stop when she closed the door.

She let herself out.

The hallway buzzed and slanted, first left, then right, until she felt drunk.

Words followed her down the impossible halls. Her grandmother's hands smoothing her hair, turning the pillow to the cool side. Singing in different tongues, older languages that Hildie couldn't understand, though she felt them sizzling in her blood. Words guarded and passed on by mothers and mothers and mothers from across a still sea.

The elevator doors opened. Hildie saw wet hoofprints on the carpet.

The kelpie must be wandering.

She walked up to the front desk, expecting to see Shar staring at papers. Instead, she was talking on the phone. When she got closer, Shar placed her hand over the mouthpiece. The phone was from the 1920s; it looked like a piece of art, with a golden cradle.

"It's your mother," Shar said.

"Why is she—?" Hildie noticed Shar's fallen expression, and her insides flipped. "Oh."

Shar nodded. "Another knight."

12

WAYNE

𝕿he world knocked loudly.

There was whistling and barking and construction noise and people watching tinny videos on their phones, all treble and crackle. But there was a counterspell to that. Wayne could close his door. Put on a record. Duke Ellington or Edith Piaf or even electronic tango—anything with a regular beat. It would match his heartbeat, and the outside noise would fade, until there was just this space.

He was showered and dressed and ready to step into the unknown, but he couldn't quite open the door.

He put on an old Pet Shop Boys album. He'd found it in his dad's collection, and there was this funny song about love being like rent. How splitting the cost of an apartment could be the purest form of desire. They sang from a different time, when AIDS was decimating a whole generation. He'd read about the hospices in Toronto, where men died in hallways, staring at fish tanks meant to calm their nervous visitors. Men and boys dying alone, knights bleeding on their own separate battlefields. The album was tinny and fun but also sad. He replaced it with the new

Lana Del Rey. Kai always made fun of his grimdark music choices, but she'd spent a summer listening to Kim Petras at ear-splitting volumes. Her music had a jellybean exterior, but the core was something different.

Now he had to meet Aunt Vera, for what promised to be some fresh horror.

But that's not what he was thinking about.

He swiped through his phone again. Bert's message hadn't disappeared. *Got shrinked and survived. Food?*

They'd been texting since they exchanged numbers, and Bert's texts were as enigmatic as his conversation. Wayne was still trying to decode it. No *hey* or other salutation, as though they were already in the middle of a conversation (but this was his first text). Did *food* mean *tonight*? There were a few places that Wayne loved—when he had the cash to eat out—but would Bert love them as well?

He needed to ask Kai, but she just kept responding with one-word texts, or the ellipses would appear only to vanish. She was clearly pre-occupied, but he needed an editor. Someone who'd make sure that he didn't mess everything up.

He'd spent about an hour trying to figure out a response. Finally, he texted back, *Thumbs up!*

He hated the thumbs-up emoji, so he always texted back *thumbs up*, which enraged Kai but also made her laugh.

Twenty minutes passed, and there was no response from Bert. He must be working—though Bert seemed like the kind of person who'd text under his desk.

The album came to an end.

Wayne sighed, lifted the needle, and closed the cover. The door had to open eventually. Until he managed to turn his bedroom into a working Holodeck, he'd need to actually leave from time to time. He didn't want to keep Aunt Vera waiting.

Like every nerdy kid who'd trusted books and cats more than people, he'd always wanted to believe that magic existed. And it did: runes were legit magic. But they didn't quite listen to him. Wayne had practiced Kai's homing rune, but the most he got was a pop of color, like a short

118

circuit. Maybe there really was a spell that fixed things. Maybe if he combined the right herbs together in a copper cauldron, he'd be able to attend parties without hiding under the bed. Maybe there was a dragon waiting for him somewhere, ready to play rooftop Sudoku or calcify his enemies or whatever affable dragons did.

No part of him had ever wanted to be a knight.

He'd *never* been the knight in this story, whatever it was. In his wildest dreams, he was always some weird bystander with low-key powers. Always something more subtle, more queer, less battle-ready. More of a world-builder than someone on the front lines. What did he know about swords? He never chose the knight when he played an RPG. His *Skyrim* character was basically an interior decorator with a passing interest in telekinesis.

His phone vibrated, and he nearly dropped it. There was a reply from Bert: *dope dope dope.*

Wayne tried to mirror Bert's text voice: *u decide on a place and leave dessert to me! ;-)*

But what kind of dessert? A box full of Timbits, half chocolate, half glazed? Or something fancy from one of those downtown bakery cafes where you had to wait in line for a macaron? Or was Bert more of an apple pie at the Templeton diner sort of guy?

Wayne texted Kai: *Code red! Need your text-deciphering abilities!*

There was no response.

He sent her an instant message. Nothing.

He thought about calling her. It was a bold move this early in the day, when she hadn't responded to any texts. She'd be annoyed. Probably wouldn't answer. And, really, who answered the phone? Sociopaths. That's who.

His bedroom door exploded.

Not literally. It was just his dad knocking, but it sounded like a gunshot. Wayne buried his phone under the covers, as if it was dangerous. "Enter!"

His dad opened the door a crack. They'd long ago passed the danger zone—from age twelve to fifteen, approximately—when knocking prevented them both from being psychically scarred. But he still knocked and sort of winced as he opened the door.

"It's fine," Wayne said. "I'm wearing pants and everything."

His dad opened the door wider. He had his work uniform on. He'd taken a job with Canada Post for the benefits, since he wasn't exactly making mad cash as a studio musician. Wayne missed the sound of his guitar. His dad stayed the same—smile barely quirking the edge of his mouth, salt-and-pepper hair making him look like a softer version of the guy from those Trivago commercials. He didn't used to be this tired, but he was still quiet and good-natured and generally okay to be around.

"Hi, kid. Have you got class today?"

"Nope. Wednesday's my free-floating anxiety day."

He meant it as a joke, but his dad raised an eyebrow. "Everything cool?"

Wayne would never know what cool meant. He was generally in a state of molten hot. But he didn't want to worry his dad. He didn't need to know about the meetings with Dr. Hadley, or the fact that Kai was giving him a tutorial on protective runes.

"Nah. Just same old stuff." He smiled widely, like a jack-o'-lantern, and gave him a slow thumbs-up.

"Okay then. Can you pick up some groceries later? I left a list."

"Sure but no more celery root. It *isn't* mashed potatoes. It's heresy."

"I thought you enjoyed the Celery Root Experiment!"

"I was just being polite." He suddenly felt bad. "But thanks for, like, preparing dinner. I appreciate it."

His dad frowned at the formality. "You sure everything's fine?"

"*Yes.*"

"Cool. Or—what's the word you're using? One hundred?"

"Stop trying to be relevant, Dad."

"Sure. I just worry sometimes."

His dad hesitated in the doorway. This was the man who'd taught him bird nomenclature and basic chords (no luck there) and how to level any surface. The man who'd believed him, at four years old, when he'd insisted that beach towels hurt his hair, and bought him something softer. His love was a fixed point in the universe. But he worried too much, and worked too much, and sometimes his smiles were wobbly. After Anna left, he'd barely said anything for the first week. Just played old songs,

120

gradually sinking into the couch. That was before he'd pawned the good Epiphone. Wayne knew the same hurt was coursing through them, but he didn't know how to talk about it. He was afraid that if they started, the apartment would crumble around them, and they'd be left in ruins.

Some small part of him—like a bee sting in his heart—also festered with anger. Because he must have known she was unhappy. He must have suspected how bad it was. And he'd let her go. Wayne couldn't have done anything, but maybe his dad could have stopped her.

"I'm fine," he said simply. "You don't have to worry about me."

Maybe it came out cold. His dad looked at him for a beat. Then he nodded and closed the door softly.

Wayne changed into a soft shirt and a pair of jeans that had disintegrated into almost nothing. He'd always hated socks, but he had a few pairs that had become shapeless lumps; they were okay so long as nobody saw them. People were forever buying him socks for Christmas, and he couldn't explain that new socks were torture devices. Socks, like wine, had to age into acceptability.

He managed to drag himself outside. Everything smelled faintly of coffee and weed and huaraches cooking at Rinconcito. Crows were diving, then retreating to their respective awnings. Vendors sold shirts and classic DVDs near the SkyTrain station entrance, wrapped in blankets as they sat on camping chairs. Wayne's stomach grumbled. Then he realized that he'd forgotten the grocery list.

Remembering something was never a straight line. It was a snarl of lights that needed to be untangled, except that he couldn't, because all of the lights were connected and winking at each other. Sometimes it felt like he remembered too much, rather than not enough. He knew it had something to do with what various psychiatrists called executive function, but it was way more than that. Memory was different for everyone. His mother used to say that he took the scenic route, and he liked that. More chance for photo ops.

He scanned his student pass and jumped on the SkyTrain. It was one of the slick new trains that didn't make any noise. Everyone puffy in their winter coats, even though it was never truly cold in Vancouver. Just damp, like bathwater cooling, making you shiver. He watched East Van moving in reverse. A crow kept pace with them briefly, and he wondered what birds thought of the flying monorail. More people got on as they drew closer to the downtown core. Wayne loved the train because it was the closest thing to a flying carpet he would ever experience. For a moment, he thought he saw something weaving through the crowd—something dark and low to the ground, moving slowly. But when he blinked, sunlight filled the space, and it was gone.

Aunt Vera and Nuncle Gale lived in the West End, which was sort of like a semicolon on the edge of the downtown core. It was one of the most densely packed neighborhoods in North America, though nobody ever seemed like they were in a rush. Lawyers, drag queens, and seniors all coexisted in a state of relative peace. Wayne had been coming here since he was a kid—long before he'd come out—and seeing all those people together had always filled him with hope. Now it was pretty much impossible to live here unless you were a millionaire.

The West End seemed to hold the ocean in its grasp. A lot of tourists didn't actually know how to get there. At least once a day, he was approached by someone asking, *So, where's the water?*

He crossed Davie Street and turned onto Thurlow. Vera and Gale lived in a walkup, surrounded by other low-top buildings from the '20s. He noticed that a few buildings in the next block had *rezoning* signs out front, which meant that they'd be torn down and replaced with space-age condo towers.

Wayne leaned on the buzzer. A moment later, the door clicked open, and he walked up the carpeted stairs that always smelled like smoke and cooked fish. Their door was ajar, so he let himself in. He'd always loved their apartment. It was how he imagined a professor's living space: old teak floors, lilac walls, and books everywhere. Plants thrived in the sunny window, trailing leaves down the walls in green-fired patterns. He heard the percolator bubbling in the small kitchen, which always smelled like the ghosts of delicious dinners past. Gale was a fantastic cook.

This felt undeniably weird. His dad didn't know he was here. The universe was crashing down, and he didn't want to keep secrets from the only parent he had left.

Gale emerged from the kitchen with two cups of coffee. "Hiya, chaval."

"Hey, Nuncle." They'd decided on that word because it made them both laugh, and because Gale said it was avuncular. He basically collected words for a living.

Nuncle Gale's place in the family was one of those things that didn't fit in a box. He was almost always gently stoned and surrounded by ancient languages. As a translator, his work mostly seemed to revolve around cracking open words and staring in puzzlement at invoices from different countries. Aunt Vera said his taxes were apocalyptic.

There was no way to put what he felt for Gale into words. So he just said, "Te extraño." *Miss you.* His Spanish was crap, but he could say that much.

Gale kissed him on the cheek. "Yo tambien, chiquito."

Wayne wrinkled his nose. "I'm a bit old for chiquito."

Aunt Vera laughed as she stepped into the room. "You're always wee to someone, no matter how big you get."

He hugged her, but a part of him remained wary. When she'd asked him to come, he hadn't exactly known what he was in for. The last time they'd all been together, Mo Penley had lost his head.

Vera gave him a long look. "I wasn't sure you'd come. After what happened. You'd be justified in screening my calls."

"Auntie. Nobody calls anymore."

"You know I'm old school." She smiled. "Come with us."

"This sounds like kidnapping."

"We won't let anything bad happen to you," Gale said. "We're family."

They left the apartment, though Wayne lingered as they passed the bookshelves. Reading was the only thing he'd ever been truly addicted to, and Aunt Vera was a supplier. She had everything you could imagine, from obscure Latin texts to erotic poetry (which he used to steal in his tweens—Catullus was illuminating).

Gale led them up the stairs to the roof. The penthouse apartment had been empty for as long as anyone could remember. The rooftop was covered in gravel. Wind licked at him, and he wished that he'd brought a better jacket. A seagull regarded them with skepticism. Wayne's heart nearly stopped when he saw two crossed swords, arrayed delicately before them, like cryptic pop-up art. The sun made them almost painful to look at, a deadly shimmer under the too-blue sky.

Aunt Vera turned to Gale. "What should we start with?"

Gale looked thoughtful. "How not to be a pin cushion?"

Wayne didn't like the sound of that.

Gale took up one of the swords. Girded? Was that the word? Wayne's mind was about to explode. The sword had a hilt wrapped in wire and a clear stone that burned in the light. There were runes along the hilt, but he couldn't read them.

He almost mentioned his rune lesson with Kai, but didn't want to implicate her any further. Plus, she wasn't answering his texts. She had her own life. She didn't exist to offer him encouragement; he understood that. But he also got nervous when he didn't hear from her. It violated their unspoken safety contract.

Both Aunt Vera and Gale were studying him. Their gaze made him uncomfortable, and he had to look away.

"You can use your aunt's sword," Gale said after a moment. "You're kin, so it should recognize you."

Aunt Vera's sword was blue-tinged, and he could see waves etched into the steel. The hilt was engraved with figures that he couldn't make out. Sometimes they looked like birds, and sometimes like wolves. He wasn't sure if it was a trick of the light, but they seemed to move in liquid procession, becoming one thing and then another.

"Don't be afraid," his aunt said, coming up behind him. "You've touched it before. You used to play with it when you were a babe in arms. Didn't earn me any popularity points with your mum, let me tell you."

Wayne couldn't imagine a universe in which toddler-him played with a sword.

Carefully, he grasped the hilt. "It's heavy."

"You'll get used to the weight," Gale said. "The balance is in the pommel."

He moved the sword experimentally. It was impossibly solid in his hand. But it also felt somehow diaphanous, like it could vanish at any moment. He felt himself sweating. His heart was machine-gunning in his chest.

"It feels weird."

"Just breathe," Aunt Vera said.

He remembered Bert's fingers tapping out a beat.

Da-DUM.

Da-DUM.

Da-DUM.

He felt his heart slow. Then it wasn't just his heart. Everything slowed, until the world was honey dripping. The seagull watched him, unmoving. The sky was a blue screen. He felt the hairs on his arms standing to attention. He felt the stones shifting under his feet. The taste of snow in the air, even though it hadn't quite fallen yet. Like the thought of winter uncurling.

Somewhere in the back of his mind, he could hear a buzz. Then it was like a song drifting through the neighbor's wall. He couldn't make out the words, but they were there under it all, persisting.

Gale winked at him. "Working, isn't it?"

"*What's* working?"

"Just listen."

Wayne felt a ripple of nausea. He closed his eyes. The sword was heavy in his hand. The sword was water and light and smoke from a thousand fires. His atoms were having a freaky-ass kiki as they fizzed and smashed into each other.

He felt something brush his shoulder.

Wayne almost dropped the sword. He turned around, and what was there—he couldn't quite describe it. There was a dark seam in the air. Something inside the fold was watching him, with intensity.

He took a step forward.

The sword made a noise—like a cat's hiss.

Then something near the edge of the roof caught his eye. A teenage boy with long hair. He wore a mail jacket that shimmered, like in TV clips from the '70s where the camera winks against spangled outfits. They were both looking at the seam in the air. Then the kid laughed. It was a sly sound. And a familiar one. Wayne could have sworn that the boy knight had his laugh.

125

The sky was gray again. The ghost and the shadow were gone. Wayne could feel sweat pooling down his back, and the sword made his hand ache. Gale and Aunt Vera stood on either side of him.

"What did you see?" His aunt's voice had an edge to it.

"I'm not sure."

He couldn't escape the feeling that she'd wanted him to see something very specific. And he didn't know what that could be.

"Enough playing with the dial." Gale raised his sword. "We're going from abstract to concrete. Lesson one. I call it Dirty Parry."

Wayne blinked. "Is that supposed to be funny?"

"Never mind. I'm going to come at you."

"What?" He took a step back.

"It's easy. Just knock my sword away. I'll move slowly."

"I don't know how to parry or whatever."

"You do," Aunt Vera said. "You just have to remember."

"Great," Wayne mumbled. "That's my superpower."

"Okay," Gale said, leveling his sword. "On three. One, two, three."

His sword flashed forward.

Wayne jumped out of the way, then nearly stumbled. "That was so fast!" His arm was on fire from holding the sword. His aunt's sword. A weapon designed for a middle-aged professor of literature.

"We'll try again." Gale was grinning. The sadist. "On three. Okay?"

Wayne sighed. "Okay."

"One. Two—"

The sword seemed to move on its own. It flashed in a diagonal line—a snake whirling through the air. Wayne saw it coming. His stomach flipped.

The line it made was perfect. Golden.

He'd seen it before.

Years ago. How many? He couldn't tell. It was another winter. Snow dusted his mother's jacket. The blade sang in her hands. She wasn't angry. Her face was right. She danced with the sword as her partner. The world hummed. Everything shrank to the line in her hands. She was balancing an equation that only she understood. The snow in her hair. The wind held at bay. The sword, the dance, the marriage.

She saw him and cracked a smile.

Everything was perfect. Everything was pre-ruin.

A snowflake touched the blade, then fell in two halves.

An atom, a marriage, splitting.

For just a second, as the latticework divided, he saw the knight again. Not solely one self. Dozens of reflections, gleaming in the ice. Old and young, familiar and distant. Men and women and nonbinary ancestors, all him, yet somehow irreducible. Like when you see a relative in an old photo, and you're in there *somewhere*—your eyes, your cheekbones, your stance—but they're still entirely themselves.

He saw himself in a slash of ice, armored, on horseback. In a gown, writing by firelight. Sitting on a dais, next to beautiful, dangerous people. Staring into a mirror that crossed centuries. Swimming in dark water. Writing, fighting, kissing, laughing, fucking, pleading, promising, even as it all slipped away. He knew them all, though they'd never met. He'd seen them in his dreams. All the possibilities. Everything he was and might have been, with no end in sight. A crystal with endless branches, dividing and divided until the world became a bright chorus.

Like the line, he was perfect. And he knew it. Knew himself.

He brought the sword up in a parry.

The blades scraped, sang against each other. He felt the impact in his wrist. There was a blossom of pain, but even that was familiar.

Wayne smiled unexpectedly.

Gale leaned in. "It's a start."

When he got home, he tore through the box of letters, searching for that memory—the winter night when Anna stood on the edge of her marriage, sword in hand, offering him something. There was nothing. No hint to suggest that he'd remembered the night correctly. But in one letter, Anna wrote, *I never asked to be a knight either. I never wanted a sword. But after I forged it, I knew it was mine. I trusted the edge.*

An edge sharp enough to cleave a snowflake.

She'd added, *Love forges a sword.*
Instead of sleeping, he thought about what that might mean.

HILDIE

You didn't expect a knight to live in a condo. But knights weren't what they used to be, and condos were the new castles, especially in Vancouver. His apartment was on the sixth floor. A neighbor had noticed something dripping from the glass balcony.

Not water.

Knights, like millionaires, were nothing special in this city. Lots of millionaires rode the bus and shopped at No Frills. Knights were the same. There were hedge knights who could barely make rent, squires who still lived with their parents, and people who could change the course of history by sending a text.

There was a fluttering around the edges of the building. *Dim.* A power valkyries borrowed, from the same place their spears lived. You couldn't do it too often—like folding paper too many times. The air would crumble and let weird things in. But Grace was good at it. She had a surprisingly light touch.

The rest was spin. Placate the neighbors, keep everything off social media, baffle anyone nosy enough to pass by. It wasn't as hard as you'd think to purchase silence.

Hildie got a text from Grace. *Other door.*

She stared at her phone.

What other door?

Then she remembered that a lot of new developments in the city had a few units which counted as social housing. They had separate entrances, which the media had started calling "poor doors."

Sure enough, there was a second entrance with a minimalist lobby. No marble or rainbow fish swimming in tanks.

Hildie thought about how you could live in a tower and never leave. You could have groceries and toiletries and books and clothes and sex delivered through various apps. There was a gym, in case you wanted human contact at a respectable distance. It seemed lonely, but a part of her couldn't deny that there was something relaxing about it. Staying at home in your stillness, like a cell with a semipermeable membrane. Curated visits only. Her awkward teen self—still very much alive and kicking in her thirty-five-year-old body—would have loved it.

The sixth floor had plush white carpet with an abstract pattern. The more she squinted at it, the more it resembled something sinister, like skulls with laughing mouths. It reminded her of that weird little skull from *The Last Unicorn* who kept cackling at the soft boy magician.

The suite was small but efficient. There was a galley kitchen with rose-flecked marble countertops, and a nook where you could just fit a bed and a nightstand. The dark laminate floors were spotless, unlike the destroyed floors in her own apartment. Bookshelves lined the walls. She noticed textbooks of every kind, from academic writing to introductory physics. The place smelled like chemicals, which masked anything else that might have been lingering. There was a corner desk stacked with more books, and a white leather sofa that had never experienced a single cat hair. There was no blood on the rug. Nothing had been disturbed. Either the killer could fly, or they'd found an interesting means of escape.

She stepped carefully onto the balcony. It was one of those glass squares that seemed to hover directly over the city. She could hear street noise from below, and the wind rasped in her ears, whipping up her hair. Grace was bent over something that Hildie couldn't see.

Hildie shut the door as quietly as possible, but it still screeched.

Grace didn't bother turning, but she did step aside.

Hildie swallowed.

He sat cross-legged and propped against the corner of the deck. The pose was contemplative, as if he'd sat down to consider something in the sunshine—maybe a family problem or some misfortune in love. He wore faded jeans and a threadbare shirt that probably came from Value Village. There was a hole in one of his socks, and Hildie could make out a toe. She couldn't tell if he'd been posed this way, or if he'd settled himself into a familiar position. Hildie imagined him coming out here every day to read. Squeezing into that last fragment of space on the deck, no chair, just chill glass against his back. It could have been a postcard, save for the parts of him that were missing.

Mo Penley's murder had been an odd mix of scalpel precision and animal rage. This was all rage.

The knight's face was a shatter pattern. Something wild had torn him apart. The blood pool was spiderwebbing around the edges, more like mud now, and his clothes were a brutal map of stains. An arc, still tacky against the glass patio, reminded Hildie of a painting she'd recently seen at the gallery downtown. Something with deep reds and purples. The more she looked at the body, the more she could feel his heart as it tried, and failed, to keep pumping.

The heart was gone. Something had opened his chest, leaving a bare cupboard.

"This is Percy," Grace said. "A freelance copyeditor. Part-time grad student studying"—she squinted at her tablet, which had a splotch of blood on it—"philology. Didn't know they still taught that."

"Sounds very employable." Hildie tried to look at his face—which resembled a blasted tree—without actually looking at it. Blond hair matted with blood. One eye, blue, staring at something above her. "What did this? A wild animal?"

Grace scanned through her notes. She didn't seem to notice the bloody thumbprint on the screen. "No idea. You couldn't even suggest a copycat. But that's not all that doesn't add up. There's no way that a copy-editor would have been able to afford this place. We've requested a copy of the rental agreement."

Hildie nodded. "Somewhere, an absentee landlord just shit himself."

"Now that you're here," Grace said, "we can try to listen. Two works better than one. As long as everyone focuses."

"I'm focused," Hildie muttered.

"Good."

Neither was willing to join hands, though it might have improved the contact. Valkyries could retrace a death thread, but not like the sisters. Shar had access to the whole loom, while Hildie felt like she was worrying a loose seam before it unraveled completely.

Hildie tried to empty her mind. She'd always been terrible at meditating. You were supposed to let all of your thoughts drift past you, like they were being carried away by a summer breeze. Her thoughts stuck, like something damp and moldy.

Gradually, she relaxed. The edges of the body rippled slightly. She could see that familiar black cord, extending like a stray thread from his foot. The bookmark of his life. She looked at Grace, who nodded.

It wasn't quite like flexing a muscle. More like a curious balance of reach and surrender. She listened with her body. The more deeply she listened, the closer that thread seemed to grow, until it hovered before her.

This is Percy, she thought. *All that he was, all that he could be—punctuated.*

The thread unraveled as they worked at it gently. It clung in parts, like sodden rope, but slowly they teased it loose. Every fiber required attention.

Not like unwrapping a present, Nan's notes scolded. *Uncovering a secret. Work slowly. Respect the life, and the death. We're all stitched to the same pattern.*

Hildie did feel it. A dull ache at the bottom of her heart. Something you could explain away as a mere buildup of enzymes, though it felt primal. Organ memory.

They worked to map out each layer of his thread. They spread it in glowing lines before them, a map of burning striae. Grace had been doing this longer, and she could find every strand. Hildie's talent was less technical.

She could see the snags. The shadows that signaled some tremendous impact. She'd always felt the death thread more closely than others, for as long as she could remember. It lay before her in stark contrast to the everyday patterns of life. The moment of death blossomed cold within her, and she could practically taste it.

Once the thread was laid bare, they could see his life in patterns of fire. The sisters had left their mark. His difficult breach birth, when Clywen had brushed his forehead, coaxing the roots of his ancestral tree back to life. The bout of adolescent cancer, when Braeda had left a fog of breath on his ultrasound reports, watching and worrying with him.

A familiar face flashed by. A girl. Hildie couldn't place where she'd seen her—the image flickered by too quickly. She tried to go back, but it was fraying already.

And there was the death thread. The sudden stain, like spilled ink. Rather than falling from above, it rose from the very center of him.

Grace looked at her. "Can you amplify it?"

Hildie straightened her shoulders. She didn't want to. She was tired of hearing these final recordings. But it was her job. She was her mother's daughter. And if it told them something, the discomfort would be worth it.

She listened closely.

Death was sensate. You had to feel it with everything. That was why she always carried breath mints.

She was with Percy now. She heard his stomach gurgling. Felt the acid in his throat. The sky was gray with dawn light. The air was ocean-heavy, and gulls screamed. Or was it Percy screaming? The sounds gelled until they were hard to separate.

Hildie sat cross-legged on the patio. The hairs on her arms stood to attention. Her mind was white noise with an ichor of panic somewhere underneath. Thick animal fear, millions of years old, more efficient than anything she'd been taught. She heard something close by.

What was it?

A scraping. Like metal against stone. Or claws.

Percy's lips were dry. His tongue convulsed. It was impossible to speak, even though that's all he wanted to do. Terror hung like dew over everything. His body wouldn't obey.

Hildie concentrated.

She dimmed the background noise. Tweaked the world like an equalizer, sharpening the contrast and dimming what she didn't need. It made her sweat. Something's ragged breathing. Heat on her neck. She tried to see it, but she couldn't quite make it out. She focused back on Percy, trying to hear his last words before they vanished.

Hildie smelled death, sweet and thick, filling up everything.

Then Percy screamed, "I did what you asked!"

A hand around her heart. Squeezing.

Hildie staggered backward.

Grace was holding her by the arm. For a second, her authority dissolved, and she wore a mother's expression. "Are you okay?"

Hildie nodded slowly. "That was . . . a lot."

"What did you hear? Quickly, before it fades."

There you are, First Valkyrie.

Hildie ran a hand through her hair. She wanted to tear out clumps and take a scrub brush to her memories. But Grace was right. It would all fade. That was how she kept doing her job. Like pain, the memories dulled, until you couldn't quite feel them anymore.

"Something did it with their bare hands."

Grace considered this. "Even a knight couldn't do that."

"I'm not sure—I'm getting a weird vibe."

Grace looked at her. "Vibe?"

"What's your specialized word for it?"

Unexpectedly, her mother smiled. "Razzle dazzle."

Hildie chuckled in spite of herself. For a second, they were family. Then she remembered the body.

"Percy said, 'I did what you asked.' Those were his last words."

Grace's look went distant. "Possibilities."

Hildie tried to ignore the heartburn. "There aren't many people who could do this." Aside from Morgan Arcand, there was only one name that occurred to her. But she almost didn't want to say it.

Grace seemed to hear her thinking. "You're considering someone other than the provost."

"I mean, it seems unlikely. He's currently in prison."

Her mother exhaled. "Arthur."

"Maybe he's escaped. Is he capable of this?"

"Not with his bare hands. But with help. He's always been motivated to get exactly what he wants. Most kings are."

Hildie pictured the old king pacing a cell. "Who put him there, exactly?"

Grace managed to look annoyed. "Your nan's records on that were surprisingly incomplete. And I wasn't involved. But I doubt any place could hold that myth for long."

Hildie leaned over the railing. Tour buses roared down Burrard, where they would inevitably fail to turn onto Robson—owing to their size—and beach themselves diagonally across the city's busiest intersection.

"I can't think of a connection between these victims," her mother said, though she seemed to be talking to the gulls. "Mo was a famous conservative with an eye toward administration. Percy was a pauper who edited textbooks for a living."

"Vera Grisi said that Penley might have been more radical than we thought."

Grace raised an eyebrow. "She could also be misdirecting you."

"What would she get out of lying?"

"She's a queen, Hildie. Her kind *always* want something." Grace cast a glance into the apartment. "Though in this case, I'm not sure what. Or if that old dog Arthur is involved." She shook her head. "I can't imagine why he'd strike at someone who was barely a squire. The kid was an editor, not a warrior."

Hildie thought about that for a moment. How Percy's job had been to improve people's writing. Maybe that was its own battle. Maybe someday a future scribe would collect this story—collate her and everyone she loved—into a slim volume.

Then she remembered.

She opened the sliding glass door.

Grace frowned. "Where are you going?"

"To check something." Hildie stepped back inside the living room. It felt hot and stuffy after being outside. The walls seemed to close in on her. It couldn't have been more than four hundred square feet of space.

She scanned the bookshelves. She'd seen *something* when she walked in, but it had barely registered as conscious. There were titles like *Critical Conversations* and *Thermodynamics without Fear*.

She found it on the nightstand—a pop of color that her mind had barely registered when she walked by. Hildie fished a pair of gloves out of her bag. It was probably nothing. But sometimes nothing proved to be everything.

She stepped back onto the patio. She showed the textbook to Grace.

"*Medieval Times: Voice of the Shuttle*." Grace looked at her. "What's the clue here? It looks like any overpriced textbook with a nonsensical title."

"Come on. Let me be right." Hildie flipped to the frontispiece. There was no mention of Percy, but she had a hunch. She flipped to the acknowledgments. Near the very end, there was a line: *And gratitude to my copyeditor, Percy Bianco, a living saint.*

Grace raised an eyebrow. "So he copyedited a textbook. That's his—" Then her expression changed as she saw the name below. "Dr. Vera Grisi, editor."

Hildie grinned. "That's the connection. Percy must have spoken with Vera while he was working on this doorstop."

"Vera knew both victims." Grace looked like she was on the verge of smiling, which was either very good or very bad.

"This is probable cause. I can question her again."

"Probable cause? You're not a cop, Hildie."

"Well, what would you call it?"

"A break." Grace cracked her knuckles. "You have my blessing to make Vera Grisi's life as complicated as possible. But keep it quiet. She has an old name, and that means power. Push her too hard, and she'll retaliate." Her mother gave her an unfamiliar look, which might have been close to maternal pride. "Right now you're close to her, and you can use that. But remember that Vera has been through a lot. She's been broken down and built herself back up. People like that have nothing to lose."

"Almost sounds like you respect her."

Grace nodded faintly. "You can respect someone without trusting them. Remember: you're the one driving. Don't let her distract you."

"I know how to drive."

"I did realize that when you stole my car." Grace touched her shoulder lightly. "I see you, Hildie. I see your skill, your potential. I also see all of the things that are holding you back. I trust you to make the right choices."

That was a Grace compliment—the slap was subtle. But Hildie focused on the first part, which was actually warm. Then her eyes narrowed. "Did you suspect her from the start?"

"I suspect everyone," Grace said.

"Even me?"

She thought of her own suspicions. Did Grace really trust her, or was she maneuvering her, like a piece on a game board?

Grace seemed to consider her question. Then she replied, "The people you love are the usual suspects."

For a moment, Hildie remembered Grace lecturing her on weight loss when she was seventeen. Recommending cayenne cleanses and celery snacks and trying to convince her to go jogging along the sea-wall. *I love you*, her mother had said, *that's why I'm worried. I want you to have a long and healthy life.* But was it about love or control? If everyone was a suspect to Grace, what did that make Hildie?

Her mother idly flicked through pictures on Percy's phone. They sat in companionable silence on the couch, watching his life scroll by. Photos of book covers and PDF scans and a flash of beach every once in a while. Grace stopped when a girl appeared. They both stared at the image. She was young, with red highlights in her dark hair. Her expression was a blaze of confidence, but beneath it was something fragile and unspoken, as if she didn't want to give too much away.

It was the girl she'd seen in Percy's memories. And Hildie knew who she was.

"Well." Grace tapped the screen with a gloved fingertip. "The knot tightens."

14

WAYNE

Bert had texted him a couplet:

My only skill in a dystopia would be growing herbs.

If u were here we'd be having the thyme of our lives.

For days, he'd heard nothing. Now this. Texts like microfiction blazing to life.

His mind was still spinning when he got off at Granville Station. The crowd pressed against him, and he used his mental force-field exercise to keep from pushing back.

They were supposed to meet later today, but Wayne had research to do in the meantime. Kai was still chronically unavailable, and he tried not to let his anxiety about that reach a boil. He'd chosen the next best course of action.

The public library loomed over him like a modern-day colosseum. The closest thing he had to a church. Wayne made a beeline for the stacks. Most people looked like they were doing homework, killing time, or working in the media lab. He found the book he was looking for: *Medieval Beasts*. It was a bulky hardcover that smelled sweetly of binding glue.

He flipped through dragons and hippogriffs and salamanders, until he came to a manuscript image. A beast with eyes like tunnels. It was a chimera. A storm of wings and tails and claws. It loomed over a pool, about to lap up the water. Its tongue, a shock of gold leaf on the page. He felt his hands shake.

We've all seen the beast in our dreams.

"Secret project?"

The words made him jump. He whirled around, clutching the book to his chest.

Bert's face peered at him through a gap in the shelves; his smile looked disembodied. Uncomfortably like a floating head. "I knew you were up to something."

This was not their designated meeting time, and it threw him into a panic. It felt weird. Like running into a crush at church.

Wayne shoved the book into his knapsack.

Bert walked around the aisle. He wore a Sasha Velour tee, black and tight around the stomach. He'd cut his hair into a sort of pompadour, with the sides shaved. Wayne thought about how those prickly sides might feel, like freshly mown grass, then immediately discarded the image. You couldn't go around touching people's hair.

Bert pointed at his knapsack. "Whatcha got in there, Baby Yoda?"

Wayne made a face. He didn't like being called baby anything, but he also wasn't in any position to explain things. "It's for a class presentation."

"That's very specific."

"I don't have a thesis yet."

Bert smiled. "I could help with that."

Finding a thesis with Bert was possibly the most exciting thing he'd considered in his life. He felt goose bumps. But it would lead to no good. A date was probably safer than reading together, which could lead to real attachment.

Bert glanced at his smart watch. "Are we hanging out yet?" He was smirking.

Wayne wanted to wipe that smirk off his face, preferably by kissing it multiple times. But he was also terrified. The thought of Bert getting closer made him feel like he had a low-grade fever. He worried what that touch would do to him. The burning prints it would leave behind, for everyone to see.

It was hard to hide when you wanted so badly, for once, to be seen.

His phone buzzed. He hoped it was Kai, but it was probably Aunt Vera, inviting him for a friendly duel on her rooftop again. Life was getting a bit surreal.

Or maybe it was the Student Success Office, demanding some new form that would tear open his body and soul.

Or maybe—

"Hey," Bert said gently. "Where'd you go?"

Wayne shook his head to clear it. "Sorry. Mental traffic jam."

"What?"

"Never mind. Yes. Let's do it. Hanging out. Like . . ." *Don't say bats. Don't say it.* "A pair of chandeliers." *What the actual eff?*

Bert leaned in close, grinning. "Sounds magical."

For a moment, there was only a sliver of space between them. Wayne smelled rain and ashes and Old Spice. Their magnetic fields were practically making out already. Could they date on a quantum level? That seemed unsustainable.

It was too much, looking into Bert's eyes. Like an electric current that was both sweet and painful. He looked down and noticed lines of ink creeping along Bert's collarbone, just visible from the tee's neckline. A tattoo that looked suspiciously like a rune. Wayne couldn't quite make it out, and he didn't want to be caught staring.

He clutched his knapsack like it was a support animal.

"What could go wrong?" he murmured.

Bert took him to a hole-in-the-wall Vietnamese restaurant on Robson Street, slightly removed from the chaos, where they ate bánh mì. It was weird to be on a date; Wayne rarely dated. Now he was hanging out with a guy he barely knew—a guy who probably saw him as nothing more than a cuddly kitten—instead of doing actual research to figure out how to be some kind of knight.

He sipped his tea. It had magical properties—of that he was sure.

"I love this place," Bert said. "Plus, daikon is underrated."

"By whom? The people who rate vegetables?"

"Exactly. The veggie editors." Bert had already drained his tea and was fiddling with the cup. "So what were you actually working on at the library?"

Oh, nothing. Just questing beasts.

Wayne stalled by taking another sip. "Just a class presentation on—" *Don't say beasts.* "Um. Ecology. I'm worried about my participation mark."

"Those are mostly bullshit."

"Not if you're trying to hang onto a scholarship." He stared out the window. "Professors always want you to be 'engaged,' whatever that means. It's hell for people who don't love socializing."

"I always liked presentations. That's kind of why I decided to do my MA." Bert smiled. "It felt good—being at the front of the class. It made sense. Like being a good host."

Group projects terrified Wayne. He hated standing at the front of the class, with all those eyes on him, even when he was in control of the topic. He imagined Bert standing at a lectern, probably wearing a velvet blazer, leaning forward dramatically to catch everyone's attention. People would want to hear that lecture.

"I might like teaching," Wayne replied. "But I'm not sure. It's scary."

"That doesn't ever change. It's called imposter syndrome."

Wayne chuckled. "Is there a version for everyday life? Like, when you're impersonating a functional human?"

Bert inched closer on the stool. Their knees were touching, and Wayne tried to still the white noise in his head.

"I think we're all doing that," Bert said.

The tea was making him sweat. Wayne shrugged off his jacket. Someone opened the door, and cool air rushed in from the street. He wasn't panicking exactly. He just felt uncomfortably present. There was nowhere to hide in this small space. Bert was looking at him, and there was no closed captioning to explain the look. Either Bert was into him, or merely found him curious (likely), or he just liked Vietnamese subs.

"What's that?" Bert pointed to his shirt. "Neuro Queer? Sounds spicy."

Oh.

Suddenly he was twelve again. His mom was pointing to the laptop.

Why are you visiting all these sites? Why are you checking them every day?

Wayne had forgotten that he was wearing his rainbow brain shirt. He'd planned on changing before seeing Bert. He rarely wore the shirt because it started too many terrifying conversations, just like this one.

He lost his voice. He kept looking for it, but it was stuck. He seemed to be viewing the whole incident from an aerial perspective. His voice was struggling to free itself with the jaws of life. He just stood there, saying everything on the inside, speaking entire volumes without opening his mouth.

Bert's look was bemused. Patient. But how long would that last?

Wayne had to say something, or it would get really awkward. But what was he supposed to say? How could he explain something that was so fundamental and inexpressible at the same time? Something that he was still negotiating with every day?

"Is it like . . . brain pride?"

Wayne closed his eyes for a second. He wanted to freeze this moment. Everything after would be shit. Everything would be sketchy and ill-defined and vibrating with awkward silences. Bert would say the worst thing. All of his kindness would evaporate, and he'd just become another Wikipedia-trained expert on the subject.

Say something. Say. Something. Now.

"It means—" He cleared his throat. "It's like being on the spectrum?"

It sounds like you're asking a question. Be confident!

"Oh." Bert's look brightened with recognition. "Like that show? *Love on the Spectrum*? I watched an episode and it was—"

"Nope. That show is—" Wayne tried not to sound sharp. "It's more complicated."

Bert smiled. "Okay."

Wayne thought he'd keep talking, but he just had this gently expectant look on his face.

Okay. He's listening. This is it. You've got maybe thirty seconds before this goes off the rails, so no pressure.

"So—" Wayne couldn't look Bert in the eyes. No, not *couldn't*. It was just too hard, thinking and talking and looking at the same time, especially when Bert's eyes were that deep shade of brown that reminded him of good things. "So, like, neuro queer means that there's no such thing as a correct brain. Different brains, different operating systems."

"And some systems are fruitier than others?" Bert was still smiling.

Please don't make this a joke, Wayne thought. But Bert didn't seem to be. His expression still looked inviting.

"Your mind can be queer, just like your body," Wayne said. "It's not just an autistic thing. People with all different kinds of brains will use it sometimes, like an umbrella term. Though there's sometimes drama—" He shook his head. "Never mind. Yeah. It's a brain pride thing."

Bert nodded slowly. "So you're saying that you're"—he frowned for a second, choosing his words with care—"on the spectrum?"

Look him in the eye and say yes.

Look him in the eye.

Say yes.

Say anything!

He could feel the meltdown fluttering around him. Not fully manifest yet, but on its way, like a Dementor slowly taking shape.

Wayne took a deep breath. His hands were shaking.

Bert's expression was measured and careful. He wasn't smiling exactly, but there was something inviting about the look. Something safe. Or maybe that was just Wayne's wishful thinking. He'd been burned so many times before. A part of him knew already that telling this impossibly cool guy would be a disaster. Often, the most liberal-seeming guys were the ones who had the most toxic opinions about how a person's mind should work.

What if Bert asked about his diagnosis? Wayne was so tired of talking about it. Tired of never quite feeling valid enough. Like an essay that people kept reading for mistakes. Tired of being told that he just wanted attention, or special treatment, or he couldn't possibly be *like that* because he didn't match up exactly with someone's brother or cousin or the one person they'd met who they decided were autistic enough. He didn't want to see that look in Bert's eyes, like, *Oh, maybe he's just weird.*

But Bert had never looked at him that way before. Never pushed him. Never made him feel small or peculiar.

It would be easier to just kiss, Wayne thought. *To be honest that way. But why is this so much harder? Why is it so hard to just tell people who I am?*

Steam rose from the tea. Everything had slowed down. Bert's eyes were soft. His hand so near. Wayne took a breath.

"I'm autistic, yeah," he said.

The words hung between them, like a small clap of thunder. Now his body was shaking. He tried to angle himself away from Bert, so he wouldn't see. But it was hard enough just *not* falling off the stool. Any sudden movement seemed like it would unleash tragedy.

"Cool." Bert tapped Wayne's knee; it felt like a wild drumbeat. "Thanks for telling me."

"You think it's . . . cool?"

Bert smiled. "If that's what makes you *you*, then it's great. Because you're brilliant and hilarious, and you own it. You're literally wearing your brain on your shirt." He blinked. "Which sounds a bit like a zombie thing, but in this case, yeah, it's cool!"

"I forgot I was wearing this shirt, to be honest. I'm not totally comfortable . . . Anyway, it's not something I can always talk about it."

"I'm glad you did though. Now I know more about you."

Wayne frowned. "Do you have—I don't know—questions? Comments?"

"You're looking for peer review?"

"Actually, no. It's just—normally, people have questions. Or they disagree with me. Or they want to explain me to myself. Which gets kind of meta. The reality is . . ."

Stop shaking.

Control yourself. Sit still. Be normal.

But he was tired of the control. The endless masking. His body felt like it might crumble if he had to keep doing it forever.

"The reality," Wayne said, "is that I spend a lot of energy trying to hide. To move and speak and act like I'm fine, like the world was made for me. But it's not fine. I'm always tense. And there are days when I feel white-hot rage directed at, I don't know, the entire universe that wasn't built for people like me. I just want to smash everything, but then I look erratic, and I can't get the classroom accommodation I need."

Bert said nothing. He seemed to be absorbing this.

"Sometimes it's painful," Wayne continued, "being looked at. Judged. People are always trying to figure out what my deal is, why I'm just a little bit off. It's like that Taylor Swift song where her life is a mirrorball. Always spinning and changing, even though people are always trying to figure her out." He closed his eyes. "Of course I'd use a Taylor Swift metaphor. Kai always says I'm a music snob, but, like, I *do* listen to all sorts of things, not just—"

Bert put his hand on Wayne's knee. He stopped talking. It did nothing to stop the shaking, but it hadn't reached his knees yet.

"Nobody gets to judge how you see the world," Bert said. "And for the record, I really, really like how you see it. I see that you get nervous sometimes. That you're not a big talker, but you tend to say interesting things. That you see people. Like me, for instance." He looked slightly embarrassed. "I feel like you see right through me, sometimes. Not in a bad way. You see through my bullshit. Most people don't."

"Maybe they're nearsighted," Wayne said.

Bert laughed. "Maybe. But in case it's not clear, I like you rather a lot."

"*Rather a lot?* Are we on *Bridgerton?*"

"I'm more old-fashioned than I seem. And you're a little bit of all right."

Bert steadied him as he tried to get off the stool. His hand on Wayne's back left a spiderweb impression.

⧉

They walked down Granville Street, past the Commodore, where a line was already forming. The art-deco valkyrie atop the Orpheum theater seemed to watch them from above. Everyone was bundled up against the cold. Dozens of languages floated around them. Collectives of street kids gathered beneath the awnings, surrounded by dogs. Every few moments, they'd hear another siren, like birds calling to each other a few blocks away. Seagulls moved like a white carpet over the street, which had been carved with stars dedicated to obscure Canadian actors. Wayne saw an old woman sitting with a duck in her lap, periodically stroking its head.

"This is my favorite street," Bert said. "The whole city used to be called Granville, before it burnt down in the nineteenth century. Now there's just the street. They try to gentrify it, but Granville is like a wild plant that can't be pruned."

They shared a large Fritz fries with curry dip and turned onto Davie Street. Wayne liked the feeling of his legs in motion—the pleasant burn of wandering. Bert moved with this effortless gait that made him jealous. He just seemed to know where he was going. Wayne kept dancing around crowds and hand-holding couples, nearly tripping himself, muttering apologies, while Bert somehow wove in-between them. He seemed to anticipate the empty spaces and pour himself into them. At one point, he guided Wayne around an excavated tree stump. It was oddly familiar, as if they'd walked this way many times before, dodging the same crowds and stumps and city rubble.

For a moment, he imagined the glass condos as Douglas fir trees, which had towered over everything before settlers cut them down. Bert was guiding him through a forest grove that smelled of moss and mushrooms and unraveling leaves. They knew where they were going because they'd been there countless times, under different skies.

"The first time I saw Davie Street," Wayne confessed, "I was terrified."

"How old were you?"

"Twelve, maybe. I was with my dad. We walked past the PumpJack, and there were these two guys smoking outside. One of them kissed the other, and it was like someone just plugged me into an electric current. I wasn't clueless—I had the internet—but I guess I'd never seen that in real life before. Like, a real possibility. They weren't young either."

"Like the guys in porn?" Bert waggled his eyebrows.

He shook his head. "Those guys—I mean, don't get me wrong, I *watched*. I'm not made of stone. But they never looked like me. These guys, standing on the corner—I don't even know what their situation was, married, open, whatever. But they were real. One of them had a bushy beard, and the other had this beautiful long hair that they wore in a ponytail, and they were smoking and laughing about something that only they knew. And I thought, *How does that happen? How do you get there?*"

Bert chuckled. "I'm not the person to ask. I don't usually date."

"Not usually?"

"Not as a habit, no."

"But you're open to it, under certain circumstances." Wayne couldn't help grinning slightly. "Like, for a matter of national security, you'd do it."

"For Canada," Bert said, also smiling, "sure."

Wayne suddenly realized that he was flirting. That he was *successfully* flirting. This was as rare as an eclipse, and he wanted to take a moment to congratulate himself. But it was sort of like when you become aware of tying your shoes: as soon as he thought too closely about it, the whole thing seemed confusing. He tried to think of the next thing to say, but it wouldn't materialize. So he just squinted at the sun.

They walked to the corner of Davie and Denman, where the city gave way to ocean. Bert led him past Yue Minjun's laughing statues, which seemed like good-natured guardians of the beach. It was cold enough that the beach was only dotted with tourists and dog-walkers.

They sat on a vacant log and stared at the tankers. Bert counted them. Wayne thought he was the only person who regularly did that. They were close to the spot where the *Komagata Maru* had been turned away in 1914. Wealthy white Vancouverites didn't want to let South Asian families into the city.

An old couple was sharing a skunky roach nearby. The cherry glowed between them. He heard one of them ask, "What exactly *is* daylight saving time?"

The other shrugged. "What's *time*?"

Bert laughed. Then he inched closer on the log.

If they were in a movie theater, they might hold hands in the dark. They could feasibly hold hands in the daylight. Though people still got bashed on Davie Street. And he didn't necessarily want to draw attention. His hand itched though. Would Bert even want to?

What would life be like without an unending commentary track?

Was this all he'd ever wanted? To stare at the ocean with a guy who actually liked him? Someone with great hair and bushy eyebrows and a tricky sense of humor?

Bert suddenly looked at him. He seemed about to say something uncomfortable. Ask a question that Wayne couldn't answer. But he wanted this to keep going.

Wayne blurted out, "I keep thinking about that night. At the provost's house."

Bert's mouth hardened. Why wasn't he saying anything?

"We were in the same room," he said. "With . . . *him*." He couldn't say *the body*. "I don't understand who could do something like that."

"People can surprise you." Bert's voice was low. It was a strange thing to say.

Wayne's mind constructed a brutal list in that moment:

1. Bert is a suspect.
2. I am a suspect.

"My friend Kai said that wonderful things and terrible things happen side by side," he said, not quite willing to push the conversation either way.

Bert just nodded. He didn't inch closer. Their hands were no longer in the danger zone.

Wayne missed Kai. What was she doing?

What was *he* doing?

Maybe he should have told Aunt Vera about Bert. She had so many sharp opinions though. And he wanted something that was his alone. Just sitting on the beach, counting tankers. Suddenly full of silences, still touching gently like a humming circuit.

15

HILDIE

Hildie glanced at the bottle of gin. It had a top hat for a lid, which had struck her as funny when she'd bought it. It was half-full. She mixed herself another drink, then squeezed in some lime juice. Often, she lost track of her sacred spear in whatever aether it happened to be floating, but she always knew where the lemon squeezer was.

She remembered Mo Penley's barb: *Like mother, like daughter.*

Hildie stink-eyed the gin and tonic. Then drained it.

She wasn't like her mother in every way—just some.

Her phone reminded her that she had an unread message from Grace. Her mother loved to leave curt voicemails in which she introduced herself. *Hildie, this is your mother.* Grace had let her old phone convert them to text, so that it garbled them. *Tilly, this is your brother.* It never failed to make her laugh.

Vera Grisi wasn't returning her calls. Hildie had even made another trip to campus, but Dr. Grisi had posted a *back in a moment* sign on her shared office door. A moment had stretched to an hour. She wasn't keen to talk.

Hildie stared at her nan's notes. She'd written everything in neat, sloping cursive, though some words remained stubbornly illegible. Nan would sometimes make jokes in the margins. Once, when investigating a fight at a bar called Numbers, she'd written *Witnesses distracted by Donna Summer song.*

Her own notes made little sense. She still liked using yellow-lined paper, because the autocorrect on her phone was such a travesty. Two headless bodies, one killed with precision, the other practically torn apart. Ylf shot that wasn't meant to kill, only to induce a profound stupor, like a paranormal anesthetic. An adjunct professor who stood no chance of profiting from either death. A provost that nobody could get close to.

And two college kids who'd blundered into the middle of it all, like goslings crossing a freeway. A clueless squire and a born runesmith. It sounded like a teen show about sexy monsters—not a coherent case.

Sutton meowed.

In the light of the living room, he resembled a curl of gold leaf. Hoo, his calico sister, slept near her feet. They'd been Nan's cats. She'd inherited them, along with the notes and everything else that Grace wouldn't claim. Nan's ghost, haunting her closet and sleeping on her bed at night. She would have found that hilarious.

Hildie raised an eyebrow. "Got any leads?"

Sutton pawed her knee. One claw faintly detectible.

"Food isn't always the answer, you know."

His cry sounded like a harp on fire.

"Fine, fine."

They both followed her into the kitchen. She refilled their dry food and gave them a small sliver of food from the can. Though he'd initiated dinner, Sutton waited for Hoo to eat. She was the queen.

Vera Grisi had been a queen once. In her own mind, she still was. Morgan was also from a royal family, though she transcended the court.

Hildie rubbed her forehead. The myths were giving her headaches.

Just as she was about to pour herself another drink, her phone buzzed. It was the text that she'd been waiting for. *Meet me at Mary's.*

Hildie had suggested the spot because it was busy and they'd both blend in. She hadn't really expected a reply. The contact info had come from Grace, and she felt like reaching out might be a gamble. But she didn't have a choice at this point.

Hildie tore a brush through her hair, swearing the whole time. She threw on layers and walked to the diner. The brunch rush had given way to a more sparse afternoon crowd. The girl in question sat at a booth near the back.

Hildie slid into the booth. "Thanks for meeting me."

Kai's expression was wary. "I don't usually lunch with valkyries." She said the word at full volume, as if daring the other patrons to notice. But no one was actually listening. "Wayne said you were at"—now her voice did lower—"her house. When it happened. That you were investigating. He's a terrible judge of character, but he didn't seem too freaked out by you. Though I'm not sure where I fit into this. I wasn't there. He's barely told me anything."

There was a lick of fear, under the defiant note. She had power— Hildie could smell it—but she was also young and inexperienced. Worried about her best friend.

Hildie slid her phone across the table. She'd snagged the image from Percy's phone, and now it was on her screen. Kai, honest and vulnerable and maybe hopeful, staring at the camera. Maybe he'd taken the photo, or maybe she'd sent it to him. Whatever the case, she was woven into his life in an unexpected way.

Kai's expression darkened. "Where the fuck did you get this?"

Hildie felt Kai's power rising. Like someone had just flicked on a space heater.

"Dial it down," she murmured. "We're in public."

Kai ran a slightly shaking hand through her hair. The heat faded somewhat. Hildie realized that Kai had good reason to be suspicious of virtually everyone. Seeing her photo on a valkyrie's phone would be ringing alarm bells.

"Kai," she said gently, "Percy's dead."

Something shut in her eyes. She said nothing. Just stared at the photo. Then, with a deliberate flick, she deleted it from Hildie's phone. Folded her hands in her lap. Stared at the Formica surface of the table as if it was flecked with real gold.

Kai didn't look up, but some part of her remained watchful. "We met through Wayne's aunt," she said quietly. Her voice was flat. "He was editing her book, and one time he showed up at her apartment with some galley proofs or something. He was—" She swallowed. "He was sweet. When he looked at me, it felt real. He made me feel . . . like it was okay to be real. I lied to Wayne about meeting him online. Sometimes he spirals, and I didn't want him to have one more thing to worry about. But we did mostly text. We were going to have dinner tonight." Her voice rose on the last word. "At this pizza place I like. Drink a jug of merlot and just sort of exist with each other, no walls up, just a runesmith and a poor knight eating way too much cheese. Like that was ever fucking possible."

They were silent for a bit. Then Kai asked, "Have you ever really liked someone, but you knew it was doomed? And your idiot heart just wouldn't get the message?"

Hildie thought about a person who fit that description. A relationship with that same arc of impossibility. Her own heart was pounding beneath the floorboards, but she'd never do anything about it. How would it even work? First, she'd need to figure out what she wanted, and that had only taken three decades so far. Nobody had that kind of patience.

This girl was staring at her with raw honesty, and she had to say something.

"Yes." She swallowed. "My heart is also an idiot."

Something softened in Kai's eyes. "You should just tell her."

"How did you know—?"

"Oh please. I'm fucking a sorceress. I know a Sapphic paradox when I see it."

Hildie laughed softly. "It's not that—I don't even know why I'm telling you this. It's inappropriate."

"Because low-key stalking two college students is the height of ethics?"

She rubbed her temples as if that might erase her brain. "She's . . . complicated. And my sexuality is . . . I think the technical term is a fucking riddle?"

"Welcome, sister."

"I'm sorry. We have to get back to this case." Hildie didn't want to push, but they were also running out of time. Two murders would soon become three, if they didn't find out more. "You said Vera Grisi was friendly with him. What about her roommate?"

"Nuncle Gale?" Kai laughed helplessly. "I've known him since I was little. He's a knight, for sure, but he wouldn't hurt anyone."

"And the *ex*-roommate?"

Kai thought about this for a second. "Lance, you mean. He's been gone for years. Nobody has seen him—not since Wayne's mom left. Besides. Lance—" Kai frowned. "He could be a dick sometimes. Entitled, I guess. And hot. People liked him, and sometimes he used that. But he was loyal to—" Kai almost said a name but stopped short. "He loved Wayne's family. Loved Vera and Gale. I can't see why he'd come back and do something like this. And Wayne would know if he was around."

"That leaves Vera," Hildie said. "She knew Percy. Knew where he lived. She was a warrior in her day. She could have done this."

Kai laughed weirdly. "Is everyone I love a suspect?"

Hildie pulled back slightly. She didn't want to push Kai to a dark place. She needed her to stay wary but articulate. "We're exploring everyone," she said. "Vera has no clear motive, but she's been around for a long time. Maybe Percy threatened her?"

"I can't see it. Vera . . ." Kai seemed to consider all her memories of the woman. "She's kind but strong. I mean—she's a queen, right? She once held the bloody Tower of London during a siege. She's done shit. But I can't see why she'd do this. And Percy was—" Her voice faltered again. "His whole job was making people's words better. He was a helper. I'll bet he organized all his bills and receipts in a little drawer. He wasn't the kind of person to get involved in whatever this is."

The mention of receipts made Hildie think. "Did you visit his apartment?"

Kai's eyes narrowed. "No. I really liked him, but I'm not going to some dude's place before we've met a couple times. I know he lived downtown, in some kind of rent-controlled place, like the grail."

The word made Hildie's stomach clench. The last thing they needed to think about right now was a legend that dangerous.

"How did a poor copyeditor manage to find a place like that?"

"I think Vera might have given him a tip; she knows lots of people. Maybe she knew the last friendly landlord in the city." Kai stood abruptly. "I need to—not be here anymore. I'm not going to tell Wayne about this. I get you're probably watching us both. But can you back off for a few days? I'm working on something that'll protect us—but I need to think."

Hildie nodded. "You two look out for each other, eh?"

"He'd die for me." Kai's eyes burned into her for a second. "I'd kill for him. That's the main difference between us."

Later that night, Hildie's hand touched a wrapped bundle as she was rooting around in the closet for a coat.

She paused. It wasn't something she'd used in a long time. But maybe. She slid it into her coat pocket, just in case, already knowing what was going to happen.

Outside it smelled like rain. Workers at donair and pizza joints were psyching themselves up for the night, like warriors preparing for battle. She walked past a number of suitable bars and clubs, with inviting patios. She wasn't going anywhere suitable. She was following her dark heart, which always led her to family.

Being kin meant a lot of bad things. But it also meant that you always had a place to be your duct-taped self.

Hildie walked to Gastown. She navigated the still-wet cobblestones and narrow streets, until she reached Blood Alley, where the butcher shops used to be a century ago. Now it was a slice of color in the dark, flanked by gleaming cafes. She imagined what it used to look like: rivers of blood, hoarse cries, the *snick* of knives.

She disappeared down the alley. A rookie move, if ever there was one.

She avoided the deeper puddles and the people sleeping near dumpsters. Hildie laid change in their cups, careful not to wake them. At the end of the alley, there was a quizzical door. Quizzical because it was made of old wood, and it stuck out as much as she did in this alley full of rain and stark smells.

She pulled out her phone and pointed it at the peeling green paint. She swiped with her thumb and switched on an LED light.

Except that it wasn't an ordinary flashlight. It projected a design on the door in red. It looked vaguely like a diamond with two protruding arms. Kind of a geometric squid, or a tower with a glaring eye. She wasn't a runesmith. That wasn't in her toolkit. But she could fumble with runes as a distant third language, which opened certain doors. The digital revolution had made things more accessible, though actual runesmiths got annoyed at the pixelated versions of their hard-earned script.

The door opened an inch.

She forced it open further, one inch at a time. It was heavy as death. Which made sense, because parts of it shared the same neighborhood. Trembling blue light shone through the crack. It reminded her of the chemical reaction from luminol—its glow rising from blood that refused to depart a surface.

She negotiated the stairs carefully. You never knew what you'd find, and she wasn't in the mood for a confrontation. This was technically a safe space, but valkyries weren't always welcome here. They had a reputation for observing things too closely, and there were secrets that this place kept locked tight.

Just before stepping over the threshold, she unwrapped the bundle. She hadn't worn it in ages, but what the hell? There was a strict masquerade dress code here, and who was she to disobey the rules of her community? Hildie slipped on the mask. It was slightly stiff and cold at first, but warmed quickly. As soon as she put it on, she felt different. That was partly the magic of the place, but also a common reaction. Even a simple mask changed you.

Imagine a party that's been burning forever. A blast of warm air hits you. It smells . . . not bad. It's people. Laughing and dancing and spilling their drinks on the scarred floorboards. There's a cloud of messy conversation and bitching and judgment and unexpected kindness. Everyone's hazy around the edges, like a tree in a Bob Ross painting. You can't tell where one life begins and another ends. The lineup for the bathroom is its own subparty, complete with drama and recrimination and that one hedge knight who's always watching a YouTube video on their phone, something about cats and football and lasers. You know the music's there, you can feel it, but you can't make out the lyrics. You feel as though you don't quite belong, and at the same time, there's nowhere else to go. That was the Castle.

The lanterns destroyed edges, making everything soft and motile. The high ceiling, also wood, rested on a series of vaulted arches. It reminded her of stave churches in Scandinavia: miracles of wood and stone that resemble Seussical towers. The walls were knotted and speckled with luminescent moss. Several health violations were at play here, but nobody cared. The whole night could crumble around her, but it's all she had, the warm, close danger.

The bar counter was scarred iron that had seen way too much in its time. People clustered along it, screaming their drink orders in various languages. She recognized Anglish and Cornish, as well as the burr of Breton and the liquid syllables of Old Irish. Someone in the back was speaking what might have been Sumerian, but that was above her pay grade.

Hildie ordered a double gin and tonic. The ylf bartender gave her a generous pour. She had no idea how they mixed drinks without visible hands, but they were swift and efficient. Their eyes burned like vape lights in the dark. She reached into her purse and pulled out some wild carrot—not the best tip, but it would suit.

Two knights were making out furiously near the bar. They were young, blurry, ecstatic. She'd never been that bold. Not even in a space like this.

She went to the patio to escape the heat. The gin was cool fire.

On her way there, she thought she saw someone familiar. Was it a knight? Where did she know them from? She blinked, and the shadow was gone.

The enclosed deck afforded a view of multiple neighborhoods; it was part of the magic.

She saw slumbering trains and old cathouses on Powell and Alexander Streets. The murals that burned between warehouses and dark tracks of unceded space. The Imperial Rice building with its dress of scaffolding, insensate to the loft parties and street markets and complex lives on every block. The survivors' totem pole rising from Pigeon Park. For a moment, she felt herself moving along tracks that tore up worlds, the steam works and whale-roads and telegraph lines that broke open Vancouver. And beneath it, the foundations of čəsnaʔəm, the Musqueam settlement that had been here for thousands of years before contact and would be here when the skyscrapers fell.

People were smoking, laughing, exchanging stories, leaning into each other. There were bright spots and dark spots. She headed for the latter, ice clinking in her glass.

There were vines growing on the walls. Hildie could hear a low, soft keening somewhere, like a night animal. The moon waxed above her. She smelled pot and mistletoe. Beneath the smoke, there was clay, rain, barnacles.

Hildie leaned out as far as she could, taking a long, cold sip.

She saw the beachfront tower with the tree growing from its roof. It made her think about the world tree from Nan's stories, the ash whose branches stretched across multiple universes. With a gossipy squirrel running up and down its length.

A nearly dead tree on a condo rooftop. That was Vancouver. And maybe her world was that tree. The old worlds retreating. The colonial myths had spread like kudzu over the stories that already lived here. The Romans and the Celts and the Bretons and the Welsh and the Saxons and the Normans and the Vikings and Spaniards and the French, spinning myths out of bloodshed, piloting their stories across oceans, carving their beliefs in stone, wood, and flesh.

She drained her glass.

"Hello, stranger."

She turned, and a current of surprise ran through her.

A woman in a black dress stood next to her. She was holding a drink that might have been a margarita, though it was shifting colors, from gold to red and back again. Hildie thought about how many things had started with a woman in a black dress.

She was familiar, but the mask concealed just enough. Hildie tried to puzzle out who she was, then stopped. Wasn't not knowing the whole point?

The woman saw her staring and smiled. "This drink is almost definitely what magic was made for."

Hildie stumbled over a reply.

She should go.

That would be smart. Definitely.

The woman's tattoos were moving in the dim light. One of them was something long and sinuous, like a snake or a thread. She knew that mark.

Their eyes met. Something passed between them. Hildie felt herself make a decision that was possibly irrevocable. But maybe this, exactly this, had been happening for ages. The flame was there. All she had to do was cup her hands around it.

"The real magic," Hildie said at last, "is the bartender serving triple pours."

The woman raised an eyebrow. "You aim to misbehave?"

Hildie considered an answer to the question.

She stared at the tiny sun in the woman's glass.

Then asked, "Where can I get one of those?"

They both smiled.

⁂

Hildie's mouth tasted like too many things. Her stomach burned, and someone had sucked all the moisture out of her eyes. At least she'd eaten before falling asleep. The cats hadn't been so lucky, which explained their accusatory looks.

She swung around to a sitting position. Weird parts of her body hurt, like her ankles and possibly her spleen. Hildie moved slowly into the kitchen, where she flicked on the coffee maker. She dumped dry food into the cats' bowls, spilling some in the process. Hoo gave her a disgusted look but proceeded to eat regardless. Sutton continued to study her from a distance, as if absorbing details for a report later.

"I don't judge you," she said, shrugging on a pair of old jeans. She had to reverse her shirt twice before she got it on the right way. It was going to be a fine day.

She went back to Mary's.

Shar was sitting in the same booth where she'd met Kai. Like she knew. Or maybe she just had a sense for the best spot in the diner.

Hildie slid into the booth, trying not to wince. All textures felt equally bad.

Shar took one look at her, then flagged down a server. "Coffee and a gallon of water," she said. "And the West Ender with extra bacon. Please and thank you."

Her stomach flipped at the thought of food, but Shar's choice was on point. She wanted all the pancakes in the world.

Shar wore a cardigan with birds of paradise that preened before Hildie's eyes. The flowers side-eyed her, then went back to whatever they were doing. The movement didn't help her blooming migraine. Shar handed her a vial of something green.

"Drink this now."

Hildie scowled. "Your herbal remedies always taste like sour ass."

"That's fine. It's only a thousand-year-old hangover cure. I'm sure that Motrin will do the trick instead."

Hildie downed the green shot. "*Gah!* Why is my tongue frozen?"

"It'll pass."

The coffee arrived, along with a massive plate, including a satellite plate for bacon. Hildie devoured her breakfast like a creature unhinging its jaw. Shar checked emails on her phone and occasionally dictated a note, but always out of context. *Check on the singularity. Pick up Tums and apples for the kelpie.*

Hildie pushed the nearly empty plate away. Her body was thoroughly confused, but she felt better. Less dry and empty. The coffee thawed her brain. Moments from last night shimmered before her. Dancing. Sun in a cup. The woman making a joke that wasn't quite a joke, though it split her with laughter. The woman's cheek pressed against hers. Pleasant sweat smell, arms laced around her neck, that effervescent grin.

Shar smiled—almost shyly. "How was your night?"

Hildie spread her hands. "Don't you already know?"

"That's not how it works." Shar folded her arms. "The future is a spectrum. It's woven into the past and present—the most complicated threadwork you can imagine. I see lots of things, and they're not always clear. It's a fucking headache is what it is."

"Sorry."

Shar shrugged. "It's fine. When you've got a weird thing, people tend to be curious about it. But it's never what they think."

Hildie ran a hand through her hair, which felt like a smashed haystack. "It was . . . it's a bit hazy. But it was good. Yeah." She felt a flush slowly rising to her cheeks, and glanced away.

Shar grinned. "Interesting."

"It's just—" Hildie sighed. "This stuff always gets so complicated. I'm tired of explaining who I am. Especially when I don't always know from one day to the next. It's different with each person. Do I have fluttery feelings? Sure. Do I want the exact same things? I don't know. I've been in bad situations before, and it's astonishing how quickly the bad arrives. People are all, 'Ooh intimacy,' but what they want is an orgasm."

The server appeared as she said *orgasm*, but this was Mary's. No one was fazed. He refilled their coffee and gave them some cantaloupe wedges on the house.

"Well," Shar said, "maybe you're down for something more, if the stars align."

Hildie felt a small wave of anger. "Right. Because I just need to fuck the right person, and my sexuality will correct course like a GPS."

It was Shar's turn to sigh. "Sorry. I didn't mean it like that." She seemed almost flustered, which was strange for Shar. She practically flossed with nuclear forces. She didn't get flustered by anything.

"I know." It still stung a bit though. Shar usually understood her. This was starting to feel like a conversation with Grace, who wanted to pay for her premium Bumble account.

Shar stretched. "Shit doesn't fit in a box. I'm just a Wyrd Sister having brunch with a valkyrie, asking her if she's going to eat her last pancake."

They stared at each other. For a moment, Hildie thought Shar would say it. A being like her knew how to compartmentalize. What had even happened, really? Some close dancing? An almost kiss? What did that mean in the long arc of who they'd always been?

Shar's finger danced across Hildie's knuckles. Just for a second.

She remembered.

Hildie said nothing. She just pushed the plate forward. "Go nuts."

Shar finished it in one bite. "How's the case?"

"Well, I made great strides on it last night, as you know."

"Uh-huh."

"How's the hotel situation?"

Shar frowned. "I don't even want to talk about it. The legal fees alone will keep us from renovating the place for the next century."

Hildie massaged her forehead. "I do have something. Maybe a lead. Maybe a cul-de-sac. But it's better than nothing."

"I heard the latest victim was basically a pauper."

"A pauper living in a segregated luxury suite."

Shar shrugged. "Knights can never just chill. They take day jobs, start families, sell shit on Etsy. But then the lure of the quest comes along. They always stick their heads out of the ground to investigate. It's no wonder someone's killing them."

Hildie frowned. "You think they deserve it?"

"No. I think they love the risk, because it reminds them of the good old days." Shar played with a single remaining hashbrown. "Living for the grail. What a joke that was. But they still want it. Nostalgia can be dangerous."

Was that it? Was someone picking off blue-blooded knights with a conservative streak? Wannabe proud boys with deep family roots?

That didn't explain Percy, the copyeditor who shouldn't have been able to afford his posh apartment. Or Mo, the prickish administrator. They had nothing to do with each other.

Shar's phone rang. "Sorry. Gotta take this. Back in a lunar revolution —I mean a second." She headed for the door, and Hildie heard her say, "Okay, but *how* cursed?"

Hildie soaked up the last of the egg with her toast crust, watching Shar talk on her phone. The last thing that made sense in her life. She thought of Kai's expression when she learned Percy was dead—when she felt it. The death of all those sweet possibilities. That was all they had really. And Shar saw every one of them. Weighed them in her hands.

Cut them when she had to.

WAYNE

Sun poured green through stained-glass windows. Wayne crossed the nave. His boots made a faint crunching sound in the snow. It was falling in soft drifts from the vaulted ceiling. *Crunch. Crunch.* It sounded like a monster gnawing on bones, though he tried not to concentrate on that. Sun from the windows, snow from the roof, and a wind whistling across unseen plains. He checked his weather app, but it was just a picture of a sad kitten.

So that probably wasn't good.

Light painted him green. He waggled his fingers, and the light curled around them, like delicate strands of moss. He remembered reading that moss was the simplest tree possible. It thrived close to the ground, in the spots where everything stayed warm and still. Sometimes it spontaneously gave birth to itself.

Wayne had conflicted feelings about church. His mother had been religious; he didn't know if she still was. She hadn't been dogmatic, but she liked the concept of God. A sort of waveform love that touched everyone across the universe. She also liked medieval architecture. She was forever taking pictures of Gothic churches and telling him about graffiti frozen in time. His mother had taught him that the word *grammar* meant *to scratch* in a distant language, and that's really all we were doing. Just scratching our lives onto a tricky substrate.

A fox stood at the altar, cleaning snow from his paws.

"I should have known you'd be here," Wayne said.

The fox nipped at his tail, gave him a level look, then dashed behind the altar. Wayne followed, but by the time he peered around the corner, there was only a set of delicate paw prints.

He heard a small cough.

Wayne turned and saw that the pews were no longer empty. Bert sat about halfway back, reading a book. Snow fell on his black T-shirt, which, for once, was plain.

He walked down the aisle. *Crunch, crunch.* Why did it sound like bones?

Bert looked up from his book. It was *The Paper Bag Princess* by Robert Munsch. Every page was covered in sticky notes.

"Hey," Bert said. "Just studying up for my thesis defense. My supervisor's a dragon, so I'll need all the help I can get."

Wayne smiled. "Does that make you the princess?"

Bert put the book away. "Shit doesn't fit in a box."

Wayne had just heard this but couldn't remember where. "If it was Schrödinger's box," he said helpfully, "shit both would and wouldn't fit."

Bert got up. He grinned, then kissed Wayne swiftly on the cheek. "You're my favorite footnote."

Wayne's heart hammered. Normally, he'd freak out at breach of his force field. But it didn't appear to function quite the same way around Bert. He was still nervous about physical contact, but a part of him—a surprisingly insistent part—was constructing arguments about why it might be okay. Every thesis statement ended in how kissable Bert might be, and how further research was required.

"Tell me a fable," Bert said. He laced his hand through Wayne's. The contact fizzed hot and cold. Soft flakes made a crown in Bert's black hair. He seemed to be an unstable collective of crow feathers and weather systems and forest smells. It wasn't unpleasant, but something about it remained worrisome.

"Once I got cedar itch," Wayne said. "And my mom wasn't home, so my dad gave me a bath. It was weird, because I was, like, eight. Too old for communal baths, you know? And my dad kept trying to distract me. He did all the voices from *Jimmy Neutron*, and then he'd break character and say, 'No scratching.' And I laughed so hard that I farted in the bathtub, and then we both killed ourselves laughing. When my mom got home, that's how she found us. My dad was wheezing on the floor, and I was shaking with a towel around my shoulders. She just kept yelling, 'What's happening?' And she was so frantic that it made it funnier."

"But she still left," Bert said.

Wayne blinked. "How did you know that?"

He smiled. "I know things. In this place, anyway."

They walked past the altar into the vestry. Wayne expected it to be full of clothes, but instead it was brimming with plants. They were everywhere, and it was muggy. The snow had retreated. Bert picked up a watering can with a Chi Ro inscribed onto its surface: an ancient cross that was halfway pagan. He placidly watered a red fern, then moved on to the others. Sometimes he spoke to them with quiet encouragement. Wayne felt like he was seeing something too private. But it was also routine, as if Bert had been watering plants since the beginning of time.

"Your turn," Wayne said. "What's your fable?"

Bert sat on the counter. Wayne joined him, uncertainly. Their hands were almost touching again, but neither moved to close the circuit. *If I had air roots*, Wayne thought, *they'd all be straining toward him right now.*

"Typical story," Bert said. "Boy meets world. Then everything goes sideways."

Wayne swallowed around his nerves. "Tell me who you are."

Bert nudged him. "You already know that."

"Do I?"

"We've met before. We're always meeting. It's all we can do." His smile was a bit sad, but maybe that wasn't the word. It quirked slightly. "Knights and monsters. They're made for each other."

167

"Who's the monster?"

Bert shrugged. "That's not for us to decide."

"Where were you born?"

"Is that a low-key question about immigration?"

Wayne rolled his eyes. "No. I'm just curious."

"In a forest."

"What? Like a foundling?"

"See for yourself."

The plants grew, twisting, until they were a forest canopy. Wayne sucked in his breath. He heard something in the distance. A low keening that was also an earthquake.

"Don't worry. That's just the beast." Bert was now holding a bag of white-cheddar popcorn. "Want some?"

He saw a boy playing *Legend of Zelda* in the middle of a forest. Wayne recognized the game: *Majora's Mask*. The one where he kept getting stuck in a time loop. Link wore a mask that looked like a golden fox. But when he took it off, there wasn't a boy underneath. There was something with burning-hole eyes and a mouth full of bloody roots.

Wayne stiffened. Bert's hand tightened around his own. "It's only a game."

The boy and the forest both vanished.

They were standing in Wayne's room. He was horrified to see his unmade bed, his records strewn all over the place, a pair of boxers crumpled on the floor.

Bert walked over to the turntable. He lowered the needle. It was variation number fifteen. The plaintive end to the record's first side. The same variation he'd heard at the dean's house, when they first met.

He felt nervous and filled with the desire to explain something. "These were written as a lullaby," Wayne said. "For some cranky Saxon count, who couldn't sleep."

"They were written for you," Bert said.

Wayne said, "Um."

Bert wrapped an arm around his waist. Pulled him closer.

Wayne shivered.

He put his hands on Bert's shoulders. He was hot, like an element. He smelled like hardwood floors and cinnamon oatmeal and everything Wayne had lost, every apartment they'd bid farewell, every friend who'd grown exasperated with him, every boy who'd touched him in the dark and then quickly shrugged his shirt back on.

"It's only a game," Wayne repeated.

Bert smiled. "But we all have to play."

He leaned in for a kiss.

The door blasted open.

The doorway was a tunnel. Wayne saw something flying through the darkness. Eyes like blazing holes in parchment, cigarette lighters glowing in red coils. A mouth large enough to swallow the whole apartment.

He screamed.

When he opened his eyes, he was on the floor, panting, covered in sweat.

He looked down at his boxers and sighed.

Monsters would be his fantasy.

⁂

When he got to Broadway Station, he saw Kai sitting on the bench outside, reading. She put the book away, then popped out her earbuds. There was a new red streak in her hair. She didn't quite smile when she saw him, but he could tell that she was happy. She handed him a greasy paper bag, which contained a giant warm muffin from JJ Bean. They picked at the muffin together, waiting for the train.

"How's your guy? The one with the funny name."

Her face fell. For an awful moment, Wayne thought she might cry, and Kai almost never cried. She was the strong one.

Instead, she put her head on his shoulder. Her hair smelled clean and familiar.

Wayne wasn't sure what this meant. Did they break up before meeting? Did he say something horrible? Did it all just unravel?

169

"Once," he said, as if he was telling a fairy tale, "I gave a hand job to this guy who wouldn't stop talking about the power of NFTs. We were in his truck, and he brought his dog, Ranger, who was by far the most interesting person in that truck. When the guy came, Ranger started barking like *crazy*, and then I hit the gear shift and the truck rolled forward, and we bounced slowly off the wall of the parking garage. Then Ranger peed on my shoe. That was the second most awkward hand job I've ever given."

Kai snorted into his shoulder. "Never tell me the first. Not until we're on our death beds. I want that to be the last story I hear."

A subject change seemed necessary. "How's your programming class?"

"I'm not really paying attention to it. I've got this other project on the go." She chewed her thumb. "If it works, it could be something. But I'm not sure yet."

"Is it sketchy?"

"Sketchy's, like, my main neighborhood."

"Kai." Wayne suddenly realized he was about to tell the truth. "I've been dreaming about a monster."

She frowned. "Like a dragon or, like, Elon Musk?"

"I think it's something called the questing beast. It hunts knights— or they hunt it—I don't know, it's old and weird and hard to define. Do your people have anything to say about something like that?"

"My *people*?" She chuckled. "Runesmiths aren't fancy like knights. We're more scattered. But—yes. Everyone knows about the beast. It's one of those things like the grail, or whatever. You never actually find it. I don't think it's even real."

"I just feel like—" He shivered. "I don't know. It's closer to *being* real, somehow. But maybe my anxiety is the beast. I don't know anymore. I just hope you're being careful."

"Nobody ever died from Java programming."

"Just promise."

"Yes!" She punched him on the shoulder. "No questing for this nerd."

They both went to class. Aunt Vera lectured about the poet Marie de France, who wrote about a knight called Lanval who seemed low-key gay. In the poem, Queen Guinevere actually says to him, "I hear you don't even like women. You prefer sailors."

Dr. Grisi laughed as she read the Old French aloud. "Imagine—a queen saying that! Lanval is a foreign knight, with no family, no connections. Guinevere is almost a predator here. All she cares about is getting what she wants."

Wayne surprised himself by putting up his hand. He never spoke in class. Half of the lecture hall was engaged in a group chat, and the other half just looked sleepy.

Dr. Grisi gave him a curious look. "Yes, Wayne? You have a thought?"

"It doesn't make sense," Wayne said. "In the twelfth century, wouldn't that kind of accusation be really serious? Is Guinevere so fickle that she'd risk this dude's life just to—you know—smash?" Some of the students chuckled at this. "Then Arthur's so mad at her that she ends up nearly getting executed, and Lanval can only save her with the help of this secretive fairy woman. I'm just not sure what the lesson is."

"Don't mess with a queen," one student said.

Dr. Grisi nodded. "Perhaps that's it. Guinevere and the fairy woman do seem like the prime movers in this story. Maybe the lesson is *don't underestimate medieval women.*"

Wayne would have to ask Nuncle Gale about Lanval. If there really was another queer knight hanging around, cruising stevedores by the docks, he'd probably know.

After the lecture, Aunt Vera told him to meet her later that night. Probably for another dueling lesson, which filled him with dread. Kai was great with runes, and sword-fighting ran in his family, but he was shit at just about everything. How was he supposed to fight when the sword made his hand go numb, and his childish runes fizzed like weak ginger ale?

He ran to the Student Success Office and signed more forms. A stern secretary went over each accommodation, asking if he was sure that he needed all of this. He bent on a few things but fought for the extra time on assignments. He barely looked up from the paper. It was easier to be stubborn when you weren't dealing with someone's skeptical look.

Dr. Hadley met him for a late-morning session. He looked slightly rumpled. He couldn't have been more than forty but already had salt-and-pepper hair. Wayne thought about how that must sneak up on you. How he wouldn't always have this nineteen-year-old body, which he barely wanted right now.

Hadley sipped his coffee. "How are you?"

A cosmic disaster. A psychology textbook on fire.

Wayne forced himself to drink more coffee, though he was already vibrating. "Fine. Some . . . things have happened."

The counselor raised an eyebrow but said nothing.

"I met someone." He thought of Kai's breakup. Easier to discount it than to hope. "I'm sure it won't work."

"Why not?" Hadley had set his notes aside. For a moment, it felt like they were having a real conversation, without any diagnoses.

"He's basically perfect." Wayne stared at the ground. "I mean, I'm sure he has flaws. But not like mine. He's goofy and confident and now he's haunting my dreams."

"You had a dream about him?"

He flushed slightly. "Let's not mention it."

"But you think it's not going to work."

Wayne sighed. "I told him about"—his eyes glanced around the room— "you know. The spectrum thing. And he was super supportive, but now I feel like he's being—I don't know—*too understanding*. Like I'm his little neurodivergent buddy. And I don't want that. I want to kiss his face off."

Hadley smiled slightly. "Have you shared that with him?"

"No. Our knuckles have brushed, but that's about it."

"What's holding you back?"

He spoke before he could think about it. "How much do you know about knights?" He'd suspected for a while that Hadley was part of the community. But he couldn't quite tell. They didn't have a Spidey sense for that.

Several expressions crossed Hadley's face. He settled on neutral. "It's been a while since I've read the *Morte d'Arthur*. But I've got a decent memory."

"Well. They follow a code, don't they?"

"Yeah. Monsters on the battlefield, lovers at court. But nobody can do that, right? You can't just be two different people."

Wasn't that his life?

"He's a knight," Wayne continued breathlessly. "He gets the code; I don't. I'm nothing. I'm like a monk who wandered onto the battlefield, and not even a *good* monk. Like, a remedial monk who failed catechism or whatever."

The counselor's expression was a mystery. "You think he's too good for you."

"No. Yes. I don't think I fit with anyone."

He expected Hadley to say, *Everyone fits with someone.*

Instead, he asked, "Could this be about your mother leaving?"

Wayne felt like someone had dumped ice on him. "I—what? Why are we talking about my mother? How do you even know that?"

Dr. Hadley's expression didn't change. "It's in your file. Not that she left, but that your father has sole custody, and you live with him. We don't have any contact info for your mother. But she's in the system"—now he looked slightly contrite—"for her brief stay at a facility."

Wayne's mouth was dry. "When I was nine," he mumbled. "She didn't stay there for long. She said she was sorting her head out."

"And when did she leave?"

He felt a pressure on his skull. His vision swam slightly, and he thought the ugly carpet might devour him, like the swamps of sadness from that old kid's book. Anna used to read it to him. All about Bastian, the fat, bullied kid who got to ride a dragon. Where the fuck was his dragon? Did it get lost in the mail, along with her last letter?

"Six years ago," he said, in a monotone. He could feel his defenses breaking. His ability to mask was rapidly falling apart. If he didn't get out of here soon, the meltdown would come. Maybe this was the perfect place for it. But he didn't want the shaking, the gut punch, the exhausting comedown afterward.

"You know," Dr. Hadley said carefully, "your mother's choices, her ways of dealing with anxiety, pain, and depression—they don't determine how you move through the world. She must have left for her own reasons.

As a thirteen-year-old kid, you had no way to decipher that. And all this time, you've been doing your best with the information you had. What I'm saying is that there's no prophecy here. She left, but that doesn't mean everyone else will. You don't have to keep holding your breath, waiting for this guy, or anyone else, to pull a disappearing act. Your mother acted in her own best interests, and you have to act in yours."

She'd left him with ruins and riddles. There were no new letters. Was that it? She'd prepared him this much, and there were no words left? She'd never supplied a return address, so he had nowhere to send his love and his rage and his choking sadness. And every time he saw his irritatingly loyal and simple dad, just hanging around like a load-bearing wall, he had the most terrible thought. *It should have been you that left.* Statistically, dads were the ones who booked it more often. But Anna had been a scientist—maybe she crunched the numbers and decided to buck tradition. A scientist with a sword. She'd taken the blade with her, so she must be fighting her own monsters. But why had she left him unarmed?

His hands gripped the arms of the chair. "I was just a kid. I still feel like a kid. Shouldn't her best interests have been . . . mine?"

"We can't know why people do things. What she did, Wayne, doesn't have to define you. It's possible for you both to live and thrive, apart from each other."

The meltdown was so close. He could feel its breath on his cheek. The beast hovering over him, warm and catastrophic and oh so familiar.

"It still fucking hurts," he whispered.

Dr. Hadley nodded. "Of course it does. Because you're alive. You're free. The pain is real, but so are all the possibilities. You can make your own rules."

Wayne leaned back in his chair. He could feel, oddly, that the beast had withdrawn. It was still in the room, but its stinking breath wasn't so close. He could think again. "Sounds fake," he said, though he didn't quite believe his own disbelief.

"Maybe you're stronger than you think."

He drained the coffee cup.

Then remembered Gale's advice about the sword: *You'll get used to it.*

Maybe he needed a different kind of weapon. Maybe he *was* a different kind of weapon. Something without instructions.

There's no prophecy here. He thought about Dr. Hadley's words on the bus home, as the mountain unscrolled itself.

He read a letter in his pajamas, with a mug of tea balanced precariously in his lap. The more he read, the more he felt like he could hear her. She was getting closer. Though a part of him was also forgetting what she sounded like.

Dearest Wort,

If you're reading this, I know that you're ready. Don't run, like I did. Arm yourself with more than weapons. Stand and fight, in every way that you can.

You always wanted to know the future. I remember you crying out, "I wasn't expecting that!" Your sweet, indignant look. But some part of you has always known this was coming. You've lived many lifetimes, darling, and you'll live many more.

You're never alone. You have a chorus of ancestors. So many versions of you have lived and loved and changed the world, just so you could be here, reading this, feeling whatever you're feeling right now. Every version of you has been complete, and if you listen, I promise you'll hear them. Your heartbeat.

leof,

Anna

17

HILDIE

She'd already left two messages for Vera Grisi, who had an honest-to-God *answering machine* that beeped loudly. It reminded Hildie of her grandmother's old answering machine. The way the cassette tape rewinded with a low *squee* sound. How it seemed to actually contain all those voices, like a treasure chest. She remembered Nan scowling as she fast-forwarded through messages from the Canada Revenue Agency. She'd always been fairly mellow about paying taxes. *It's not even their land*, she used to say.

It should be easy to keep tabs on someone. But Vera kept ghosting her.

As it turned out, they were neighbors. Hildie decided to go over for a cup of sugar and a light interrogation.

Her apartment was off Thurlow Street, just a few blocks up from the chaos of downtown. You could hear birdsong. Highly groomed dogs patrolled their territories. The building was a classic three-story, with a tiled front entrance and a heavy door that looked like it should lead to a principal's office. Hildie pressed every button on the intercom. A few seconds later, she heard a soft click, and the door opened.

Some dude waiting for his lasagne will always let you in.

She walked up two flights of garishly carpeted stairs. It was hotter on the second floor, and the hallway smelled like ghostly meals.

Hildie rapped once, sharply, on the door.

There was no response at first. Just as she was about to knock again, the door opened. Gale Amadís leaned against the frame. He wore a rumpled shirt, with an image of Sor Juana Inés de la Cruz on it, and what looked suspiciously like cargo shorts. Not exactly a knight's uniform. He smelled faintly of weed and dryer sheets, which was an odd combination.

"Detective." It wasn't quite a greeting or a question. "I haven't seen you since the beheading." He blinked. "Sorry. I have a dark sense of humor sometimes."

She walked past him. Gale was slow to react. People didn't expect you to barge into their home.

He limped after her. "Can I help you? Vera isn't here."

Hildie took in the living room. Two very different people lived here. The bookcases were arranged meticulously, with perfectly aligned spines. But there were also piles of books in the corners, a shirt thrown over a chair, an open wardrobe with various things spilling out. The mantle displayed pictures and cards arranged at perfect angles, while the couch was covered in loose papers. She saw a joint cooling in a Bakelite ashtray. The place was like a *House Hunters* episode. *She likes things orderly, but he just wants his man cave—will they be able to compromise?* Clearly, they had, but you could still see the lines of tension all over the small apartment.

"I know she's not here," Hildie said. "That's the point. We were supposed to meet, but she's not texting me back."

Gale reached for his cane. This one was less formal than the one she'd seen at Morgan's party. It had stickers on it, in various languages. "She's at work."

"I don't doubt that. But right now, she's in the middle of an investigation that's gone sideways. I need to talk to her."

Gale stretched his leg. "Vera's careful. And consistent. She'll get back to you soon."

"She doesn't know about the second body."

His eyes widened. "There's been another death?"

177

"A regular feudal serial killer." Hildie leaned toward him. "Here's the problem, Gale. Your roommate is connected to the victim. In fact, right now, she's the only connection between two dead knights. So I'd say it's in her best interest to stay in contact with us."

Gale was silent for a moment. Then he ran a hand through his hair. "Feudal serial killer," he repeated, in a soft voice. "¡Joder! Sounds like a show on the History Channel." His tone still had a dreamy quality to it, in spite of the profanity.

Hildie settled into an old wingback chair that was surprisingly comfortable. "You people have been killing each other since the fall of Rome. Maybe before then, depending on what stories you believe. There's no shortage of absurd violence among knights. But this feels more targeted, less crusade-y."

"I was born in Córdoba," he said mildly. "I know all about what Christians called *crusades*." His eyes went distant for a moment. "I miss hearing the call to prayer. Those days—al-Andalus—it was an explosion of art and poetry and science. We felt like the world was changing. And it was. But then it kept changing, and now we don't even teach that time anymore. *The Dark Ages.* I remember it being full of light." He reached for the joint. "Want some?"

"No thanks. I'm working." It sounded a bit uptight, given how much gin she'd consumed earlier.

He shrugged, took a long drag, and let the smoke curl like dragon's breath around him. In the hazy air, she could almost see a different person. A knight who was sadly beautiful, with dark eyes and a resigned expression. "I'm working too," he said, gesturing to the piles of paper. "I've got several translations on the go. Knights have to eat. And Vera never knows if her contract will be renewed."

"I never quite thought of her as a knight."

He chuckled. "That's your first mistake." He stubbed out the joint. "Valkyries aren't exactly peace-loving. Didn't they used to call you slaughter-companions?"

"We don't *start* wars though. We just deal with the spoils."

Gale shifted his leg again. "Old injury. Comes back in every life—isn't that funny? Not that I can remember them all. It's not like I just wake up in a new body, with all that knowledge. It feels more like dreaming, sometimes. And in every dream, there's pain. Is it like that for your people?"

Hildie wasn't sure she liked where this interview was going. "Not exactly. I mean, I see ghosts, obviously. And sometimes I have dreams that are, like, Ambien-level weird, full of giant spear maidens. But I don't have a clear line to my ancestors, like you."

"Sometimes it feels more like an old Nokia struggling to connect. We can't always tell what they want from us. If they *are* us." Gale settled back on the couch. "I guess you've got questions about"—he gestured to the apartment—"my home life."

"We have a file on you and Vera." Hildie kept her expression neutral. "Separately. There's nothing really on your relationship. Or—"

"Lance?" Gale's expression shifted. Something slightly dangerous flashed in his sweet, stoner eyes. "No three-part file on us?"

"There are . . . connections." Hildie resisted the urge to check her notes. "Do you think Lance has something to do with this? Or is he in danger? Nobody's quite sure where he is, at the moment. According to our records, he left town years ago."

"I saw him at the party."

"Morgan's party?"

Gale nodded. "He was there. But I don't know if he's involved. He's always been a big deal, so if this person is targeting knights, he might be the next target."

"Why did he leave?"

Gale rubbed his eyes. He looked tired all of a sudden; his face seemed to go soft. "He never really said. Vera thought he wanted to start over somewhere. Vancouver's like a small town sometimes, and there are knights in other places. Maybe he just wanted to vanish."

"Is that what you think?"

"No. Lance liked attention."

"Then why is he lurking like my mother on Facebook?"

Gale shrugged. "I stopped trying to figure him out a long time ago. But he's definitely back in town, and someone's bound to notice."

Hildie glanced at the papers again. He was translating at least five languages, and a lot of it looked like poetry. There'd been a note in his file that she couldn't decipher at first. *Always dies of a broken heart.* Now it was starting to make a bit more sense. Gale was a romantic who had the bad luck to fall in love with two people at the same time.

"How long were the three of you together?"

Gale smiled slightly. "Long time," he said. "The first time I saw them, we were in France. Vera was coming down a stairway, her ladies walking behind her. Lance on horseback. We met on the castle green."

"You brought them together?"

He shook his head. "It wasn't like that. It was barely even conscious. I loved them both, from that first moment. I just wanted to be near them. I never intended to be a go-between. But then he got weirdly shy, and she was so imperious back then. So I encouraged it. Just one kiss." He grinned. "A very complicated kiss."

Hildie could only imagine how strange it had been. They'd practically brought down a court, a whole way of life. But desire had that effect sometimes.

"The body that we found—it was Vera's copyeditor."

"Percy?" Gale eyes widened. "He was a puppy. Why would anyone kill him?"

"We think he was involved in some kind of deal. He owed someone." She couldn't tell him exactly what she'd heard from Percy's ghost. But she felt like Gale was about to crack. He would lead her to Vera.

"That's all we have left sometimes," Gale said. "Old alliances. Words and bonds."

"Vera and Lance could both be targets. I can't keep chasing her. We need to talk before it's too late."

Gale sighed. Then he stood. "Give me a minute to get ready."

"Burn those shorts," she called after him.

While he was changing, Hildie scanned the bookshelves. It only took her a second to find what she was looking for. The same textbook, with its optimistic cover.

Everyone loves to imagine the past. As long as it's white and god-fearing and men still get to do whatever they please.

Gale emerged from a cubicle-sized bedroom, wearing black jeans and an old leather jacket. The wild one was still in there, it seemed.

He led them outside. "No Car 4 Us. That's fine. We'll need something faster anyhow."

It was Hildie's turn to look surprised. "You're going to boost a car?"

"The verb is *borrow*." He stopped in front of a cherry-red 1969 Mustang Spider, which was parked a few blocks down. It was wedged into a spot next to an old Geo Metro. "This will do. It's only got two seats though. We'll have to squeeze in."

Hildie frowned. "You're going to steal the most conspicuous car on the block?"

Gale smiled. "This is nothing. Yesterday on Robson, I saw a guy driving a spaceship." He reached into his pocket and withdrew a Sharpie. One of the mini-sized ones that resembles a tube of Chapstick. Then, as if this were an everyday occurrence, he drew a rune on the car door. It looked like a jagged *R*, only the legs of the shape weren't quite connected. Almost more of a bend than a letter. Hildie felt the air pressure around them shift slightly. She heard hoofbeats and felt wind on the back of her neck. It was the rune for riding. She hadn't realized you could use it for carjacking.

She blew out through her nose, to make her ears pop.

The car door opened. Gale clucked. "Works every time."

Hildie stared at the symbol. "Wasn't that for horses?"

He nodded. "Lots of similarities. Cars also like to go fast."

Gale lowered himself into the driver's seat, carefully. His expression was more irritated than pained—the look of someone who lived with chronic discomfort.

Hildie glanced at Gale's leg. "I can drive, you know."

He tapped the dashboard. "That's okay. It's nice to be back in the saddle."

"How are we—" Hildie started to say.

But Gale ignored her. He cocked his head, as if listening to something else. Then he chuckled. "Well, it's not a destrier—but they might handle the same way. Excuse me? That was *planned*. I didn't just fall into a river." He noticed Hildie staring at him. "Ancestors. Don't yours talk to you?"

Hildie thought of her grandmother. "Not as loudly."

"Right. Well, my relatives like to keep in touch."

Then he withdrew a small screwdriver from his bag and used it to pop the dash open. He touched a wire, swore when it shocked him, then found another. The computer screen blinked to life, and read *Welcome back, Christian.*

"That better be a joke," Gale said. Then he whipped out of the parking spot. "Hang on."

They roared down Barclay and swung like a slingshot onto Burrard. As they wove in and out of traffic, Gale smiled more, like he was in his natural element.

An old blue Bronco was tailing them. It had chipped paint, and she couldn't make out the driver through the dirty windshield.

Hildie tapped his shoulder. "You've noticed our friend?"

"Of course."

"Any idea who it belongs to?"

"That depends. How many people want to kill us?"

"It's your kin. You'd know more than me."

"Hard to say." Gale took a hairpin turn down Smithe Street, slowing into dense traffic.

The Bronco rear-ended them. The Mustang would have crumpled if the chase hadn't slowed. The impact still whipped them forward. Hildie felt it in her neck, burning along the nerves. It was going to take a bit more than comfrey tomorrow morning. She'd have to slam back some Motrin. Hildie turned around in spite of the pain and, for a second, caught a glimpse of the driver through a clean spot in the dirty glass. Buzz cut. Square jaw. Wearing sunglasses. Big hand wrapped around the wheel. Built like a knight.

Or a hockey player, she thought, remembering the force that had nearly dislocated her shoulder back at Morgan's house.

Gale whipped onto Granville. The Mustang shot through a red light, cutting off a bus. The SUV was still close behind. *Murderous knights in the mirror are closer than they appear.* Hildie reached for something to hold onto, but there was nothing. The cabin was too small. It was like riding a wild horse onto a battlefield.

Gale's eyes flashed.

They flew past the old Bay building—leaning over them like a dowager at tea—then turned onto Hastings Street. No police cars yet. Maybe the driver of the Bronco was diverting them. Maybe the driver *was* a cop. Some knights had gone that route.

The Spider roared through Gastown. The cobblestone streets were hell on the suspension, but that would work in their favor. The Bronco was more likely to flip. They flew past the fancy shoe stores and micro-cafés. All this wealth blooming just a few blocks from Main and Hastings Streets, where police had driven out all the sex workers and drug users in the name of gentrification. Like Edinburgh building a whole new town in the eighteenth century, so nobles could escape the poor confines of the old city.

The Bronco was still keeping pace. Gale jumped a concrete divider and swung onto Water Street. "We've definitely voided the lease. Sorry, Christian."

Gale drove around buses and cyclists and confused tourists. He took them down more rattling cobblestones on Cordova, which split at Water Street. Hildie could still see the Bronco. Horns followed them like trumpets heralding a royal progress.

They drove down Blood Alley, past the line of dumpsters and the power lines that hung like heat-stunned snakes.

Hildie remembered her night at the Castle. *Not relevant at the moment!*

The Mustang was just lean enough to wedge through another alley, though the brick walls licked at the cherry-red paint. Gale winced.

"I think this is how James Dean died," she said. Her voice wavered. "Except it was on a country road."

"I appreciate the comparison," Gale said.

They doubled back onto Cordova. Hildie could see the busy harbor and the slice of blue that lay beyond. Anything could be hiding in those waters.

Hildie peered out the window. "Did we lose them?"

"Perhaps we're supposed to think that."

Hildie imagined all the people who might go to this much trouble. It was actually a short list, but everyone on it was dangerous. And the person at the top was unimaginable.

They rattled down the cobblestones.

"Vera can take care of herself," Gale said, as if trying to convince himself. Then his eyes widened. "Oh *shit*."

"What?"

"She's meeting chiq—I mean, Wayne. Our nephew. They were supposed to meet for her class at the downtown campus."

"We're close."

Gale pressed the accelerator. The car screamed with joy as it blasted down Cordova. For a moment, Hildie remembered the feeling of a horse beneath her. Hooves tearing up the turf, steaming flanks, spear tasting blood.

"We all remember how to fight," Gale said.

WAYNE

It was Wayne's day off again, but his brain didn't know that. He sat in bed, thinking about Bert and the beast and then Bert again. He'd done research on both of them, but it hadn't yielded much. And he dreamed about both—sometimes, disturbingly, with the same results. His body was a traitor.

He got off at Waterfront Station and met Aunt Vera by the angel statue. Her sweater looked slightly wrinkled, and she was sorting through a pile of essays in her bag.

"Hi, doll." She kissed him on the cheek. "Ready for chivalry?"

"Have I ever been?"

She smiled. "You're doing fine. Come on."

They stepped into a bodega, the kind that were vanishing in Vancouver. She grabbed a handful of granola bars, which would soon disappear into her bag, never to be seen again. Wayne saw her pause before the cigarette cupboard, her eyes sweeping it. But then she seemed to decide against it and only bought the fistful of Nutri-Grains.

The tired employee took her card. "Thank you, ma'am."

It was strange—hearing her called ma'am. This fiercely intelligent woman who'd partially raised him. A legend who lived in a shoebox apartment that she could barely afford with a sleepy knight. A fractured fairy tale.

"I was a queen once," she said flatly. Wayne froze. Aunt Vera was always careful. She never talked about court stuff in the open.

The employee blinked. "A drag queen? Like Shangela?"

Vera laughed. "No. I was Gray-Eyed. My false sister tried to impersonate me. My husband tried to burn me at the stake. I sinned beneath hedges. I schemed. I was jury and executioner. I faced down enchantresses. I felt the bloody breath of the questing beast and didn't tremble. I held a naked sword in my hand. I walked down a winding staircase with an army of women, and on the greensward, I saw the loves of my life. We came to each other like soft animals, like words in a prophecy. And now—"

There was a silence.

He cleared his throat. "Do you have our points card?"

"Come on, Auntie." Wayne grabbed the hoard of granola bars. "Let's go."

The waterfront campus was all glass and deep '90s greens, with fluorescent lighting that made everyone look like holograms. Aunt Vera's class was upstairs, and taking an escalator reminded him that part of the building was a mall. It was attached to Harbour Centre, where you could look out over the rain-soaked city from a fancy revolving restaurant. It must have been like eating in a space station. Wayne knew he should be studying for midterms, but he kept sketching ominous runes instead of actual notes. It was hard to concentrate on in-class essays when your family legacy might devour you at any moment.

There were twelve students in the class, and Wayne immediately felt like he was on display. They were seated around a table, so there was nowhere to hide. He sat next to a girl that he dimly recognized, and then realized it was the student he'd seen at the Student Success Office—the one reading the *Squirrel Girl* comic. She had a rainbow brain sticker on her laptop.

"Nice sticker," he whispered.

186

She gave him an odd look—obviously not recognizing him. Then she seemed to decide something about him, and her expression softened. "Thanks," she said. She returned to her beautiful color-coded lecture notes. Dr. Grisi showed them a manuscript image of the Green Knight. His head was off, and blood shot out of his neck stump like a sprinkler. The drawing was much cruder than other manuscript images she'd shown, and he wondered if the artist had been unskilled or bored, or some kind of precocious child who was gleeful about bloodshed.

"What do we know about the host, Lord Bertilak, and the Green Knight?"

Squirrel Girl said, "They're the same person."

Wayne realized that nobody in upper-level classes had to raise their hands. You just talked whenever you felt like it.

Dr. Grisi smiled. "Are they? We know that this quest, Bertilak's fairy castle—maybe the entire poem itself—is part of Morgan le Fay's plot to scare Guinevere. She's engineered all of this through enchantment. So is Bertilak real? Is the Green Knight real?"

"They both are." Wayne was always surprised when he spoke in class. Especially a class he wasn't registered in. "Sorry. I don't mean to be, um, impertinent. I'm a guest here."

"Like Gawain," Squirrel Girl said. "If anyone offers you a green girdle, just say no."

The class laughed politely. He suddenly felt very visible.

Dr. Grisi could have made a joke about beheading and hospitality, but she didn't. Maybe she, too, remembered Mo Penley's headless body, the blood in the sheets, his elegant cold fingers.

This whole poem was supposed to be about Wayne, but the more he read it, the less he understood. A knight defends Arthur against a monster, then goes looking for the monster, knowing he'll probably die. One beheading for another. He ends up at a weird dude's house, gets seduced multiple times, and then—he hadn't finished it yet.

He didn't know the young knight who rode his loyal horse, Gringolet, across Welsh forests and scrubland to an impossible castle. Like a distant relative, he could barely see anything of himself in that boy. Dr. Grisi's eyes were on him. But then, out of kindness, she shifted her gaze, so that it lingered above his shoulder. An act of love. "How do we know they're both real?"

He shifted uncomfortably. "Gawain knows. He has physical evidence—the scar on his neck, from where he was nicked by the Green Knight's axe. To remind him, I guess, that it's okay to fail. Like, to fail at *everything*. At being a good knight. Completing a quest. Solving a mystery. Doing what you're told—what you believe in. None of that matters in the end."

Another student—a guy in a hoodie who looked like a grad student—leaned forward. "That proves the Green Knight is real, but what about the lord? We don't ever see him again. Maybe he was just a dream."

"He wasn't." Wayne thought of Bert, and his own certainty was a fire.

Dr. Grisi's smile quirked ever so slightly. "How do we know?"

He felt himself flush. "Because of the kisses," he said. "Gawain kisses him—what's the word in Middle English?"

"Sadly," Squirrel Girl said. "Which is weird. Was it a sad kiss?"

We haven't even kissed yet, he almost said, *except in dreams*. But this wasn't about him. It was about a fourteenth-century knight. What could they possibly have in common?

"Remember," Dr. Grisi said, "that in the dialect of the time, *sad* meant *strong*."

Hoodie Guy frowned. "But isn't the Green Knight a monster?"

"Depends on what you consider a monster," she replied. "If so, he's very hospitable. Invites the hapless knight into his castle. Feeds him, kisses him, gives him nice clothes and a soft bed."

Squirrel Girl made a face. "And his wife."

"Well." Vera smiled. "The lady's motivations are never clear, are they?"

Hoodie Guy said, "It is just a story." As if he'd already lost interest.

Dr. Grisi shrugged expansively. "Aren't we all? Think of it as a myth. In the end, Gawain learns that failure isn't the worst thing in the world. He has to forgive himself for being human."

It seemed so much easier said than done.

After class, they stopped by the library. Aunt Vera crammed even more books into her bag. He made a note to ask Kai if there was a rune of infinite holding—something to turn his aunt's bag into a parallel dimension so she didn't have to haul around so many books.

"What do you really think of the poem?" Aunt Vera gave him that sweet iron look that said the conversation could go several ways, depending on his answer.

"I like it," he said. "I haven't gotten to the very end yet. The language is tricky."

"West Midlands? You spoke it once."

"I guess so." He tapped his fingers on the library table in a rhythmic stim. It took him a second to realize it was Bert's pentameter beat. "Do you think the Green Knight is actually a monster?"

"One student called him a 'horny tree' in her essay, so any interpretation is possible."

"For real, though."

She seemed to consider several replies. "Monsters show us things," she said finally. "They tend to arrive at turning points. They aren't always bad."

He thought about Bert and Morgan Arcand. Were they the same? Or was she in a class all her own? How could you tell the good monsters from the bad?

"What about the beast?"

Vera frowned. "There's no beast in the text."

"No. The questing beast." His voice was a bit too loud for the library. "The thing with all the claws and tails and the"—Wayne swallowed—"the burning eyes. I see it in my dreams. Is it real, or is it like a myth?"

For the first time in a while, Aunt Vera looked uncomfortable. "That's a part of us," she said at last. "Our myths are braided. But you can't run from the beast."

"That's what she—" Wayne shook his head. "Never mind. Let's get some hot chocolate and warm up."

There was a figure standing in the tiled entryway. At first, Wayne thought they were a security guard. Then he realized they were wearing a full-on Boba Fett costume, helmet and everything. It looked almost too real. Maybe it was a promotional stunt for that new show.

"We'll have to squeeze by," Aunt Vera said. Her voice was odd—chipper and nonthreatening.

"That's what you've done for years." The voice from the helmet was distorted. "Squeeze by. Aren't you tired of it?"

Wayne felt himself go cold.

Vera took a small step back. "You know, in polite circles, we issue a challenge face-to-face. Are you afraid to look me in the eye?"

"Not afraid." They still hadn't moved. "Not stupid either." There was anger coiled in the voice, and something else. A flicker of uncertainty.

Wayne stared at Boba Fett. "What's going on? Who are you?"

The mask regarded him coldly but said nothing.

Vera spread her arms. "Clearly you have the drop on us. I'm unarmed, and he's just a kid."

"No such animal." They snatched her bag. Dumped it on the ground.

"Hey!" Wayne stepped forward. "Leave her alone!"

"Wayne—" She stepped between them.

The purse produced a pile of detritus—books, gum wrappers, hand sanitizer, a few stray keys that might have opened anything. What were they looking for?

"You're errant," Vera said. "Who sent you?"

They kicked her bag away. "No more questions."

"The security booth is around the corner."

Their laugh sounded alien through the mask. "They're lucky I only put them to sleep."

Aunt Vera's voice remained steady. "*Who* sent you?"

They placed a gloved hand against the dark glass of the nearby window. Wayne saw it ripple—moonlight through stained glass. Then they reached *through* the glass and pulled something out. Bastard sword. A hand-and-a-half monster with runes on the hilt. The iron steamed beneath the fluorescent lights. It reeked of stale blood.

Wayne made an inarticulate sound, like a surprised cat.

Aunt Vera kept herself between Wayne and the figure. Her expression was a still river.

"You've got heart," they said. "Can't wait to eat it."

She dropped to one knee, which surprised him. "Do it, then. Make it a clean cut—don't dishonor me, boy."

Wayne felt a cocktail of fear course through him. "Auntie!"

As Boba Fett swung the blade down, she spun around and reached into the window. The reflection of the mountains rippled. Wayne watched it happen again. Maybe glass was conducive to this sort of magic. Sand and fire: the blades remembered it, somehow.

Something long and thin came out in her hand, like an icicle forming.

Her fingers curled around the hilt, and she brought up the sword in a rough parry. Their swords locked together. Then she slid her blade upward and used the momentum to stand. They were bound, arms in the air, like two statues.

"Wayne," Aunt Vera said, without looking at him, "*run.*"

But he was frozen. He watched her unbind their blades with a sly movement. They made a *snick* as they came apart. Before Boba Fett could advance, Aunt Vera passed her finger along the edge of the blade. Red smeared along the fuller runes, and one burned like an ember.

"I'll show you a trick," Aunt Vera said. "Don't try this at home."

Wayne felt a flash of recognition. It was an iron rune, he realized, old and toxic and partial to war. That's why it still listened to knights.

Thunder rang in his ears. The air swirled into a dark helix, then *flexed*, coming sharply undone between Aunt Vera and Boba Fett, as if something had wrung out the space like a rag. The *crack* made his skull vibrate. It threw the knight across the room. They bounced off the glass double doors and slid to the ground in a heap.

Students were filing curiously out of the library.

"Oh my God," one whispered. "They're filming *Shadowhunters.*"

"Get out of here!" Wayne tried to wave them away. "This isn't TV!"

"It's so meta," the same guy said, his voice tinged with delight.

The knight was already getting up. Aunt Vera grabbed Wayne and pulled him in the opposite direction. He stumbled, then ran alongside her.

"How—" His eyes were wide.

"Just *move*," she said. "We'll talk iron runes later!"

Wayne saw the security guards—snoring on the couch by the picture window.

The knight closed the distance between them. Limping slightly, but still very much in the game. Their longsword came down. Just as it was about to bite into Aunt Vera's shoulder, she moved to the side and brought her blade up. The hilts snagged—bucks locking antlers. She twisted her blade and drove it upward, straight at the Halloween mask. Wayne could see it for a second—the mechanics of the dance. He remembered it faintly, remembered practicing it endlessly with another version of her. Sweating and swearing while she laughed at him and cried, *Again, nephew, again!*

The movement was like a pool cue aiming for the corner pocket. The knight was slower to move this time, and her blade scraped along their helmet with a sharp sound.

They both took a step back.

"Pretty good for a senior." Boba Fett's voice dripped condescension, but there was a flicker of doubt there as well.

"Pay attention," she replied. "Maybe you'll learn something."

Before they could respond, Aunt Vera attacked with an overhead swing. Her blade was slight but, Wayne realized, that made it maneuverable. Their hilts clashed again. For a moment, everything slowed down. She leveled the blade, going for the pool-cue move again. She let the blade move on its own, sliding forward—but then the knight moved their blade up, taking hers with it.

They were frozen for a moment.

Wayne heard a sound like a bear growling. He realized it was him.

A voice said, *Move now, Gawain. You remember how to fight.*

He didn't. Not really. But he *did* remember the chaos of playing rugby in middle school. The unexpected joy of slamming into the boys who'd tormented him, driving them into the ground. Once, he'd even tackled a teammate—a kid who'd been making his life hell, following him around, pushing him, calling him stupid and crazy.

I'm on your fucking team! He spit out grass.

No, Wayne had said, *I'm on my own fucking team.*

He crashed into the knight, ramming a shoulder into his stomach. They both staggered back. Had he ever moved with such purpose? No time to think of that now.

The distraction gave Aunt Vera the chance to free her blade, and she struck the top of the knight's plastic helm. This produced a satisfying sound. Sparks danced. She'd hacked off part of the disguise; Wayne could see pale skin beneath, a tuft of black hair.

Boba Fett reversed their blade and slashed at her face with the hilt. She managed to leap away, but Wayne saw her ankle twist. She crashed to the tiled floor.

He ran to her side. Boba Fett raised the blade. For a second they were frozen in some kind of techno-medieval tableau.

"You're no knights." Boba Fett stood over them. "You're nothing relevant."

Wayne watched his aunt. She seemed to be noticing all the phones pointed at them, which were recording everything. Maybe technology didn't have to be their enemy. Hadn't their kind survived by adapting? Wayne had figured out pieces of his myth long before anyone in his family decided to talk to him about it. He'd Googled recklessly and found weird corners of the internet where people shared theories. *Knights on the streets of Vancouver? Have you seen a woman with a sword?*

"You know who I am," Aunt Vera said. "But not what I've been. What I'm capable of. Otherwise, you'd run."

Wayne moved to help her up and noticed her etching something into the peeling '90s tiles. A rune. Aunt Vera stood.

Boba Fett laughed. "You've got nothing."

"Wrong," she said. "I've got everything."

The rune burned with its own light. The tiles shattered.

"I'm Guinevere." His aunt's voice rattled the windows. The power shook its hackles, eager for a fight. Then it poured into all of those screens, into their matrices of light, unchaining it. Wayne felt it. All the

TikTok videos and recording screens and photos on the verge of being posted, shimmering in the dark. The phones blazed up. Their owners murmured to themselves but didn't drop them. He heard someone say, "Is this like *Pokémon Go?*"

Then light cracked the screens. Light burst forth in a waveform and surrounded the knight. They shielded their eyes, but it only grew brighter. They screamed.

Wayne felt his aunt's hand on his shoulder. "Run for *real* this time! Head for the elevator!"

He spotted the fire alarm and pulled it. A mist of water flooded the lobby. The security guards had roused themselves and started directing the students. The light was fading—they had to move fast, because soon Boba Fett would be right behind them.

Her limp slowed them down and Wayne didn't want to push her. She was middle-aged! But she was also a queen.

They crashed into the elevator. Wayne pressed the button for the observation deck on the top floor of Harbour Centre. They shot upward in silence.

Wayne leaned against the glass wall, breathing hard. He looked down for a second, but the city was too small, and he had to look away. They were nearly five hundred feet above Vancouver, and the view was dizzying.

The doors opened, and they piled into a dark lobby. Vera led them to the circular roof, which resembled a giant muffler and was, thankfully, not turning. She used her sword like a bolt cutter, and it parted the chains around the door.

"That thing's like a sonic screwdriver," Wayne said.

She rolled her eyes. "You and your science fiction." They burst through the door, and the freezing air took their breath away. The city was a glowing chessboard. Spires blinked like stars around them. Wayne heard a helicopter in the distance.

"When he's distracted," Aunt Vera said, "you get the hell out of here—understand? Run for the elevator, and once you're downstairs, call Gale. Don't wait for me."

He stared at her. "I'm not leaving you."

"I'm an old dog." She smiled grimly. "I'll be fine."

The elevator chimed. The knight stepped onto the roof. They looked a bit worse for wear but didn't show any signs of slowing down.

"Merry chase," they said. "End of the line though."

Vera came at the knight with a controlled swing. Their blades met in an X. They were rugby players in the rain now, circling, joined by the bind. Her neck was inches away from his blade, though she pulled closer. Then she made a light movement, almost a thrust but subtler. The blades reversed. Now she was on the other side of the knight, drawing her sword up in a swift motion.

That's it! The part of him that remembered battle was coming awake. *Move like water. Keep them guessing. Close the trap.* He wasn't totally sure where these ideas were coming from, but he felt them in his bones. His hand twitched to grip a hilt.

The edge of Aunt Vera's blade raked across Boba Fett's exposed arm. Blood misted and they screamed. Then they lunged and smashed the blade's pommel into her stomach. Wayne saw his aunt fall. Her hand was empty, her blade on the ground. The knight was shaking ice off his sword, the way you'd shake off a snow brush.

Boba Fett wasn't paying attention to him.

Wayne saw his aunt's blade, inches away. He remembered Gale's comment when they were sparring on the roof. *It knows you.*

"I have a message for you," the knight said to Vera. "Are you ready?"

Aunt Vera's eyes pierced the knight like an X-ray. She said nothing.

Wayne inched forward. Touched the hilt. It was warm. He gripped it, felt the weight, the balance of the pommel. His wrist ached for a moment, then the pain vanished. He stepped forward and leveled the blade at Boba Fett. Fire coursed along his arm. He remembered a battle long ago, at a castle called Joyous Gard. Whirling through mud and sparks and screams, the sword an extension of his body, his heart.

"I can't think of anything cool to say. But I'm pretty sure I know how to use this."

The knight laughed. "Your stance is crap."

Wayne spaced his legs apart.

Aunt Vera gave him a look of pride.

The knight moved, and Wayne swung.

He swung wildly. He swung as he had his whole life, lacking even the most basic technique. He thought of all the hockey and lacrosse and baseball games where he'd failed to distinguish himself, the middle-school years when your swing was what made you a man. He seemed to swing against that. Boba Fett parried with a startled look. Their blades bound. Wayne held onto the stance.

Desperate, he thought, *but sometimes desperate works.*

His hand was about to slip off the pommel. But he held on.

Then he slid the blade up. Boba Fett compensated, raising both arms. Their hilts slid into a second lock. Wayne slipped his blade from the bind. He switched grips, then used his free hand to push the knight's arm even further up. Wayne thrust forward with the pommel, using it like a hockey stick. The blow caught the knight in the temple. They staggered.

He heard the chime of the elevator. At first, he thought it must be the two security guards. But it was Gale and—he blinked—was that the valkyrie? She held a wine-dark spear. They must have seen them running through the lobby.

The knight scanned the four of them. Even beneath the mask, Wayne could guess what their expression must be.

"We figured you'd run for higher ground," the valkyrie called. "Now you've got nowhere left to go."

Boba Fett made a distorted sound that might have been a laugh.

The valkyrie and Gale fanned out, circling. She was right. There was nowhere to go, except empty space.

They charged at Hildie.

Her spear flashed overhead. Wayne had never seen a valkyrie's spear before. It was eerie, like void pressed into a shining, deadly angle, with barbs at the leaf-shaped tip. It created afterimages as she slashed with it, mirrored shadow spears that trailed her.

Boba Fett's blade caught her spear, slotting into the barbs. She used the momentum to angle their weapons. As they pushed against her, Hildie's spear slid at an angle. Like its owner, the spear was stronger than it looked. A line of dark matter.

Hildie used the knight's momentum against them. Her spear danced in a zigzag pattern that was mesmerizing. Then she thrust forward. The edge slashed Boba Fett's leg. Blood fanned across her hands.

They yelled and charged again, limping. Hildie brought her spear up to cross-check, but their momentum drove into her, knocking her off balance. They slammed the pommel into her cheek. Hildie seemed to partially anticipate what was coming, because the blow glanced off her face, instead of crushing it like a pop can.

She went down on one knee. Gale lunged at the knight, but they were already running for the stairwell. By the time Hildie struggled to rise, the echo of their footsteps had already vanished. Wayne saw the elevator doors close. Boba Fett must have called it a few floors down. They'd be gone in a moment.

"They had a brain after all." Vera leaned on Wayne for support. "You were brave, doll."

He flashed her a foolish grin. "Right?"

She turned to Hildie. "Are you okay?"

The valkyrie held a hand to her cheek, which was already swelling. She'd put her spear away, though Wayne wasn't sure how. It seemed to slide into some pocket of space, vanish.

"Amazing," Hildie muttered. "So glad I came. What was your plan again?"

"It had"—Aunt Vera winced—"several stages."

"Like taking on some mystery knight in single combat? On a *roof*? With nothing but a squire as backup?"

Wayne glared at her. "I *was* backup."

Gale stared at the sword. "Is this your blood?"

Aunt Vera waved him off. "Just a little."

Hildie shook her head. "You're both lucky to be alive."

Aunt Vera looked at Wayne for a moment. Something passed between them. She smiled. "Luck had nothing to do with it."

Gale laughed. The sound was pure and echoed in the cold air. "Still thinking like a damn queen."

19

HILDIE

She stared at the coffee maker like it was a Sphinx that would unravel every mystery. It was old and kept threatening to overflow, but then it would right itself like a wobbly cup. Sutton and Hoo danced around her feet. She nearly tripped over Sutton, yelled "Okay, okay, okay," and filled their bowls. Hoo hung back slightly, as if studying her.

"I know," she said, reaching for the biggest mug.

Her face ached. She scanned the liquor cabinet, but the only thing left was an ancient bottle of Malibu with a crusted top. Hildie sighed and mixed some in with the coffee. It burned sweetly. Her cheek felt like crushed strawberries. That's what happened when a *Star Wars* enthusiast smashed their very real sword into your face.

She carried her coffee to the bathroom. The medicine cabinet was unusually bare, as if she didn't have an actual body. Just Band-Aids and floss and painkillers. Hildie caught a glimpse of herself in the water-spotted mirror, pulled her long black shirt down over her leggings. She trusted her body. It was strong and generous and marked by joy. Occasionally, she'd feel eyes on her, a man on the SkyTrain, judging her. But whatever he felt was his business. Also, she could manifest a spear from thin air, so men's opinions weren't really her problem.

She popped three Motrin and washed them down with tropical coffee. Her stomach did the equivalent of a double-take at this ill treatment. In response, she wandered back to the kitchen, opened a bag of dinner rolls from the Independent, and ate two of them dry.

Hildie stretched herself across the couch. Sutton immediately curled up on her feet. A rock with fur. She tried to space her feet further apart, but he just rearranged himself for optimum coverage. Hoo perched in her spot on top of the couch, where she could issue judgment and spy on her brother.

Hildie pressed her good cheek into the pillow, which was awkward, because it meant that she had to bury her face in the couch. Everything took on a dark muffled quality, aside from Sutton's steady purr. She hovered between sleep and anxiety until the pain lost some of its teeth. Then she finished the coffee.

Valkyries were strong and healed quickly. But they weren't mutants. She'd found that out after her first emergency dental surgery. All the fire and adrenaline in the world couldn't reverse the laws of physics. Not usually.

Shar had called yesterday with a message about the brooch—the one that the intruder had left behind on Morgan's property. *Clywen says they're ultrarare—made by someone with a ton of power. Two were forged, and that's it. She might be able to use one like a homing pigeon. No. Beacon. That's the word I was looking for.*

No telling how long that would take. In the meantime, more knights would die.

She fumbled with the Bluetooth function on her phone. Eventually, Robyn popped through the speakers. An old summer playlist favorite and still relevant content for her life. It reminded her of driving to Victoria. Blaring music in the hold of the ferry, as she waited to board. Cruising through Sidney, a seaside town full of bookstores that seemed to ache for a murder mystery.

Now she was in the middle of one.

She thought about these brooches with their weird animal eyes—separated like two lovers. Clywen said only someone powerful could have made them. That could mean Morgan. The brooch might have belonged to Bert, her cute dogsbody. He could have dropped it while he was hiding in the bushes. Or perhaps Mo Penley had made a deal with someone higher up, and the brooches were a symbol of that. Had he been wearing a brooch at the party? She couldn't remember.

"I can feel you judging me," she told Hoo. "You're too little to be so self-assured."

But Hoo had gone to sleep.

Sometimes she was certain that both cats had part of Nan's spirit. Sutton got her indefatigable sense of caring. Hoo got the rest.

Nan would have made her a foul-smelling nettle tea. Something that tasted like wild forests and smug satisfaction. Hildie drained the dregs of the coffee. The Malibu sediment at the bottom tasted like her past. Camping with Shar. Drunk on sweet things. She'd fallen into a riverbed, laughing, her shorts caked in mud. Shar breathing next to her in the tent. Occasionally saying something, a word plucked from a dream that Hildie couldn't understand. What did a sister of fate dream about? She remembered Shar drifting closer, like something drawn home. Throwing off so much heat. All she could do was hold her breath in the dark. Wondering what this was, and what it wasn't.

Shar guiding her back to camp through the mud. Weaving back and forth.

What's the difference, Hildie hiccupped, *between warp and weft?*

Shar's hand on her back. *One skims the surface. One cuts across the pattern. Changing everything. You'll feel it when it happens.*

There were no pictures from that time. Shar didn't photograph well, anyhow. Not that she didn't look good. But cameras didn't always register. Sometimes she was just a sunspot, a blur, a dancing brightness in the corner, just out of frame.

Did you see my thread? Hildie whispered the question, as Shar was falling asleep. *When I was born? Did you see me and know everything I was, everything I'd ever be?*

Shar's eyes flashed with some knowing fire. *I saw what you could be. All the glorious maybes. Every one beautiful.*

Hildie's buzzer chirped.

She searched her memory. Had she ordered something? She'd been trying to do less of that lately, since the last rent increase.

She pressed the button and hovered by the door.

There was a short sharp knock. Hildie sighed. She knew that knock.

She opened the door. Her mother stood in the hallway, wearing a pair of wide dark sunglasses that made her resemble a harried celebrity. She wore what Hildie could best describe as activewear—the type of pants and jacket that you would never actually wear to the gym, though you *could* go at any moment. She radiated health and power. It made Hildie's face hurt even more. She grunted and let her mother in.

Grace said nothing for a moment. Then she took off her glasses and squinted at Hildie's face, like she was trying to solve a puzzle. Unexpectedly, she reached out and touched her cheek softly. Hildie winced but didn't move. Her mother's touch was a rare thing.

"So the report was true. You did collide with a sword butt."

"Sword butt." The phrase made her chuckle.

"Maturity, Hildegard."

"It was always my strength. Coffee?"

Grace nodded. It was one of those days where they actually seemed to be on the same wavelength. Maybe that meant the lecture wasn't coming.

There was room enough on the couch, but Grace sat on the chair. She'd never been a fan of the cats. Hildie used to think she just didn't like animals, but over the years, she'd come to suspect that the cats reminded her of Nan too. They weren't particular fans of Grace either. Hoo watched her warily, and Sutton kept one eye open.

"Well," Grace said, after a beat. "How would *you* say things are going?"

Hildie laughed, then winced from the pain. "You want a self-evaluation?"

"Hildie."

She rubbed her temples. "You can't blame me for things going south. Vera was the one who cut ties. I had to chase her onto a roof!"

Grace said nothing. Just sipped her coffee.

"I'm trying to protect them," Hildie said. "And they aren't making it easy."

"You were conspicuous."

"Is that really our biggest problem? Some knight in a Halloween costume tried to murder one of our suspects. The nephew's involved, too, and the stoner uncle. Who was a bit *too* experienced at lifting cars if you ask me."

"We're talking about you, Hildegard. You're the current problem."

She rose. "You gave me this assignment. You dropped these bombs in my lap and told me to deal with a cagey ex-queen. Who's very much involved, by the way. I have a growing list of things that link her to these murders. Why aren't you yelling at her?"

"You know why."

Hildie rolled her eyes. "Because I'm the easy target."

Grace gave her a long look. She didn't seem angry. "This was a mistake. I want you to take some time off."

Hildie started to laugh. "Oh my God. You're *benching* me? Is this an episode of—"

Her mother's eyes flashed. "This isn't TV, kiddo. People are dying. And you've taken on too much. I'm telling you to step back. I'll handle Vera Grisi. Just leave your phone on. I don't want any more surprises."

She bit down on several replies. "Perfect."

Grace looked like she might reach out again. But then she lifted her chin slightly, as if she was pushing something back. "I want you safe," she said. "You're my daughter before you're a valkyrie."

"I thought there was no difference between the two," she replied flatly.

Grace seemed to take in her apartment for the first time. The pizza box, the empty bottles of gin, the glass on the coffee table. Her eyes narrowed. "Is this really what you want?"

"What does that mean?"

"It just feels like—"

"I'm repeating your mistakes? Drinking in the middle of the day?"

Grace almost flinched. "That was a long time ago."

"Oh yeah? I saw how generous you were with the wine at Morgan's party. And the Scotch hidden in your desk?"

"Hildie." Her voice was flat. "That Scotch was ancient. And Morgan has the best Malbec. I had two glasses, when I was off the clock. This . . ." She gestured helplessly around her. "What you're doing is deliberate. You're numbing yourself. Trying to make bad decisions."

"And who the fuck did I learn that from?" Hildie's anger was awake. She could almost feel the spear, humming in the dark. Waiting to be drawn. Spears didn't care about family. They were weapons. They just wanted to sing. She tried to calm down, but they'd been here so many times before, this battlefield. It was too late to stop. "Even before Nan died, you'd go through a bottle. Wandering around the house, turning on all the lights. What did you think you were protecting us from? Or the times I'd catch you leaving him messages. The way your voice sounded. Like you were a completely different person. You weren't strong—not the way I'd always pictured you. Valkyries don't cry on their ex-husband's answering machine."

Grace's eyes went dark. For a moment, Hildie thought her mother might hit her. She'd never done that before, though she'd come close. Instead, she exhaled. "Hildie, is it possible that you're fixating on my past mistakes because you don't want to deal with your current ones?"

The logic was almost gentle. That was what threw her. For some reason, it was worse than being slapped. "I—" She tried to tamp down her anger. "I know I could be doing better. I get that things look a bit messy around the edges. But I'm trying."

Grace shook her head. "Trying what, exactly? To relive my greatest psychological hits? Hildie, I've numbed myself in the past. It was a mistake, and I'm not proud of it. But you can't live like this"—she pointed again at the gin bottle—"and then glare at me every time I take a drink, like I'm going to become that person again. It's a part of me, yes, but it's not who I am *now*. And I don't think it's who you are, really. It's just familiar. And I'm sorry for that."

It was maybe the most that Grace had ever talked about her drinking. Hildie wanted to respond like an adult, but she could feel the resentment like a wad in her throat. "You're the one who set this fucking example. Now every time I see you with a glass full of ice, my heart sinks. It was so exhausting—watching and wondering what would happen next."

Her mother's face was very still. "We're not just repeating myths," she said. "Knights or valkyries. We're disasters. Like regular people. You don't have to make the same mistakes I did. There's always a bit of choice threaded into fate. You can reach for the life you want." She exhaled. "Your father was a bad story in our lives, but I still missed him. And I miss your nan. She was my mother, Hildie. We fought, but I miss her every day, just like you. Her awful tea. The way she held her spear. Her absolute refusal to pay taxes."

Hildie laughed. "Remember all the paperwork?"

"It was like an epic poem. All the forms that make up our lives. All the phone calls just to say, yes, she's gone, really gone. And I drank. I tried to escape. Just like you're trying to."

"I can't though." Hildie rubbed her eyes. "I never asked for this, but I still can't get away from it."

"Hildie . . ." Grace looked tired. She wore the full force of years on her face, all those memories, those ancestors. Maybe even a bit of Nan peeked out of her eyes. But there was still a spark there. "Do you remember when you used to sneak out at night? To practice?"

The question threw her. "Yeah. I'd roll your car down the road and start it up. No way you heard it."

"I heard it."

Hildie frowned. "So we're making me feel bad for past transgressions now?"

Grace's look was oddly soft. "I always knew. I sat in the living room, under the lamplight, picturing you with that spear. Thinking of all the dread things you'd meet with it when the time came. All those monsters I couldn't protect you from." She seemed to sink into the chair for a moment. Then she shook her head, as if to clear it. "I turned myself inside out, worrying about you. And when I heard you rolling that car up the driveway, I made sure I was back in bed. So you didn't see me."

Hildie stared at her. "Why didn't you say something?"

"Because I knew my mother did the same thing. Generations of spear mothers, waiting and worrying and hoping our lessons were enough. You had to learn on your own. But I was there, Hildie. I was always there. Even if I couldn't say it."

Grace stood. They both looked at each other for a beat. Then she nodded, as if deciding something, and let herself out.

Hildie didn't know what to do.

She wanted to whirl in circles, like a figure skater locked in a death spiral, until her anger exploded outward.

She got dressed and washed her hair in the sink. In the end, it looked like a collapsed curtain. Hildie went downstairs. It was dim in the lobby. The familiar hole in the ceiling had become an architectural feature. Moving on autopilot, she checked her mailbox, then stopped.

There was a folded note, on top of her phone bill and a pile of pizza flyers.

She examined the note carefully. It was written in Anglish. Each letter neatly composed, as if the writer had used a fountain pen.

She had a quick-and-dirty translator on her phone, but a message like this required context. She huffed back up the stairs, pulled the Bosworth-Toller dictionary from under her bed, and sat down to translate the message by hand. The cats were startled at first, then sat down next to her, intrigued by this turn of events.

It took about half an hour. By the final word, she was sweating, and her tailbone hurt from sitting on the floor. The shaky message was probably full of her own mistakes, but it made sense.

Meet us in the lost place.

Bring yourselves.

She chuckled at the last part. Ylves didn't really have a singular self-concept, and that bled into all the languages they spoke. She stared at the note. A bead of sweat dropped from her chin.

So she was going to ylf territory.

Step back, she thought.

In another world, a different daughter would have taken that advice. She'd be more petite, with a heart-shaped face and an optimistic

206

worldview. She and her mother would be shopping for clothes at Value Village instead of sitting on opposite edges of a divide.

Hildie pulled her selves into a standing position.

She'd need a different outfit.

And a sacrifice.

WAYNE

*I*t definitely wasn't a vacation.

But after the incident on the roof of Harbour Centre, his aunt had suggested a trip.

It was an excuse to get out of town, while Hildie tracked down the knight who'd attacked them. "You can't be underfoot," Aunt Vera had said. "You're a target, and Kai is by extension. You need some distance."

He hadn't realized that she'd meant the ocean.

Grayish light hung like spiderwebs as they waited in the ferry terminal at Tsawwassen. It was too early in the morning to form thoughts. Wayne held his coffee as if it would unravel mysteries, though not quickly enough. Kai was working on her laptop. Some kind of project for her comp sci class. Every time he tried to look over her shoulder, she minimized the window and replaced it with an otter meme. Normally she wasn't this secretive, and he wondered what had enraptured her.

But here they were, about to embark on the *Spirit of British Columbia*, a colonial fantasy taking them to Victoria. The provincial capital was an odd fusion of government buildings and artist communities, where everyone was either stoned or late for parliament. He'd been there a few times to visit family friends. There were newer buildings downtown, and rent had clearly skyrocketed. Dad agreed to the trip, mostly because he knew there'd be light supervision. Wayne knew that he didn't need permission, but over the years, they'd become like an independent company, the two of them. Wayne had held back so much already, and the wrongness of it made his teeth ache. So it was only fair to explain where he was going.

"As long as Kai's there," his father had said. "She'll keep you out of trouble."

Kai's mother liked the idea of the trip, anyhow. Kai could get in touch with her runes, and he could do . . . whatever he was supposed to. A map would be nice. A footnote, even, that told him how to be a knight. Wasn't it an impossible category? How could you kill people on the battlefield, then go dancing?

Kai put away her laptop, and they watched the ferry pull in. He'd told her about the fight on the roof, but she hadn't said much about it. Maybe she was worried. Or preoccupied. Lately, she'd been hard to reach, and he had to keep reminding himself that she had her own journey. He'd pulled her into this, but she wasn't just following him into danger.

"Thanks for coming," he said.

She yawned as the ferry docked. "Mom thinks it'll be good. Like Rune Honors Studies with—what's her name again?"

"Viv. She and Wally are friends of the family."

Her eyebrow shot up. "Are they a couple?"

"I dunno. I haven't seen them since I was nine. At that point in my life, all I cared about was a series of books about prophesied cat warriors. I wasn't analyzing their partnership."

"I would have been. Boys miss so much. So, one is a runesmith and the other is—what—an *actual* smith?"

"They're both actual smiths. They just do different . . . smithing. Is that a word?"

She cocked her head. "Makes sense. We're just hammering different forces. Even coding is like that."

Before she could elaborate, the boarding announcement came. They rushed to grab an optimal spot in line. Someone's massive MEC backpack kept hitting Wayne in the shoulder, but he did an excellent job of not freaking. Once they handed over their tickets, they ran up the shuddering gangplank. Wayne remembered his dad running ahead, years ago. Finding them the best seats. Later, they'd split a piece of lemon meringue pie, which always tasted metallic for some reason, unearthly golden and tart.

Now they did the same thing, demolishing a breakfast at White Spot and splitting a piece of pie. The waves had brought him full circle. Kai dragged him onto the deck, where the wind and spray cut through them. She leaned over the bar and pointed out a dark shape, which might have been a selkie. The green water churned white as they cut their way toward Swartz Bay. The horn blew at one point, and Kai screamed, then doubled over laughing.

When the ferry docked, they ran to the head of the bus line. Wayne loved the double-decker bus, which felt like it belonged to another time. He was too wired to sleep, though Kai dozed intermittently. It reminded him of a middle-school trip years ago, when she'd fallen asleep on his shoulder. Her hair was shorter then, and it had caused a bit of a scandal. The school's gay-straight alliance hadn't known what to do with this odd friendship between a trans girl and a socially awkward kid still in the closet. Kai had joked about making a PowerPoint, but Wayne couldn't quite see the need. They weren't a cause. They were just two dancing quarks who'd found each other and refused to let go.

They had a brief hour to be tourists. They raced through each floor of Russell Books. Kai found a book of poems by Larissa Lai, and Wayne found a funny autism memoir by Sarah Kurchak. They pooled all of their mad money to buy a single cocktail at the Empress Hotel, which they sipped slowly, while the staff watched them with visible distrust. Wayne stood guard while Kai used the family bathroom. When someone wandered by, he said that his wife was in there. "Our baby exploded" was all he could think to add in clarification. The stranger left with a frown.

A second bus took them to the edge of the city. Viv and Wally lived in a Tudor-style house surrounded by hedges. The flora was so wild, he thought it might bite back for a moment. But the house itself was well-kept, and Wayne felt an odd sense of peace as he approached the front door. His knock was answered by a tall woman in a yellow dress with pockets. Her hair was swept up in a chignon. Her expression wasn't precisely warm, but it was familiar, in a way that made him feel recognized.

"Gawain." Now she smiled, delicately. "It has been so long. How old are you now?" Her voice was low and smooth, and her tone had a kind of formality to it.

"Nearly twenty."

She nodded. "You have grown." Then she extended her hand to Kai. "I am Vivian. You are welcome in our house."

"Kai." She took Viv's hand gently, a tad uncertainly. For a moment, they looked at each other, as if confirming something. Then Kai's smile widened, and Vivian returned a more knowing version of it.

"Lunch first," she said. "Then to work."

Wally was in the bright kitchen. They swept up Wayne in a bear hug that he didn't entirely consent to, though he'd been expecting it.

"Zounds, kid! Look at you!" A dark braid ran down their back, and they wore a T-shirt that looked like it might be covered in cigarette burns. "And who's this?"

Kai introduced herself, somewhat shyly.

Wally favored her with a wink. "Be sure to put Viv through her paces, eh? You'll know if you're doing a good job, because her face'll get all scrunched, like a dry apple."

"Thank you for that," Viv pronounced.

They ate fresh bread, smoked herring, and a Stilton cheese that made his eyes water. It reminded him of what he'd come to think of as medieval brunches, which he'd shared with Vera, Gale, and sometimes Lance. The meals had always ended with laughter and a story about some distant cousin soiling his armor.

They split up after the meal. Viv and Kai walked through the tidy garden, talking about whatever runesmiths talked about. Ecological grief, or perhaps how to conjugate fire runes without burning your shoes. Wally took Wayne to an outbuilding around back. It was made of white-washed brick and had a chimney that hissed smoke. Wayne had the sense that they were breaking several bylaws, though the forge did seem relatively self-contained.

The inside was dim and hot. Tongs, hooks, and other tools hung from the white walls. A chain dangled from the ceiling, and Wayne felt the smell of rust and earth taking him back to another time—not wholly unpleasant. The anvil was an imposing structure. It reminded him of a massive iron stump. A bar of steel was sitting on top.

"That's for you," Wally said.

His eyes widened. "No. I'm not—" He stared at them. "You don't expect me to *forge* something. Have you seen my arms?"

Wally's arms were ropy with muscle. They shrugged on an apron. "It's not power that makes a smith," they said. "It's skill. Listening to the metal. Knowing when to hammer, and when to rest. By the end of this weekend, you'll have a sword."

Wayne swallowed. "I seriously doubt that."

Wally pulled the chain. Wayne heard the whoosh of the bellows, and the coals stirred.

"Doubts are assholes." Wally stoked the flame. "Everyone's got 'em. But they're no use here. Trust in the tempering, the quench. Trust the steel, and your memory."

He watched them heat the steel, until it sang, white-hot and brilliant. Then Wally handed him gloves and a hammer.

"Start with the weakest point, and work your way forward. We're all swords. We all have weak tips and strong bases. We all have edges. Any part of us can be a weapon. Now get hammering."

It felt unnatural at first. After a few blows, he was already sweating. His muscles ached. Wally adjusted his angle a few times, as he sculpted the tip of the blade. After a while, they just let him strike the metal, over and over, until he found a rhythm. He heard the blood pounding in his ears. *Dum-DUM. Dum-DUM Dum-DUM.* The sound of his weapon forging itself. He remembered Bert's hand on his own. The meter of the poem that fired his blood until he was a molten core. The hammer's song was a charm for living, a way to keep singing himself into existence. He gave himself to the rhythm, to the dim light and warmth of the forge, which felt like a ruined hall. There were things outside that space—thoughts, seasons, animals scratching to get in—but he held himself within the forge. Was held. Dance and skitter, beat and recoil, muscles burning, again, again, forging a newborn star.

Wally taught him how to strike ripples into the steel until it crested like a wave. It was a living thing—no longer a lump of metal. It was somehow his. By the end of the day, his whole body was trembling, and his arms felt as if they'd been torn from their sockets. But he had part of a blade. His blade. Wally led him back inside, one hand gently on his back, the way you'd guide a sleepy child. They all sat down to a winter feast: hare stew with wild mushrooms, date pies, and sage wine (it had a spicy taste that woke him up). Kai was flushed and devoured the food. At one point they looked at each other, like two live wires, throwing off sparks. They texted under the table because they were too tired to talk.

holy shit I'm making a SWORD

SO MASC

are you learning dangerous runes

it. is. intense.

After dinner, they sat in the living room, which was full of perfectly comfortable mismatched furniture. Viv told him the story of his parents meeting. He'd heard it before, but not this particular version. His mom was working for a government-funded project at the university. Her team was developing eye-tracking software, which was still in its early stages. They wanted to see how people's eyes moved as they read, and his mom suggested that they use one of her favorite poems. The one by Emily Dickinson about volcanoes keeping their secrets, or

213

something like that. All he remembered was the last line: "The only secret people keep / is immortality."

They brought in subjects who were trained to take instructions under pressure—pilots and nurses—but they also invited more artsy types. His dad was a studio musician, and he came in to read the poem (the study paid twenty dollars and included lunch). He was supposed to be looking at the poem, but he was looking at Anna instead. She made him repeat the test. Apparently, his eye tracking was unique. He'd focused on a word that nobody else seemed to notice.

"Your father was an unaccountable variable in your mother's study," Viv said, sipping her wine. "A favorable inconsistency."

"She means they hooked up," Wally supplied.

"I kind of figured." Wayne laughed at the thought of his dad, skewing his mom's study.

They drank birch wine, which tasted like crisp apples and pine and smoothed out their heads. Kai did an impression of Hildie, which mostly involved her scowling and saying, *But I'm a vaaaaaalkyrie.* Which she'd never actually said. But Wally thought it was hilarious.

Wayne felt his thoughts drift back to the rooftop. Both Aunt Vera's roof, where he'd held a sword for the first time, and the Harbour Centre roof. Where, he had to remind himself, things might have gone a lot worse.

"Do you have any idea who's doing this? Who might be killing knights?"

Viv and Wally exchanged a look.

"Plenty of knights gone bad," Wally said. "Kings and queens too. When you keep getting reborn over the centuries, you're bound to come back shite one time or another."

Viv stared toward the window. Sometimes she had a faraway quality, like she was peeling apart layers of reality. He wondered if Kai would become like that.

"Someone will always be willing to burn down the order," she said. "Often, they are closer than they seem. We belong to a small community, after all. Some of us are beasts. But that is a matter for daylight talk."

After that, they went to bed. Wayne and Kai were in separate guest rooms, but Kai knocked on his door in record time. She wore *Adventure*

Time pajamas. He was just in his boxers, so he made an attempt to slide beneath the blanket.

"Oh please." Kai sat down on the bed. "I've seen it all before."

"When we were eight," he muttered.

"Sorry." She tilted her head. "I'm sure you've made tremendous strides since then."

"Can we talk about something else?"

She pulled her hair into a ponytail. "Yes. Oh my God. Viv is like—" Kai shook her head. "She's a freaking goddess. Or almost. Some of the stories she told me—like, this one time, she managed to trap—" Kai shook her head again. "Never mind. It's not important. Anyways, I shared a little idea with her, and she's been really encouraging. How's your sword coming along?"

"Still in pieces." Wayne rubbed his aching arms. "I can't believe Wally thinks I can actually do this. It's going to look awful in the end."

"It'll be perfect." Kai grinned. "It'll be you."

She seemed to have gained confidence over the course of the afternoon. They were both vibrating with excitement but also *so* tired. Kai had snuck in a book from Viv's library and showed Wayne a manuscript page: it was a sword-fighting manual written in Latin. Someone who looked a lot like Wally held a sword in the illustration. Their full name was Walpurgis.

"Look how cool they were," Kai said.

"Still are."

They curled up in bed and watched an episode of *She-Ra* on Kai's phone. She smiled at Bow's dads fussing over him. Kai reiterated her theory that Bow was a trans boy, since he'd been wearing a binder in one episode, and they agreed that it must be canon. Wayne was nearly asleep when the episode finished. He heard the door close softly, then fell into the dark.

The next day, they worked on the sword hilt. At one point, Wally squinted at him, and said, "What kinda pommel are you? I think tea cozy."

Wayne had no idea what that meant. But it did sound right.

He hammered until his arm fell off.

He hammered until he could feel each individual bone in his hand.

The forge was hot and dark, like a volcano's spirit. It only took about an hour for him to sweat through his shirt. He took it off and kept working the steel. He didn't even care that his belly was on display, or that his hair was a disgusting sweat mop. At one point, Kai peeked her head through the door and catcalled him.

Wally showed him how to make a raised bump in the steel, which he could then distribute across the surface of the blade. They showed him how to pattern-weld different pieces into the weapon, making it stronger.

"Same as your heart," they observed. "Break it, and it only gets stronger."

Before the day ended, he used a hot chisel to slice through glowing white steel. It parted seamlessly, like it was made of silk. Even his fingernails hurt. But he had more of a blade now. Something recognizable.

For dinner, they had pike in pepper sauce, which made his eyes water. Spiced pear soup, which had an odd taste that didn't quite make sense, though he enjoyed it. Rose pudding for dessert, which reminded him of a fancy Jell-O no-bake cheesecake. They drank ginger mead in the living room, which was *strong*, and Wayne felt himself growing tipsy.

Wally told a story about a blade they'd forged. It broke, and so they reforged it, and then it broke again. They kept packing it in clay and reheating it, but every time they requenched the blade, the same crack would appear. Finally, Wally just let the crack be.

"Made me sad at first," they said. "Seeing that crack. But I stopped thinking of it as an imperfection. The blade had scars, like its owner."

Wayne was nearly too tired for words. But something occurred to him. Something he couldn't help but ask about.

"Aunt Vivian, you said some knights were beasts. Did you mean, like, the questing beast? The monster from the old stories?"

Viv and Wally exchanged a look.

Vivian started to say something but instead walked over to the bookshelf and withdrew a book that seemed to have been stitched with several types of bindings. She undid the clasp on the front and turned the vellum pages gently, until she found what she was looking for. Nestled within the Latin text was an illuminated miniature of the beast. It looked part dragon, part hyena, with a wolf's mouth and eyes that burned holes in the page.

"Your relatives looked for it," Vivian said. "Someone always looks for it. But the beast isn't something you find. It's something you carry."

Wayne frowned. "You mean it's inside us?"

"More like *around* us," Wally said. "The beast's a living quest. Something we made. Like a riddle gone wrong. It's the dark side of every story. And some dipshit—" They saw Viv's distasteful expression. "Some *overconfident soul* always thinks they can find the beast and get it to do whatever. But the price is too high. Some stories eat you."

"On that note." Vivian shut the book. "To bed, chickens."

Kai crept into his room. This time, they didn't talk. They listened to a podcast, hovering on the edge of sleep the whole time. It was *One from the Vaults*, and Kai laughed once, when Morgan Page said that history was like gossip. Wayne didn't hear her leave. In his dream, he wore a heavy suit of armor. He could barely move and he had to swim, until the armor crumbled and he was sinking. He woke up on the floor.

Wayne's body screamed at him as he entered the forge. He wanted to wrap himself in ice and lie on the couch for a week. His arms trembled. Wally said nothing. They seemed to be waiting for him to decide something.

He took up the hammer again.

He worked past the point of exhaustion. He hammered and cut and scraped until he seemed to be tearing off layers of his own body. He was the sword, and the fire was destroying him from the inside. He was the one being scraped away. Wayne felt his sinews unravel, his muscles calcify, until he was pure carbon. He remembered all the times a boy had struck him. Pushed him. Laughed at him. Called him fag and shit-for-brains and fucking weirdo.

I'm weird, he thought, as he shaped the blade.

Clang!

I'm wyrd.

Scree!

I'm a sword.

Ssssh!

I'm a sword.

I'm a sword.

He shaped and pounded and wove the steel, until there was nothing left, no separation between blade and boy. Just a white-hot trembling core.

Wally took the hammer and tongs from him.

"I'll finish the last few details," they said. "Rest, Gawain."

He didn't even notice that they'd used his full name.

Wayne barely tasted dinner (veggie and herb pies). He drank orange wine in silence. Kai watched him but said nothing. The hearth burned low. Viv was tracing something on the table. Perhaps it was a rune. Her finger moved back and forth, weaving a shape that seemed to have been there all along.

"I remember the wedding of your mother," she said. "Anna was not fond of the institution."

Wayne just listened.

"She came from an old family. A noble daughter. And your father"—Viv looked askance for a moment—"was more of a hedge knight. But he fit. He wore an orange suit! Can you imagine? A suit like that, in the middle of a heatwave. I thought he would melt. But Anna thought it perfect. He had worn the same color when they first met, and he so rudely disrupted her experiment."

Wayne had seen pictures, but for some reason, he had never really *seen* that orange suit until Viv described it.

That night, they sat around a firepit in the backyard. Wally played a drum. Vivian danced, her feet swift as she leapt over ashes. Kai joined her, and they whirled in the half-light, two Beltane torches, silent but grinning. He could have watched them forever. He wondered if his mother had ever danced like that.

Kai didn't knock on his bedroom door. He knocked on hers. She let him sit at the foot of the bed, silent, full of words but unable to say anything. She sat very close to him, saying nothing, for what might have been hours. Something moved between them, a rune neither fire nor water, but something else—some nameless element. The outline of it was a comfort, because it joined them in bright lines.

Wally presented him with the sword the next morning. It had a wire grip, which he could hold with one hand. The pommel balanced it. They'd acid-etched his name rune along the fuller. It gleamed in purple whorls against the Damascene steel. There he was.

He stared at it. As his eyes adjusted one last time to the dark of the forge, he watched the lines tremble and rearrange themselves. The rune was an X, but it meant gift, and Gawain, and other things that thrummed silently but were impossible to speak.

"All that you are," Wally said, "is a gift. And this is my gift to you." They drew him close and touched their forehead to his. Normally, that would have made him uncomfortable. But they'd come to know each other in the heat of the forge.

"Now. Let me show you a trick."

Wally pulled out a hand mirror. It was old—more polished metal than glass. They touched the blurry reflection, and it rippled. As he watched, they reached into the mirror and pulled out a bright line. It was their own blade, whose pommel gleamed with a carbuncle.

"Shitballs!"

"Scabbard, actually," Wally said. "There is a place where weapons wait for us. Valkyries can use it, too, though sometimes our weapons get into fights with theirs." Wally chuckled. "Viv would call it 'esoteric.' Just old rivalries, I think. You need a reflective surface. First, place your hand on the fuller, on top of your name rune. You'll feel a thread."

Wayne did as they asked. He pressed his palm against the graven rune. After a while, he did feel something—a tickling. It reminded him of the time he'd filled his pockets with woolly caterpillars. Their tiny hairs had tickled his fingers.

"Good. Now find that same thread elsewhere—like tuning the dial until you find the proper frequency."

He frowned at them. "Dial?"

"God, I forget how young you are. Just touch the blade to the glass."

It was awkward, but Wayne managed to press the tip of the blade to the burnished surface of the glass. It snagged on something, and he felt the same tickle. The vibration ran up his arm.

"Feel it? Now, push."

It felt strange, but he pushed the blade. It slid into the mirror. Then it was gone.

He stared at his empty hand. "This is what Aunt Vera did with her sword. But—is it . . . ?" He frowned.

"It'll be there when you reach for it. Just don't leave it for too long. It'll get restless." They laughed suddenly. "Your face. How else did you think we stored our blades? This isn't *Outlander*. Or *Highlander*. You can't just walk around with a sword at your hip. This is more efficient. And it's magic that we all share. But always be careful around mirrors. Use them too much, and they'll start to use you."

He had no idea what that meant and was too tired to ask.

When they walked into the living room, Kai was packing the last of her things. Viv handed her a small leather-bound volume.

"This should help with your endeavor," she said. "Take care though. These are not forces to be trifled with."

It reminded Wayne of his dream about Bert. How he'd said all of this was just a game. But it clearly wasn't.

"I get that now," Kai said. "I get . . . a lot. Thank you."

Viv placed a hand gently on the back of Kai's head. "You are the ember," she said, "that will light the way."

"I'd rather burn shit down."

"That too." Viv smiled. "All your relations are proud."

Wayne had a sword.

He *was* a sword.

Wally hugged him, which he allowed. Viv brushed his forehead lightly but said nothing. Just gave him a fond look. As if she had no worries about him whatsoever.

Kai opened the front door, and her expression rearranged itself.

"Um. Wayne?"

He peeked around her, and his jaw dropped.

His father stood on the front porch. He looked tired but happy.

"Thought you might want a ride back to the ferry," he said.

Wally laughed. "Oh, your face! You should be surprised more often!"

Wayne stared at him. "How—I mean—Dad, what are you doing here?"

He rolled his eyes. "You think I don't know what you're up to? There's only one reason Vera would send you here."

"Might as well show him," Wally said. They handed him the mirror.

Wayne felt for the thread and reached inside. His hand closed around the grip. The quillons were cold, like a specter's touch. But still his.

He pulled the blade out.

"Shitballs!" It was Kai, this time.

His dad grinned. "Well. I always knew you had that in you."

"But . . ." Wayne's voice faded to a whisper. "Would Mom hate it?" He sounded like a kid in the dark. But he wasn't anymore.

"My boy." He kissed Gawain on the cheek. "She would want you to be armed."

HILDIE

Shar listened to Bush as they drove to Lost Lagoon. She was on a '90s kick, and Hildie had convinced her to drive, so she couldn't say anything about the music. Thready guitar rumbled in waves through the car. She leaned her bad cheek against the glass, taking comfort in the cool sting of it. Night was falling, and most of the tourists had gone back to their Airbnbs to upload photos. She watched the trails branching off like pathways to other worlds. Water lapped against the edges of the park. The lagoon was a nature preserve on Squamish land. Pauline Johnson, the Haudenosaunee poet, had named it as an antidote to the industrial Coal Harbour. She'd called it a "sheltered little cove." It sheltered far more than birds and poets.

Swallowed . . . swallowed. The lyrics rang through Shar's surprisingly loud speakers.

"So." Shar parked off Georgia Street, and the car idled for a while before she finally turned it off. "Things are going well?"

Hildie laughed. "Super."

"And are you going to tell me more about this ylf assignation at dusk? It sounds like something from a Tennyson poem."

Hildie shrugged. "Not much to tell. The ylf staying at the hotel gave me a tip. I'm coming to collect the information."

"And"—she peered into the backseat—"the rat?"

A white rat peered out of a small cage. He was terrified but silent.

"Payment. I wasn't sure precisely what the exchange rate would be, and the pet store didn't have any guinea pigs."

Shar sighed. "Some things never change."

Hildie stretched, though it did little to relieve the ache her body had become. "Before you ask, no, Grace doesn't know."

"Hmm." Shar tapped the wheel with a purple nail. "That strategy has worked well in the past, no?"

"Hush." She'd never tell one of the sisters to shut up, but she and Shar had known each other for a long time. Long in her estimation. To Shar, it was probably just a siesta.

Shar didn't look at her. Instead, she fiddled with the tchotchkes on the dashboard. Little monster puppets with wiggly arms. "Have you considered that this might be beyond the capacities of a single valkyrie? Even one as determined as yourself?"

Whenever she sank into formal language, it meant that she'd seen something. Usually not a good something. Hildie felt her insides turn to ice.

"You think I shouldn't?"

"I couldn't say. Wyrd moves as it will, and all that."

"Shar."

Shar stared fixedly through the darkening glass of the windshield. The park lights were winking on, like Narnian lampposts. Fauns weren't nice though. Hildie had learned that the hard way, needing half a bottle of antiseptic.

"Ylves follow their own timeline," Shar said at last. "Different from ours. Mine, I mean. They're more like trees. It takes them a long time to decide on things, and they don't see swift life—*your* life—in the same way."

223

"I know they're tricky."

"What I'm saying," Shar persisted, "is that their solution to your problem won't be immediate. And they could very well see you as part of the problem. So choose your words carefully, and avoid distraction."

Hildie smiled. "I know the drill. Don't eat anything, don't listen to the music, and get out before the moon shows up."

Shar simply nodded. She wasn't saying something. But there was no way to pry it out of her. Slim chance at best that she'd even want to know.

"Remember when Nan used to invite you over?"

Shar smiled. "She made the best powdered orange juice."

Her grandmother had died of lung cancer, but that didn't necessarily diminish the happiness of the memory. She'd died of other things too. After the funeral, Grace said she was going for a walk. She came back hours later, smelling like night, smoke, and gin. Shar had come over. Stroked Hildie's hair as she sobbed into a sour pillow. Cried so hard she thought there must be blood somewhere, from what was breaking inside her. Shar's voice in her ear: *She was a warrior, and so is your mom, and so are you.*

Desperation blooming inside. *But you can weave her back. Just one stray thread. Who'd even notice? You could do it.*

But Shar couldn't. And Hildie knew that. She cried even harder because she knew it. Shar held her like a broken animal.

"Your hair was rainbow then," Hildie said. "I loved it. You told me that I was a warrior and I never forgot that."

Shar had a funny expression. "Was that what I said?"

"Maybe I'm misremembering."

Shar smiled at her. "She's proud of you."

Hildie stiffened. "You mean my grandmother?"

"You must feel it."

She stared out the window, allowing her focus to haze over. "Sometimes. Hopefully that's enough."

"I'll see you in a bit."

Hildie gently lifted the rat's cage. "You don't think it'll take long?"

"Time works differently in their place. It's always a bit."

Helpful, she thought. But she knew that Shar was trying. There were some things that she couldn't explain because they required a whole universe of context.

"Don't misbehave."

Her mind flashed to a dark patio, Shar holding a small sun in her hand.

Aiming to misbehave?

"What was that night?"

Shar frowned. "Is this a riddle? Does the answer have something to do with stars, or maybe onions?"

Don't wriggle out of this moment, Hildie thought. *Spear it.* "You know what I mean." She held Shar's gaze. "At the Castle."

Wind rattled the windows of the car. It might snow. Shar was silent for what felt like a thousand years.

"I don't know," she said. Normally, her voice was so certain. She knew about fate and dark matter and how to get blood out of merino wool. But she didn't seem to know about this. A future she hadn't anticipated. A weft crashing across both of them.

Hildie couldn't look at her anymore. She was like the flicker in photographs. Like staring at the sun. Hildie looked out the windshield instead. "But it was something."

She could hear Shar breathing. Thinking. Or not thinking.

Then the warmth of her hand. Fingers weaving.

"It was something, Hildie."

How long did they stay like that? Watching the park grow dim. Listening to the rat squeak in the cage.

Hildie climbed out of the passenger seat. Shar stared at her for a moment through the window, then started the car.

She walked to the edge of the water. Its surface was cloudy in parts, and willow trees bowed, keeping quiet. Not that she could hear them. That had never been one of her talents, though Nan had always insisted that tree roots had a crackling language. She'd comment on arguments between trees and fungi like they were newspaper headlines.

Hildie took the rat out of the cage. "I'm putting you in my purse," she said. "Please make yourself at home, and don't eat anything."

The rat popped himself into her purse without comment. Maybe he knew. She walked along the edge of the water. Smoke hung in the sky from distant wildfires in the Okanagan, giving everything a papery feel. The moon was still indistinct. Hildie stopped near a copse of trees. Or maybe it was a coppice? She should probably get her ecological vocabulary right if she was going to deal with ylves. She waited. The rat squeaked quietly in her purse. She reached in and stroked his fur.

The light changed. Colors leached out of the trees. Everything took on the feeling of grayscale. She felt her breathing quicken. Carefully, she reached into the space where her spear was. It was not a particularly friendly space. It was very dark, like the mind of a mountain, and shot through with gleams of something. The spear twitched, but she passed over it, searching. Listening. Finally, she heard a faint tone, like a musical note played through some kind of filter. Not a human sound.

She followed it through the trees.

From the outside, the canopy wasn't dense. The inside was a different story. It grew dark almost immediately, as the trees linked their skeletal crowns above. The light that filtered through was blue and cold. Hildie felt herself shiver. It wasn't the damp cold of the West Coast; this was the cold of another planet. It took up residence in her lungs and crystallized her breath. She saw flakes on her boots. But it wasn't unbearable. She got used to it with each step, which should have bothered her.

The faint floating note led her to a clearing. There were shifting lights in the trees, as if something had draped long strings of Christmas bulbs. They flickered and danced in the leaves, occasionally whispering. The more Hildie strained to hear what they were saying, the colder she got. She could feel a curious blankness spreading across her mind, like a stain across linen. It was more difficult to feel herself, to know who she was and what she wanted. Everything bled into trees and winter and prismatic nothing.

Hildie tried to think more about it, and her thoughts developed trails. Someone else was thinking with her. Multiple someones. It was disorienting, and as she tried to hang onto who she was, she felt a growing nausea. Like a diver fighting against the bends.

She came to an overgrown stave church—one of those ancient tall structures that looked more like trees than buildings. Choppy towers mingled with crowns of leaves, until you couldn't tell what was made from what had always been there. It reminded her of a twisted Disney castle. Something that had decayed into peculiar glory.

The floor was made of packed earth. It was dim inside, save for minerals that flared within the walls. To make sure that she didn't fall and break her ankle, Hildie turned on the flashlight app on her phone. She heard a loud hiss in her brain. It wasn't a welcoming sound.

"Sorry." She turned off the light.

There was silence for a while. Then, gradually, she became aware of eyes regarding her from dark corners. Old red pitiless eyes studied her, as she might study a weird bug that had turned up in her house.

Hildie brought out the rat, who began to squirm. Now he got it.

"My gift," she said.

Stick to the script. Don't improvise. Rituals can keep you alive, or they can kill you, if you fail to obey them.

She looked into the rat's eyes. "I'm sorry, Madonna," she said. "Thank you. Go in peace."

Then she let him jump to the ground. He took off into the darkness.

Hildie heard a short sharp noise, like a screeching wheel.

Afterward, nothing.

She didn't move.

The eyes were closed now, but still watching her.

After a time, she became aware of a nearby shadow. It lengthened, and somehow she knew it was the ylf she'd spoken with in the hotel room. Some twinge of familiarity within the ripples of dark.

She inclined her head, and said in Anglish, "Well met."

They immediately switched to English, like she was a tourist in Montréal. "You received my note."

"Yes." Hildie didn't mention how creepy the note had been, or ask how the ylf had slipped it into her mailbox.

"How goes the adventure?"

She blinked. It took her a moment to realize that the ylf meant *investigation*. She remembered that *adventure* used to mean a lot of different things. "There's been another death," she said. No use hiding anything at this point. "A hedge knight. We have a slim connection between murders, but nothing more."

"Murders are always riddles," the ylf said helpfully.

Hildie nodded. "Okay. Do you have something for me?"

The eyes glanced away from her. They seemed to be conferring with the shadows in the church.

"We will give you something," the ylf replied, still listening to something beyond. "In exchange for your gift."

"That's great—thank you."

"But," the ylf continued, "we'll need something more."

Hildie felt a dull pain in her skull. She tried to brush it away, knowing it meant that she'd already spent too much time in this place. "We can . . . talk about it. But I'm not authorized to offer you anything more on behalf of my people. I'd need to confer with them."

"You mean you'd need to ask your mother."

That seemed like a cheap shot, even for an ylf with a perverse sense of humor. "If you want to put it that way," she said, trying to ignore the buzzing in her teeth.

"You will owe us a favor," the ylf said. "Only you."

She frowned. "What kind of favor?"

"You will know when the time comes. But we ask nothing of the Wælcyrian." This point seemed to be important to them. "Only you," the ylf repeated.

For a moment, Hildie thought she saw her grandmother in the shadows. Her expression, as always, was a jigsaw puzzle. She offered no advice.

Some help you are.

Hildie swallowed. "When would you need this favor?"

"In a little while," the ylf said.

She nearly laughed. Shar was always right.

This is your only real lead.

Hildie sighed. "Fine."

"You agree?"

"Yes."

Hildie saw something flash toward her—like impossibly sharp rubies. Her hand flared with pain, and she yanked it away.

Blood welled up in two half-moon marks on her palm. They ached. More like an old wound than a new shallow cut. Hildie shook her hand.

"Was that necessary?"

"Pain teaches," the ylf said. "Come closer, and we'll show you."

The blank space was spreading now. It was the size of a province. She watched a drop of her own blood fall to the hard-packed earth. The edges cooled and scalloped immediately, rimed with frost. Hildie sucked in her breath.

She stepped forward, and all the eyes snapped open.

WAYNE

He was eight when he'd met Kai, at a private school that his parents were briefly able to afford before he had to transfer to a regular school. A lot of squires and baby runesmiths and other unmentionables went there, mingling with ordinary kids who had no idea. His parents had been fighting about mainstreaming at the time. Mom wanted him to have a conventional life, full of gaps and mysteries, while Dad pushed for something more traditional. Ironic, given that he was way more ordinary. Maybe he romanticized that life? It was tense in those days, lots of slamming doors and bruised silences whenever he'd walk into the room. Mom would pretend she'd been reading the whole time, while Dad would reach for his guitar. When you're eight, you can sense weirdness like a cat, but there's nothing you can do about it. Then he fell into Kai's orbit. Collided with her really, like something astrophysical.

Making friends was something that never happened for him. The guide book had been lost somewhere, and his only move was to stand on the edge of things, looking scared and hopeful. Which rarely worked. So he spent a lot of time wandering the school field and talking to crows. A few of them talked back, though his crow grammar was pretty bad; he just translated everything as *hungry*. The crows were happy with him, at any rate, because he shared his lunch.

At the very edge of the school grounds, there was a clutch of twisted trees that resembled two old people with bowed backs locked in a peculiar embrace. He'd once heard his mother use the word *altar* in a hushed voice, and he thought of the space between the trees as a kind of altar. He was the sacrifice. He'd sit there most days, waiting to be changed. Then a bell would chime—recess was over—and he'd go back inside.

One time, as he was settling in near the altar, he heard a rustling from above.

"Move," a voice said.

Startled, he looked up. Kai was sitting in the branches. She wore baggy clothes and had tortoise-shell barrettes in her hair. She looked like she was about to jump—like she'd done this a thousand times before.

Wayne frowned. "How did you get up there?"

"Climbed. Obviously. Now move." Kai softened her voice. "Please."

Wayne took a step back. Kai shimmied down the tree. She brushed herself off, and they half looked at each other. Two people meeting entirely out of context, unwilling to reveal too much.

Wayne wasn't good at introductions. They tended to defeat him. A person's name would blaze up, then he'd immediately forget it because they were trying to shake his hand or ask a weird question. His mother would gently remind him to make eye contact, shake their hand firmly, and smile. The smiling was the most important part, because if you didn't smile, the whole thing was ruined for some reason. Wayne practiced smiling in the bathroom mirror, but it never looked right. He'd settled on a soft grimace that most people let slide.

Kai still wasn't saying anything. She seemed to be assessing him from multiple angles. She wasn't quite frowning; it was more like a diagnostic expression. A *what do we have here*. Or maybe she was shy too. He didn't think so though. He'd seen her managing the other kids, telling them how to make their games more efficient. She didn't seem to suffer from any lack of confidence.

231

He'd learned recently that people liked to be complimented on their appearance. He'd tried it on several people, and it usually worked. Though once he'd complimented his Aunt Vera on her scarf, by saying it looked *quite serpentine*—a high compliment—and she'd merely raised an eyebrow and seemed a bit miffed.

He said to Kai, "I like your barrettes. They remind me of gemstones."

Kai touched one of the barrettes self-consciously. "Thanks. I had another pair, but"—her face went dark for a second—"I lost them."

"I could help you find them. I'm pretty good at finding things."

She hesitated for a second, then said, "They were stolen. I liked them too. They had garnets. But some kids stole them. Assholes."

His eyes widened. He wasn't allowed to swear at home, though Mom swore all the time. She said *goddamn fucking car* so often that, for years, he'd thought that was just how you said *car*. Which had caused some issues.

He couldn't imagine a roving band of barrette thieves. "Who took them?"

Her voice faltered. "Just some boys."

"Why would boys steal barrettes?"

Her face was doing a thing he couldn't quite identify. She was collapsing into herself, like a neutron star. "They said, 'Boys don't wear barrettes.'"

He shook his head. "But you're a girl."

Kai smiled shyly. "Not everyone sees that."

"I do," Wayne said. "It's obvious. But I'm also pretty good at seeing things. Like microwave background radiation from the Big Bang."

She narrowed her eyes, as if she was trying to figure out if he was joking. "You mean—like light waves?"

"Well, light is both a particle and a wave, but yes. I can show you."

Kai laughed softly. "Okay. What does it look like? The Big Bang light?"

"Well . . ." He frowned. "Sort of like Christmas lights. Only fainter. And some of the stars look like our Pokémon ornament."

Kai snorted. "The Charmander Galaxy."

"Exactly!"

She seemed to be sizing him up again. "What family are you from?"

He didn't quite understand the question. "My parents are Anna and Lot. My aunt Vera came from away—Mom says she married in. Though she's not married anymore."

Kai stared at him for a second. "You're Gawain."

He rolled his eyes. "People are always saying that to me. I never know what it means. I mean, I know I'm a knight. In theory. But actually I'm just Wayne."

"I'm Kai," she said. It looked like she was about to shake his hand, but instead she gave him a fist bump. Which he returned.

Then her face glowed with mischief. "Before you show me the Big Bang, can I show you something else?"

"Okay. But like my dad always says, keep it PG. Whatever that means."

She led him to a tree stump. It looked hardened, like rock. She reached into her bag and pulled out an old-fashioned letter opener. It looked like a sword. Not a real one—he'd seen those. More like what people *assumed* a sword would be.

Kai scraped at the top layer of the stump—there was green underneath!

"It's not dead," she said. "The other trees are keeping it alive. They're using their roots to share nutrients."

"Why would they do that?"

Her face was open. "Why wouldn't they?"

Then she used the letter opener to carve something lightly into the soft part of the tree. He'd seen those lines before, in the books that he wasn't supposed to read.

Runes.

Kai stared at the shape. It looked a bit like a lightning bolt, or a stylized 4. He could feel a ghostly warmth coming from it. A sun rune. Kai's eyes narrowed, and her whole body seemed to be flexing with concentration.

For a second, the air above the rune grew elastic. The day slowed down. He heard the leaves rasping something, felt the blood pumping to and from his heart. *Lub-DUB.*

A spark flashed before them.

It was tiny, like a spark from a lighter. But it was blue and bright.

Wayne took a step back. *"Shit,"* he said, then immediately felt bad for swearing.

Kai grinned.

Then she scraped away the rune.

It was Wayne's introduction to power.

⤜⤛⤜⤛

"Nope."

"Bear."

"We're not doing it."

"Look"—she was typing rapidly—"I just have to—*there.*" She pointed to the screen of her massive Razer gaming laptop, which had its own industrial fan to keep it from catching fire.

He squinted at the characters. "Are those runes?"

"Oh yeah. Sorry."

Kai opened a window that read *command line* and typed in a string of characters. The runes dissolved like fireworks, becoming Western characters that he recognized as actual words. As she cycled between windows, he saw something that looked like a JavaScript program, only some of the characters were definitely runes. They trembled slightly on the screen, and he had to squint to look at them.

"So, you're programming in runes now. Is that normal?"

She closed the window. "I told you I was working on something. It's a bit unorthodox—though I'm far from the only runesmith who's coding. Willow Rosenberg from *Buffy* was a programmer."

"That show is so old."

"It's a cult classic. You just pretend not to like it because of that one episode with Xander in the Speedo that made you too horny."

Wayne flushed. "Um. Not relevant. Do you really want to base your plan on a '90s cyber witch? She's not real."

Her expression darkened. "Leave this house."

He studied the website. "The Castle," he read. "An endless masquerade. Dress code strictly enforced. No unauthorized rune work on premises." Wayne stared at the address. "Wait. This is in Gastown. I've walked by this place a hundred times."

"Viv told me about it. Look, if you want the magical gossip, this is where it's at. Maybe we'll even run into *Bertram*."

He did seem like the club type. The sort of guy who leaned casually against a bar, holding it up with the gravity of his cuteness and general inaccessibility.

She grinned. "Now he's interested!"

"No."

"It's either this, or wait around for another rooftop attack."

Kai wasn't entirely wrong. She never was, and that was the problem. This did feel more proactive than just sitting around. Plus, things were different now. He had a weapon. Granted, he could only draw it from the aether fifty percent of the time, and each time it gave him a migraine, but that still felt like some progress.

"What do you think they mean by dress code?"

Kai was smiling.

"No. Absolutely—"

The trip to Value Village was basically destined. Kai immediately located their discounted Halloween stock from earlier in the year. She found a flowing purple robe described as *druid's garb*, whose package featured a blond woman holding a sacrificial dagger. The plastic dagger was extra, but she decided to spring for it. Wayne bought a suit of chain mail that sounded like it had been made from bottle caps. He also found a helmet that obscured most of his face, while Kai opted for an elegant domino mask.

They waited until dark. Wayne's anxiety equaled the first time he'd been to a gay bar; he'd accepted three blue-colored shots and immediately vomited on the patio.

Kai led him confidently down Blood Alley, which most tourists avoided because it was so dark and twisty. At the end, they reached a green door with no handle or any other distinguishing marks. She reached into her purse and withdrew a bundle that he'd never seen before. It looked like a roll of camping supplies, except that the tools felt more random. Chisels and other scrapers, spray paint, nail polish, and what looked suspiciously like a minitorch for toasting crème brûlée.

"It's like a bug-out bag," she said, "except for rune stuff."

"You're freaking me out."

"I've always been this person, Wayne." She dug through her bag. "Okay. I've got spray paint, and you've got your creepy sword pocket."

"It's a dimension," he protested feebly.

"Some smiths go fully digital," Kai said, "but I'm still a print nerd."

She pulled out a stencil and spray-painted a rune on the door. It was vivid orange. Looking at it too closely made his teeth ache. His mind did a little flip and translated the shape as *hospitality, home*. The door creaked open a crack. It took both of them to pry it open further. The wood was surprisingly dense.

They walked upstairs and Wayne felt his heart spike.

Everyone was in costume, but the costumes somehow made them more real, more themselves. Knights were dancing and drinking and making out in corners. He looked up and realized that the hazy underwater light came from tapestries of iridescent moss. There were also crystal strands that gave off their own curious light. It smelled like people and smoke and spirits, which were in liberal supply. There was a casual nonbinary feeling to the crowd. In the half dark, everyone could be who they were. Some people were on their own, but nobody seemed alone. They were all bound by threads that he couldn't quite explain.

"Stay here," Kai said. "I'm going to chat up the bartender."

"Is he—I mean, are they"—Wayne frowned at the shape behind the bar—"just eyes?"

"An ylf. Like in fairy tales, but more cryptic."

He frowned at her. "Have you talked to an . . . ylf before? Like, as a matter of your daily routine?"

Her composure broke slightly. "Well, no. But I'm less of a tourist than you, so here goes nothing. If someone touches your butt, just go with it."

"That's the opposite of consent."

Kai walked over to the bar, her druid robe swishing across the dark floor.

He wasn't sure where to stand. People kept shouldering past him. At one point, he got accidentally caught up in the bathroom line. He was pretty sure someone ahead of him was dressed as a pantomime horse. Or it was a kelpie.

Someone tapped him on the shoulder. He resisted the urge to yelp. At first, he didn't recognize the woman in the pastel confection of a gown, which had a hoop skirt and multiple layers of ruffle. Then his eyes widened.

"Hildie?"

She pulled him out of line. "Tell me precisely what you're doing here, and it's possible that I won't call your scary auntie to come drag you away."

Wayne chuckled; he couldn't help it. "You look like a furious gumdrop."

"It's cosplay night. Never mind. Did you come alone?" Her eyes darkened. "Of course you didn't. This plan has Little Miss Runesmith all over it."

"We were hoping for a lead."

"That's my job. Your job is to stay alive." Hildie rolled her eyes. "I'm going to find Kai. Stay put." She walked off, which took awhile because she had to lift up all of her skirts. She was wearing sneakers underneath.

Everyone kept telling him to stay put. He felt like a child. An overgrown child surrounded by people who were only now starting to take notice of him. Some of their expressions verged on hunger.

He saw someone familiar walk past. Wayne frowned.

Screw staying put.

He followed the shadow down the hallway. It smelled of smoke and stale beer. The shadow turned for a second, and Wayne's heart seized.

"Uncle Lance?" He was astonished to hear his own voice.

The figure paused, still half in the dark. Then it switched direction and walked through the fire exit. There was no alarm. Wayne followed—instinct kept him from opening the door again, but maybe it was disconnected? He pushed, and the door gave slightly with no alarm. He propped it open with a chair. But by the time he'd worked his way outside, the figure was gone.

Had it been Lance?

Wayne smelled something familiar. He crossed the parking lot and found a knight vaping.

He said nothing. Just offered Wayne a puff silently. Most of his face was obscured by a bascinet helm. Only his eyes were visible. They seemed kind.

Wayne inhaled, coughed, and returned it. He still wasn't sure what he thought about weed. Sometimes it was soothing, and sometimes it ramped up his anxiety.

"Virgin lungs?" The knight's voice was laced with warm humor.

"My last virginal part."

He snickered. "Doubt that. You seem cuddly. Like a medieval otter."

"Otters are actually pretty much assholes."

"I don't mind that."

They smoked in companionable silence for a bit. Everything felt a bit hazy and green around the edges. The night softened. Wayne felt oddly comfortable with this stranger, who didn't demand conversation.

"Sometimes this helps," Wayne said, motioning with the vape like he was conducting a minor symphony. "With my anxiety."

"You know what else could help?"

"What?"

"Dancing."

"*Noooo.*"

"Come on otter-butt."

"I really can't."

"It's so easy. I'll show you."

They went back inside and made their way to the dance floor.

Kai and Hildie were nowhere to be seen. Not that he was looking for them too closely. He found a little corner on the dance floor, which had a give to it, like the horsehair floors in the Commodore nightclub on Granville. He danced with the knight to a techno song in Middle English. Something about how summer was coming. At the chorus, everyone yelled *cuckoo*, which they both thought was hilarious. He was sweating beneath his chainmail, flushed and strangely happy. The song shifted to "Clearest Blue" by CHVRCHES. It started slow, then bubbled up into percussive joy. Everyone on the dance floor was leaping around them, but they formed a perfect blue stillness. Bert drew closer. Wayne smelled campfires and cinnamon gum. The knight took off his helmet. He was smiling.

"I thought so" was all Wayne said. He took off his own visor.

The knight grinned. He put his arms around Wayne, and they spun in slow circles. They were still wearing armor, but Wayne felt like they were totally exposed. Like there was nothing between them, just a breath and a rhythm they both understood. Wayne thought of the word *kenning*, which was really one word becoming two. Maybe that's what they were. Kenning.

"Told you it was easy," he said.

"With you—it is. Oddly."

Then their scales got tangled, and they had to pry each other apart, laughing.

They walked back along the beach, and the water was dark glass. Bert did a funny robot dance in the sand. Wayne nearly spit out his donair. His phone shook like a wild beast in his pocket, until he turned it off. Like going under anesthesia. Putting your finger on the beating knot of life and saying, *Just hold on for two seconds while I fall.*

Bert lived in an old carriage house on one of those weird, rambling properties in the West End that used to be the height of luxury. Now it was crumbling and broken into little suites, cloaked by a thick hedge. They walked up a formerly grand staircase, and Wayne felt the temperature rise. The place was so old that the bathroom was in the main hallway. He didn't want to think about pissing behind a thin door while the neighbors listened, but he had more important things to worry about. Like what would happen once they got inside.

The suite was cramped and warm and felt oddly safe. It was Bert. There were mountains of books in mismatched shelves, a sagging couch, and skateboards hanging from the wall. Benign piles of things everywhere: free weights and an exercise ball, multicolored yarn, strings of lights, half-carved blocks of wood, bright fishing lures, dried flowers, an ivory chess set, hunting knives, comics, watercolors, geodes that shone sea green and blood red when the light struck them, and an anatomical skeleton.

Bert smiled sheepishly. "I might be a hoarder."

"It's the greatest apartment I've ever seen," Wayne breathed. "It's Merlin's den."

He touched the spines of the books—on everything from graphic arts to foraging mushrooms. Like Bert was quietly gathering up all the world's knowledge. The cramped living room gave way to the kitchen, with black-and-white linoleum. It was full of potted plants, which all appeared to be thriving. The air smelled like something delicious. Cast-iron pans hung from the actual ceiling.

"I love green things," Bert said.

"I'm starting to see that." Wayne touched a happy fern, which felt dry and comforting against his fingertips. "They speak an easy language. Talking is too hard sometimes. The words get stuck in a traffic jam. I want people to just *see* what I mean, but it's tough when the words won't come. I mean"—he dared a glance up—"they're coming now. I'm rambling. But they're not always there."

Bert took his hand. "I see you," he said. "I won't lie. My past isn't green or pretty. There are some dark things happening. If I were you, I probably wouldn't trust me. But don't believe everything that valkyries tell you."

This surprised him. "You've talked to Hildie?" He was at the party. It made sense. But somehow Wayne had thought that Hildie was *their* valkyrie. However silly that might be.

"I know she's keeping us all close," Bert said. "Valkyries solve the case—that's their main objective. It's all they care about. Justice. Or vengeance."

240

Wayne slipped his hand away, though he didn't want to. "This is overwhelming. But I'm not freaking out. I don't know why. Here I am, getting seduced by a fairy tale in a coach house. Like it could all be real and work out somehow. Like I deserve . . . whatever this is."

Bert hesitated. "Maybe I've gone about this wrong. Maybe we both should have been open about our pasts from the start. But it's not every day that you see someone, and they see you. When I was at the party that night, I didn't really want to be seen. But there you were. That moment. When you were listening to the music—what was it again?"

"Bach," he said softly.

"The expression on your face." Bert smiled. "I wanted to know what secret thing was making you so happy. I wanted to be that thing."

Wayne looked at him, allowing the eye contact to send skitters of fire through him. Like staring at the sun. "Bert." His voice was faint. "I'm *so* messed up. I don't think you want this. My panic and my weirdness—all the times words fail me, and I can't say what I mean. All the sharp edges in me, and the scared parts, and . . ." He swallowed. "It's a lot, okay? And you're so . . . *finished*, somehow. Like you know exactly who you are. You're charming and wonderful, and you keep plants alive. I can't imagine a world in which we'd be right for each other. A place where we'd fit. I just . . . can't."

"I can," Bert said. Then he kissed Wayne.

It was warm and steady. It was like . . . it was like . . .

Bert's tongue teasing his mouth. The smell of leaves and sweat and summer, in spite of the cold wind. Bert's arms around him, the warmth of his chest, the little chuckling sound he made before their mouths met. Wayne melted. The force field dissolved. Bert was the field now, the circle of his arms, that tender compass.

Wayne pulled away.

Bert's eyes widened. "Sorry. It's too much, isn't it?"

Wayne shook his head. "It's not. I'm just worried I might knock over the plants."

Bert laughed. "You'd prefer the bed?"

241

"If I fall, the damage will be minimal." Everything was happening quickly now. It always happened so quickly. That was the only way he could avoid second-guessing it.

The bedroom was a snug den, with more leaning bookshelves and a bed on cinderblocks. The floor was that kind of wood that looked destroyed but also forgiving, like it had seen everything. The duvet had a forest print.

Wayne kissed Bert against the wall, surprising himself. Pulled his shirt over his head, and kissed all the way down his furry chest, down to his belly. The floor warm against his knees. Bert suddenly still, like he was afraid to move, to breathe. Light from the alarm clock, casting them in green-blue shadows as they crumbled into each other.

They tumbled into the sheets, flinging off clothes. Wayne tried to take off his pants, but his shoes were still on. Bert had to help him, and they both laughed as they bent over each other, shaking and hot, bodies singing.

Bert stretched underneath him. Wayne traced fingertips down his hip, trailing in the shaggy hair on his legs. Bert kissed his neck. Then sucked on his ear. The world went white along the edges. Wayne shivered. Bert wrapped an arm around him.

"I've got you," he said, rubbing slow circles along Wayne's back. He didn't normally like light touch, but this was okay.

Wayne kissed Bert's beard. "I've wanted to do that for a while."

"Oh yeah?"

"Yeah. And this."

Bert's whole body shuddered.

"That . . . *too?*" Bert asked, when he could speak.

"Yep."

Bert kissed his chest. Licked his nipple, which turned to fire. Bit softly. Wayne's mind exploded like a murder of crows.

He was reaching into the nightstand table. Pulling out condoms and lube. Wayne paused for a moment, wondering what direction this would go in. He wasn't *very* experienced, though he knew his way around this particular battlefield. Knew enough, and what he liked, and was willing to follow Bert's lead.

Then Bert winked. And Wayne realized it wasn't about leading. It was about listening to each other—not just words, but bodies and breaths and looks. And that had never been his strong suit. But with Bert, it made more sense. Like someone had turned up the volume or switched on the subtitles.

Wayne held still for a moment.

"Okay?"

Bert nodded.

"I'll go slow."

"You don't—"

"For me too. This isn't, I mean, I'm no—"

Bert put a hand on his chest. "We're good," he whispered.

Wayne gently touched the pad of Bert's foot. The scar on his ankle, which carried no explanation with it. Just another footnote.

He went slowly at first. Bert's breath quickened, and Wayne listened to that. Followed the dance, which they were both locked in. He sped up, as fire trickled through him. His mind was dim now. Shocked into a kind of silence, though he could still feel anxiety calling like a passenger stranded on the shore. It was always there. But so was he.

Bert came with a sharp sound that dissolved into laughter.

They held each other for a while. Bert's heartbeat softened. He breathed long and slow into Wayne's neck. He was bigger than Wayne, but holding him worked. His body gave way to the embrace. They whispered things, and giggled, and rearranged each other. Wayne played with Bert's legs, like he was riding a bicycle, until Bert snorted. Then Bert tapped out a tune on Wayne's chest, until Wayne guessed that it was the theme song from *Sesame Street*. Bert made a joke about Snuffleupagus, and Wayne shook with laughter. He coughed, and Bert rubbed his back, though he was also laughing.

After a time, the fire came back. Bert's body pressed lightly against his. They tried a side-to-side thing Wayne'd seen in a porn once, but Bert just shook his head. "Not gonna work. We're forks, not spoons." That made Wayne laugh. They arranged some pillows. Bert went slowly. Wayne opened like a wild possibility. Thunder moved through him. Bert reaching down to kiss him, waves crashing through him. Then later, Bert's mouth buried in his neck, one arm stretched across his chest, holding him together. Two lines in a rune.

23

HILDIE

Her life philosophy was to do the opposite of what her mother said.

So far, it was a cracking success, though it had nearly got her killed several times.

It didn't take too much effort to grab some footage of their car chase through Gastown, which a group of students from Van Film School had captured on their phones. After a night of shotgunning Timbits, she was able to pull a license plate from the Bronco that had nearly run them down in Blood Alley. It was a commercial vehicle, belonging to none other than Caerleon Corp—the company that was trying to expose Hotel Wyrd. There was no listing of the main shareholders, though she had her suspicions about who they might be.

There was, however, a listing of office employees. Which was interesting, because as far as she could tell, Caerleon's office was an empty glass box with a *for lease* sign.

The roster was a short one. The secretary had retired. She was a cagey witch who lived by the docks and had no desire to give up any information. But she did confirm that Caerleon had a casual driver: a guy named Boris, who rarely showed up.

"He smelled like mouthwash and stale food." That was all the witch volunteered, before she slammed the door of her storage container in Hildie's face.

Now she was parked outside the basement suite that Boris rented. It was in Hastings-Sunrise: hip brunch places and hookah lounges jostled next to Chinese bakeries and bodegas. Iron Dog Books was having a sale. She remembered a place that used to sell curry and giant cinnamon buns, now gone. Hildie drained her coffee. She was wired and knew this stake-out was a terrible idea, but she couldn't stop. The ideas just kept coming, like a greatest hits version of her worst impulses. She tapped the dash. Something had to happen soon.

And it did.

A red car pulled into the driveway. The door opened, and Hildie sucked in her breath.

She considered her response. She could deal with this logically, civilly. She ran across the street, just as the figure was about to open the back door.

"Am I asleep?" Hildie glared at her. "Is this a fever dream, instead of you collaborating with the enemy in real life?"

Shar sighed. She wore a beautiful black coat with polished brass buttons. "She's not the enemy. She's the First Valkyrie, and your mother, and you know I had no choice."

"I can think of several choices, other than this."

"Hildie." Shar looked so tired. "The sisters are knee-deep in this. We're tied up in a real-estate battle, and we might lose the hotel. You're the one who said that this investigation is likely connected. When Grace called—what was I supposed to do?"

"She's benched me." Hildie looked down. "I feel useless."

Shar touched her arm. "You're essential. But sometimes the answer is to hang back and wait. She just wants to protect you."

But who's protecting you? For a moment, Hildie wanted to grab Shar and hide her away in some pocket dimension. A place where they could watch old movies under Nan's patchwork quilt, and the windows were murder-proof, and nothing bad could get in.

Then the anger was back. "Nah. She wants me out of the way. No dice. Plus, I know something that she doesn't. The ylves—"

Grace appeared in the doorway. Her eyes raked Hildie. "Perfect. Could you possibly draw more attention to this active crime scene? Perhaps you could send out a press bulletin, or have an airship trundle by with a banner."

At the words *crime scene*, Hildie felt her stomach clench. She'd expected to do some light interrogation. Not find another body.

Grace seemed about to say more. Then she shook her head and stepped back inside. Shar followed, and Hildie climbed the steps slowly, feeling like the third wheel that she'd become. A chaotic and squeaky third wheel, kicking up sparks.

They wiped their shoes on the rag rug in the hallway. The living room was dim, with only a bit of light filtering through the garden-level windows. The carpet was gray and rotting. Boris hadn't done much with the place. A sunken sectional couch was pushed against one wall, and a TV balanced precariously on a broken table. There was a tower of old pizza boxes and other recycling, which swayed gently in the corner. The cupboards were mostly bare, save for dead spices and dusty taco kits. Grace found a sizeable bag of hash in the freezer, tucked underneath a stack of Michelina alfredo dinners.

Boris was in the bedroom. He was splayed atop a fur blanket. Her eyes widened as recognition struck her. This was definitely the driver who'd rear-ended them. She remembered the brush cut and the thick-set jaw.

He had the build of an athlete who'd gone to seed. *Dad bod* felt a bit whimsical for an active crime scene, but it was the thought that occurred to her. Numerous scars dotted his chest and shoulders like a lunar canyon—old wounds. His nose looked like it had been broken and reset multiple times. He was probably held together by pins and scar tissue.

But that wasn't what killed him.

Something had ripped open his side. The blood beneath him had the look of black ice, now dried. For a moment, Hildie thought of that biblical story: Jacob wrestling with the angel. The angel's touch soft, but apocalyptic. Something similar had left its mark on Boris, leaving him unstitched, his body a discarded pillowcase. Something with claws.

"The interesting thing," Grace said, as if analyzing a novel, "is what's *not* missing."

He'd kept his head and his heart.

Shar took a closer look at his leg. "What's this?" She pointed to a healing cut on his thigh. "Looks like an older injury."

Hildie touched her own cheek, remembering the knight on the rooftop. "Boris was the one who attacked Vera and her nephew. I left him that souvenir. He's also the one who tried to run me off the road." When Grace stared at her, she added, "Gale Amadís was driving. I was just an unwilling passenger."

Hildie noticed a tiny mark on his chest. At first, she thought it was a pimple. But then she recognized it, because she'd done the same thing to herself with a safety pin. She pointed to it.

"He poked himself by accident," she said. "With the brooch. Trying to put it on in a hurry." It was a funny image—a knight struggling to pin on jewelry. "He's the one who hip-checked me at Morgan's house," she said. "That means someone else is wearing its twin."

Grace walked slowly around the bed. "Any leads on that second brooch?"

"The inscription was too worn to read," Shar said. "But Clywen's still working on it."

"The first kill was a mixed message," Grace said. "A slick cut and a gaping wound. It didn't make sense. The second was more animalistic, as if something had torn Percy apart. This feels almost"—she looked dispassionately at Boris—"restrained. Like whatever did this had to end his life but didn't take as much joy in it. If I had to guess, I'd say Boris outlived his usefulness. But this doesn't help our profile."

"Considering some of our profiles are medieval scrolls," Hildie said, "I'm not sure we should be surprised by the odd, at this point."

Grace looked at Shar. "Are you up for this? I know this isn't the best time."

She nodded. "I want to help."

The air stilled. Hildie listened to her breath, letting it slow, until they were all breathing in unison. Three women joined in the dim room. Everything faded. Slowly, they unraveled the bloody threads that were Boris. The Boris that had been. He was a knight, so it had been a long life, but not a happy one. Hildie felt his pain as a boy. His father raining down blows and drunken invectives. Healing bones and bruises that went deep, like tree roots. She smelled the fragrance of a stable. A horse's soft mouth, nuzzling dried apples in her hand. Boris's hand. The gentle company of animals, who neither judged him nor expected him to be strong all the time. Lives spreading out like axons, forming dark lattices of power and heartbreak.

But then an intervention. A woman bringing him to the edge of a clear lake. Pinning his cloak with a brooch. Animals winking at him. *This is for you. And one other.*

Hildie couldn't see the other person. They were always in shadow. Boris ran alongside them, trying to keep up. Always the enforcer. Always fighting, bragging, trying to cover the fear. And beneath it all, that kid with the horses grew quiet, until he was nearly inaudible. Hildie kept his thread, letting it snag within her. Not willing to let go until the last moment.

Shar froze his death. It hung before them, blue and blurred.

A giant claw, opening a door in his side.

"Do we know anything else about him?" Hildie found herself looking around the apartment again, just to get away from the image.

"We're searching," Grace replied, "but there isn't much. He must be a fallen knight."

Hildie had felt something in his last moments. Right before the flash of pain. A different kind of hurt. Betrayal.

Whoever was watching in the background—that was what Boris was trying to see. Not the monster unseaming him.

The shadow he'd trusted.

It was still dark when she left for the office. They were open day and night, but this early she'd have the place to herself. That was what she hoped. A solid half hour without her mother scrutinizing her every move, so that she could follow up on what the ylves had told her. It was a surprising fragment of information that didn't make much sense. But ylves didn't make much sense as a rule.

Hildie walked down Pender Street, which was still quiet. People slept on the sidewalk, covered in tarps and dirty blankets. The shelters were always overflowing. Vancouver had no living space that wasn't reserved for millionaires. It must have been the same way in the Middle Ages, she thought, when aristocrats lived in castles that overlooked shocking poverty. Maybe it didn't seem as real when you were peering out of a tiny lancet window, eating peacock.

She walked into the Sun Tower, past the front desk, which was always empty (though that didn't mean someone wasn't watching from above). She took the elevator, then climbed the remaining nine floors, slowly, huffing the entire way. Hildie wanted a job on the ground.

Still, working under the dome could be soothing. And the stone women offered them some protection, though they were fickle. And when they got hungry, all bets were off. Hildie mostly steered clear of them.

The office smelled like fresh coffee. She shook her head. Grace had beaten her to the punch once again. Now her work would be impossible. What was her mother doing up this early? Was she harboring a secret Pinterest addiction that could only be satisfied in the dawn hours? Hildie thought of her valkyrie mother, pinning toy spears or weird fan art, and it made her smile. Then her stomach did a turn, and she realized she was still nauseous from climbing the stairs. Nothing said *good morning* like dry heaving in Valkyrie HQ.

A light gleamed above her, in Grace's office. Hildie considered her options. She could try to run this search as quickly as possible. But Grace had a preternatural sense for when she was up to something and would emerge from the office in no time. Hildie was ten years old again, trying to pierce her own ear with a safety pin while Grace banged on the bathroom door.

Don't you dare!

Hildie hadn't heard that sort of urgency in her mother's voice for a long time. Though she'd almost expressed a feeling when they last spoke.

That time she all but forced me into taking leave and abandoning this case.

Hildie climbed the ladder. She wondered how many other dutiful daughters had done exactly this, in other eras. She would do her job. She would follow this weird trail of ylvish bloody bread crumbs, no matter where they might lead. Grace would have to officially suspend her, and then people would talk. Gossip came from the old word *god-sib*. Family murmuring. It could be as dangerous as a spear.

She entered just as the desk chair turned. An icicle formed in her stomach. "You . . . are not my mother."

"Nope." Shar was obviously trying to get into the computer. Her mother's computer.

What the hell?

"You live here now?"

Shar smiled thinly. "I just got here. Coffee's still brewing."

That moment in a conversation—when you realize someone you love isn't telling you something—always poses an interesting problem. Do you call out the lie immediately? Do you see where it leads?

Hildie smiled slightly. She couldn't help it. She'd come here to break the rules, and here was Shar doing the exact same thing.

"So, you're just low-key going through my mother's files because you couldn't sleep?"

Shar didn't even have the decency to look guilty. "I've been trying to find out more about this company, Caerleon. Grace owes me a couple favors, and I wanted to access a few of the office files, so . . ." She smiled. "Coffee? Or?"

Hildie wasn't sure what *or* meant.

She thought about the night at the club. The drink that tasted like summer. The kiss. Every kiss was a surprise, even when she could sense that it was coming. It always seemed to be leading somewhere, but Hildie wondered if a kiss could simply exist on its own. A sweet conclusion, rather than the frantic start to something even more intense.

People said the world was supposed to fall away when you kissed someone.

But in Hildie's experience, the world stayed where it was. It just got fuzzier. And then the worry crept in. Because a kiss was supposed to be an invitation, even when you didn't want it to be. And she couldn't kiss someone without second-guessing it.

Especially Shar.

"Coffee," she said.

Shar brought her a mug with an old *Far Side* cartoon. It was a cow in pearls, staring at her husband and saying, *Wendel, I'm not content.* "This one seemed to resonate with you."

Hildie laughed and took it. "First of all, you're doing a terrible job of breaking into my mother's computer. Can't you just foretell the password or something?"

"You really don't understand how fate works."

Hildie cackled, the laugh bursting out of her. "No. I really don't."

She typed in her full name, *Hildegard*.

The desktop was frighteningly well organized. She searched for *Caerleon*. There was a note about their claim to Hotel Wyrd. They owned property across the city. One address snagged her attention; she squinted at it, then swore. It was Percy's apartment. She scrolled down to a third address on Beach Street and wrote it down. She wasn't sure who lived there, but it was worth checking out.

"They own the suite where we found the second victim." Hildie cracked her knuckles. "They're also trying to steal your home. There's virtually no data on them, and it'll take forever to dig up anything at city hall. I need to visit this property on Beach—"

An email alert flashed across Grace's screen. The sender was anonymous, but there was a video attached. For a second, Hildie thought she knew what it might be.

But when she played it, she was still surprised to see Wayne. Unmasked at the Castle, in spite of their masquerade rules. Little shit.

The video played on a loop. Bert held Wayne close. They danced cheek to cheek. There was no sound. Bert whispered something in Wayne's ear. Wayne's expression was a mystery. The club seemed to revolve around them. She felt happy for Wayne, but that was quickly replaced by anger.

Shar frowned at the screen. "I know Vera's nephew, but who's sexy Paw Patrol with the beard?"

"He works for the provost," Hildie said. "He's slippery. Look." She reached over Shar to minimize the window. Then she logged into the cloud and opened up her directory of interview questions. Bert's file was composed of wry answers, none more than a few words. He'd managed to avoid saying anything at all.

Shar watched the video again. It was cute, if you ignored the POV. "Who was filming them? And what are they trying to tell us?"

"That they're watching," Hildie said. "The ylves said as much. Someone's after Bert as well. Though he's no saint."

"What did they say about him?"

Hildie stared at the grainy footage once more. Bert's arm around Wayne, spinning him in slow circles. "That he bought a poisoned arrow from them." Bert's expression too pixelated to make out. Two shadows dancing. "Paid for it with a bottle of wine."

Shar stared at her. "Ylves don't normally love wine."

"They do if it's old enough. And this was from somebody's private stock. Somebody who collected rare East Anglian red. Somebody who throws a lot of parties."

It wasn't easy to find Bert.

When she had interviewed him, she'd traced a discreet rune on his phone case. It was sketchy magic, but it should have given her access to the phone's GPS. The problem was that it wasn't working. His location kept spinning, like when you call an Uber and it's suddenly trapped in another dimension.

There were a number of possibilities. Someone could have broken her tracking spell, which admittedly hadn't been great to begin with. She'd never had a great talent for the limited runic alphabet that valkyries could call upon.

His phone could also be genuinely confused. Smartphones tended to lose their bearings in certain areas of the city, where older powers prevailed. But that didn't make her feel any better. The final possibility was that Bert could fly.

In the end, Hildie trusted in something more reliable than magic or technology.

Gossip.

She visited the kelpie, who was sunning herself in the hotel fountain. "What do you know about Bertram?"

The horse side-eyed her. Then snorted. Hildie saw it coming, but the spray still dampened the edges of her hair.

She pulled out two bags of Wendy's hamburgers. "There's a Frosty in here too."

The kelpie looked at her more closely. As if she'd just become interesting.

"Look," Hildie said. "You've got a nice setup here. I could make it even nicer. Daily hamburger deliveries. Access to a spa. I could also conveniently lose your interview file. No more annoying questions about the produce truck that you overturned, and all the delivery people that you tried to eat."

Apples was all the kelpie said.

"You like apples. I get that. And I can supply those too." Her eyes narrowed. "Or I could call animal control."

The kelpie stared her down.

Then she said *Jacuzzi.*

Hildie smiled grimly. "Who says legends can't adapt?"

After the second burger, the kelpie gave her something. It wasn't much—Hildie still didn't even know where Bert lived—but she did get another address. A commercial space.

Good apples there, the kelpie had said. She had a one-track mind.

Hildie exited the Main Street SkyTrain station. A silver dome loomed over it all. They'd built it for Expo 86, which had propelled the city onto the international scene. It always reminded Hildie of those old-fashioned typewriter balls, which Nan had let her play with when she was four years old. A whole language in the palm of her hand. The geodesic dome, it was rumored, had been programmed to display lights in various colors. But the fabulous 1980s technology had sputtered out, and now the dome just twitched random lights at night, like flashbulbs going off. Once you got used to it, the erratic display was sort of comforting. The dome was doing its best.

A few people were boarding the Granville Island Aquabus—like a modern Venetian gondola that brought you to the realm of crafts and craft beer. Hildie briefly thought about how nice it would be to hop on. She could wolf down some perogies in the market, then gaze at the concrete silos painted by Brazilian artists to look like giants. Sometimes she liked to imagine them coming to life and smashing everything, like the giants in old Anglish poems that Nan had read to her. Grace hadn't liked that, but Hildie enjoyed the sharp sounds of the language in her ears. Nan always growled her *R*s, which made Hildie laugh.

Main and Third was an industrial corner, tucked away from the bus route. There were a few old apartments, some supply stores, and something that looked like a café that had stalled before opening. There was a door around back. Hildie expected trouble getting in, but the door was ajar. Nobody guarding the threshold. She listened carefully: all she could hear was a kind of white noise in the distance. Not exactly power. Something different?

Hildie walked down a flight of stairs into a surprisingly tidy basement space where a group of people mingled among folding chairs. There was a knit rug on the concrete floor, and coffee with artisanal doughnuts on a side table. She took a doughnut because her stomach was growling, then grabbed a chair near the back. The crowd resembled a condo strata meeting. Nobody looked like a knight or a runesmith, and the more she tried to sniff them out, the less she was able to sense.

It occurred to Hildie that this place was a dead spot. A place where someone—or something—had muted the volume on every kind of power.

Oh. It clicked.

A hush fell over the room. Then Bert appeared in the aisle. He looked more confident than she'd ever seen him, as if this was his safe space. There was something in his step. He didn't see Hildie as he walked to the front, where a makeshift podium had been set up. Just a card table with a crate on top of it. All eyes were on him.

"I'm Bertram," he said.

They greeted him warmly.

This was an MA meeting. Magic Anonymous.

"You've heard stories from me before," he continued. "All true—though names have been changed to protect the innocent. I've used people, like pieces on a board. I've hurt them. Broken them. I've done awful things. I don't even remember half of them. But all that pain and regret never goes away. The powers that I dealt with—the chaos that I caused—I thought I could pay the price. When others paid it for me, I didn't stop."

He spoke with a conviction that went beyond the experience of someone in his twenties. This wasn't just Bert speaking; this was all of his shadows. A whole line of relations, probably going back to the iron age, or even further.

"I thought," Bert said, "that it fixed things. Power. Isn't that what we're taught? I used it like duct tape. Like I was trying to hold together a condemned property, one crack at a time. I let people control me. They—" He shook his head as if to clear it. "I've been here before. And now there's something good in my life. I think—I know—I'll be okay."

Everyone clapped. As Bert took a seat, he saw Hildie, and his face went pale.

That's right, you little shit. Your cloak-and-dagger game has consequences.

256

They sat politely through the next several speakers. There was a middle-aged woman who talked about the damage she'd done in a previous relationship. A nonbinary person who had a taste for fire runes. A kid—barely thirteen—who spoke numbly about using power against a predator who wouldn't leave him alone. Grief hung in the room, but also a sense of determination and a desire for change.

When the meeting was over, they all filed outside. Bert had the decency to wait for her. No use running now.

"Came for the snacks?" The smile didn't reach his eyes.

Hildie thought about all the ways in which Bert had probably been manipulating her investigation. She remembered her conversation with the ylves. Her hand still ached.

Her mother was going to have kittens. Rage kittens who'd devour them all.

"You haven't been completely honest with us," Hildie said. "You've messed quite liberally with my case. And you're currently my favorite suspect."

His expression shifted. "It's not that simple and you know it."

Hildie drew closer. "I know you bought contraband from a bunch of ylves. Paid for it with wine from Morgan's cellar. How am I doing so far?"

Bert sighed. He looked almost relieved for a second, to be caught. Then a mask seemed to slam over his face. "It's my mess."

Hildie cycled through a number of responses. Then she asked herself, *What would Nan do?*

"Come on," she said. "You owe me a drink. For the sake of hospitality."

He half smiled. "You know I can't say no."

Myths like Bert had a connection to households. They were always attached to lavish feasts. And they never turned down the opportunity to take a shot.

They went to the Fairview, a dive bar on Cambie Street that had pretty much ignored every trend since the '80s. Hildie appreciated the brass fixtures and the crumbling vinyl booths, and there were no artisanal cocktails in sight. She ordered a vodka water to pace herself. Bert drained a pint of Granville Island lager in the first five minutes, then ordered another. He didn't seem fazed. She imagined that he could probably suck back a drinking horn of mead and still walk a straight line. Forest spirits were like that—if that's what he was.

They didn't say much for the first round of drinks. Bert wasn't quite uncomfortable, but he wasn't being charming either. She'd thrown him off by showing up at the meeting—his intimate space. Surprise could be a good tactic when nothing else worked.

"The Office of Valkyries has a long file on you," Hildie said. "It's full of holes, like a moth-eaten tapestry. Some of it's protected by passwords that people have forgotten over time. Even my mother has trouble with it."

He smiled slightly. "I have had a bit of an affair with trouble."

Hildie decided to do something odd. She pulled out her tablet, opened up Bert's file, and handed it to him. "Want to add anything?"

She watched him scan the long document, paging down with his finger. There was something in his eyes. Was it laughter? Or pride?

"Birthplace: Castle of the High Wastes." He chuckled. "That's one translation. Not where I was born though." His eyes went distant for a moment. "It was a spring near the mountains. The water was so cold and clean, like drinking from a glacier. That's where she found me." Something in his eyes slammed shut.

"You mean Morgan."

"She didn't have a name back then. She was all feathers and fangs. I guess I was her apprentice. She'd had others, but they didn't work out. The Irish kid with the spear. The wanderer. The Very Black Witch. They all failed her in some way. But she saw something in me." He took a long sip. "Maybe I was just scrappy enough. Maybe I had no one else. But when she offered me a deal, I took it."

Hildie resisted the urge to order another. She needed to stay clear-headed. "And what was that deal exactly?"

Bert surprised her by ordering garlic wings. He deflected her questions until the food arrived. He was controlling the conversation in a genial, but still tactical, way. It surprised her. Beneath the smiles and the hipster beard, he was as much of a player as Morgan was. Something slightly dangerous in the body of a cuddly grad student.

"She called it a game," he said, once he'd polished off the wings and licked the sauce from his fingertips. "I'd be her weapon, and she'd be my patron. I was an enforcer. Professional shit-disturber. I broke up fancy dinners and challenged knights. Sometimes I delivered their heads. It was"—he ran a hand through his hair—"exhausting. She cooled down a bit. Focused more on killing careers than actual people. For a while, I almost had a normal life. Then all this shit started with Mo Penley and—" He seemed about to say another name but stopped himself.

Hildie glanced around the bar. Nobody seemed to be paying attention. She noticed a nurse who might be a witch, but she was fully absorbed in a book.

"I don't think you killed Penley," she said in a low voice. "But you definitely used ylvish contraband to put him out of commission. Why?"

A weird expression crossed his face. Like he was trying to ignore something painful. "I can't say much," he said, "but we weren't trying to hurt him. We wanted to protect him—take him out of the game for a bit."

Something clicked. "The rune on Morgan's staircase. That's why it was pushing everyone away. You were trying to keep him safe in that room."

"We were too late, though. Once you wake that thing up, you can't put it back in the box."

"What thing?"

Bert stood up. "She's watching you," he said matter-of-factly. "But at least you know that. When you can't see her, that's when you should worry." He started to leave.

"Wait—"

"I have to get out of here."

"*Wait.*" Hildie couldn't think of anything to say. Instead, she grabbed a bone from his plate and threw it at him. It bounced off his green cardigan, leaving a sauce print.

He stared at her. "Are you twelve?"

She shrugged. "Valkyries excel at anger, not maturity."

"What do you *want*?"

Hildie almost laughed. *To solve this case? To keep everyone alive? To make my mother stop sighing whenever she sees me? To not set fire to the only relationship in my life that's ever sustained me?*

"I saw you," she said finally, "dancing with him."

Bert's eyes hardened. "You know stalking isn't the same as detection."

"It's on video, Bert. Someone recorded you and sent us the file. Morgan may be watching me, but someone's watching you as well."

He shrugged. "You don't stay in my position without making enemies."

"What about Wayne?"

His expression softened. "He doesn't know the first thing about this."

"He's a knight, like you. He's involved."

"I'm not a knight." Bert's smile was bleak. "I'm a monster."

"So's Oscar the Grouch. He doesn't go around beheading people." Hildie gave him a long look. "You don't have to be a single story."

"That's rich coming from a legacy valkyrie."

Hildie exhaled. "Tell Wayne the truth about your connection to Morgan. If he's going to stay alive, he needs to know."

Bert leaned in closer. "Sure. I'll tell him, as soon as you tell the First Valkyrie that you're flirting with one of the Wyrd Sisters."

That struck her speechless.

Had he seen them at the Castle? Or did Morgan know everything?

Bert's voice lost its edge. "I didn't plan for this thing to happen with Wayne. I've been involved with a lot of knights. It never really meant anything until now. Or . . ." He shrugged. "I don't know. Maybe it was always him, and I finally just figured it out. But it has nothing to do with all of this bullshit. I'm not going to hurt him. We don't get to choose our relationships. But you have to cut me some slack."

Hildie didn't trust him. But she didn't trust herself either.

"Tell me," she said, "about the monster in the box."

Bert's eyes darkened. "No need," he said. "It's always behind you."

Then he left before she could throw more bones at him.

24

WAYNE

Bert was asleep and dreaming. His legs twitched like a dog. Maybe he was chasing a cat, or leaping through a sprinkler. Whatever it was, he looked happy. His face was a blank page. No lines on his forehead. Wayne's mother had told him once that he looked like a disgruntled opera-goer when he slept, all frowns and light snarls. He watched Bert for as long as it was socially acceptable to do so. There were faint scars on his body, which Wayne felt like he couldn't ask about. Not yet. This moment—the perfectly preserved second date—was a bubble that would burst at any moment. It had to.

Bert was the type of guy that you'd see on a bus, reading a book standing up. Just entirely complete with no permeable edges. And you'd glance at him, wonder about him, never say anything. You'd watch him get off the bus with a sense of numbness, rather than piercing regret. Because why would you ever think of talking to someone like that? Someone who balanced so easily on a moving hinge, reading one-handed, smiling secretly at something on the page?

And now here they were. Matter and antimatter, colliding in bed. Wayne had to leave before everything fell apart, while he still could.

The problem was that he couldn't find his shirt.

It's fine, he thought, shimmying into his pants. *It's just under something.*

But a quiet search turned up nothing.

Wayne tried not to worry as he pulled on his socks. But by the time he'd rescued his wallet and keys, the vague nightmare was turning into a reality.

He had no idea where it was.

Wayne stood shirtless in the kitchen, slowly turning like a figurine in a music box. The turning normally helped him think. But it wasn't helping now.

It was his Neuro Queer shirt. The worn-in one that felt like wearing a cloak of air. The most identifiable piece of clothing that he owned, the one most likely to cause a weird conversation that he'd need to parachute out of. The shirt that had basically outed him to Bert in the first place.

Wayne knew what he had to do. It was obvious. Just one second, and he'd be out of the apartment. But what would it look like?

1. I stole your sweater because I'm a stalker—surprise!
2. I stole your sweater because of poor executive functioning—signed, Brain.
3. I stole your sweater to use in a love ritual that will bind our hearts forever and the only side effect is that we're going to the Bad Place.

Bert's sweater was draped over a chair, where it seemed to beckon, like a sly emerald. Wayne picked it up. *Do not inhale. Do not.* It smelled like campfires and saltwater and boy. Like Bert. Wayne tried not to think about how soft it was, how broken down in the right places, how it was nearly as comfortable as the shirt he'd lost.

There was an instrument case beneath the futon; he hadn't noticed it before. Bert continued to snore. Wayne smiled at the thought of Bert playing trumpet or saxophone. He gently flipped open the lid, and then froze.

It wasn't a trumpet.

It was an axe.

The weapon was in two parts, lying snugly in green velvet. The edges reminded him of half-moons. There was a rune carved into the blade. It looked like a stylized *B*. Wayne remembered that it meant beginnings, or was it endings? Maybe it was just his name rune. *B* for *B*. He should take a picture and send it to Kai. But he couldn't quite make his arms work.

When he got control of his breathing, he closed the lid and shoved the case back under the futon. He could almost feel the metal, pressed against the back of his neck.

Mo Penley had lost his head.

An axe like that—

Bert stirred in his sleep.

Wayne crept out of the apartment, closing the door gently.

It could be for protection.

But from what?

Wayne couldn't think about it anymore. He popped in his earphones and listened to Troye Sivan singing about how he still sees an ex in his dreams. It kept him from having to interact with strangers, but also reminded him of the dreams he'd had about Bert—and the beast. Were they connected?

The snow was thickening. No longer a playful feathery cover. It had purpose. He should go home while he still could.

Burrard Skytrain Station was oddly silent. The cherry trees had all gone to sleep for the winter, and nobody else was on the platform. The train screeched toward him—one of the old red-and-blue Expo trains that sounded like a monster.

They flew past Granville and emerged into the open air. He saw the dome at Main Street, glowing like some medieval cupola on top of a church. Nobody got on the train. He had it all to himself. He leaned against the door, brazenly.

Something flickered within the dome.

For a second, it looked like a face. Human or animal, he couldn't tell.

The lights flickered off.

Grayish sun trickled through the window, but now the car was full of shadows. Wayne tried not to freak out. *Just some computer glitch.* He tried a grounding technique. What were five things that he could see? The face in the dome. The shadows skittering at his feet. The cut of winter sky above him. The face in the dome—now just eyes. Just eyes.

The train kicked into high gear. He fell against one of the vinyl seats. The car screamed along the track now. He'd never felt it moving this fast before. Something was wrong. He tried to name something he could touch, but all he could feel was vertigo. They whipped past the harbor. The water roiled below. Something struck the window, hard. A crow?

There was an awful, grinding, scraping noise. Then the feeling of a void opening inside of his body as the train jumped the track.

He was falling and screaming and then—

—flying.

The car flew over the water. He thought he might be sick or pass out, but neither of those things happened. It felt as though they were circling, like a plane that hadn't yet been given permission to land. His ears kept popping.

Then the lights flicked back on.

He could hear something else—maybe in the next car over. Music?

Where were Kai and Hildie when he needed them?

Slowly, as if he doubted his own legs, Wayne stood. He made his way to the back of the car, holding onto the hand-grips. The music was louder. He stared at the safety door. The sticker told him *absolutely do not open this.*

He braced himself against the door and pushed.

It slid open roughly. Now the air was screaming all around him. A thin metal coupling linked his train car with the next.

Don't look don't look don't you fucking look—

Wayne took two steps onto the metal bar. Now he was fully outside, and there was no time to think about what that meant. The train bucked, and he grabbed onto the next safety door for support. He might have been crying, or gasping—the air sucked away everything.

He managed to get the door open and crumpled into the next car. His legs were toast.

It took him a moment to get his bearings, if those even existed anymore. He was still in a SkyTrain car, but this one looked more like an apartment.

Someone had wedged a couch into the back of the car. Most of the seats had been removed and replaced with bookshelves. They rattled along with the car, but they'd been secured to the wall with cable ties. There was a rug spread across the ground. *Was* it a rug? It could have been a tapestry. He saw knights that looked almost pixelated, a woman with gray eyes, dozens of beasts watching from the margins of a dense forest.

There was a record player in the corner, balanced on a milk crate. He recognized the song now. It was from one of Aunt Vera's favorites, Bonnie Bramlett. Singing about how you can need someone without wanting them.

A familiar man was sitting on the couch, next to a pile of leather-bound photo albums. Wayne recognized his uncle from old pictures, though they probably hadn't seen each other since he was six years old. He'd been an athlete once, but, like Henry VIII, he'd grown portly. His red beard was streaked with gray. His eyes danced with light. The type of person who'd buy you a drink, then challenge you to a fight in the same breath. He was barefoot—this was his place, after all, even if it happened to be on a flying train—but the sight of his pale feet was somehow unnerving.

"Gawain." He made a beckoning motion. "Come sit with me."

"Uncle Arthur." He wasn't quite willing to cozy up to his convict relative. A person he'd heard several hair-raising stories about. A person his mother had forcibly kept at a distance. But she was long gone.

"Please." He grinned, displaying a gold tooth. "Call me Artie."

He resembled Tony Soprano, not a fallen monarch. But Wayne didn't think he looked like a knight either. Soft around the edges, too quiet, too nervous, like a skittish cat who might scratch you at a moment's notice. No charming knight. No Gawain.

"Did you—" Wayne frowned. "Did you *bring* me here, somehow? I thought you were in prison."

Arthur gestured around them. "This is it, nephew. Home and prison."

"They stuck you in a SkyTrain?"

"More complicated than that, but yeah. Basically. What's your generation's version of a Hotel California? An Airbnb you can never leave?" He patted the couch. "C'mere."

Wayne took a seat on the floral couch. The springs protested, and he sank an inch or so, but it held in the end.

"I thought you'd come visit a long time ago. I've sent messages. I assume your mother dealt with those."

Wayne didn't ever want to talk about his mother. "I was told to keep my distance."

His grin didn't fade. "Smart. But you're here now. Anyway, that half sister of mine is tricky as a bag of knives, but she's keeping her eye on you. Protecting you."

Wayne realized he meant Morgan. He'd never been able to keep their queer family tree straight, but it did make sense that the two were related in some primordial way. Did that make Morgan Arcand his . . . half aunt? She seemed more likely to throw him to the wolves than buy him a snack, like Aunt Vera would have.

"She's *protecting* me?"

Arthur nodded. "Though with her, it can look a lot like chaos. Or worse. She was never great at showing affection, you know? We didn't exactly bond. I was a bastard—literally—and she always thought she could rule the kingdom better." He chuckled. "Maybe she was right."

Questions formed a traffic jam in his mind. *Why were you put in prison? What did you do to my family? On a scale of one to Babadook, how scared of you should I be?*

But he didn't look scary. He looked like Uncle Arthur. Artie. He'd always been jovial, always up for a game or a spot of mischief. People loved him. They just didn't trust him.

He was full of promise, Wayne's mother used to say, *but he threw it all away. He always throws it away.*

Uncle Artie opened one of the photo albums. They were the old-fashioned kind, with stiff pages covered in yellowing plastic. He pointed to a photo of a small boy.

"Recognize that little peanut?"

Wayne peered at the photo. He would have been maybe four at the time. His expression was slightly pained, as if the flash had startled him.

"Always with a book," Uncle Artie said. "That brain of yours. Your ma worried, but I never did. I knew what you were capable of."

That was news to Wayne. They'd never really had the chance to bond—not the way he'd bonded with Uncle Lance. But Lance had married in, as his mother used to say, so it was hard to say who was the true relative, or the imposter. Maybe they were all imposters. This was all a family game of love, death, and betrayal.

Artie flipped through the pages. He paused over a photo of Wayne's mother. She wore a sleeveless shirt, teal silk, and behind her was an explosion of lilac. Her expression was dreamy. She wasn't staring at the camera but into the distance, with a knowing smile. Her hair was tied in a messy bun, with a few strands falling out; even frayed, she was beautiful and sharp.

"Anna could play any instrument," his uncle said. "She could pick up a guitar and just strum it by ear. Beautiful voice." He closed his eyes. "I'm forgetting what it sounded like. You remember?"

"Her voice?" Wayne swallowed. "Sometimes."

She'd been gone six years, and it was fading. Everything was fading. Dad refused to talk about her. He missed their music together. The notes floating into the kitchen. The buzz of the old amp. His mother's cackle when something surprised her.

She'd seen it coming. The end of their marriage. Wherever she ran to. She'd seen it coming miles away.

"She still loves you, kid." Uncle Artie laid a paw on his shoulder. It was uncomfortable, but Wayne counted to five, then discreetly shifted away.

His uncle pointed to another image. A scrap of manuscript under glass. There was a king and queen near the top, watching, as if from a balcony. The perspective was strange. Beneath them was something—a shadow. The rest of the page had been torn away.

Wayne stared at the king. "Is it really *you*?" He blinked. "Like . . . do you remember it? Like those symbionts from *Star Trek* who inhabit different bodies?"

Artie smiled. "Don't know anything about *symbionts*. But yeah. I remember it—the way you remember a dream. It was me. It is me. And years from now, some shadow of me will look at this moment and wonder what we were thinking. What we were capable of."

"Is that how it works? We keep coming back until something changes? Or do we just keep doing the same thing, over and over?"

Artie scratched his beard. "Myths survive for two reasons," he said, "love and violence. Sometimes you whisper a story after dark; sometimes you tell it on the edge of a sword. Our kind came here a long time ago. To be close to the water. To change, maybe. Some generations come back whole, and some are like pieces of a puzzle, dragging themselves back together." His eyes grew dark. "We didn't ask permission. We took what we wanted. But the older stories—they never left. Now everything's all mixed up. Vera thought we should adapt. Cede the territory. Live with all kinds of stories."

Wayne swallowed. "What did you think?"

Artie seemed about to reply. Then, before Wayne could protest, he picked up an old camera and took a picture of them both, sitting on the couch.

"Old-timer selfie. With real film. Maybe I'll develop it, once I get out of this place."

The thought of him getting out was more than unsettling— especially because Wayne still had no idea exactly why he'd been locked up here. Wherever *here* was.

His mother had only mentioned Arthur once, in her second-to-last letter. *He was put away for good reason. Boys can be deadly, and he was always somewhat childish. Stay away from him, Wort. He thinks everything's an adventure. That's all he cares about. The beast, the hunt, the ghost story.*

Wayne summoned up a flash of courage. "Why are you here?"

Uncle Artie looked at him for a while. Not speaking. He licked his lips, and the gesture reminded Wayne of a cornered wolf. He opened his mouth, and Wayne could see his gold teeth, like coins in a dragon's hoard.

"I started a war," he said. "It's still going on. But I'm stuck on this train going nowhere." He laughed.

"But who put you here?"

Artie glanced at the safety door, as if he'd heard something. "Time's almost up," he said. "Time's a monster that way. It was nice seeing you, kid. And—if you'd be so kind—I want you to deliver a message. To Auntie Vera."

Wayne grew cold. Any message he wanted to give her was probably bad. Still, this was the first time they'd spoken in years. Maybe he'd changed.

Did he even have a choice?

Wayne nodded. "Okay."

"Tell her . . ." Uncle Artie leaned in close. Wayne could smell the whiskey on his breath, like a tongue of flame. "To stop underestimating her family."

The safety door opened a crack.

Wayne digested this message. "That's . . . all you want me to tell her?"

Uncle Artie's face softened for a moment. "She knows the rest. Now go."

Wayne paused. He knew he had to ask a question, but everything was happening too fast, the opening door, the moving shadows, his stomach lurching.

"Uncle Lance is back," he said slowly, with great effort.

"Lance. The loyal one." Darkness flashed across his uncle's face—a dangerous flush in his cheeks. "The ones we love cut us deep."

Wayne knew it was best not to ask about this. "Where did he go?"

Arthur smiled. "To hell. To a forest. To kill a quest, before it killed him." He tapped his fingers against the camera. "Not sure how he did though. Still a work in progress."

"You mean—"

"Never say its name, kid." Arthur's face was in shadow now. "Never look behind you either. Just keep moving forward."

The train lurched in midflight.

A paw broke through the safety glass.

"Why?" Wayne stared at his uncle, heart pounding. "Why did you bring me here? What is that thing? Why is any of this happening."

The record made a *screeeee* noise as the needle cut across it.

Something was climbing through the shattered window—many somethings—moving slowly and with great purpose, like blood seeping through cloth.

Artie shrugged. "You'll have to ask her."

But which *her*?

Morgan?

Aunt Vera?

His mother?

For a second, Wayne heard her voice.

Then the car went dark. His blood was pounding in his ears. He couldn't breathe.

The car lurched back onto the track. The lights flickered back on. Uncle Artie was gone. His apartment was gone. Though he saw a thread from the carpet pressed against the vinyl seat.

The next station, the train announcement said, *is Camelot.*

He stared up at the loudspeaker. It had said *Commercial*, not *Camelot*.

He was almost sure of it.

25

HILDIE

Hildie paused outside the entrance to Hotel Wyrd. The snow was coming down now. Everyone had that shocked west coast look, as if it had started raining frogs. Gastown was blanketed in white, and it reminded her momentarily of the furs in Morgan's office, soft and menacing.

Wasn't there a medieval story that revolved around Christmas? Something she remembered reading a long time ago, back when she'd tried to get a degree in something. There was a monster, and Christmas dinner, and a fairy-tale castle. But in the end, it wasn't what you thought.

Kai was gazing at the Victorian entrance to the hotel. "I've always wondered where this place was," she said. "My mom told me about it."

"Children sometimes spot it," Hildie said absently. "If you try too hard, it'll give you a migraine. Valkyries can taste it."

She wanted to keep both Wayne and Kai close. Wayne was currently unaccounted for: a fact that was giving her a planet-sized migraine. But Kai had answered her text and met her near Gastown.

Kai blinked. "Did you say *taste*?"

Hildie nodded. "Old and kind of bitter. Like a pickle in the back of the fridge."

"A fridge pickle." Kai flicked the hair from her eyes. "That's what the sisters who shape life and death taste like. Noted."

"That's how the *building*—never mind." Hildie was about to lead her through the entrance, then stopped. "Before we go any further, tell me what you've been working on. When we met earlier, you said something about protection. If this is going to backfire and make a nuclear-sized hole in my case, I need to know."

Kai's expression was evasive. "It's not like I'm doing it on my own. Vivian helped. Well . . . she gave me the frame that I needed, sort of. It's hard to explain in words. But you can think of it as a trap. For a monster."

Hildie would have to check on Vivian's file, but if she remembered correctly, it was nearly as long as Morgan's. She was an enchantress with serious firepower, though she generally kept it in the gray zone. Where Morgan zigged, Vivian zagged. She was a kind of steward, when it served her. Morgan had always been an independent contractor.

"It sounds like you're getting mixed up in some deep quantum shit," Hildie began, "and you may think you're handling it well, but you're young."

"My thoughts aren't."

Hildie sighed. "Look. This monster—whatever it is—you can't just throw a leash around its neck and hope for the best."

"Less of a leash," Kai said, waving her hand vaguely, "more of a . . . reboot."

"What does that mean?"

"Well, it's still in the beta stage." Nerdy excitement flashed across her face. "But I'm working online with a whole community of runesmiths. Wayne"—she glanced at her phone again—"he keeps talking about the questing beast."

"We're looking for a real-life killer, not a myth."

Kai made a face. "We're *all* myths. But anyways. If there really is some legendary monster involved in all of this, we need to contain it. I'm hoping this might work."

Hildie thought about it. The animal marks. The chaos of the scenes—mingled with control. It was possible. Someone could be working with . . . whatever this thing was. Not a super-powered killer, but someone trying to rein in a runaway nightmare. Could they really gamble on the kind of myth that never seemed to appear?

"What do you mean," she said, "by *reboot*?"

But then something shifted in the air around them. Something was wrong: she could feel it like a chill descending on the hotel. There was no more time.

"Tell me later," Hildie said. "We have to move. And keep texting Wayne. I can't have him wandering around like a sketchy extra."

They stepped into the lobby. There were wet half-moon hoofprints all over the carpet. Other than that, the space was empty. Weird, for the middle of the day.

Hildie rang the bell. There was no answer.

She glanced at her phone. Shar hadn't replied to her text.

"Okay," she said. "Follow me. This place is wonky."

Kai raised an eyebrow. "I need more."

"Don't get lost," she said. "Or you'll stay lost."

On a hunch, she peered behind the front desk. There was a stack of papers. What looked like a deed, though it was in Latin. She should have paid more attention before she dropped out of college. She pocketed the deed. It might come in handy later.

They stepped into the elevator.

Shar had always operated it. Hildie wasn't sure it would even respond to her.

Kai tapped her foot. "Did you forget which floor we're going to?"

"It's not a normal elevator." Hildie laughed. "As if anything in our lives is normal. It's more like the great glass elevator."

"I have no idea what that is."

She rolled her eyes. "You need an education in the classics."

Hildie felt something rearrange the plates in her skull. A violent skittering of power that went through all of them, like they were paper dolls.

The elevator lurched. Then they descended.

The doors opened. They stepped into the undercroft of the hotel. It was full-on snowing down here, visible flurries, and she pulled her jacket closer. Kai stared at the flakes in delight. She stuck out her tongue to catch one.

Hildie led them to the chamber with the bier, where the sisters performed their examinations. There was ice in her lungs now. She expected to see Shar. Instead, Clywen was sitting on the floor. She kept picking up and discarding scrolls rapidly. Braeda was having several high-pitched conversations at once on her earpiece. As Hildie got closer, she saw ghostly windows of data open above her, spinning like cards in a wind.

It struck her all at once. A blow that stole the air from her lungs.

Hildie folded her arms. "Where's Shar?" Her voice was softer than she'd intended. Not a valkyrie's voice. More like a child.

Clywen gave her a distracted look. There were tattered ribbons in her hair, and the indoor winds made them flutter. Her eyes were red-rimmed. As Hildie stared, those eyes became tunnels, leading somewhere she didn't want to go.

"Taken," Clywen said.

Hildie's heart dropped to the ground. *"Where?"*

Clywen shook her head. "The knight. We should have seen. That thread. Always causing trouble. That little gray thread—imagine what it was capable of!"

A tremor hit the building.

Hildie stumbled. A crack appeared in the floor.

She raked a hand through her hair. This wasn't just Shar popping out to the store. The hotel would only react this way if she'd been taken by force. The space was rapidly crumbling without the three sisters to maintain it.

Braeda finally noticed her. She paused all her windows. "We're looking absolutely everywhere, but she must be under some kind of veil. I'm calling in every favor." There was a pile of discarded coffee cups behind her. "Shar's smart though. She'll find a way to send us a message. She'll be fine. Fine."

They were coming undone.

"Clywen!" Hildie snapped her fingers. An aftershock made her stumble again. This was no time to be polite. "I need something—a location, a hint—anything. *Who* could have taken Shar, and where would they go?"

Clywen seemed to focus again. "The brooch," she murmured.

Hildie's eyes brightened. "*Yes*. The brooch. Did you decode the inscription?"

"He was a good boy," Clywen said faintly. "A bully sometimes, but bullies are often just children crying out in the dark. Always under his brother's shadow."

"I need more than riddles!"

Braeda grabbed the brooch and put it in Hildie's hand. "She means Bors." Bors. Boris.

"Wasn't he raised by the Lady of the Lake?"

"Fostered, yes. Along with his brother." Braeda pulled up a glowing file and let it hang in the air. A handsome knight with something hidden in his eyes. There was anger beneath that beauty. His smile was practiced, as if he was always posing for a photograph.

"Uncle Lance," Kai said.

Clywen gave her an approving look. "Both were fostered," she said. "One grew to fame. The other stayed in shadows."

Hildie's mind was working a mile a minute.

Lancelot and Bors shared protective brooches. Bors must have been working for Lance. The brooches had let them both move undetected. Was Lance the shadow she'd felt at the party?

"Lance is the architect," she breathed. "Bors was the muscle. That still doesn't explain the ylf shot, though, or Morgan's involvement. And why would Lance kidnap Shar? Braeda, what was she working on? What was the last thing she was doing?"

This was getting worse by the second. A knight who had nothing to lose.

"Fighting our legal case." Braeda was scanning through more files. She pulled up the lease agreement for the hotel. It was in several ancient languages, including Brythonic and what might have been Indo-European. Hildie's vision swam. But she recognized a word or two.

"Caerleon Corp," Hildie said. "Of course. It's an old name for Camelot. Lance was trying to buy the hotel out from under you. And Shar figured it out." Now Hildie was coming undone. She willed her body to stop shaking. "So, what? He's holding her ransom?"

Clywen shook her head. "I fear not."

Shar was the person Hildie would want to see at the end of the world, as the sun was winking out. Maybe the only person who saw her, and demanded no compromises.

"Would he"—she couldn't say *kill*—"is it even possible?"

"We're all threads," Braeda said breathlessly. "Threads can be—"

Hildie raised her hand to stop the word. "But *why*? What could he possibly have to gain by eliminating Shar?"

The sisters both shook their heads.

Finally, something they didn't know.

Hildie breathed in and out. In and out.

Threads.

Bert buys the ylf shot. Morgan puts Mo into a kind of trance. To get him out of the way? Or maybe she'd wanted something else. His power? His life?

Hildie felt herself pacing. "Okay. Morgan kills her upstart competitor. Maybe. Is Lance working with her? They've been entangled before. There was a whole thing I remember reading about in Grace's files—he was injured once and had to stay in her castle. Or maybe she kidnapped him. There are so many stories, and they rarely agree with each other."

"Stories are living things," Clywen said absently.

Hildie tried not to stare at the cracks forming in the floor. "What if something went wrong with the ylf shot—the dose was too potent? The other deaths could have been meant as a cover. So we'd think there was a serial killer."

Clywen had returned her attention to the storm of scrolls. Braeda was still paging through ghostly screens above her.

"I have to think like a knight," Hildie said. "Valkyries are different. We maintain order. Knights are all about pageantry. Ceremony. Telling stories. Maybe Lance is back because he wants something to change. A new story." She turned to Kai. "You've met him. Can you think of where he might go? What his next move could be?"

Kai looked up from her phone. "Wayne has never gone this long—"

"Kai, *focus*. Wayne is a knight—he's not helpless. Right now we need to track Lance before this hotel turns into a neutron star. What do you know about him?"

"Not—not much." Hildie had never heard her sound less certain. "He'd drop in to visit sometimes. Cute and charming—like a minor celebrity. Wayne's mother was always pissed at him. Once, I remember, she said he'd gotten mixed up with something dark. Something she wanted no part of."

Hildie was nodding. "Knights are stories. And stories repeat. They're driven by desire and conflict." Her eyes sharpened. "What did Lance *want*? What did he want more than anything else? What has he always wanted?"

"He was the loyal one," Clywen observed. "Until it fell apart."

"Loyal to Arthur." Hildie felt something else click into place. "I think I know what a disgraced knight would want. But we need help."

She slipped the brooch into her pocket. It singed the tips of her fingers, like a dragon's kiss.

❧

She was tired of knights. Tired of her own kind, even. Valkyries who mostly did paperwork and solved problems for the rich and immoral.

"Hildie?" Kai was staring at her. "Where are we going?"

"Goddamn knights."

"What?"

"The person I care most about in the world could be—" Hildie swallowed. "This is all because of their weird power trips. What does their king even do? Arthur's in prison. Morgan attends faculty meetings. Vera lives in a tiny apartment. What's so great about a crown that someone would do all this?"

"I don't know anything about it," Kai said slowly. "I was supposed to be a knight. But I went in a different direction. So I was never part of that. But . . . I don't think this is about ruling or whatever. I think it goes deeper than that. Wayne's whole family is involved somehow." She frowned suddenly. "Wait. You and the Wyrd Sister. Are you . . . ?"

"It's fucking *complicated*, Kai."

Her phone rang. It was Grace.

She's using the phone part of the phone. That's not good.

Hildie jammed it back in her purse. They were hiking up Thurlow Street, toward the West End. The sky was the color of a frozen pond. Everyone looked horrified by the weather, though it was already snowpocalypse in Alberta.

"Lance must have sent that video," Hildie said, almost to herself.

Kai stopped. "What video?"

"Shar and I saw a clip of Wayne dancing—with Bert. When we were all at the club. Lance obviously sent it as a warning. Or maybe a distraction."

"To throw you off the scent, maybe? Get you to focus on Bert so that you wouldn't notice when he kidnapped the sister?" Kai almost seemed to relax. "So maybe he's fine."

"Nobody's fine." Hildie kept walking toward the West End. Kai kept up without much effort. They were silent for a while. A single flake of snow fell in Hildie's hair. As a child, she would have loved it. Now it felt like winter was telling them something.

They came to Vera's apartment.

She didn't bother buzzing. Just let the tip of her spear manifest for a second and passed it through the deadbolt. The door shuddered, then clicked open.

"Badass," Kai said.

"Yeah, well, that's not what you're supposed to use it for."

"That thing's like a dangerous can opener."

All she could think about was the unfolding incident report, which already involved breaking and entering, ignoring calls for backup, and concealing information from her superior. Who, in this case, was her mother.

She started it.

They went upstairs. Vera's lobby smelled like cedar moth repellant, along with a faint patina of mold that was the finishing touch for every

West End apartment. Hildie knocked on the door. It opened before she could knock twice. Gale stood in the doorway. His hair was a mess of cowlicks, and it seemed as though he hadn't slept.

He blinked. "Oh. You're both here. I didn't even realize you knew each other. But where's Wayne?"

"Not answering his texts," Kai said. "Giving me a slow-moving heart attack. Putting us all in crisis mode. Hi, Nuncle Gale."

He put an arm around her. "Why do you never come over anymore? We used to see you all the time."

Her expression seemed to dim. "I know. I miss you both. Things have been *deeply* weird."

Hildie edged past him and stepped into the cluttered living room. Vera was on the couch surrounded by a stack of yellowed papers. Some of them looked like old manuscripts. Others might have been files or records of some kind. She was more put together than Gale, though her expression was also brittle, like she'd been up half the night.

Vera didn't look up. "I suppose you're here for a verbal spar."

"Oh, we're past verbal." Hildie put her hands on her hips, then second-guessed the position and crossed her arms instead. "I have questions. And not a lot of time. If you answer them, I promise not to tear your bookshelves apart."

Vera's eyes narrowed. "You wouldn't."

"Tell me the truth about Percy. And Boris." She placed the brooch on the table. "Recognize this? Your ex had one just like it."

Vera seemed to sink into the couch. She stared at the brooch with something that might have been sadness. "Percy was innocent. He did freelance editing for my textbook. He was dropping off the page proofs, and—" She stared out the window. "I'm not sure. I think he and Lance must have run into each other. An accident of fate."

Kai stared at her. "You were seeing Lance?"

"Not in any real sense. After Mo, I started to catch glimpses of him. I thought my eyes were playing tricks on me. I'd see his reflection in a café window, the shadow of him on a bus, always in passing." There was faint hurt in her eyes. The pain of seeing someone after years, only to find them unreachable. "He never said anything to me. He was always just watching. But I thought I saw him one night, as Percy was leaving."

Something hardened in Kai's expression. "But you didn't tell Wayne. Or me. You just let him—" She looked away. "Percy's dead. Because nobody did anything."

Vera looked confused for a moment. Then comprehension dawned. Her eyes softened. "It was you."

Kai looked up. "What?"

"You were the girl he talked about. The one he was excited about meeting." She smiled. "That was the last thing I remember hearing from him. 'She's brilliant and beautiful. I can't wait to meet her.' Oh, Kai. I'm so sorry."

Tears fell silently down Kai's cheeks. But her face was locked in anger. "If you'd said something, I could have protected him. Wayne too. If—"

"Darling." Vera didn't dare touch her. "You're powerful. But you can't protect everyone. There's no way any of us could have known."

"I saw him too," Gale said softly. "Once in a crowded street. Again in the supermarket—just grinning at me in the frozen food aisle. I thought I was going crazy."

Vera sighed. "When Lance left, we both hoped he was going somewhere to get help. Somewhere he could detox or decompress. He was one of the knights who imprisoned Arthur—that wasn't easy. It took a psychic toll. We worried that he was getting involved with other parties—dark forces—but we could never confirm it. Wayne's mother tried to talk to me about it once. But then—" Something closed behind her eyes. "She was gone before we could learn the details."

Hildie frowned. "Did they leave together?"

"No," Gale said. "Lance left first. We thought he might be back in a few months, or years. But when the years flew by, it seemed like he was out of the game for good."

"Well, he's definitely fucking back," Hildie said through clenched teeth. "And there are all kinds of dark forces we could focus on, but right now, he's kidnapped Shar. Knowing he was at large might have prevented this."

I could have fixed it, she thought. *I should have known. Should have kept a closer eye on Shar. I kept involving her, digging her in further. And now?*

Vera's voice fell. "I'm sorry."

"Well, *sorry* is about as useful to me as a wellness seminar at the moment. This is bigger than just your ex, whatever he was. If Hotel Wyrd crumbles, the sisters won't be able to do their job. And none of us want to think about what that will mean for the billions of souls in need of their particular talents." Hildie took a breath. "Tell me about Boris. He's the only thing we have to go on right now. Lance must have killed him. Or something working for Lance. We're still not sure."

"Lance's stepbrother?" Gale frowned. "Kind of dim, but loyal. They grew up together. He was always a bit jealous of Lance. When your mother lives in a lake, your childhood ends up being a bit weird."

"Lance and Boris were working together, no?"

"I'm sure Lance promised him something. Unless it was Morgan pulling the strings. She and Lance had a bit of a thing, centuries ago."

Vera leaned forward. "We need to work with one person at a time. Why would Lance kidnap one of the sisters?"

"He's been working to buy up the hotel," Hildie said. "Going through a shadow corporation called Caerleon."

Vera exhaled. "If he really manages to expose the hotel and split up the sisters, there's no telling what will happen. All the myths could unravel."

"Maybe he really does want to be king," Kai said. "It could be canon. King Lancelot."

Everyone was silent for a moment.

Gale disappeared into the kitchen. He emerged with an old blue cookie tin, full of photos and old thread. "I might know where he's taken her." He sorted through the photos, then pulled one out. It was the same photo Hildie had seen in Morgan's guest room.

No. Not exactly the same. It was from a slightly different angle, and Gale was in the photo, and Morgan was the one behind the camera.

Lance had his arms around both of them, like he was holding them together. Grinning madly.

"He loved you both," Hildie said.

Vera and Gale exchanged a look.

"He had a lot of love," Gale said. "Among other things."

What did that mean?

Gale pointed to the background of the photo. "The Lost Lagoon in Stanley Park."

"That's where I met with the ylves," Hildie said. "Lost Lagoon. There are woods all around that part of the park. Lots of cover."

"It was one of Lance's favorite places," Gale said. "He always thought of the park as an ancient forest."

Was that why he'd burned the photo? To destroy anything that might lead them back to his own personal grove?

But Morgan was also in that photo. They had to be working together somehow.

Vera gave Hildie a pointed look. "What do ylves have to do with this?"

"Mo Penley's body tested positive for ylf shot. When I talked to the ylves"—she used *talked* in the loosest sense, still thinking of the bargain she'd made—"they said Morgan's assistant had bought the ylf shot from them. Morgan must have used it to incapacitate Mo. But then what happened? Did everything go off the rails?"

They could have been an unholy trinity. Lance, Morgan, and Bert. Bringing down Mo and starting a new monarchy. The first step: eliminate the only powers that were older and willing to hold them accountable. First Arthur, then the fates. Split up the sisters, carve up their home, maybe—

Maybe kill one of them. Or all. Was it possible?

She thought about the photo again. The last thing Mo Penley had seen.

"How close were Penley and Lance?"

"Not really friends," Gale said. "They ran in the same circles. Mo was kind of an asshole. He loved to remind me that he was an ally."

"They drank together sometimes," Vera added. "I didn't love it. But Lance could find anyone interesting."

Hildie touched the photo. "Would Lance have a copy of this?"

Gale nodded. "He took some photos when he left. I could never really imagine them on his desk though. He wasn't that sentimental. I was a bit surprised when he took them."

Hildie stared at the image again. "Morgan's version is so close—just with Lance missing. If they were working together, and Mo looked at both photos . . ." She tried to remember that ghostly feeling as he stared at the photo in Morgan's room. "Maybe it was Lance that he saw. In his final moment. He must have wondered about it. Like the photos were two different stories. Lance could have had Boris destroy Morgan's copy, so we wouldn't be focused on Lost Lagoon. If he'd always intended to make something happen there."

Kai frowned. "It could have been Bert though. I want to trust him. But what do we really know about him, other than he works for Morgan? I sort of feel like Wayne is—" She suddenly looked uncertain. "I don't know. Keeping him a secret. I know there are things he hasn't told me. It's not like him."

Hildie considered it. Bert had said he only meant to incapacitate Mo. But he also stood to gain a lot. A position at Morgan's side. A swank home in a city where homes were castles. An alliance with the knight who'd bring in some kind of new order. He'd always been an outsider: no name, no title, no past, just a green thread in a white loom.

But now there was Wayne. Did he mean something to Bert? Or was it all part of some game he was playing?

Kai reached into her bag and pulled out her laptop.

"I've got a bit of a plan," she said. "Something I've been working on. Half program, half spell. If that's the word for it. If we can get close to whoever this is—whatever power they're running—I might be able to bind it."

Vera's eyes darkened. "Kai, this isn't a class project."

"I know that. But Wayne kept talking about a beast. We're all hunting this beast, or being hunted by it—sometimes it feels the same. If Lance somehow has control of this thing, he could be using it to kill knights. I think I've got a way to press pause on that."

Gale started riffling through papers with a look of almost feverish excitement. He pulled out an old engraving of a chimera—a hybrid beast with too many heads and tails.

"You mean this? It's supposed to be a legend."

"So are we, love," Vera reminded him.

He stared at the image. "If Lance had control of this thing, he could do unspeakable damage. But it wouldn't be one-way. Something like that gets in your head."

"We could use that to our advantage," Hildie said. "Exploit any weaknesses. But we can't put Kai in harm's way."

"I won't be," Kai insisted. "I can hide behind a bush or whatever. Besides. Lance hasn't seen me in a long time." Her eyes flashed. "Not the real me, anyway. He might not recognize me until it's too late. All I need to do is get this rune program running, and if this beast is close enough, I should be able to put a leash on it. Sort of. It's a bit more complicated than that. But myths are like programs too. They can be rewritten."

Vera stood. "We'll revisit this when the time comes. But know this, girl." Her eyes pinned Kai to space for a moment. "If I say run, you run. Your mother will absolutely murder me if anything happens to you."

Kai nodded. "Yes, Auntie Vera."

"Now." Vera's expression was set. "Where the hell is my nephew?"

26

WAYNE

After the SkyTrain incident, Wayne felt untethered. He went home to shower and to think. He hated showering—it was all transitions, dry to wet, cold to hot. Afterward, he slipped the sweater back on, like a secret layer between his shirt and his jacket. The apartment was silent. His dad had left him a lasagne to microwave later. Dad love was often like that— consumable in some way, measurable in rides and hours. As certain as a receipt. There was also a Post-it on the fridge reminding him that his socks were falling apart. Lot had left some cash for him to go to the Bay downtown. It seemed like the first reasonable quest he'd been given.

He took a bus to avoid the SkyTrain. The engine rumbled like the fear in his gut. He pulled the cord once they reached Burrard Street, then wandered through the downtown core. Snow was falling on the construction around Robson Square. He passed by a store he used to love when he was young, but it now sold sporting goods, not books. Kai texted him, but he couldn't reply. He needed to gather his thoughts first.

The detail about Morgan had surprised him the most. He'd always thought the big bad enchantress was someone to watch out for. But

Arthur had said that she was protecting him. It didn't feel like protection. At the moment, shivering in his spring jacket, he felt distinctly vulnerable. What good was protection, magical or otherwise, when your incarcerated uncle could hijack your SkyTrain car? Mo Penley had been a powerful knight, and where did that get him? Dead in the middle of a party. No one had seen it coming.

His dad was trying to protect him in his own way. He kept food on the table, kept a roof over their heads. But when he'd appeared at Viv and Wally's place, there'd been a look on his face. He was out of his element. This had always been more his mother's world, and she wasn't dispensing any more advice. He'd come to the end of her letters.

His phone buzzed. Kai again. He put it back in his pocket.

Then he took it out again. Nearly texted Bert.

What do I say?

1. Is it possible that you might be a teeny bit of a serial killer?
2. Did you find my shirt?
3. Can't we just be kissing right now?

Though Wayne wasn't even sure he wanted that. The kissing part. Not that it wasn't lovely, but right now he wanted simpler things. Bert's hand on his own. Bert's whisper in his ear, distracting him with a joke.

Something flashed past him in a nearby alley.

Too small to be a person. Or a monster.

Wayne made his way carefully down the alley. The lights of Granville Street faded. He saw the shadow again; it nearly leapt over his feet. Wayne made the decision to stand still and wait. He ignored every alarm bell in his head that was screaming for him to run.

A fox emerged from the trash.

"Hey, buddy." Something in his heart soared. "I didn't realize you were still around. I guess things can't be all that bad, if you're still in the world."

It couldn't possibly be the same fox he'd seen on the mountain. There was no way. It looked the same though. Its dark eyes regarded him with something between curiosity and understanding. It wasn't afraid.

Wayne took a step forward. "I don't have much to offer. You could live under my bed, maybe. What do foxes eat?"

It stared at him for a long moment. Then it moved further down the alley. Wayne followed it to a ring of dumpsters. The fox jumped atop one of the giant trash piles and kept looking at him.

"What's your message, bud? I don't speak vulpine. Are you leading me somewhere?"

The fox made a chittering noise. Almost like a puppy's whimper.

Then it dashed down the alley.

"Wait!" Wayne chased the orange blur. "What are you always running from?"

The fox disappeared near the intersection of Granville and Davie. Wayne struggled to catch his breath. He was in terrible condition for a knight.

He could walk uphill, toward Aunt Vera's place. But then he'd have to answer all kinds of questions, or submit to a lecture. His mind was still grinding its gears.

Could you really date someone who has an axe under his futon?

Something had taken off Mo Penley's head like a dandelion. It couldn't have been Bert. They had been together. But there was that moment, when he'd left to replace the book. Could he have done it then? Maybe he was involved in a subtler way. Like how an inquisitor wouldn't *exactly* kill you, but they'd make your death possible. Thinking about subtext made his teeth hurt. He just wanted a clear answer.

Wayne sat down in a tiny industrial parklet. There used to be a famous gay bar across the street. The Odyssey. It closed before he was old enough to go—replaced by condos and an upscale fried chicken place—but he'd heard stories. He'd always wanted to go. Together and alone on the dance floor. A normal queer kid, instead of a weird, half-assed knight.

Shadows lengthened on the grass.

For the first time, Wayne didn't care if the beast caught him. What was the use of all this hiding when bad things could get you anywhere?

An odyssey was like a rambling quest. He'd read parts of it in a survey course. What stuck was that Odysseus wasn't the strongest hero. But he was clever.

Maybe it's more about knowing the right things. Knowing yourself.

He ignored his buzzing phone.

Someone was making their way across the park. A tall man in a wool greatcoat. He sat down on the bench next to Wayne. They hadn't seen each other in years. But Wayne recognized the laugh lines, the slightly arrogant cut of his smile, the eyes that invited you in and promised that everything would be fine. Though it never was. There was a silver brooch pinned to his coat. Two wolves—or were they ravens?—whispering into someone's ears. The three figures were braided together. Man wolf bird whispering. Wasn't a rune a whisper?

"Uncle Lance."

"Hey, nephew."

His voice was warm. The way he used to sound. Maybe he hadn't changed after all.

"I thought I saw you at the party."

Lance nodded, looking straight ahead. "Crazy night."

"Why did you come back?"

"Well." Lance sighed. "It's complicated. Remember what I told you the last time we saw each other?" He looked at Wayne. His smile was open. The old Uncle Lance.

"You told me to remember that I was a knight."

"That's right." Lance touched his shoulder lightly. "Before this is all over, make sure to hold onto that. Nobody can take it away."

"Uncle Lance—"

His fingertips brushed against Wayne's shoulder, a weirdly light touch. And he knew Wayne didn't like that. Which was odd.

Lance lifted his hand. Wayne saw that his fingertips were ink-stained. He'd traced a rune on Wayne's shoulder. It looked like a crooked finger. A watery rune. He heard waves lapping in his ears. The soft tattoo of rain. Felt himself drifting to sleep. The water. That had always been Lance's realm. He'd been raised on the beach. That's why he loved Vancouver so much.

"Why . . ."

"Hush, pup." Lance gently caught him as he fell. "All in good time."

The only light was green.

Funny that Bert still had an old-fashioned digital clock, instead of using his phone like a regular person. Wayne stared at the green numbers. 5:55 a.m. That probably meant something. Five points? Five fears? Five chances to make this work before the bottom fell out of it? The lines of green light seemed to form a five-pointed star. He remembered the poem. How Gawain needed to understand five wounds and five virtues. But he hadn't finished reading it.

His brain was racing like a runaway Mario Kart. He should be studying for finals. Deciding on his future. But it seemed impossible to escape the past. Especially when it was literally hunting him.

Wayne shifted in bed. He could feel Bert's warm body, close but not touching. He threw off a lot of heat. Also was a duvet thief. Wayne tried to readjust it, but it was tangled up like an impossible knot. One of his feet was cold, the other sweating.

There was an odd familiarity to this moment. Knights were always being retold. You spent your life remembering parts of that story, taking what you needed, forgiving yourself for the rest. Holding your past stories and realizing that they did their best, that you were doing your best now. Bert seemed to know a lot more about this. His story was dynamic and fun and sometimes a bit scary, but he always seemed to know what was around the corner. Who was Wayne though? What was his story?

"I can feel you being anxious from across the bed."

Wayne tried to find a cool spot on the pillow. "Sorry."

"S'okay." Bert's voice was still partially asleep. "What can I do?"

"Um." Wayne considered the question—not one that people normally asked. Usually it was *When will you stop?* "Well. I guess . . . some pressure would be nice?"

Bert rearranged himself. He wrapped his arms around Wayne from behind and draped a leg over him, pulling him in tight. He nuzzled his nose into Wayne's neck. It felt like being hugged by a brown bear.

"Like this?"

Bert's warmth moved through him, and Wayne felt himself relax a bit. "Yeah."

"Good. I'll be your weighted blanket."

"I bought one of those once, but all the beads fell out. It was a nightmare."

"I won't fall apart." Bert squeezed him. "I'm very well made."

The phrase made him curious. "Where *are* you from?"

Bert was quiet for a moment. Then said, "It wasn't really called England then. I was born in Ceastershire. Chester. On the border of Wales. Kind of like the Canadian equivalent of . . . the prairies?"

"Do you remember your parents?"

It took Bert even longer to answer. His breath was warm and even. Wayne gently ran his fingertips down Bert's wrist, tracing little circles.

"No," he said finally. "I remember Morgan. She fostered me."

"Oh. So, she's like your stepmom?"

Bert chuckled. "I dare you to call her that."

"But she took care of you."

"She was something." Bert didn't elaborate. "What are your parents like?"

Wayne thought about this. "My dad was a musician. But he hasn't written any new music in a while. He's kind of a dork, but sincere. My mom." He wasn't sure how to quantify Anna. "She left when I was thirteen. She was an awful cook, but she gave incredible deep-pressure hugs. It felt like we were partners in crime. She would feed me lines in bad social situations, steer me out of danger. At the end of each day, we'd always find something to laugh about. Just how strange it is to be a soul in a body, pinballing off each other. All the ragged stories we dragged around like blankets."

Bert nuzzled into his shoulder. "She sounds wonderful."

"She understood me, I think. More than my dad—though he always tried, and in the end, he was the one who stayed. But she could give me this laser look from across the room, and I'd know exactly what she meant. She was the only person I could read like that. The only one who wasn't a storm of hidden things. I could relax around her, because I wasn't trying so hard to decode something. She was clean paper with a solid font. And she saw me too. We could read each other all day." He shifted. "But she was always trying to edit my life. She could never figure out if I should be a knight or a normal person."

Bert kissed the back of his neck. "You can be both."

"I don't think so."

"Well, normal is overrated anyway. I lived in trees for a while. Chatted with fungus. They're basically the Wi-Fi of the forest. I like plants more than people."

It was easy to talk this way—not looking at each other. "But you seem so confident. You chatted me up at the party."

"Are you sure? Maybe it was you."

"I'd never start a conversation with a stranger."

"We're not strangers." Bert smelled familiar, like home. "We've been doing this forever. We've got forever to do just this. If we do it right."

Wayne felt something odd. "Wait. Is this a waterbed?"

Bert said nothing.

Wayne felt cold water spreading all around him. The bed was dissolving. Bert was gone. He was alone in the dark room, floating.

He struggled out of the bed, which was rapidly becoming a lake.

The floor was covered in an inch of water. He could feel it rising. He splashed into the living room, and it felt steamy, like a rainforest.

You really ought to wake up.

Someone else's voice rang in his ears. Not his own internal monologue. It was low and musical, but slightly imperious. A voice that knew the answer to everything.

Bert's painted decks were floating in the water. His books were dissolving. Wayne opened the front door, and an ocean rushed in, pushing him back. He grabbed onto the couch like a life preserver.

Clever of him to use that rune. He always loved lakes. Water is so mutable. It can be anything. The perfect rune for someone who needs to wear masks.

Wayne struggled to stand up as the water rose all around. "Who *is* this?"

Gawain, there's no time for inane questions. You need to wake up.

He blinked. "Morgan?"

The longer you stay asleep, the less time you have.

He struggled back to the door. Pulled with all his might, but the water held it shut.

"Is there a rune for upper body strength?" he asked with a tinge of desperation.

Wayne heard splashing. His father emerged from Bert's room, wearing hip waders and carrying a fishing rod. "You always did hate boats. And camping. I remember trying to get you into the water. You'd just yell back, 'I'm a human, not a gill-bearing craniate. Different taxonomy, Dad!'"

He stared at his father. "Were you here the whole time?"

Lot grinned. His eye crinkles were at full strength, and he looked like he had years ago, discovering a new song. "I'm always here, Gawain. Now let's pull."

They both tugged at the door. Eventually, inch by inch, it came open. The hallway was completely submerged. Wayne looked at the stairs, which were dark and murky.

"How do I wake up?"

"Silly billy." Lot ruffled his hair. "You're made of water." He squeezed Wayne's hand. "Our blood runs through you."

Dive now. Morgan's voice was crackling. *Dive.*

Wayne stared at the dark water.

Held his breath.

Dissolved.

He was in the ocean.

No. Wait.

He was driving past the ocean.

Wayne saw tourists walking along the seawall. He knew that if he opened the window, he'd be able to smell the damp salt air.

He couldn't though. His hands were tied. He looked down and saw something wrapped tight around his wrists. He thought it was a scarf at first. But then he realized it was Bert's sweater. Torn and slightly stained, but still very much recognizable. It was thin—the only way that Wayne could tolerate a sweater—and that had made it easier to knot.

A woman was next to him in the back seat. Wayne didn't recognize her. She had multicolored hair cut at odd angles. Her eyes also seemed to change color, though that might have been a trick. Was he still dreaming?

He was about to say something. The woman seemed to sense this and shook her head gently, once.

The birds on her dress were flapping their wings in irritation.

He must still be dreaming.

But the ache in his wrists was real.

Lance saw him in the rearview mirror and smiled. "Hey-o. Don't struggle, kid. It'll only chafe your wrists. I promise to cut those once we arrive."

"You . . ." His tongue was still thick. "You drugged me with a rune."

"Just a lull-a-bye," Lance said. "Not like I slipped you GHB or something. You'll have a wee bit of a hangover, but that's it."

Wayne looked out the window again. "Are we heading to Stanley Park?"

Lance kept driving.

The woman gave him a warning look, as if to suggest that questions might be dangerous. Had he seen her somewhere before? He remembered her, faintly, like something from another life.

What would Kai do in this situation?

Kai had a razor-sharp mind. She'd ask questions. She'd figure out Lance's motive and talk him out of doing whatever he was planning to do.

He remembered Morgan's voice in his head. *The longer you stay asleep, the less time you have.*

To do what?

He needed to focus. To assess his environment. He looked around the back seat, trying to appear idly curious, or like he was still in shock. A part of him still was, but another part of him was slowly turning white hot with fear.

They were in an SUV, leather seats, new car smell. A rental? Not good. Lance could hose down those seats afterward, and no one would be the wiser.

Don't think like that. He's a knight and so are you. So think like one.

"I thought knights were supposed to protect damsels." Wayne tried to keep the quaver out of his voice, to sound like he was just making conversation, one cavalier to another.

Lance chuckled, but it had a dark sound to it. "She's no damsel. Guess you don't recognize her. She's one of the Wyrd Sisters. The future."

"Shar." Her voice was scratchy, like she'd also been drugged. "I have a name."

"We've all had so many," Lance said. "Who can keep them straight?" His hands tapped a song against the wheel. It was impossible to tell if this was an act or if he was totally comfortable with the situation. Like he drugged and kidnapped people all the time.

Wayne tried to remember everything he knew about Uncle Lance:

1. Good biking and swimming teacher. Excellent grasp of flying/falling.
2. Gives a lot of one-armed hugs and high-fives.
3. Seemed to piss off his mother just by existing.
4. Loves both Auntie Vera and Nuncle Gale. Or used to.

Lance had always been a minor celebrity in the family. Charm, good looks, and a knack for crushing life. He'd always seemed talented at just about everything. His clear, easy laugh cracking through silence. His sure hands untying knots in Wayne's shoelaces. His actual dad was slightly more reserved. A studio musician, not a rock star. Lance was the one with star quality. Was that useful at all? Was it anything?

Wayne decided to go for the more obvious weakness. "Aunt Vera's looking for me. She'll go nuclear when she figures out what you've done."

"I can deal with your aunt's temper," he said smoothly. "She's left me in the lurch more than once—expected me to save her from the flames. She isn't all generosity, you know. I've seen her beg for her life. She's as selfish as the rest of us."

"Lancelot." Shar's voice was firm, like someone much older was speaking through her. "You don't need the boy. Stop the car and drop him off."

"Shut it, sister." Lance's voice was cheerful, but underneath there was a pulsing threat. He needed both of them, and he wasn't letting anyone go.

They were driving through the park now. Trees growing thick. It was twice the size of Central Park in New York. Lots of places to hide. Winter had driven most of the tourists away. The winding streets that led to the park's heart were empty.

"Closest thing we have to a forest in the city," Lance said. "The king used to own the forest. He'd parcel out the land, or charge exorbitant rents, like a modern-day slumlord. But the forest is older than anything." He tapped the wheel. "That's why I've brought the four of us here. To get away from the distractions of the court."

The four *of us?*

Who else were they going to meet? Wayne ran quickly through the worst calculations. Kai in a grove somewhere, tied up. His dad. Aunt Vera, stripped of her weapons.

For just a second, he imagined his mother in the forest. Waiting.

Lance parked in an empty gravel lot. He ushered them both out of the car. Being tied up threw Wayne off balance, but he could still walk, slowly. And the more he concentrated on his hands, the more he realized that there was a gap in the knot. Maybe some moment of tenderness had kept Lance from tightening it. A small space. But it might be enough.

Now was the time to run.

But where?

All he could see were empty paths and thick trees. No heroic park ranger in sight. If he ran, like an errant horse, Lance would catch him.

There was no use. A real knight would have freed Shar, told her to run, distracted Lance while she got away. A real runesmith would have set Lance's arrogant face on fire.

But he was neither.

They marched through the forest in silence. It grew darker, the quiet grew deeper, as if the animals were waiting for something.

Wayne heard a growl in the distance.

Oh. Oh no.

He didn't want to keep walking. He thought of Bilbo Baggins, who was so afraid of the dragon but walked into his lair because he had to. Because being brave meant being scared first.

Wayne put one foot in front of the other.

"Why?" The question burst out of him. "Uncle Lance. Why are you doing this? Why are you doing *any* of this?"

Lance didn't turn around. "You'll understand when you're older," he said. "In another life, maybe. You'll get it."

"I want to understand *now.*"

For a second, Lance lost his composure. He turned. "I wanted a lot of things too," he snapped, "when I was your age. I wanted to swim in the lake, and save people, and go on quests to haunted churches and enchanted valleys. I wanted—" Real pain flashed across his eyes. "What I wanted, I wasn't worthy of. Not my decision. Everything I got was always twisted, always double-edged. Because it's a losing game, being a knight. That's what I'm trying to change."

"You sound like—"

But he didn't finish the sentence. His shoe hit a rock, and he went down hard. Instinctively, he tried to break his fall. It sort of worked: he landed painfully on his side. The roots concealed a rock's edge, and it sliced his palm. He felt the edge of the rock, pushing against that gap.

Lance moved toward him, but Shar said something. He didn't hear what, but it made Lance turn. She knew. She was buying him these seconds.

He could just manage to strain against the weak knot. Sawing up and down, unable to see what he was doing, because his eyes were on Lance.

He was sweating and bleeding and rubbing his bind against the rock, push-ing, in spite of the burn. One hand slipped out. Numb and painful but free.

For a second, he lay there in shock, staring as the blood welled up. It reminded him of something—long and sinuous. A rune. He remem-bered what Kai had shown him. The runes that called for help. The ones that remembered home.

Lance was walking toward him now.

There was a stump next to him, ashy and overgrown with mold. But he saw one clear spot. He traced two shapes in his own blood: the angles embracing, the slantwise cross. *Harvest*, the first rune said. *Need*, the other. Like a longing for plenty. The feeling of coming home to a firelit hall, a table of food and friends. Knowing you belonged. He joined them with a rough slash.

Nothing happened.

He slipped his hand back into the fabric, against his back. If you squinted, the bind might still look secure.

Lance hauled him up by the arm. "Watch yourself, nephew."

Wayne kicked dirt over the blood.

For a second, he thought he saw a flicker, deep in the wood grain. But it might have been a trick of the gray light.

It was truly snowing now. Winter at their heels. Covering them in a soft blanket that would eventually root into their bones.

They marched on in silence. The trees thickened, narrowing, like the roof of a church closing in. They seemed to whisper and watch. This was their entertainment. A tournament where almost-immortals fought each other for—what, exactly? That was what he'd never under-stood. There was no grail. At least he'd never seen it. No sword pulled from the stone. No round table, like in the stories. Just the metallic taste of fear in his mouth, the ache in his wrists, as he marched toward fate.

Now the gray light barely filtered into the woods. Animals and shadows moved among the moss and decaying logs. Hundreds of eyes on them.

He heard the growl again, closer this time. Like a bull. Or some-thing larger. What had they been called in medieval times? An aurochs.

The thing you tested yourself against. If you could bring it down, that meant something.

When they broke into the clearing with the soaring trees, his breath caught.

It had been waiting for them.

27

HILDIE

"**T**ell me where you are."

Grace's voice was iron over the phone, but Hildie knew her. Beneath that control, there was something she'd rarely heard in her mother's tone: fear.

She was in the back seat of Vera's car—a gray Pinto from the late '70s with no shocks. They might as well have been on horseback; they could feel every bump in the road. Gale pushed it to the red line. The engine screamed, and Hildie could feel the car shaking, like it might come apart at any moment.

"Heading to Lost Lagoon," she said. She'd pulled out her tablet, with a crack down the middle of the screen. "I need full access to Lancelot's file. Everything you've got. There could be some detail that will help."

"Stanley Park is huge. Even the Lagoon—"

"I know how big Stanley Park is, Mother!"

Grace sighed. "That file goes back to the twelfth century, and some parts—"

"Just give me access! We can talk about medieval history later."

There was a silence. "Okay. You've got access to everything I do. I'm getting in the car. Keep your phone on."

"Don't bring backup. There are already too many moving parts to this."

"Hildie."

"I'm serious. From what I can tell about this knight, he's overconfident. But he's also strong. If we push him, that could be it." She didn't say *for Shar*. She couldn't.

"Fine. Is the nephew with you?"

Hildie's blood froze. "You don't have eyes on him?"

"He vanished about an hour ago."

She closed her eyes for a second. "All right. I'll be in touch." She put away the phone and opened Lance's file. Grace hadn't been kidding. It was long and colorful.

"He's got Wayne." Kai's voice was dangerously quiet. "Right?"

Hildie scanned rapidly through the centuries. "Lance isn't a killer. If he *has* to"—she tried to look reassuring—"but normally he doesn't. He's all about chivalry. If he's got both Shar and Wayne, he obviously needs them for something. He won't do anything drastic."

Kai said nothing, but the temperature in the car started to rise.

The water flew past them. Water. That was what Lancelot had always known. Raised by the Lady of the Lake—a woman about whom almost nothing was known, save for the fact that she appeared during moments of crisis. A woman, a weaponsmith, a political player, who happened to be Lance's foster mother.

There was a statement from her in the file: *A knight's sword has two edges. One is sharp, to punish the wicked. The other, soft, to save the righteous.*

Which one was Lance? Wicked or righteous?

"He still has that brooch," she said, almost to herself. "But we've got one too." She thought for a moment, then handed it to Kai. It was heavy and slightly warm. Once, Clywen told her, there'd been gems for the dragon's eyes. Now they were shadows, staring. Waiting. "When things get wild, put this on. You're the best chance we have at this point."

Kai took it with an expression that verged on hunger.

"It's not a toy," Hildie said.

"Good," Kai said. "I'm not playing."

Hildie desperately scanned through the file. The list of ex-girlfriends and boyfriends was numerous. Elaine Astolat—she'd killed herself after he refused to commit. A knight named Belleus whom he'd met at a tournament. Vera and Gale had been the core. The thing that pinned him to this world.

The knight Galehaut died of grief for Sir Lancelot.

Hildie stared at the line; it kept coming up in multiple parts of the file.

She looked at Gale. He smiled as he cut someone off. Like he was coming alive for the first time.

She read further. There'd been countless battles between Lancelot and Gawain. They were always pitted against one another: Gawain fought for Camelot, and Lancelot fought for—what? Freedom? Guinevere's honor? A new way of life? It happened again and again. Arthur always died. But now he was in prison. That had to change things.

"Vera, what does Camelot even mean?"

She turned around in her seat. "It was always more of an idea than a place. A society based on honor and spectacle. But everyone had blood under their nails. Everyone was secretly frightened. I don't know that it was ever truly a home."

"We made our own home," Gale said. "Or tried to."

She found a note deep in Lance's file. Something she hadn't seen before. It was a scan of something scrawled on paper. She recognized Nan's graceful handwriting.

Lancelot is water. He drowns the world. Wave by wave, he wears everyone down. A new castle rises from the deep. His joy. Their sorrow.

She remembered the old stories about Lancelot. How his castle was called Joyous Gard. How he broke Camelot for different reasons. To be with Guinevere. To protect her from Arthur. But maybe he was just another kind of Arthur.

He drowns the world.

She wasn't thinking about the world. Just Shar and Gawain.

Lance was going to kill them both.

Maybe he didn't want to kill Wayne, but he'd do it if he had to. She remembered her mother telling her that some knowledge was dangerous. Had she known that it was Lance the whole time? Or was Nan's note not considered an official report? Something closer to poetry than evidence?

Hildie could smell death on the wind.

But whose would it be? She looked at everyone in the car, trying to divine something. But it was too early yet. The blizzard was on its way.

Kai suddenly took a deep breath. Then she started to laugh. "That sweet little nerd," she said. "He remembered the lesson."

Hildie stared at her. "What are you talking—"

"*There!*" Kai pointed to the tree line. "There it is!"

Hildie blinked. At first she thought it was a trick of the light. But the flicker was two distinct shapes. Two runes, turning slowly in the winter air.

"I know exactly where he is," Kai said.

WAYNE

It was much larger in person.

In his dreams, it was always sliding in and out of focus. A flicker of movement in an empty room, or a sound that might just be the house settling.

Now that the questing beast was in front of him—chained to a tree—he saw that it was massive. It had three heads, numerous tails, the pelt of a wolf, and a thunderous cry that was all of these things—a lupine howl, a big cat's vibrato, a dog's snarl, the piercing wail of a hawk. The sound filled him until he could hear nothing else. Until the beast was clawing to get out of him, screaming in his own voice.

It pawed the earth, leaving claw marks in the wet grass. Its eyes pinned Wayne. They were glowing tunnels that led to some fathomless interior. There was intelligence pulsing in those eyes, and a vast uncontainable appetite. It opened its mouths and roared. The force of it drove Wayne back—nearly brought him to his knees. The grove shook, and the trees seemed to recoil.

"Don't run," Shar whispered. "Never run from something like this. If you do, it'll know that you're prey."

The beast was looking right at him. Those ancient eyes working things out. Maybe it was thinking of all the knights it had cleaved in the past. But there was something else. A kind of recognition.

"Well met." Wayne said it before he could stop himself. The words were incantatory. He'd said them before, in some other life, and he would say them again.

The beast strained toward him. All of its heads moved closer, until only a few feet separated them. If it broke the chain, he was dead. But it wasn't pulling on the links, at least not yet. It seemed to be drawing closer, like a spectator at a tournament. Or someone who was about to hear a story, wondering what might change this time.

"The questing beast," Lance said. "Odd word—*quest*. It means to seek, but did you know it also means to scream?"

"Lancelot." Shar kept her eyes on the beast, the way you would a bonfire about to get out of control. "You can't possibly go through with this. You've never been the one to tame the beast. It's not even part of your story. Do you think you can rewrite everything? That killing me will do that?"

Wayne stared at her. It became real as she said it. Lance had brought this woman here for one purpose.

But why had Lance brought *him*?

"No." His voice was almost reasonable. "You're right. It's not part of my story. I've always been the antihero who loses everything in the end. The grail. The queen. The prince. I lose *everything*. And all so the story can keep going."

Wayne's mind was racing. He'd always had a brain for details—a bottom-up processor. Lance was the detail he'd never been able to sort. But he could feel all the stories and memories in his hand now, like glittering marbles. He moved them to and fro. A new pattern began to emerge.

"That's why you imprisoned Uncle Arthur," he said slowly. "The story—our story—is supposed to be about him. I may only be halfway through Aunt Vera's class, but even I know that he dies in the end. You needed to keep that from happening. You froze the myth."

At the mention of Aunt Vera, pain flashed across Lance's face. But he recovered quickly. "It's never really been about Arthur," he said, with a kind of exaggerated patience. "I'm on every page. I'm the heart. What's he? Just an instigator. An abusive husband. A terrible monarch. In the version we've all come to accept, Mordred kills Arthur in the end. And he *never* sees it coming. There have even been Arthurs who survived the final battle. Mordreds who saw reason. Guineveres who escaped the obscurity of the convent. But the real ending—the ending in our bones—that never changes. The heroes are always forgotten."

Lance saw himself as a hero. Someone who could topple a dictator. And wasn't that why people loved antiheroes? Because they didn't follow the rules? Beneath that easy smile, that swagger, Wayne saw the feverish glow of someone who saw himself as a rebel. Someone who believed he was right. Believed it so clearly that he was willing to destroy one of the sisters of fate, and possibly his own nephew. That belief was more dangerous than any sword. He saw now that Lance wouldn't—couldn't—stop. Not until this new story burned itself onto the unexplored page. And it would start with the beast.

"You needed to get Mo Penley out of the way first," Wayne said. "Not just because you didn't agree with his politics. But because he couldn't exist if this"—he gestured around him—"was going to happen. Like you said. Change the story. Uncle Artie's in prison, Penley's out of the picture. Headless." He shuddered. "I was there. You were there too. I saw you."

"I was surprised to see you." Lance smiled, and it was almost gentle. "Happy though. I missed you. It was nice to see you, all grown up and flirting with Morgan's lackey. Watch out for him, by the way. Knights like that, they don't change."

Wayne flushed slightly. But he wouldn't take the bait. He continued, in spite of his fear. "That's why you took his head off. I saw that axe." He almost said *under Bert's futon*, then stopped himself. "You wanted to throw the suspicion on someone else. It looked like some wild animal had mauled the provost, but then there was also that cut. Like a scalpel. That must have confused Hildie."

Lance shook his head. "Still trusting valkyries. Your second mistake."

The beast roared. It passed through them like thunder.

In the distance, Wayne thought he heard something else.

Lance seemed to refocus. His eyes were bright. "Mo was Team Beast for a while," he said, as if dispensing a bit of gossip. "He helped me throw Arthur in prison, and he was all too happy to eliminate anyone else opposed to our vision. A new kingdom—without the king. But he choked at the last second. Maybe it was the myth in him, pulling toward the familiar. Maybe he lost his nerve. I had to act on my own."

Shar glanced at the edge of the clearing. She'd heard something as well. Her expression shifted from a kind of resignation to something different. Like she was seeing something new.

"The ylf shot wasn't you," she said. Her voice was distracted. She seemed to be working out something much larger. A beast-sized problem that was about to tear through them.

Lance chuckled. "You know whose work that was."

Wayne thought about the axe. He remembered what Bert had said in his dream. How he'd been found, as an orphan. The look he'd given her that was far beyond annoyance directed at an employer, but more like anger toward someone you trusted, even loved.

"Morgan," he said.

"Just like her," Lance cut in, "always working from the margins. And it was a decent plan. She wanted to incapacitate Mo without hurting him. Drag him away from the party. Lock him in a room until things calmed down. But Mo was drinking that night—and wine does funny things to old magic. The ylf shot didn't quite work as it should. He kept weaving in and out of the party, appearing, then vanishing. She couldn't isolate him. That was all we needed in the end."

Shar was moving slowly. Placing herself between Wayne and the beast. It looked at her through hooded eyes. Curious. A cat willing to play with its prey.

"So, what?" Shar gestured to the heads, which now turned toward her. "This is it? You feed a Wyrd Sister to the beast, and you think everything comes up roses? You get your happy ending? That's not how this is going down, and you know it."

"Are you sure about that?" Lance favored her with an angelic smile. "You've been fairly preoccupied with your legal case. Fighting to keep the hotel unseen, to keep your family together. Are you sure you *really* see what's coming? You certainly missed this. Maybe you're off your fortune-telling game for good."

A tremor passed through the grove. Even the beast seemed to notice.

"This is what happens, sister," Lance said. His voice was firm—no more playing. "The beast does its job. Eats the future. Leaves a blank page where you used to be. Your family splits. The remaining sisters will lose control. Your home will collapse. And then I'll build a new kingdom from the ruins. I'll be greater than Arthur. More just. More real. I'll rule the way he should have from the beginning."

Wayne stared at him. "But why am I here?"

Lance managed to look a bit guilty. "Well. I wish it was a more honorable reason. A heroic battle, like in the books. But really, nephew, it's not precisely about *you*. It's more about who loves you."

His stomach lurched. "Aunt Vera."

"The queen needs to be here. One way or another."

"And Gale?"

Lance's face almost softened. "I'm sure he'll come too. But what's he going to do? He can't translate his way out of this."

Wayne looked up at the beast. Now it was pulling. Eager.

He saw something flash across the clearing. It might have been a shadow.

Or a fox.

29

KAI

Kai preferred to be invisible most days. And now she was.

Well, not exactly.

The brooch was a pretty bit of runesmithing. If she ever met the Lady of the Lake in person, she hoped to geek out about what exactly had gone into it. It made her difficult to notice, like a thought that slips past when you try to grasp it. It must have made it easy to commit murder. Not its original function—Hildie thought it was for protection— but power could always be twisted.

They'd sent her in a different direction. Hildie, Vera, and Gale were approaching the clearing from another angle. She'd gone on ahead. It was easy enough for Gale to track them down the path. But it was Kai's idea to split up.

She worked better on her own, anyhow. Not always a fan of playing with others.

Her namesake was an old knight—one of the very first in the stories that were mostly just a whisper around the fire. Stories that resisted being written down, because they were too slippery. The knight was hot-headed. Always getting into fights, saying the wrong thing, or maybe it was the right thing. In many ways, they'd been the same. But Kai had slipped away from being a knight. She'd seen who she really was, inside the armor. Every once in a while, someone would shift to a different story. She knew that she was a runesmith. That was one of her powers: Kai had always known who she was.

She hadn't seen Uncle Lance in ages.

Not her uncle. But when you spent enough time with someone, their relatives became yours. Her father had died of lung cancer when she was young. He'd been a cook at a hotel in Yaletown—the sort of place they couldn't afford to stay. What she remembered was the smell of garlic and scallions late at night, as he made her a twilight meal. Watching him chop vegetables so fast they bounced and spun, like a magic trick. The crunch of gai lan as he laughed at her Cantonese. *You sound like a book.* Teaching her words that were faintly scandalous. During the day, she'd eat carbs and sugar. Her mom would make a disappointed sound and walk out of the kitchen. But at night, she relished whatever her father prepared.

When she started hormones, her appetite flourished. She wanted all those old meals. She found herself walking through Chinatown, in search of the places that hadn't changed. As a teenager, she'd been embarrassed by them. She'd dragged her father to the high-end places downtown, where you could get remixes of traditional food. It never tasted the same. There were upscale ramen spots on East Georgia now. But she could still find the restaurants and shops he used to haunt.

She worried about being noticed there. This place where she'd never quite belonged. But she moved invisibly. Just a tall girl with a plastic bag full of greens. Knowing she'd never be able to make something that tasted the same. But she could sometimes see him in the kitchen. A shard of carrot would leap from the knife, and he'd catch it, grinning.

Her mother was a lecturer, which meant she got paid to talk to rooms full of students about history. But when she got home, tired and bright-eyed, she often lapsed into silence. Kai talked enough for the both of them.

She'd always been good at describing things. She'd started speaking early, naming *moon* (月) and *talk* (講), demanding endless narratives. When she was barely eight years old, she'd seen Wayne and knew exactly how to speak to him. She'd approached him sideways, the way you would a skeptical alley cat. But the words had come. They'd always come.

Careful, her mother had said. *Careful with your power.*

But there was so much inside her. So many runes. A spiral galaxy full of possibilities, turning, always turning. If she got close to Lance, for instance. There were runes that she could draw on him. You could draw them on bark, stone, even air, but skin was an excellent medium. Especially for the bad ones.

She'd grown up with so many warnings. *Treat the runic alphabet with care.* There were runes to help, runes to keep you safe, runes who'd listen to your appeals in the dark. The way Sappho had prayed to Aphrodite: *Don't fill my heart with care.*

There were powers that you learned to guard against, but never embrace. Some runes were like wild animals. You never knew what they were up to, what damage they might create. But they were a comfort too. Her name rune meant torch. It was knowledge and fire. The pain of understanding. The sweep of a well-lit room. She'd always been friends with fire. It had gotten her into trouble, but it had saved her too.

She looked at Wayne. He couldn't see her. A part of him was distant. But another part of him—somehow—seemed to be looking exactly at the spot where she hid, behind a tree. Like he could see her no matter the magic, even if the world was about to end, he could always see her.

For a long time, she'd wished that she could be a computer—just free-floating data. Then she read about Ada Lovelace, Lord Byron's genius daughter, who was an actual coder. She could calculate anything. And the women who worked as living computers in the nineteenth century, solving thorny problems for men. The industry had been made by women like her.

Kai clenched her fists.

When her mother was a teenager—only slightly younger than Kai was now—she'd been hurled through the open window of her car. Seatbelts weren't as big of a deal back then, and the impact threw her into the street.

Kai asked her what she'd thought as she was flying.

Her mother had blinked. Then grinned. *Here goes nothing.*

Kai felt her palms warm. She reached for her laptop.

Here goes something.

WAYNE

It felt like Kai was here, somehow. He couldn't quite explain it. But a storm was on its way, and she was dancing in it.

Wayne felt a scrap of hope.

He turned to Lance. "What if the beast won't listen to you anymore? Can a monster be loyal? What if it sides with the valkyries, or the Wyrd Sisters? You've bet everything on this working. But what if it doesn't?"

The heads turned toward him. Infinite eyes peered at him, not just the beast's. The whole forest was watching. Lance had said the beast and the forest were one. That meant that the forest had its own vote in this.

Lance gave him a look, as if he was dismissing a child's complaint. "Is that meant to shake my confidence? The beast understands one thing: hunger. And I'm the one feeding it. I've given it more than anyone ever has. Sir Pellinore sniffed around a forest, chasing after it for a few years—that was nothing. I've given it three knights. My own foster brother." He looked pained for a moment. "He was shooting his mouth off at the Castle. Trying to make himself sound like the real hero, the conquering knight. I loved him." He blinked. "I did.

He protected me. He was kind to me. The scars on his knuckles, the broken bones—I loved every inch of him. But this. This was more important."

"And the squire?" Shar had managed to get closer to the tree where the beast was chained up. "Did that make you feel like a man? Killing a sweet kid?"

"Percy?" Lance's eyes grew dark. "He wasn't that innocent, you know. You think he deserved to see it—the grail—when I couldn't? Just because he hadn't lived or loved or made any hard choices?" His voice roiled with anger. "He deserved what I gave him instead. Plus, he was too close to Vera. Over to her apartment at all hours. That's where we ran into each other." Lance smiled, pleased with himself. "It was easy. I've got a face like a real estate agent. *You can trust me.* I set him up in an apartment, one of the properties I owned. Easier to keep an eye on him that way. I asked him to check on Vera, to bring me little updates. It worked for a while—I got to know her patterns—but then he started asking too many questions. Easier to make him a sacrifice. He died beautifully though."

Percy.

It hit Wayne then. The boy with the funny name. The one who'd joked with Kai about what kind of animal he'd be. How swans sang at the moment of their death.

He died beautifully.

Did she know?

What would she do in return?

"You can *stop inching now,*" Lance said sharply. He knelt down. Reached his hand into a reflective patch of ice and drew out a sword. Runes curled along the hilt—runes, Wayne knew, that spelled out Lance's name. That sword knew him. It would do anything for him.

Shar stopped where she was. "You've fed it knights," she said. "But this is different. I'm a fixed goddamn point in space and time. You're not even sure it can kill me. I'm not sure that *anything* can kill me."

"But has anyone tried this hard before?" Lance gestured toward the beast. "Let's just see. I'll loosen the chain. It's quite famished. We'll see how long it takes. What it has to do. All the things you might live through—or not. Either way, it'll disrupt the pattern enough that we

313

can start from scratch. If it takes more pain?" He shrugged. "I'm fine with that. My life has been pain. Loving someone I could never have, and another who was never sure they wanted me. Following a king that I couldn't trust, and watching him bluster and fumble and fuck everything up. *Let's hear a marvel.* That's what he was always asking for. Well, here it is. A marvel. A monster."

"Lancelot—" There was a note of real fear in Shar's voice.

He brought his sword down on the chain. Rune-forged steel cut through it like water.

The beast screamed in delight.

That was when Wayne saw Aunt Vera, sword in hand, running.

31

VERA

Seeing Lance after all these years felt exactly like she thought it would.

Vera tightened her grip.

Lance's gaze swept to her as she broke into the clearing. Blue eyes cold and dancing.

She remembered his mouth on hers.

The jokes he used to whisper, to make her laugh at mass. So long ago. Then later, standing at the engraved window. Ladies falling asleep around her. Ladies reading and batting at flies and stabbing embroidery. She looked out the window and saw him, astride a piebald horse. Long hair, a scrap of mourning cloth against the sun. Another man, with a dark beard and kind eyes, was talking to him. They had the ease of brothers, though there was something else, something in the man's expression. Maybe it was longing.

She walked down the endless flights of stone stairs. Her ladies, frantic, followed her, like a trail of clouds, all the way to the base of the keep. She walked across the greensward. She did not run. He saw her coming, had always seen her coming, but affected surprise.

He bowed. "Majesty."

Vera did not give him leave to rise. He stayed there, one knee growing wet from the grass, which had already stained the hem of her gown.

His friend chuckled.

"I like you there," Vera had said. "Where I can see you clearly."

"Majesty"—he switched stiffly to his other leg—"you see mischief where there is only joy."

"And service," his friend added, pragmatically.

"Of course." He beamed. "I am forever your majesty's servant."

He moved beneath her, a warm fixed point. She smiled and kept him down, always, where she could see him. *Keep the devil in your sight.*

But then she lost sight of him.

And now they were here.

Because she'd loved him, and Gale, and herself.

Because she'd tried to make another life. Tearing out the old threads for the new.

The questing beast loomed over them, a many-headed shadow. She'd never seen it this close before. It was magnificent and wrong and deadly. An aurochs with wings and the cold eyes of reptiles. All those mouths. It had been made to devour them, knights and stories and queens, like field mice.

The sword hummed in her hand.

The swordsmith Walpurgis had taught her to fight. She remembered striking endless targets, until both arms ached. Remembered Vivian's calm, clear voice. *A queen must fight. But she must also be more clever than anyone else.*

She was queen and knight both.

Lance's face split into an unexpected grin at the sight of her.

Then she was dancing. She threw away the old guards, the fighting positions, the lessons. She let the blade guide her. Lance was almost startled as he parried. The impact jarred her wrist, but she pushed forward. The long quillons of his sword were like fingers, tangling her weapon. But she remembered them well. She unbound her blade, reversed the hilt, and drove the pommel into his stomach. He grunted and took a step back. Something flickered across his eyes. Was it joy? Or the edge of surprise?

"You're outmatched for once," Vera said. Though she wasn't sure she believed it.

Lance looked at the beast. It hadn't moved. It was watching them closely, like whalebone pawns on a board. Then Lance looked back to her and smiled. There was incurable love and darkness in his expression.

"Majesty. You've been right about a lot of things. But not this."

32

GALE

He knew Lance's weak spots. The positions he loved. Those elegant moves that he favored, even when they weren't practical. Lance was pretty and charming, and that was a distraction. You didn't notice him reaching for a blade.

He'd broken Gale's leg once, while they were sparring. Delivered a blow that rattled through Gale's body, and *snap*.

This was before hospitals. Lance had torn up his tabard to make a sling. Then set him delicately in the saddle. The pain gave everything a red margin. He was shaky and thought he might be sick. Because he couldn't properly hold on, Lance held him in place from behind. One arm gently around his waist, the other guiding his horse, who snorted in protest against the extra weight.

I'm sorry, he'd breathed into Gale's ear, as they rode.

It never healed. A part of his myth. Always coming back, an ache, a memory, a storm thrumming within and rattling every bone. Sometimes it was his arm, sometimes his leg, sometimes a dull fire below his heart.

He arrived late to the fight, as always. His unreliable body, dragging its shadow of pain. But Gale had learned to love it. His disability wasn't a flaw. More like an unexpected vein in clear quartz. A flash of something unpredictable. And the thing about being constantly underestimated was that nobody expected you to swing.

He got there in his own time. On his own terms. Ready.

Lance finally saw him. Love and cruelty turning in his eyes.

Gale knelt down and reached into a patch of ice. Drew his sword. The hilt was cold from lack of use. His whole arm shuddered. But then he felt the leather warming, the runes waking up.

The beast screamed at him.

The sound brought him up short.

It was unbound now. It could leap in any direction. Mince them or break open their bone chambers. What did they used to call the body? The life house? Where the soul's mystery slept like a saint's finger in a reliquary. He'd died and lived so many times, different shadows of himself, each with a sadness in common.

He kept his eyes on the beast. Leveled his blade.

"I missed you both," Lancelot said. Already smiling.

Gale's leg flared with pain. He let it move through him like a guest in his home. You couldn't send it away, but you could live with it. "We forgot to RSVP to the end the world," he said, "but we showed up anyway. We're annoying like that."

"Please." Lance was watching Vera, but a part of him—a shadow Gale remembered—was giving him all of its attention. "You're a poet. Not a warrior."

The night they walked by the water. Fish gleaming like silver coins in the shallows. The sound of the boats, knocking against the pier that had been there since Rome. Lance's hand in his. Whispering *I grew up by the water.* Pulling him beneath the rotted slats, where shells crunched under their boots. Sharp tang of seaweed. Gale had never trusted him. Never known who he was with him. But then Lance's mouth was on his. Wine and hot breath and a smile he could see in the dark. What had he felt that first time? Like a poet, maybe. Or a boy in a fairy tale. That knight from the poem by Marie. Only this time, he kissed the sailor.

"I think you'll find," Gale said, tightening his grip, "that I'm a goddamn knight."

He exchanged a look with Vera. A sign of love and battle.

They both leapt forward as the beast howled. .

33

HILDIE

She approached the clearing from a different angle. Trying to flank him. The spear was cold in her hands. Cold like the knight's eyes, which seemed to be skimming them all for weaknesses. She tried not to look directly at the beast, which was enormous and no longer chained up. Muscles rippled beneath its hide, but it wasn't moving just yet. Deciding who to eat first, maybe. Her spear knew the creature. A scream was trapped within the wood, and the beast heard it. Stared right at her.

You can't take that on. Focus on what you can *deal with. The knight.*

He'd kidnapped one of the fates. Not just one of them—*her* fate. Her Shar.

She tried to edge around the beast. But it saw her. It saw everything. And it was going to crash over them.

The knight, Hildie. Valkyries deal with knights. Just do your job.

Vera and Gale circled Lance. Gale was quicker than she'd expected. He danced. His blade cut like wind. But Lance seemed to know where he'd be at all times. Their weapons skittered, true edges kissing, sliding in and out of an embrace. Vera moved in with a surprising overhead slash—she hadn't realized the woman could move like that—but Lance also saw that coming. He glanced over his shoulder and spun to meet her blade, while elbowing Gale hard at the same time. They both stepped back. Gale was breathing hard. How long had it been since the sleepy knight was on a battlefield?

The beast was still watching. Its heads moved in time with the sword strokes, following each attack, each retreat.

She locked eyes with Shar.

What was she seeing in the beast's many eyes?

Knowing could be a terrible thing.

Hildie knew, for instance, that Gale and Vera were going to lose. They could only keep this up for so long. Wayne was inching closer to the beast. What was his plan? She'd thought he was bound—she'd seen something around his hands—but now it was gone.

Even if he drew his clumsy new sword, he'd only gain them a few seconds of confusion. Then Lance would hurl the beast at them. At Shar.

She was looking at Hildie now. What was in her eyes? Defeat? Resignation? Or something else?

If I were a different person, Hildie thought, *I'd have a spear wall around me. Loyal sisters on either side. Even the beast couldn't take us down. Maybe.*

But that wasn't who she was. Not the kind of person who called for help. Not a detective who fostered relationships with anyone else—at least anyone that mattered. Her mother was on the way, but there was no guarantee she'd arrive in time. And the beast might just tear her apart.

Suddenly, she saw the ghost of a smile play across Shar's face.

Not defeat. A sliver of hope. Shar was trusting her to do something.

Hildie tightened her grip on the spear.

What if there was a world in which this all made sense? A place where she could have everything she wanted? Not just solving the case. Not just making her ancestors happy. What if it was possible to be a warrior and still have a life worth living?

At one time, valkyries like her had chosen the slain on the battlefield. *You.* They'd heard a note rising, a blood cry. *You will fall. So that others can rise.*

Maybe it could be the opposite. She could choose who lived, instead.

Her body was already moving.

But so was the beast. Its spiny tail whipped out, like a hockey stick, slashing at Vera. The force of it sent her tumbling into the snow. As she rose, Hildie saw red against the white. The spines had cut through her jeans, leaving ragged edges behind.

Gale looked torn. That moment of indecision was enough for Lance to thrust low. Gale half saw it coming and managed to ward off the strike. But it threw him off balance. He went down hard on one knee.

Then she heard something unearthly. She thought the sound was coming from the earth. Until she realized it was Shar. Singing. An old high song, without words, just a threnody swirling with the snow. Piercing. A song that women had always sung in the face of battle. A mourning and a reckoning.

The beast stopped. It stared at the singing fate. All of its eyes were questioning. Curious. It had heard such a song before, but perhaps not like this.

Hildie ran toward Lance.

She heard Nan's voice.

She hadn't heard it in so long, but it soared in her mind. A tremendous whisper.

Don't you know that you can do anything? My spear child. My magnificent gift. When you strike, it's with all of our strength.

Lance barely had time to raise his sword. Hildie's spear point was level. An extension of her own gaze. She thrust long, with the power of her shoulder. He parried with the flat of his blade, and she switched to a diagonal slash. It knocked his weapon off course. She danced in a Z, gaining power with each step. Tapping out a heartbeat. Short thrust, slash, long thrust. The tip of her spear was a hungry tooth, an exquisite black hole, its event horizon skimming closer and closer to Lance's unprotected throat.

He deflected her blows, but she could tell that he was slightly disoriented. Knights were used to meeting other swords, not spears. She'd trained in both. The spear had always been a neglected weapon. The sword was sexier. Medieval reenactors loved it, because it was full of bullshit symbolism. But spears had been winning battles since long before Rome. As she aimed for his soft parts, she remembered, somehow, being part of a spear wall. So long ago. How her sisters, her ancestors, had been there with a long reach to defend her. The love and the fury.

She sent a thought down the length of the spear. It shivered and grew longer. A shadow lengthening. Snow glittered like stars in the dark of it.

His eyes widened for a second. Then he smirked.

Lance renewed his attack. Even with her longer reach, it was hard to find a weak point. He moved like water. He was, maybe, the greatest knight in the world.

Who was she?

Shar's song was a beautiful thorn, pressed to her skin.

Hildie danced and slashed, danced and slashed.

Who was she? A valkyrie. But more than her myth. More than her family. More than her need to solve things, to untie knots and riddles. What had Grace said on her first day in the office? *A warrior doesn't win every battle. A detective can illuminate problems, but they can't solve the heart. They can't go back in time; they can't make people stop needing and hurting and betraying each other.*

Shar's song was coming to an end. The spear grew heavy in her hands. The beast had noticed her now. Its dark eyes were on her.

Hildie slashed high and wide. Lance anticipated it. But then she reversed the motion. Spun her spear around. Slammed the spike on the end—what Nan used to call the lizard killer—into Lance's shoulder. He moved an inch, just enough to keep her from tearing through an artery. But she still cut him. First real blood.

There was something feverish in his eyes.

He looked at the beast. Hildie could see him making a decision. Even with blood seeping through his jacket, he seemed entirely in control.

But there was something he couldn't see.

34

KAI

Over and over, line by line, she painted a rune on bare skin that showed through her torn leggings. Flesh meeting data, and somewhere in the middle, her soul. She'd bought these leggings from Value Village, while an employee frowned at her. Getting clocked at a charity shop was always fun. Too many people to make a scene. They'd never kick her out, but there was that *look*.

She'd learned so many lessons as she transitioned. The way men were allowed to look at her. The catcalls when they saw her from a distance. The whiff of violence when they got too near and their faces changed.

But Kai knew who she was. Knew her own skin. And the rune was so familiar. Neither bad nor good. A rune she'd thought about for so long. A golden firework hanging above her in the dark, as she scrolled through possibilities on her phone.

The rune for change.

Its heat bloomed against her skin.

But it wasn't for her.

She could do that on her own—*was* doing it on her own—because she was already magic. She didn't need runes to be true.

This was for something else.

She stared at the screen. A network of runes swirled around the more pedestrian code. Bits of code and magic that she'd borrowed from other runesmiths around the world, plunging headlong into secret threads: Discord servers and Reddit holes and sweet old blogs. Weird community spaces and furtive DMs and old BBS sites that shouldn't have existed anymore. Watching the beautiful runes unfold in ASCII code. All about the possibility of stopping the beast.

Not trapping it. *Stopping* it. Getting it to pause and reconsider. Like getting a dragon or a black hole to blink.

Wayne had done some research, but his thinking was too medieval. Kai stopped thinking of the beast as a relic and more as a kind of artificial intelligence. A program that all knights encountered, at one point or another. Everyone was always looking for the beast, and if you offered it the right things—as Lance had done—you could harness its power. Make it kill for you. But nobody ever asked what it wanted. Instead of using it, she wanted it to be still, to listen, to wait. Just like it had paused for the sister's creepy song. But more permanently. A pause that meant something different.

It might just eat them all. But maybe.

Kai traced the rune until she could hold its angles in her mind. Until she was living it. Until she could exhale it, letting go of all the pain and fear, so the only thing left was change.

This could go badly. Of course it could.

But she'd shared pieces of the code with other runesmiths. They'd all contributed something, all agreed that it just might work. Even Viv, who disapproved of the gambit, even if she admired its power.

A song to soothe the beast, she'd said.

Kai inserted the rune for change. The same rune for water. It looked like a delicate claw, or a sickle. She remembered her mother reading the old rune poem to her, when it was clear that she wouldn't be a knight—that she'd chosen to be herself instead. The water rune almost floating before her, as her mother whispered the verse.

And se brim-henges brindles ne gymeð.

And the wave-horse heeds no bridle.

All the water surrounding them. Delivering colonizers. Drawing invisible boundaries. But still enduring as older territories. The water that answered to no knight.

And the beast. It could change too. There was a way out of this myth, for all of them. Or a deepening of it. Love hiding fathoms below.

She hit *debug*.

Compiling, the screen said.

Let's see, she thought, *what you really want. Doesn't* quest *also come from* question? *What are you asking for?*

A warmth began in her chest and spread out. She felt the other rune-smiths around the world, hitting *run*, lending her power from their own fragments of code. Felt their love and their pride, felt seen, as the power compiled. All the nerds and coders and systems librarians and gamers and stealth runesmiths who were like her. And Vivian, sitting in her living room in Victoria, smiling slightly, as she traced the same rune on a square of parchment. Lots of things could be screens.

The Wi-Fi lit up with their runes. A cloud of unknowing fire and possibility.

Lance noticed her for the first time. She was burning now. The runes had made her visible.

He stared at her in astonishment. *"Kai?"*

WAYNE

L ight poured through the clearing. Not the gray light of winter, but something more like a solar flare. He saw Kai at the heart of the light, sitting cross-legged on the ground with her laptop. For a second, he thought, *This is the volta—the part of the sonnet where everything turns.* Kai on fire with purpose.

Then the beast screamed.

All of its mouths were windows into a different fire—one that would consume them.

Wayne saw forms in the light. Hildie's spear was a negative space. His aunt's blade reflected the light in a thousand stars.

Wayne and Lance both turned toward Kai at the same time.

If he could just get in front of her. Before.

Lance was so fast. Closing the gap between them in an instant. Kai's expression, backlit by a quasar, was one of almost mild surprise. Like she couldn't believe any of this was happening, let alone the reality of that sword meeting her.

Lance swung.

Wayne saw the arc. The line of violence that Lance had followed for ages.

Wayne heard a voice in his head. His own voice from worlds away. Some shadow of himself from another time.

Kill the fear.

What was that supposed to mean?

What was he most afraid of?

A world without Kai.

Kill the fear.

He saw it in Lance's eyes. A flicker, even as he swung.

He's afraid too.

The world seemed to slow. Was this magic? Or did time always do this when things were about to change?

Wayne moved faster than he ever had in his life. Faster than when he'd run from the boys who wanted to hurt him in middle school. Faster than the streams of text he and Kai sent to each other every day. Faster than apocalypse. Like he'd always been running, his brain on overdrive, his thoughts careening photons. For the first time, maybe, he put a hand on that pulse of movement. *I control where I'm going. I can run toward something.*

He fumbled with his jacket as he ran. Reached into the little mirror Wally had placed in his pocket, that medieval fragment linking them. Pulled out the blade, so cold it numbed his hand, but unmistakably his weapon. *His* sword.

He was faster than he knew.

Their blades locked. The impact made his wrist ache. Their hilts caught like dueling horns in a move that Gale had shown him.

"Should have made that knot tighter." Lance chuckled, and it was almost a snarl. "That'll teach me to use what's on hand."

Wayne thought about Bert's sweater. Wrapped around his arm now, like a badge or some queer garter. Wondering if, in a way, it had saved him. Tight but not too tight, just like his bear hugs.

Not the time to think about this!

Lance pressed against the lock of their blades. He was barely trying—still just playing with him—but Wayne could feel his own strength giving way.

Hildie was running with her spear. Vera was behind her, yelling. But they weren't fast enough. None of it could ever be fast enough.

Then Kai stood up.

"Run!"

But she wasn't telling them to flee. She was talking to the universe, to the program she'd just unleashed. Telling it to do what it had to.

A rune turned in the air before her—a rune made of pure white flame and heart song and the blood that moved through them all. The star matter that wove them. The synapses leaping over darkness to make them who they were.

He knew that rune.

It was something his mother used to trace on his back, when he couldn't sleep. Lance had used a similar water rune, but this was far more expansive.

Possibility, she'd called it. The opposite of the rune he'd seen carved into Mo Penley's chest. Kai had said it was a thorn: a sign that the universe was about to cut you. Something you endured, maybe, for the right kind of power. But Kai's rune wasn't about pain or power. It was about claiming a future.

The rune sang. For a moment, Wayne saw a loom of letters, revolving in a starstruck pattern around them. Every possible combination of rune codes, as if Kai had tapped into the source and spread it all before them. Not some isolated magic. A language that was alive, a voice that was searching for infinite variation.

Lance stared at the curtain of runes like it was a coming storm.

36

HILDIE

Her feet were growing colder in the snow. She'd never frozen like this before. But maybe time itself was frozen. Maybe this was all happening across a thousand lifetimes, every sister watching her, waiting.

What was she waiting for? It was all happening. It was all joy and surprise and unfathomable hurt. This was it. When her time was up, another valkyrie, just like her, would smell death on the air. She'd see the black thread coming loose. She'd unravel Hildie, in search of something she wasn't even sure of.

This sweet burning moment was everything. And she could choose. She could move toward the life that she wanted.

The beast was staring at the runes as they came down, like burning snowflakes. Kai's magic was getting to it. Slowing things down. But not enough.

Lance pushed Wayne into the snow. Vera and Gale were getting closer, trying to circle him, but he seemed to know their every move. A familiar story.

Shar was staring at the beast. Struggling to free herself. All those eyes drifting from her to the runes and back to her. Torn between fate and whatever this new magic was.

For a moment, all Hildie could see was Shar.

Hildie knew she had a duty to protect the nephew and the rune-smith. She should back up Vera and Gale. Raise her spear against Lance. With enough force, they might even win.

But the beast.

The way it was looking at Shar, even through that rune haze. Drifting between curiosity and hunger.

Shar.

Hildie felt herself moving.

I wanted to be a part of something.

Breaking into a run.

I wanted a house like the one in Strathcona, and two difficult cats, and your laughter in the kitchen. Dancing on the hardwood.

Leaving Lance and Wayne and the chaos of knights behind her.

Your flannel and my leather. My spear and your song.

Shar's eyes on her. The barest hint of a smile on her face, beneath the beast's shadow.

I wanted it.

Slipping in the snow, running as fast as she ever had.

I never said it, because my body is tricky, and my heart even trickier, and for a long time I didn't know if there was a love that fit. But there is.

Now she was between them. A question mark separating fate from beast.

Shar stared at her. "Hildie. What are you doing?"

She took Shar's hand, gently. Used the edge of her spear to cut the restraints. She rubbed Shar's wrists to get the feeling back in them.

"Hildie, you have to run. Call for more valkyries. Find Grace."

"I've got my own grace," she said, smiling. "And you know there isn't time."

The beast was snarling now. It wasn't a full-throated rumble—more like the half growl of a dog who's noticed someone at the door. But on the beast, it shook the earth.

"Remember that trick we did with my spear once?"

Shar laughed, even though she was crying a bit. "Your mom *hated* it. She thought you'd burn the house down."

"No time like now."

The mist of runes were all around them. Hildie could feel them on her face, like moth's wings. A fluttering of power.

Shar reached out and plucked one from the air. It perched on her finger. A shimmering soap bubble that reminded Hildie of a raven's hungry beak.

As Hildie watched, Shar drew a silver thread from the air. Her hands worked swiftly, over and under, stitching it to the spear blade. The beast watched in fascination.

"Ready?" Shar grinned.

"Yes. Always. Let's make a Very Bad Decision."

The spear warmed. She felt the fire rune coursing through the grain, until the blade was alive with light. A little star above them, throwing off heat.

All of the beast's eyes landed on it.

"Let's hope it loves a laser pointer," Hildie said. Then she waved her spear in an arc, leaving bright afterimages behind. "Who's up for a wild hunt?"

The beast howled. All of its sinuous necks followed the motion of the spear.

She kept her eyes on the beast but spoke to Shar. "Get out of here."

"Not a chance."

"There's no reason for us both to be dumb."

"If you think that, you don't know me at all." She grabbed a branch and lit with another stray fire rune. A stitch so fast Hildie almost didn't see it. Smooth as silk. Now they both had brands.

"Copycat."

"Just *run*, babe."

Everything shot forward, like a universe waking up, burning itself into being. Hildie ran with the spear held high. Shar was at her side, waving the branch like a flare. Behind them was storm and nightmare and snapping jaws. They tore through the tree line. All those manicured trails that were supposed to be safe. Shar wove steadily beside her. She'd done track and field, Hildie remembered. She was the youngest thread, and the fastest.

They startled the sleeping birds as they ran. Geese crying out in the distance. *Intruder!* But the trees seemed to guide them forward. Hildie could hear the beast as it hammered the forest floor, but she didn't dare turn around. If she stopped for a moment, it would pass through her in a wave of blood and blasted bone. She'd be nothing but a stain on the snow.

She heard Lance in the distance, yelling. At first, she couldn't make out his words. But then she heard him scream, *I still own you!*

The beast stopped. Digging its claws into the snow and earth.

Fuuuuuuck.

She had to turn around. She had to. Shar sensed it too. She slowed down. They turned as one, still holding their brands high.

Hildie waved the burning spear. "Eyes on us. Don't listen to the angry knight. We're way more compelling. And you don't need to *only* hunt knights."

"Hildie," Shar murmured, "are you really trying to make it *hungrier*?"

She could see the hesitation in the beast's eyes. Some of the heads were still very focused on her, but some were winding in other directions. Was it Kai's magic? Was it the call of Lance's voice?

Hildie lowered her spear. She addressed the beast like an unwelcome guest. "I think you know what you want. There must be something that'll make all of this *stop*." It felt like leaning into a blizzard of teeth and ancient rage. But she had to try.

"Hon," Shar said, "maybe *don't* force Cerberus into a staring match?"

The beast moved toward her. Snarling. She could smell the blood on its fur. The charnel house breath.

When Hildie was little, a rottweiler had snarled at her through a fence. Jaws snapping. Fear spiking through her six-year-old body.

Now that moment engulfed her, amplified by a thousand cursed mirrors into an infinity of adrenaline. The beast rose to its full height, muscles straining, spittle on its maws. All those eyes pressing down on her. Hildie saw for the first time that its pelt was a mix of fur and scales. She could hear its wild hearts beating, grim thunder in her mind, wiping out every thought except *run*. A paw scraped the ground close to her. Each nail was the size of her spear blade.

This was the actual Very Bad Decision. Standing here. Negotiating with a nightmare.

She stayed focused. "Is it really hunger? Or is it the chase?"

It was too close. There was no running now. Not enough space between them. If it lunged, she wouldn't be able to react in time.

You're not six years old anymore. You're every possibility.

Hildie stood her ground.

One of the canine heads pushed closer, until it was inches from her face. She could see the pink blush of its throat, the bloody gums. The long, low growl rattled every bone in her body. She resisted the urge to plug her ears. Let the menace vibrate through her.

Then its legs seemed to quiver. As if it was fighting the urge to move in a totally different direction. Battling an instinct more powerful than Lance's hold over it or even Kai's rune cloud, which still dusted them in ash and magic.

"Hild," Shar whispered. "Look."

At first she thought the trees were on fire.

Then she saw the eyes. Pair upon pair of ember eyes, winking into being. The feel of a different kind of hunger. The whole forest seemed to be holding its breath.

All the eyes snapped into motion. Will-o'-the-wisps tearing through the air. They danced around the beast, pulling tighter and tighter, like a cord of flame.

Ylves.

Of course. This is their forest.

She heard a voice that was leaf rustle, moss song, the pop of the sun sinking into the ocean. The humus of dead things making dark new life in the soil. The forest became a mouth, and it sang directly to the beast:

Feathers in the frith
Fishes in the flood
Wild with the hunt
Bone and blood
Wild with the hunt
Bone and blood!

They prodded at the beast, singing *wild with the hunt, bone and blood* until the words filled Hildie's being. She wanted to run too. Run for joy. Run for sorrow. Run with Shar until they outpaced the world.

The beast howled once more, but it was in a different register. Some piercing note between happiness and despair.

Then they were all running. Pounding through the woods. Ylf light gleaming around them. Strings of rubies dancing in the dusk. The beast smashed through undergrowth. Hildie felt her lungs straining but knew she could run forever. Until she was bone and blood. They skidded and danced and panted through the forest. She didn't know if the beast was chasing them anymore. She didn't know up from down. Only that Shar was nearby, and the ylves were a kind of grease that made them glide forward. Until the ground was ice and they were skating, whirling, freezing in the dance. Was she howling? Were they all making the same ungovernable cry?

She ran from her job. From her mother's need. From the edge of her own spear, which had always decided her life. From the unanswerable mysteries that kept her from ever really learning anything. From the endlessness of myths. The enormity of the stories that were told and retold until they had a life of their own. From gin and love and another woman's heat. But the flight was so fast it nearly felt like standing still. Shar's hand was right there. She could take it. She could crack her own myth wide open, drink the dew within.

She heard Lance in the distance, coming closer. Felt the hunt begin to dissolve. Her body screaming from exertion. The beast shuddering back to consciousness.

They broke into the clearing. Hildie realized they'd made a circle. That they'd been circling this whole time, a plane in a blizzard. And now Lance was screaming, and Wayne was next to Kai, and Vera's sword was liquid moonlight. They were all panting. They'd all been caught up in the wild hunt. Chasing their own nightmares.

The beast saw the glint of Vera's blade. Saw the queen in its way.

If Hildie looked close enough, she could almost see a spark coming to life in its eyes. Runes revolving. But they turned too slowly. She shot a glance at Kai and saw the same fear on her face. Knowing the change wouldn't come fast enough. Slamming against the world with your will in the hopes that it would *open*. But time fell slow as honey in that moment.

Vera raised her sword.

The beast hurled itself at her: a perfect line to cut the story.

GALE

He saw the beast move. Almost gliding.

Gale was watching the runesmith to see what she'd do. The beast exploded through the trees. Hildie was behind it, yelling something, her spear on fire. And were those *ylves*? He saw their eyes dancing in the dim.

He tried to keep Lance in view. But he couldn't see everything. And then Vera was moving. Leveling her sword.

The beast charged.

Gale remembered once reading that if the universe stopped expanding, ground to a halt, there would be light everywhere. Light flooding all the cracks.

Lance was calling to the beast. Gale thought he heard him say *Wait!*

And Vera rising. Vera's sword a line, glittering in the valkyrie's light. Vera calm and unafraid, like an inevitability.

The beast would unbolt her. Undo all the locks and let everything fly out. All the grace and the love and fury.

It tore through the snow.

Hildie's spear moving but not quick enough. An angel might dance on it.

He thought of a poem he'd once translated: a single angel dancing in her socks on the head of a pin. Answering an old medieval question.

They were all dancing on spears. Dancing on stories.

This is what always happens. This is all that happens.

Gale shook his head.

No. The text can swerve. You don't have to grieve all the time. You don't have to be the knight who sleeps in a beautiful tomb. You can wake up.

He swerved.

Now he was in the path with no future. He was the line break. Or maybe the thorn that struck unexpectedly. He saw its eyes coming for him. The many mouths. The nearly geometric precision of this— the fate he'd reached for. A strange laugh bubbled up in him. Like the fountain in Gascony they used to wish on. Vera holding one of his hands while Lance held the other.

"Gale—"

Was it Lance's voice? Was it Vera's? Who remembered his name? The knight who'd been written out of most stories.

Not written out. Mistranslated.

His whole body flamed into a verb. A sword. A tear along the parchment.

He raised his blade.

Then the beast danced through him.

38

WAYNE

He saw Gale fall. Saw the beast unbraid his side. Blood spread through the snow.

He screamed his nuncle's name.

Vera knelt by him. Pressed her hands to the wound. Kai was there too. She was using her jacket as a bandage. Crying as she pressed the fabric to the awful door in his side.

The beast circled them. Leaving bloody pawprints in the snow. Just turning and turning, like it was broken. Not snapping at anyone, but not still. Lance watched it. Vera's attention was on Gale.

"Stay," she was saying. "Stay with us."

Blood seeped over Gale's fingers. His eyes were bright.

"See?" He struggled to speak. "I'm full of surprises. I never saw this coming."

"Stop moving," Kai admonished, though she was still crying. "You're much too old for this kind of adventure."

He laughed. Blood on his lips.

Vera held him in her gaze. A queen ordering him to stay. "This is *not* the end."

"Isn't it?" He looked at the beast through a mask of pain. Those eyes held something that none of them could decipher. It was still dangerous, still worrying their circle of light with its massive bulk. But something was happening to it.

Light softened all its angles.

Shar had followed Hildie. She approached the beast now, as if she might do something. Hildie made a half gesture, as if to pull her back. But she was uncertain.

Lance knelt by Gale. Took his hand. There was something in his expression that Wayne had maybe never seen before. Regret thick as pitch.

"We made a pact," he said. "Remember? The three of us swore to always be together—the marvel of us—no matter what the king did. Together in Joyous Gard. For me, it was always that little apartment in the West End. All our joys so close to each other."

"Lance—"

"Don't try to talk. The time for talk is over."

He stood. Walked over to the beast.

"Lance, don't." Vera couldn't leave Gale. But her eyes stayed on the recreant knight as he walked toward all of their worst fears.

"Joy turns to pain," Lance said. He examined his own bloody palm. Then he held it out to the beast. "You're hungry. Remember?"

It sniffed his hand like a cautious horse.

Lance touched his hand to one of the beast's heads. He stroked it with surprising gentleness, moving closer. It looked at him with an alien expression. For a second, Wayne thought he saw something in the beast's eyes. Something like a rune, burning.

Shar was moving toward them, as if she wanted to try something. She was a fate, right? Maybe she could heal him. But her expression was tricky, and Wayne was trying to keep his eyes on everyone at once.

"Poor old beast," Lance said. "I still own you. The magic wasn't even that hard. All I had to do was kill Mo. That started the new story. Other knights spent their lives searching for you. But it turns out that all you wanted was blood."

With one hand still on the beast, Lance moved quickly, too quickly. He grabbed Shar and pulled her toward the beast. Wayne saw Hildie level her spear.

"Bad valkyrie," Lance said, without turning. "Take another step and see what happens."

He was holding Shar the way you'd drag a recalcitrant toddler through a mall. She didn't resist. Maybe she couldn't. Maybe this was some kind of destiny. Did fate have a fate? Wayne had known Shar for less than an hour, but she seemed human, real. Unafraid.

Lance smeared his blood in her hair. She stood before the beast.

Vera wouldn't leave Gale. Lance's eyes were on Hildie. That left Wayne.

"Here's the future," Lance said. "Take her."

The beast bent all of its heads down low. Its breath must have been hot in Shar's face. He saw her hair rippling in its exhale. Her expression set. The beast's eyes were open wide. Glittering with that familiar hunger. But there was something else there: the uncertainty he'd seen before.

Kai had done something. Maybe the magic hadn't worked exactly the way she thought it would. The light was fading now. But there were shadows and afterimages, still flickering.

I hope she's safe, Wayne thought. *I hope she gets away.*

The beast touched one of its muzzles to Shar's neck. Bore its fangs. A thread of saliva settled on her cheek. She remained still.

Hildie was a lightning rod. Thrumming in the uncertain light. She was about to move. But time was weird. Like someone had sprinkled sand in the gears. If they both ran, would they make it? Would they die in the same moment? A mouth to devour each of them?

The beast exhaled. It sounded like a steam engine.

Then it drew back.

Shar let out the breath she'd been holding. She moved to the side, leaning against a tree. Now he saw her fear. What had she seen in that moment? Had the life of the whole universe flashed before her?

342

"This was never going to work," Hildie said. Her voice was rusty, like she'd forgotten how to speak in those few seconds. "It doesn't want her."

Lance rubbed his eyes. "You're right."

Then he grabbed Wayne by the hair and pulled him in close. Lance's grip was iron. Dragging him toward chaos. He could feel the beast's hot breath in his face. It smelled like a charnel house, like roadkill and landfills and scraps at the bottom of a dumpster. A thin line of drool splashed against his cheek. The beast's growl in his ear was thunder. He shook. Every atom in his body was screaming.

"I don't want to do this," Lance whispered in his ear. "I think I can do it without killing you. I promise I'll try. But it needs more. We're so close. And I should have known it wouldn't want the sister. Knights are what it wants—what it lives for. So we're going to build a new kingdom with your blood. Gale's too weak. But you've got some fight left in you. Old magic like this—it needs a bit of feeling."

There were runes in all the beast's eyes now. Turning. But which ones? He didn't know enough. He needed Kai's mind or Hildie's spear or—

No. It's just you. That's all you have right now. And you don't get much longer to think about this. You can't think your way out of this moment. You just have to be.

"This world that you want to build," he said. "It won't matter. Because Aunt Vera won't willingly be a part of it. Gale will be gone. It'll just be you alone, ruling over a dead kingdom. The people who love you—they won't serve you. They'll turn away." He swallowed. "Just like my mother did."

Lance's expression darkened. "*Run* away, you mean. That's what Anna was good at."

At his mother's name, the beast rumbled. It seemed almost curious.

Wayne realized that there was shared pain between them. Lance missed her too.

"If I have to die"—Wayne's voice was numb—"that's fine. But tell me why she left. You *know*. It had something to do with you. Tell me."

"That's not what you really want to know." Lance's eyes were almost human. "You want to know if she's still alive. Where she is now."

The beast opened its jaws wide. Fear pierced him from every angle, but Lance was right. He needed to know.

"Where?"

"The truth is"—Lance shrugged—"it doesn't matter."

Wayne tried to raise his sword. It was a reflex. Past selves screaming through his body, telling him what to do. Lance grabbed Wayne's wrist and forced the hilt from his fingers. The sword fell to the ground. Lance's hand was a vice, and Wayne felt his wrist break. The pain electrified him.

"Anna was also looking for a new kingdom," he murmured. "We're not so different." His cheek was pressed to Wayne's. "Maybe you'll come back as someone you never dreamed of, walking into a brand new world. Either way—you're a story, and this is the end. I can make this quick and give the beast what's left. Or I can let it have you whole."

"I—" Wayne looked around. Everyone was a blur. His aunt was trying to say something, but he couldn't hear. Shar's expression was set, as if she knew what was about to happen. Hildie looked torn, as if she was about to move, about to do something stupid.

He still had this choice.

"I choose the beast," Wayne said.

Lance let go of him. "You're brave, nephew. You've always been brave and stubborn, every time." The light made him beautiful but also terrifying, like a true angel. "You don't remember, but we've been here many times before. And you always manage to surprise me."

Wayne realized that they *had* done this before, in other places and times. He'd followed Lance into the woods. He'd struggled to hold a sword in nerveless fingers. He'd smashed his young will against the older, more powerful mind of Lancelot, in a struggle for power that wouldn't ever stop. Until now.

Wayne reached for the beast.

It growled long and low.

He pressed his forehead to the beast's pelt. It was soft and dangerous and humming in the painful light. It was a part of the grove, and the ocean beyond, and the heavy sky, and the lamps that lit the tourist paths. It was inside him too. Life was the quest; the beast was just part of it. This was the most reasonable ending. Maybe it was how his mother had felt when she walked out the door. Struck by possibility. Reaching for some different story that she couldn't quite explain. Had it felt like a death? Were the letters an apology, or proof of her love, or a game she was playing?

He remembered her last letter: *You can live with the beast. You can live through heartache, disappointment, apocalypse. Make room for monsters in your life. We're all in this den together, all little beasts looking, always looking.*

His wrist was on fire. But he let his tingling hand move down the beast's ruff. The fur was mottled with blood but still soft.

Gawain.

He looked up, startled. The beast was looking through him.

Gawain. He knew that voice.

Wort.

He drew back with a start. His wrist still hurt, but it was distant now. The clearing was gone. He stood on the suspension bridge. On one side, he could see the beast. Waiting. Not quite obedient. But calmly assessing. Blood on its great paws.

On the other side.

At first, he didn't recognize the figure walking toward him. It had been years. But as she got closer, Wayne felt ice in his gut.

She wore blue jeans and a mail cuirass, links gleaming in the winter light. Her sword was as he remembered it. The blade could still cut a snowflake. Her hair was tied up in a messy bun. Her dark eyes knew him.

"You found me," she said.

He stared at her. "Mom. What are you doing here?"

She shrugged. "When you mess with time and space, sometimes, you get a fuzzy variable. Here I am." She glanced at the beast. "You know it's not house-trained, right?"

"Mom, what the *fuck*?"

She touched his face. Squeezed him tight, with just the right amount of pressure. He felt himself slipping away. Melting like snow in her arms.

Then she stepped back. "You've found your way to the heart of a mystery. But I'm not sure it ends the way you want it to."

"I don't care. I just want to know why you left."

She smiled sadly. "I had to. That's the only answer I've got."

"I don't—" He shook his head. "No. I can't accept that. Mothers don't just leave. You. You . . ." He was crying now. The tears scalded him. "You always protected me. You were *my* knight. And you fucking disappeared when I needed you most!"

Anna didn't touch him again. But there was a fierce, almost frightening love rising from her. Wayne could almost smell it, like ozone. "You made it here all by yourself. To this moment. You forged it, Wort. Without me."

His voice was small. "Will you come back?"

But she was already walking away, toward the beast.

He screamed, *"Mom!"*

Anna half turned. "Did you finish the poem? About the Green Knight?"

"I skimmed the ending. It's about forgiveness. And wearing a garter, for some reason."

"Yes and no." She looked at him. "It's about scars that never go away. Learning to love what's under the skin. What's beautifully bent and remade inside of you. We're all scrolls that get reused from age to age. Palimpsests. But don't scrape away the good stuff. Let it bleed and come to the surface." She looked at him for a long moment, as if she was memorizing his face. "I may not be here, but don't think for a second I haven't watched you grow up. I see you, Wayne. I always have. And I always will."

Then she was moving away again. As she passed the beast, she reached up to touch one of its faces. They recognized each other.

Wayne's face was a wreck. He was crying, and there was snow in his eyes, salt and snot and blood. He felt stretched like a canvas, about to break.

The bridge was stretched too. Shaking. A ribbon about to tear. He felt it move. Dancing him into gray skies, black waters.

Then he remembered why he'd always loved the suspension bridge. Why he'd come back there again and again. How it rocked. How it stimmed alongside him, back and forth, lulling his fears and letting him move queerly, slyly, in this world that wanted him to only be one thing.

Wayne blinked.

He was back in the clearing, a sharpness against his cheek. It was a fang. One flinch, and it would tear through the parchment of his body, his life.

Except that he wasn't fragile. Anna was right. He'd done this without her. He'd forged himself, and this moment. Beneath the anxiety was iron. Beneath the fear was an edge that would always cut true. Because love forged a sword.

"I'm ready," he breathed into the pelt.

The beast shuddered. When he looked up, he saw it for sure this time. Kai's rune turning in the beast's many eyes.

"We can change," he said. "Everything can change. Even when your heart breaks. Even when the world ends." He pressed his lips to the shaggy head. "The story doesn't."

The beast let loose a deep howl. There was the sorrow of a thousand wolves in the sound. It shook the earth.

It dragged its tongue along Wayne's cheek.

Then it crumbled to ashes.

Lance stared at it, confused for the first time.

The ashes moved slowly. They were liquid. They might have been anything, for a moment. They twined in shadows, weaving themselves into something vaguely animal. A black unicorn stepped from the pile. The one from the tapestry.

"Oh," Wayne said.

Lance stared at the unicorn. He didn't seem to have any words left.

Which was just as well. It moved with terrifying grace. Sliding its alicorn deep into his shoulder. A sword meeting a scabbard.

Lance fell.

Blood dripped down the alicorn into the unicorn's eyes. It looked at Kai. Its expression, Wayne thought, verged on a kind of subtle surprise. As if it hadn't anticipated this possibility.

Kai whispered, "You're free."

The unicorn seemed to know that.

Lance made a small sound. His breathing was shallow. He collapsed next to Gale. Wayne crouched by them. His wrist was red iron. He wanted to hold them all together, but he couldn't.

Lance tried to speak, but it came out as a ragged choke.

As the light began to die, three women came into sharp relief.

One was Hildie, leaning on her spear. The other was an older valkyrie who looked quite a bit like Hildie—her mother?

The third was Morgan.

Hildie's mother wrapped an arm around her. They swayed slightly.

Morgan crossed the clearing. She seemed to take the light with her, like gathering fabric, until it was winter again. She kneeled down next to Gale. Blood kissed the hem of her dress.

"This," she told him, "will be a magnificent scar." She placed her fingertips against the wound. "Daughter of fire, help me with this."

Kai blinked for a second. Then she crouched down next to Morgan.

The older woman favored her with a look that was almost kind. "I have need of your strength. Let us see if my sister Vivian has taught you well."

Hands slick with Gale's blood, they traced a rune. Two swords meeting, or two bodies. An X that meant gift.

He gasped. The blood slowed. Fire sealed him shut again.

Morgan turned to Lance. "My errant knight," she said, "do you remember when I trapped you in the Valley of Lovers? When you startled me so that I fell out of bed and nearly killed you? People think I hate surprises. But I do love them."

Lance tried to speak. It might have been Morgan's name, or Vera's, or a different word entirely.

"For a time," Morgan said, "we were connected. Though I could never break into the knot you'd woven with Galehaut and Guinevere. But I enjoyed being in your orbit, if only for a short while. I loved you—as much as someone like me can." She placed her hand on Lance's heart. "This wound is too difficult to heal with a rune. It's already cold. But don't despair. The joy you remember is still there. The place is still open to you. My once and future knight—however awful you may be. The universe still might forgive you."

Morgan glanced at Hildie. "Thank you, Valkyrie. This story surprised even me. But you were always right where I needed you." She looked at Wayne. "And the nephew. Full of surprises. Just like your mother."

She pulled Lancelot onto the beast with her. Held him carefully. The unicorn snorted and walked slowly out of the grove.

Hildie blinked. "Are you fucking *kidding* me? After all that, she leaves us knee-deep in blood and riddles?"

Wayne grabbed Kai's hand. He was in shock, but he managed to smile. "You maybe changed the universe," he said.

Kai laughed. "All I did was ask it a question."

"You debugged a primordial monster. Can you submit that for your final project?"

"I feel like it'll be too hard to explain."

His face fell. "I'm sorry. About Percy."

Kai's expression was too complicated to decipher. She nodded. But there was something in her eyes. A spark. Was it hope?

Hildie leaned into her mother. "You were right about Morgan being difficult. Nana called her a knot."

She gently brushed a wild lock of Hildie's hair. "They're both riddles."

Shar stood by the bloodstained tree. Hildie walked up to her. She approached gently, the way you'd suss out something feral. Shar seemed not to see her for a moment. Then her eyes cleared.

Hildie said, "You got kidnapped." As if it had just occurred to her.

"Apparently." Shar's voice was dry.

They stared at each other for a moment. Something very old passed between them. And something new. Hildie took Shar's hand, cool and strong, in her own. She pressed her lips to it, sealing a pact. "Don't do it again," she whispered.

They swayed together for a bit. Shar's soft laugh was music.

"I like your singing voice," Hildie whispered into her neck. "You should sing more often."

"Do you want me to break out my *Big Shiny Tunes* CD?"

Hildie cackled. "Yes. Please."

Vera stepped over to Wayne. She almost touched his cheek, then thought better of it. "You're a knight now," she said. "Truly."

"I think I always was."

They heard footsteps. Bert came crashing into the grove. There were leaves in his hair, and he was wearing Wayne's Neuro Queer shirt. It looked like it was covered in fox hair.

"Sorry!" He gasped. "She turned me—for protection—it's a long—never mind." He crossed the distance between them.

Wayne laughed; the sound surprised even him. "*You* were the fox."

"I tried to lead you away from him. But then I saw a raccoon. Foxes are easily distracted. Also, I have your shirt."

"I see that."

"And you've got my sweater."

Wayne looked sheepish as he held up the torn and bloodied thing. "There's a hole in it now."

Bert's smile was indulgent. "That's fine. More character."

Now they were both holding the green fabric. Wayne cocked an eyebrow. "Is this like some kind of gay handfasting ritual?"

"Maybe." Bert managed to look almost shy. "I think—maybe—we're both free now?"

Wayne grinned. "I guess so."

Gale yelled, "I'm still very much in need of *medical attention!*"

"Hi." Bert's smile turned the whole universe.

"Hi. You were hiding in that fox pelt."

"Apparently."

"But I caught you."

Bert touched his cheek. "You did. The question is, Are you foolish enough to tame me and keep me around?"

"Taming sounds like hard work. I learned that from *The Little Prince*. And you're responsible, always, for what you've tamed."

Bert was grinning. "I'm apartment-friendly. Highly tameable."

"Oh my Goddess, just kiss already," Kai snapped. "Someone in this goddamn myth cycle should have a normal relationship."

"We're not normal," Wayne said. "Nope."

Bert smiled. "Nope."

"Overrated."

"Last century."

"*Hospital*," Gale yelled again.

"I like you fox and all."

"Good. Cuz I'm lots of other animals too. And a few trees. I might be cursed."

"Well." And then Wayne kissed him. Softly once. Then sadly, as knights did. Then with a kind of delicious green joy.

EPILOGUE

WAYNE

Wayne tried not to kick the chair leg, though it did make a remark-ably pleasant noise. The last thing he wanted was another note in his file about stimming. Kind of a weird term for what, he reasoned, was a natural extension of someone's body. A way of thinking and moving through the world. There was no form for that, though, and the Student Success Office loved to issue forms in different colors.

Dr. Hadley was looking at his notes. He'd glanced briefly at the sling on Wayne's arm, and Wayne had told him it was a fox hunting accident. That seemed to end the inquiry. Hadley'd offered coffee, but Wayne was already too keyed up about a decision he'd come to recently. Well, pretty much immediately after nearly dying in Stanley Park. Hard to put it into words though.

Hadley looked up. "How are you feeling?"

Like I watched my uncle get impaled by a nightmare unicorn.

Wayne swallowed. "I'm okay, actually."

"How are your classes going?"

Finals had gone surprisingly well, even though he had to write a bunch of in-class essays one-handed. He'd received an A– on the final paper for Aunt Vera's class. She hadn't totally appreciated his queer reading of the Green Knight, though she'd written *very interesting theory* in the margins. He hadn't cited enough sources. Most of the evidence was material, in the form of a mouth that he very much enjoyed kissing. Though sometimes that got too intense, and he needed to cool off by playing *Assassin's Creed*. As it turned out, Bert was complete shite at gaming. He accidentally killed a turtle in the game, and Wayne kept teasing him about it. *Were you going to make a tiny suit of armor?*

I'm a monster.

He'd taken the controller from Bert's hand. Kissed him. *Yeah. My monster.*

"Good," Wayne said simply. "Turns out college is interesting."

"Oh?" Hadley raised an eyebrow. "Expanding your horizons?"

Wayne remembered the weight of the sword in his hands. The brilliant snowfall of Kai's runes, so real that it had hurt to look at them. He'd seen all of his reflections and known, maybe for the first time, that he was never alone.

"I'm trying new things," he said.

"That's good."

"So, you know, defying stereotypes."

Hadley frowned slightly. "I never thought rigidity was one of your issues."

"But it's definitely one of the *DSM*'s greatest hits."

Hadley looked at him kindly. "I know that you're more than a constellation of data. You're a person, with all the powers and flaws that go along with that."

"Still borderline though."

Hadley shuffled through a series of forms. "Well. The assessment is . . . inconclusive, I agree. But that isn't necessarily a bad thing. Not fitting into a box."

Wayne stretched. "I guess I could be fine. With the not fitting. And I do fit—with the people who matter."

Hadley nodded and made another note. "Diagnosis isn't fate. Like family. We feel like they control us, but we're always making our own fate. These are boxes to unpack, not spaces to live in. They mean what we want them to."

"Like a sword. Or a rune."

Hadley smiled. "Well, I wouldn't know much about either of those things. I'm just a counselor named after a knight."

"You're a good counselor," Wayne said.

Hadley shrugged. "We're all trying our best."

The Tsawwassen ferry terminal was an explosion of tourists and exhausted commuters and families crossing the water for New Year's. It had been an interesting Christmas, to say the least, with *interesting* standing in for a number of words and metaphysical phenomena. Wayne had roasted a turkey with his dad. They hadn't cooked together in what felt like a lifetime, and it was nice to soak and dice and chop. After Wayne called out *why so tough, turnips*, it became their exclamation when anything went wrong in the kitchen. Pots boiled over, and the pie crust looked like it had been mauled by wild dogs, but everything tasted like it used to. Almost perfect time travel.

Bert had arrived with mushy peas, which he claimed was an English delicacy. Wayne thought they tasted like green oatmeal. Then he ate too much pie, and when they were alone, Bert rubbed his belly while he groaned halfheartedly.

His dad was a bit shocked at first, about the move. But he took it well in the end.

"I've got a lead on some studio gigs," he said, after dinner when they were stuffed and calm. "Things will be different when you get back. You'll see."

Wayne leaned against the railing. The coffee cup warmed his hand. He watched the *Spirit of British Columbia* making its way to the harbor.

Soon there'd be all the metallic whirring as it attached to the gangplank. Then they'd board, anonymous, surrounded by strangers who had no idea what they were planning.

And wasn't it normal? Didn't people do this sort of thing all the time?

He sipped the coffee with his left hand. His sword arm was still in the sling. His wrist ached. It would always ache—a mark left by his family, added to all the rest. The bruises, visible and unseen, that reminded him of his complex kin. Bert always touched the spot gingerly, but Wayne was tougher than he appeared. He was made of scar tissue and failure and calcified memory. He'd survived two near-deaths already. Moving to an island would be simple. Safe as . . . islands.

Reading Ursula K. Le Guin had taught him that islands could be dangerous. But they were also the cradle of life, and there probably wasn't a lot of dangerous magic in Victoria. Just mellow island magic.

Hildie joined him on the deck. She was drinking a massive tea in a travel mug so large that only truckers would actually need it. "All set?"

He gestured to the incoming ferry. "It's nearly here."

Hildie cocked her head. "You know, *banishment* is an ugly word."

"Hildie."

"I don't think it's what we meant when we made the ruling."

"Your mother made the ruling."

She bristled slightly at this. "I was part of the council," she muttered. "Anyhow. We had to do something: he was complicit in Mo's murder, even if he didn't deal the death blow. Plus, it's for his own safety. But you don't have to follow him."

"I'm not," Wayne said with a small smile. "He's following me."

"You're sure about that?"

He nodded. "It was my decision to transfer to Island U. Maybe I'll finally figure out what the hell my major is supposed to be. And I've got family on the island. Viv and Wally are psyched. Bert knows some people as well. And basement suites are almost five percent cheaper."

Kai burst onto the deck, a duffel bag slung over her shoulder. "My data says closer to three percent. And I'm not looking forward to sharing space with two hairy boys who are going to absolutely clog up the sink."

"I'm not hairy."

"Yes, Wayne. You're unclassifiable. That's why it's impossible to construct a Scruff profile for you."

His eyebrow shot up. "I'm also *dating* someone."

"So?"

Hildie smiled at their bickering.

"How's Shar?" Wayne asked.

Hildie leaned over the railing. "She was quiet for a while, afterward. Something's definitely shifted between us. For the good. When I look at her now, I can see the future." She laughed. "It was always there. I was just too . . . whatever to really notice. But now there's this space where I fit. I'm not just my job, or my past, or any of that. I can be who I want. I'm channeling my mother. Don't ask for permission."

"Valkyrie goals," Wayne said.

Hildie rolled her eyes. "Anyway, we're back to fighting over the radio station. Or the fact that she listens to the radio at all, when there are a million streaming stations that don't exclusively play '90s grunge."

"You can't fault her taste," Kai replied. "Kurt Cobain was a trans icon. She wore a dress on the cover of *The Face* in '93."

Wayne smiled. You couldn't argue with fate. Or with one of them, anyhow.

The ferry reached them. It docked slowly, as ferry employees in orange jackets ran around, making small adjustments.

People crossed water all the time. People were made of water and came from water. It was home. But you still needed to respect it and fight for it.

Bert stepped onto the deck carrying a fistful of Twizzlers.

"For the journey," he said, when he saw Wayne's look.

Hildie eyed him up and down. "You knights take care of each other," she said. "You're both one of a kind."

Bert kissed Wayne on the cheek. "I'll protect him from dragons, as long as he reminds me of the Wi-Fi password."

"It's *on* the router," Wayne said, though there was no exasperation in his voice.

This was all so new. And now they were testing it by living together? It might be an awful mistake. But that was sometimes what *adventure* meant, in the old books. *Aventure*. A left turn, a leap, a magnificent failure.

"It's more likely that I'll be protecting them," Kai said. "Dragons are one thing. But I can yell at student loan officers until I'm blue in the face."

"It's your power," Wayne said.

She winked. "That, and burning the apartment down if you cross me."

Someone called *all aboard*.

Wayne laughed. People still said that? Did people still do this?

All the time. And he was people. He did this. He made his own choices. You didn't argue with the fates. You lived with them.

Hildie gave him a quick one-armed hug, respecting that he wasn't big on contact. "I'll visit as soon as I can. I've got business on the island, anyhow."

"What sort of business?"

"Don't you worry about it." She clapped Bert on the shoulder. "Be good. Kai, if this one gets out of hand, turn him back into a fox."

"Hey—"

Kai smiled. "In a heartbeat." Then she leaned in to whisper something in Hildie's ear. Wayne didn't hear what it was, but Hildie nodded, smiling.

They walked up the gangplank. Kai grinned as she breathed in the salt-tinged air. People bustled around them, but they weren't in any hurry. There would be a place for them. There always was. Though, Wayne realized, that place might be near the children's play area, which was way too noisy, so maybe they should hustle.

He nearly stumbled. Kai grabbed his hand.

"Don't get ahead of yourself," she said. "You're wounded, after all."

"Sage advice from someone learning to tame fire."

Kai chuckled. "I've always played with fire. If you're nice, I might even teach you a few more things."

Teach me to see this, Wayne thought. *Just this moment. Teach me to be happy and not keep stretching toward the future. Teach me to love what I have, and be who I am. Teach me to trust that the words will come, eventually, and they'll be right. Because they're mine.*

They squeezed through the small entrance. For a moment, it was dark, as they moved through the in-between space that led to the main deck.

He felt Bert's hand on his back. "Winter's over, knight. Time for something new." Wayne kissed him. Felt him grin. The shadows passed over them, briefly, and then he saw water. The way was clear.

ACKNOWLEDGMENTS

There are a number of teachers whose work and care helped to shape this book. My high school English teacher, Muriel Morris, introduced me to Chaucer and *Beowulf*. I remember my teenage mind being blown when she told us that the Pardoner and the Summoner were dating. To say that in Chilliwack in 1996! While I was doing my undergrad degree at the University of the Fraser Valley, John Moffatt taught me to love poetry in Middle English. Harvey De Roo ignited my love for Old English—poems full of wolves and riddles—and Sheila Roberts taught me so much about King Arthur (and never to underestimate Guinevere).

While writing this novel, I was nourished by the work of so many medieval scholars, including Gabrielle M.W. Bychowski, Dorothy Kim, Taylor Driggers-McDowall, Jonah Coman, Kavita Mudan Finn, Ellis Amity Light, Jonathan Hsy, Miles Smith, Mary Rambaran-Olm, and Rick Godden. I was also energized by the work of neurodivergent writers and scholars: Nick Walker, M. Remi Yergeau, Julia Miele Rodas, Sarah Kurchak, Richard Ford Burley, and Z.R. Ellor.

Thank you to my wonderful agent, Lauren Abramo, who always believed in this project. And to my editors at ECW, Jen Knoch and Jen Albert, whose care and enthusiasm and attention to detail have made this a better book. Thanks to Crissy Calhoun and Shannon Parr for excellent copy-editing, as well as Jen Sookfong Lee and Alex Werier for their attention to the manuscript.

I hope this story leads you to all the queer possibilities in medieval literature.

For every book sold, 1% of the cover price will be donated to TransSask, a Saskatchewan non-profit organization that supports and acts as a resource network for trans-identified, genderqueer, intersex, and gender non-conforming individuals, their spouses, family, friends, and allies.

This book is also available as a Global Certified Accessible™ (GCA) ebook. ECW Press's ebooks are screen reader friendly and are built to meet the needs of those who are unable to read standard print due to blindness, low vision, dyslexia, or a physical disability.

At ECW Press, we want you to enjoy our books in whatever format you like. If you've bought a print copy just send an email to ebook@ecwpress.com and include:

- the book title
- the name of the store where you purchased it
- a screenshot or picture of your order/receipt number and your name
- your preference of file type: PDF (for desktop reading), ePub (for a phone/tablet, Kobo, or Nook), mobi (for Kindle)

A real person will respond to your email with your ebook attached. Please note this offer is only for copies bought for personal use and does not apply to school or library copies.

Thank you for supporting an independently owned Canadian publisher with your purchase!